PRAISE
MARK MORRIS

"Mark Morris is one of the finest horror writers at work today."
—Clive Barker

"Mark Morris is a stellar talent. If you haven't read him before, now's the time!"
—Christopher Golden

"Mark Morris is one of the best horror writers we have. If you're not reading him you're missing out."
—Michael Marshall Smith

"Mark Morris is the irreducible rock of modern horror literature. Unafraid to push the boundaries of his art, he nevertheless has one foot firmly entrenched in the good earth of tradition."
—Conrad Williams

PRAISE FOR THE SHIRLEY JACKSON AWARD-NOMINATED NOVELLA, *IT SUSTAINS*

"Morris weaves together a boy's troubled adolescence and inexplicable supernatural doings in this subtle, elusive, and unforgettable tale. Morris elicits the supernatural from his rendering of ordinary life, and anguish and despair from understatement. This engrossing novella promises to sustain the reader through multiple encounters."
—*Publishers Weekly*, Starred Review

"A remarkable study of grief, first love, and what it's like to be a child when everything around you is new and exciting and dangerous. Mark Morris's skill is he can flip you between shocks and scares, and b
— ert Shearman

PRAISE FOR
THE WOLVES OF LONDON

"A new novel from Morris is always cause for celebration, and this first in a brand new trilogy ushers in his greatest, most complex and compelling work yet."

—Tim Lebbon

"In *The Wolves of London*, Mark Morris not only crosses genre boundaries, but creates an entirely new territory in the landscape of dark fiction. Part crime novel, part fantasy, part science fiction— entirely engrossing."

—Sarah Pinborough

"Fantastic. . . . I couldn't put the wretched thing down."

—*Bizarre Magazine*

"A rich, imaginative combination of chilling nightmare and SF adventure . . . a riveting ride through time and across genres."

—*Horrorview*

"Morris not only excels at character development, but suspense and build up as well. You'll have trouble putting the book down."

—*ScienceFiction.com*

ALSO BY MARK MORRIS

NOVELS

Toady
Stitch
The Immaculate
The Secret of Anatomy
Mr. Bad Face
Longbarrow
The Uglimen
Genesis
Fiddleback
The Deluge
The Black
The Wolves of London (Obsidian Heart, Book One)
The Society of Blood (Obsidian Heart, Book Two)

TIE-IN NOVELS

Doctor Who—The Bodysnatchers
Doctor Who—Deep Blue
Doctor Who—Forever Autumn
Doctor Who—Ghosts of India
Torchwood—Bay of the Dead
Hellboy—The All-Seeing Eye
Spartacus—Morituri
Dead Island
Vampire Circus
Noah (official movie tie-in novelization)

NOVELLAS

The Dogs
Stumps
It Sustains
Albion Fay

SHORT STORY COLLECTIONS

Close To the Bone
Long Shadows, Nightmare Light

AS EDITOR

Cinema Macabre
Cinema Futura
The Spectral Book of Horror Stories
The 2nd Spectral Book of Horror Stories

MARK MORRIS

WRAPPED
IN
SKIN

CZP

ChiZine Publications

FIRST EDITION

Wrapped In Skin © 2016 by Mark Morris
Cover artwork © 2016 by Erik Mohr
Cover design © 2016 by Samantha Beiko
Interior design & interior artwork © 2016 by Jared Shapiro

Distributed in Canada by
Publishers Group Canada
76 Stafford Street, Unit 300
Toronto, Ontario, M6J 2S1
Toll Free: 800-747-8147
e-mail: info@pgcbooks.ca
Distributed in the U.S. by

Consortium Book Sales & Distribution
34 Thirteenth Avenue, NE, Suite 101
Minneapolis, MN 55413
Phone: (612) 746-2600
e-mail: sales.orders@cbsd.com

Library and Archives Canada Cataloguing in Publication

Morris, Mark, 1963-, author
    Wrapped in skin / Mark Morris.

Short stories.
Issued in print and electronic formats.
ISBN 978-1-77148-357-5 (paperback).--ISBN 978-1-77148-358-2 (pdf)

    I. Title.

PR6113.O78W73 2016   823'.92   C2015-907523-8
                                             C2015-907524-6

CHIZINE PUBLICATIONS
Toronto, Canada
www.chizinepub.com
info@chizinepub.com

Edited by Don Bassingthwaite
Proofread by Ben Kinzett

Shelfie

A free eBook edition is available
with the purchase of this print book.

CLEARLY PRINT YOUR NAME ABOVE IN UPPER CASE
Instructions to claim your free eBook edition:
1. Download the Shelfie app for Android or iOS

Canada Council   Conseil des arts
for the Arts   du Canada

We acknowledge the support of the Cana[da]
million in writing and publishing throug[h]

ONTARIO ARTS COUNCIL
CONSEIL DES ARTS DE L'ONTA[RIO]

an Ontario government agency
un organisme du gouvernement de l'On[tario]

Published with the generous assistance of

Printed in Canada

WRAPPED IN SKIN

To Nel, David, and Polly, all of whom I love more than I could possibly say. Home truly is where the heart is.

TABLE OF CONTENTS

Normality Gone Bad:
An Introduction to Mark Morris's *Wrapped In Skin*
Stephen Volk

When you meet Mark Morris, he doesn't seem like a horror writer. He's probably wearing a T-shirt (albeit emblazoned with a Clash motif) and faded jeans, and is smiling, and friendly, and chatty, and humorous, and not at all socially inept or inclined to invade your personal space. In fact, he seems perfectly normal.

Don't let this fool you for a second.

For a start, if you find out his age it's clear he must have a Dorian Gray-style portrait in the attic.

Secondly, read his stories. Apart from being blown away, you'll be convinced in no time at all there's a mind at work here with a taste for the deeply peculiar, not to say creepy and downright sinister, under that extraordinarily affable exterior.

As this fine collection is about to demonstrate.

A brilliant collection, in fact—by the best British horror writer we have working today. That's my opinion. You're entitled to disagree with it, but if you do I'll wrestle you to the ground and burst your eyes with my thumbs, just because you're *wrong*.

I first met Mark on a long-haul flight to Canada for a fantasy convention. Some time that weekend I remember standing on the plate glass floor high up the Toronto Tower with a bunch of other genre scribes and publishing bods, looking down at ants that were people way below, feeling (as horror writers do about life in general): "How safe is this, exactly? Is it as strong as they say it is? What if this is the exact moment they find out it's not? What if it cracks and I fall through?"

What if I fall through reality? What then?

The great thing about a gathering of such minds is that we know how each other think. And there's comfort in that. We don't have to apologise for what we do or what we like, as often happens when we're amongst the rest of society. We can cut to the chase, and as a consequence feel liberated. Feel our true selves. As Christopher Golden once said, we were once all misfits, oddballs and loners in the playground, kids who liked monster movies and ghost stories, but if we're lucky we find a place where everybody in the room is an oddball.

That chimes with me. And I'm sure with Mark. Because he's an oddball too—even if he's wrapped in the skin of an ordinary person.

A safe, respectable, *sane*, human being.

Like I say: how wrong can you *be*?

Before that flight to Toronto, our mutual friend Tim Lebbon had said to me: "I think you two will get on." *Get on?* You know that feeling when you've been with someone for a few hours and you feel like you've known them all your life? *That.*

As I think Mark would agree, we clicked immediately. Right off the bat I told him I'd loved his first novel, *Toady*. He said he adored my BBCTV Hallowe'en "hoax", *Ghostwatch*. (Mutual admiration always being a great way to kick-start a friendship.)

By the end of the weekend we realised we shared an abundant (and possibly irrational) love of genre literature, had grown up on the same childhood reading, and enjoyed the same (i.e. pretty much *all*) horror films, with a fondness for Hammer fare in particular, as well as old and obscure TV shows—often ones frowned at, even by other fans.

In short, I knew I'd found a like-minded soul.

Over the coming months we bonded over our seemingly endless common enthusiasms: Peter Cushing, the portmanteau films of Amicus, television writers like Brian Clemens and Nigel Kneale, and the various incarnations of modern mythic characters like Frankenstein and Sherlock Holmes, to name but a few—as well as the more private concerns of being a freelance writer, with all the attendant hurdles, hardships and delights.

A good ten years later, our respective wives (both visual artists) joke that we are—physical dissimilarities notwithstanding—so alike in our foibles and personalities that we must have been twins separated at birth. They chuckle at our geekish relish in things they find blatantly naff (like *Tales from the Crypt* or Basil Rathbone's *Hound of the Baskervilles*), and shake their heads in dismay at the fact that both of us seem to be afraid of virtually everything—finding some hideous prospect inherent in the most banal of situations.

I admit, okay—there *are* similarities. . . .

Notably, we both bask in our influences. We enjoy reanimating them and reliving them in discussions—but also in the stories we tell. Not because we want to cleave ourselves to a tradition, but because that tradition has blessed us with a way of seeing the world. The only way that makes sense.

Because the only thing that makes sense to us, really, is—*fear*.

The common public, by and large, has this erroneous notion that the impulse to write horror is some kind of sadistic urge, usually one step away from being a full-throttle serial killer. I've always railed against that as a theory, saying the reality is the complete opposite—horror practitioners are not more *sadistic* than most, they're more *neurotic* than most.

You only have to ask people who know—or live with—horror writers.

Put simply, we're more prone to see things to be frightened of. That's why we respond to, and value so much, the kind of fiction that reflects our varying degrees of terror of the outside world in a metaphorical and symbolic way. (After all, Hitchcock, when he was asked what frightened him, answered: "*Everything*.")

As I've also written, while that psychological bent gives us a perhaps enviable career and (albeit erratically) enables us to earn a crust, unfortunately the same sensitivities make us susceptible to anxiety and stress.

The benefit of which is that, when you have a close friendship with another writer, close enough to share their day by day highs and lows, their triumphs and frustrations, it becomes a rare and special delight to see them hit a story out of the ballpark, Or simply nail it, seemingly effortlessly.

Time, and time, and time again.

As you are about to discover. Believe me.

And as someone who has just read these stories—some for a second time—I can only envy you the thrill, and heady satisfaction, of the journey ahead. . . .

Dare you switch off the light and get a taste of absolute darkness? In "Fallen Boys" a school trip to a mining railway becomes a bone-chilling encounter with the past.

A different school project provides a grotesque and surreal twist on our most basic and positive urge, to nurture, in "Biters". This story shows that when identity, and even life, is eroded, a tiny sliver of humanity is to be cherished.

Suburban small talk turns awkward for Len and Phyllis in "The Name Game" when they learn the peculiar rules of The Avenue. And in a deeply affecting and multi-layered story, "The Red Door", psychologically brittle Chloe's crisis of faith is tested to the limit when an extraordinary and inexplicable image haunts her.

"The Complicit" uses several recurring Morris themes—a return to the past, and childhood as a realm of fear and vulnerability—rendered in shards of memory and acute sensory precision. This searing tale is imbued with an aching regret of things undoable, unsayable, inescapable, and most of all, unresolved. Above all, it portrays the nauseous immortality of terrible acts, and the culpability of place itself in the perpetuation of misery.

In an abrupt change of tone, "Vicious" imagines in a startling act of foul-mouthed ventriloquism what might have happened if a certain punk rock bass player had had his "Robert Johnson" moment at the crossroads.

"White Wings" and "Bad Call" are tales of the unexpected in which a sense of growing dread ratchets up in increments of matter-of-fact observation.

A horror reader's dubious reading material, deemed by his peers "distant from reality" turns out to be anything but, in "Feeding Frenzy", while in "The Scariest Place in the World" a visitor arrives at Holly's home to have a look at the house he grew up in, opening the door to an oppressive childhood.

Another common Morris trope is the use of health problems as emblems of mental distress. Never more so than here, in the wonderfully bizarre and surreal "Eating Disorder"—which is one of those *"How the hell does he come up with ideas like that?"* ideas. To say more would be to spoil it.

Upsetting and unsettling in its evocation of crimes within recent memory, "Essence" starts at a watering hole where an innocuous middle-aged couple plan to lure their prey, the writer allowing us to be privy to their mundane thoughts of depredation with an unblinking eye and an unflinching pen.

"Puppies For Sale" is quite simply one of the best horror stories I have ever read, centring as it does on a parent's fear for his children's health and wellbeing. Nothing could be more chilling—or horridly convincing—than the slow-drip way that the youngsters in this story are affected by a strange force of malignancy. In the end, as a universal truth, this reminds us vividly, we just want our children to be well.

Finally, in America, a group of friends go on a risk-free thrill ride where, as in *Westworld*, nothing can go *wrong*. But events take a drastic and cataclysmic turn, undercutting all genre expectations like a razor-cut to the face. "Waiting for the Bullet" is, again, to my mind, an absolute *Desert Island Discs* classic of horror: another encounter with the past, but a time travel story as far from *Doctor Who* as can be imagined. And a perfect, unforgettable note on which to end.

What unites these multifarious offerings—all outstanding examples of the craft of the short story—is the consummate skill of the writing, the muscularity of the storytelling (gripping, without seeming to lift a finger), and an elegantly unshowy prose style.

All of which I've come to expect from the author of *The Immaculate*, *It Sustains*, *The Wolves of London* and the brilliant *Albion Fay*.

And all the better to give you nightmares, and peck at your unease, for many years to come.

But there's more to Mark Morris than scaring the pants off you, or even getting under your skin.

The key thing you have to know about him is the joy he finds in what he does, and for that reason alone I'd say he is the greatest ambassador for horror in existence. He not only executes it with impeccable grace, he also knows what horror is *for*.

And that's for the illumination of humanity—not *inhumanity*. Because however dark we sink in these stories, a heart of a human being beats.

This is what great horror stories give us. Not vampires that sparkle or heads that come off or tentacles that squirm. But connection. Empathy. The truest rendering of feelings when the impossible happens. When normality turns bad.

Under that smiling exterior, Mark Morris gets this. And how.

In my view, these tales are amongst the best our beloved genre has to offer right now. They sit right up there with the best of the past masters—Aickman, James, Machen, King, Dahl—and I can honestly promise that, if you have a taste and love for the genre, they will enrich you.

Savour them.

Stephen Volk
Bradford on Avon
August, 2015

FALLEN BOYS

FALLEN BOYS

When the child screamed, Tess Morton felt guilty for having to repress the urge to snap at it. She was aware that it wasn't Matthew Bellings who should be punished, but his tormentors, and yet the boy's cry of pain or distress was so *whiny* that it grated on her nerves.

The reason she felt little compassion for the child was because she knew it took almost nothing to provoke a wail of complaint from him. Matthew would cry out whenever someone barged into him in the school corridor; whenever a football was kicked towards him in the playground; whenever a classmate flicked a paper pellet at him, or snatched a text book out of his hand, or pushed in front of him in the lunch queue. Indeed, the merest slight would cause Matthew's red-cheeked, strangely wizened face to crumple, his mouth to twist open and that familiar, toe-curling bleat to emerge.

Tess liked children; she truly did. Unlike many of her more world-weary colleagues, she was still young enough, and optimistic enough, to regard teaching as a noble and worthwhile profession. She looked back on her own school days fondly, and regarded many of her former teachers with great affection. And as such she liked the idea of feeding and enthusing young minds, of equipping her pupils for the trials of life that would inevitably lie ahead.

All of which made her feel doubly bad for the way she felt about Matthew. He wasn't a naughty boy. He wasn't disruptive or snide or cruel. He was just . . . unlikeable.

Physically, he was stick-thin and uncoordinated. When he ran his limbs resembled a collection of slender twigs loosely bound together. He had no real friends, and as far as Tess could tell had made no particular efforts to acquire any. Breaks and lunchtimes he could most commonly be found in the library, cowering behind an open book, as if hiding from pursuers. He was the sort of child whose parents—of whom Tess had only ever met his nervous, bird-like mother—did him no favours whatsoever. Whereas the other boys carried rucksacks or sports bags, Matthew had been provided with a satchel of gleaming, conker-brown leather. Additionally, his shoes were too shiny, his trousers too short, and his old-fashioned crew cut gave him the look of a child actor in a wartime drama series.

For a while Tess had taken pity on the boy. She had put herself out, spent extra time with him, in an effort to prise him from his shell. Matthew, however, had remained not only unresponsive, but so sulky and ungrateful that in the end she had given up. She still felt a bit ashamed of abandoning the cause, but she consoled herself with the thought that at least she wasn't as downright hostile towards Matthew as some of her colleagues. The other teacher on this year eight field trip, Yvonne Harrison, who most of the kids loved for her friendliness and good humour, frequently referred to Matthew Bellings as "that snivelling little shit."

Turning now, Tess saw that Jason Hayes, his back to her, was hopping from foot to foot, waving his arm in the air. Her immediate thought was that Jason had snatched something of Matthew's and was taunting him, holding whatever-it-was out of reach. Then she saw Jason lunge forward, lowering his arm in a thrusting motion, which made Matthew squeal again. Some of the other children, especially the girls, squealed too, though there was laughter in *their* voices.

"Eew, you are *so* gross!" one of the girls (Tess thought it might be Francesca Parks) shrieked delightedly.

Muttering at the child behind her to halt, Tess strode towards the knot of pupils at the back of the queue. "*What* is going on here?"

Jason Hayes looked over his shoulder guiltily, and then flicked his arm, tossing away whatever he'd been holding. Because of the other kids milling around, Tess couldn't tell what it was, though she got the impression of something black and ragged sailing over the edge of the metal walkway and disappearing into the scrubby bushes below.

"Nothing, miss," Jason said innocently, turning to face her.

"Nothing," Tess repeated. "Do you honestly think I'm stupid, Jason?"

Jason was a sporty, thick-set boy with spiky hair. Often cheeky and excitable, but essentially a good kid.

"No, miss. No way."

"I'm very glad to hear it. So perhaps you'd like to tell me what you were doing to Matthew?"

Tess still couldn't see the smaller boy. It was as if the other children were purposely shielding him from view.

"Nothing, miss," Jason said again, and then added quickly, "I was just showing him something."

Tess sighed inwardly. She knew that to get to the heart of the onion you had to patiently peel away the layers one by one. "I see. And *what* were you showing him?"

"Just something I found, miss."

Tess stared at him silently for a moment, and then very deliberately said, "Do you *want* to go on the Mine Railway, Jason?"

"Yes, miss."

"Because it's no skin off my nose to take you back to the coach. For all I care, you can sit there for the rest of the afternoon, writing an essay on how important it is to be a positive representative of the school. Would you like that?"

"No, miss."

Francesca Parks, a precocious thirteen-year-old with a pierced navel, shrilled, "You can't do that, miss."

"Can't I, Francesca?" Tess said coolly. "And why's that?"

"You can't leave Jace on his own. It's against the law."

"He wouldn't be on his own," Tess said. "Mr. Jakes would be there."

Mr. Jakes was the school coach driver. He was a scrawny man in his early sixties who always stank of cigarettes. He had a collapsed cavern of a mouth and bad teeth.

Francesca's eyes, still bearing the trace of the eyeliner she applied every afternoon the instant she stepped out of the school gates, widened. "You can't leave him with that old perv."

Tess stared at her unblinkingly. "I beg your pardon?"

Francesca's eyelids flickered and she bowed her head. "Sorry, miss," she mumbled.

"I don't want to hear another word from you, Francesca. Not one. Do you understand me?"

Francesca's head jerked in a single, sullen nod.

Tess paused just long enough to allow her words to sink in and then she focused on Jason again. "Now, Jason," she said, "I want you to tell me exactly what you were tormenting Matthew with and I want the truth. This is your one and only chance to explain. Don't blow it."

Jason braced himself. "It was a bird, miss."

"A bird?"

He nodded. "I found a bird on the path back there, miss. A dead one. It was a bit manky."

Tess could guess what had happened. Jason had picked up the bird, waved it in Matthew's general direction, and Matthew, as ever, had over-reacted. It wasn't much more than boyish high jinks, but Matthew's response—and the fact that Jason must have known from experience exactly how his classmate *would* respond—meant that she couldn't be seen to condone his behaviour.

Curtly she said, "What did I tell you before getting on the coach today, Jason?"

"You told us we were representing the school and we had to be on our best behaviour, miss," he replied dutifully.

"Correct," said Tess. "And would you say you've adhered to those stipulations?"

"No, miss."

"No," she confirmed. "You've let us all down, haven't you?"

"Yes, miss. Sorry, miss."

"I appreciate the apology," Tess said, "but it's not me you should be apologising to."

"No, miss."

Raising her voice, Tess said, "Step forward please, Matthew."

The gaggle of Jason's classmates, who had been hovering in the background, now half-turned, shuffling aside to create an aisle. Revealed at the end of the aisle, crouching against the chain-link fence which enclosed the metal walkway leading to the mine entrance, was Matthew Bellings.

Tess immediately saw that Matthew was trembling and that he had something dark on one cheek. She wondered whether the incident had been more serious than she had thought. Surely Jason hadn't *punched* Matthew, knocked him down, bruised his face? Despite the antipathy that the other children felt towards the boy, she couldn't believe that any of them would actually resort to violence. As Matthew shakily straightened up, Tess saw one of the girls—Charlotte McDonald—silently hold something out to him. Something small and white. A tissue. And immediately Tess realised what was really on Matthew's face.

It wasn't a bruise. It was blood.

It wasn't his own blood, though; she was sure of that. His face wasn't cut or swollen, and the blood was too thin and brownish to be fresh. As Tess looked at Matthew staring at the tissue but not taking it, her brain made another connection.

It wasn't human blood. It was the bird's blood. Jason must have swung the dead and rotting creature—whether intentionally or not—right into Matthew's face. The thought of it made her feel a little sick.

However, the fact that Matthew was doing nothing to help himself, that instead of taking the proffered tissue and cleaning himself up he was simply cowering against the fence, elicited in Tess a wave not only of revulsion, but of an almost contemptuous irritation towards the boy. Marching forward, she snatched the tissue from Charlotte's hand and brusquely applied it to Matthew's cheek. Matthew was so surprised that he half-twisted away, releasing another of his plaintive squeals.

"Oh, for God's sake," Tess muttered, "don't be a baby."

Instantly she knew she'd overstepped the mark, shown too much of her true feelings. She was aware of shrewd eyes on her, could almost hear the identical thoughts forming in half a dozen thirteen-year-old heads: *Miss doesn't like him either*.

"Jason," she snapped, trying to make amends, "didn't you have something to say?"

"Er... yeah. Sorry, Matthew," Jason said, but there was a smugness in his voice that left Tess in no doubt that the damage had already been done. Despite his behaviour, Jason *knew* he was still the popular choice, even with his teacher, and that could only mean more trouble for Matthew further down the line.

"Everything okay?"

Tess turned briskly and straightened up. Her friend and head of department, Yvonne, older and more experienced by five years, was standing behind her. Yvonne had returned from collecting their pre-booked group ticket from the kiosk at the foot of the walkway.

"Just a little incident with a dead bird," Tess said. "All sorted now."

She glanced at Matthew, who stared resentfully back at her. The boy still had a faint brown stain on his red cheek. If she had been his mother she would have spat on the tissue and rubbed it until it was gone.

"I don't want to know," Yvonne said jovially. She was a large, rosy-faced woman with a mass of red hair. Raising her voice, she looked up and down the queue and called, "Right you lot, nice, straight line. No pushing or shoving. Who's looking forward to a terrifying plunge into the centre of the earth?"

Most of the kids cheered and raised their hands. A few of the girls looked gleefully terrified.

"Excellent!" Yvonne said. "Come on then."

For the next few minutes, Tess and Yvonne busied themselves handing out yellow hard hats and getting the children settled into the wooden seats of the open-sided train which would transport them underground. Aside from the bird incident, it had been a good day. Even the weather had held up, though the clouds were gathering now and a few spots of rain were beginning to patter on the plastic canopy of the walkway overhead.

They were at Porthellion Quay, a tin mining museum and visitor centre surrounded on three sides by towering Cornish cliffs. The museum was a sprawling affair, set in two hundred acres of hilly countryside, and consisting of a long-abandoned (though beautifully-preserved) mining village, and a small quayside and docks beside the fast-flowing River Tam. The children had been given a tour of the village and assay office, had had a lesson in the Victorian school (after first dressing up in period costume, much to their embarrassment and hilarity), had made rope on the "rope walk", and had enjoyed a picnic lunch down by the quayside. Now it was the highlight of the trip—a journey on a rickety narrow-gauge railway into the tin mine itself.

"Everybody wearing their hard hats?" asked the driver, a grizzled, wiry man dressed in blue overalls and an old miner's helmet with a lamp on the front.

Tess glanced at Francesca. She was the only one who had protested about the headgear, but even she was now perched sullenly in her seat, the strap tightly fastened beneath her chin.

"All ready, Mr. Hardacre!" shouted Yvonne, looking around and raising her eyebrows in gleeful anticipation.

"Let's be off then," Mr. Hardacre called.

He gave an unnecessary double-blast on the whistle, which made several of the children jump, and then, to a smattering of cheers, the train chugged jerkily forward.

Tess settled back, enjoying the rattling motion and the feel of wind on her face. She knew that the train cut leisurely through half a mile of woodland before plunging downhill into the mine itself, and she half-closed her eyes, relishing the sensation of light flickering across her vision as it forced its way through the gaps in the passing trees and bushes.

Raising his voice above the noise of the train, Mr. Hardacre began to deliver what was obviously a well-rehearsed spiel, providing them with various facts about mining and the mine itself. Tess listened as he told them how arsenic was a by-product of tin smelting, and how one of the often lethal jobs given to women and children was scraping the condensed arsenic off the walls of the calciners, which drew toxic fumes up from the smelting houses.

She phased out when he started to quote facts and figures relating to ore production and the length and depth of the mine's various shafts, and only knew that the mine entrance was coming up when several of the children sitting near the front of the train began to whoop. Opening her eyes, Tess saw the glinting thread of track, like a long zip, disappearing into the centre of an approaching black arch. Dazzled by the flickering sunlight, the arch seemed to her to be not quite there; it was like an absence of reality into which they were being inexorably drawn, its edges fuzzy, its heart of darkness utterly impenetrable.

She blinked fully awake just in time to be swallowed by blackness. A palpable ripple of fearful excitement ran through the group at the sudden claustrophobic chill emanating from the rocky walls, and at the way the light from Mr. Hardacre's lamp slithered and fractured across the tunnel's myriad planes and surfaces. Tess swallowed to ease the sudden pressure in her head, but even after the silent pop in her eardrums the previously guttural rumble of the train's engine sounded thick and muffled. She imagined the thick, dusty air clogging her throat and had to make a conscious effort not to cough. After a couple of minutes of travelling downhill, Mr. Hardacre eased back on the brake and brought the train to a grinding halt.

He gestured towards a tableau on their left. Illuminated by the light of a number of ersatz Davy lamps, fuelled not by oil but by electricity, was a family of mannequins. There was a father, a mother, a boy and a girl, all dressed in the drab clothes of a typical mid-nineteenth century mining family. The father's shiny, chipped face was streaked with black paint, evidently intended to represent subterranean grime. Like Mr. Hardacre, he wore a mining helmet and was resting a pickaxe on his shoulder.

"They're well creepy," Tess heard one of the girls whisper. She glanced in the direction of the voice and placed a finger to her lips, though she couldn't disagree.

The wide, painted eyes of the family seemed to stare blankly at the newly-arrived group. The little girl was missing a chunk of plaster from the centre of her face, which gave the impression that some hideous skin disease had eaten away her nose and part of her mouth.

Mr. Hardacre told them about life underground, about how the father would toil away for ten or twelve hours at a time in stifling conditions, while the children would sit waiting, often in pitch darkness, looking after his food and matches and whatever else he might bring down the mine with him. Meanwhile the women—if they weren't scraping arsenic off the walls of the calciners—would be at home, cleaning and washing and cooking the Cornish pasties that their husbands ate every day.

"Any questions?" Mr. Hardacre asked finally.

For a long moment there was silence, and then Simon Lawson tentatively raised a hand.

"Is the mine haunted?"

The shadows occupying the wrinkles in Mr. Hardacre's face deepened as he frowned. "Haunted?"

"Yes . . . I mean . . . well, people must have died down here. Accidents and that. So I just wondered whether there were any, like, stories or legends or anything. . . ."

Tess glanced at the boy, but in the gloom he was nothing but a hunched shadow.

"Ghosts, eh?" Mr. Hardacre said, and this time he smiled, the shadows flocking to his widening mouth. "Well, I don't know about that, but have you come across the story of the fallen boy on your travels today?"

There was a general shaking of heads.

"There's a bench with a plaque on it outside the sweet shop," Mr. Hardacre said. "It's dedicated to Michael Rowan, who died at the age of thirteen on March 16, 1865. Did anyone see that?"

A few hands went up, though Tess herself had not noticed the plaque.

"Well, there's a strange little story associated with him," Mr. Hardacre said. "Not a ghost story exactly, but still . . . sad. And a bit creepy.

"The mine, as I told you earlier, was founded in 1832. However there's a secondary shaft, which we'll see in a few minutes, which was created in 1865. The reason for this was that after thirty years of mining, the seams on this level were all but exhausted. It was decided, therefore, to mine deeper—and so the secondary shaft was created, in the hope that further seams would be discovered on a lower level.

"One of the most prominent miners at that time—he was a sort of manager, answerable directly to the mine owner—was a man called William Rowan. By all accounts, Rowan was not popular. He was a bear of a man, and something of a bully, and he had a son, Michael, who was apparently much the same.

"One of the victims of Michael's bullying was a young lad called Luke Pellant. The story goes that Michael chased Luke into the mine one night and that, in the darkness, Michael ended up losing his way and falling down the secondary shaft. It was just a big hole in the ground at that point, and back in those days there were no safety barriers or anything like that. Anyway, when Luke told everyone what had happened, a rescue operation was mounted, but of course it was too late—the lad had fallen eighty feet or so onto solid rock and was pretty much smashed to pieces.

"Although Luke claimed that Michael had fallen, Michael's father, William Rowan, didn't believe him. He accused Luke of pushing his son down the shaft, of murdering him, and he swore he'd see the boy brought to trial and punished. The general view, however, was that Michael's death had been nothing but the result of a terrible accident, and one that he had brought on himself. When nothing came of Rowan's campaign to see Luke brought to justice, Rowan was furious.

"A few weeks later, Luke disappeared, and it seems that although Rowan was initially suspected of having had something to do with it, Rowan himself put it about that the boy had fled out of guilt or shame for what he had done. In any event, nothing ever came of the incident—until about twenty years ago, when they were excavating the ground down by the quayside to lay the foundations for the information centre. During the excavation some bones were found—an almost entire skeleton, in fact—which tests revealed were about a hundred and fifty years old, and were those of a boy somewhere between the ages of ten and fifteen." Mr. Hardacre shrugged. "It's never been proven, but the general consensus is that William Rowan abducted and killed Luke Pellant and buried his remains down by the river. Of course, the Rowan family, who are still quite prominent in the area, refuse to accept it, and had the bench erected as a sort of . . . well, a sort of statement of defiance, I suppose."

"Are there any members of the Pellant family still about?" Tess asked.

Mr. Hardacre shook his head. "Not that I know of. Not in these parts anyway."

"So the bad kid gets remembered and the good one gets forgotten," one of the girls piped up. "That is *so* not fair."

Mr. Hardacre shrugged. "I don't think it makes much difference after all this time. Although if it's any consolation, Michael Rowan, despite the commemorative bench, is not regarded fondly around these parts. The locals call him the 'fallen boy', not only because he fell down the shaft, but also because, in their eyes, he—and his father—had fallen from grace."

"So does Michael Rowan's ghost haunt the mine then?" Simon Lawson asked.

Mr. Hardacre smiled. "Not that I know of. Shall we carry on?".

He started the train up again and they went deeper, the engine creaking and grinding as they chugged downhill. The tunnel became narrower, the walls more jagged and uneven, and Tess had to suppress a wave of claustrophobia when she looked up at the black ceiling and got the impression that it was crushing down on them, closing them in.

She was relieved several minutes later when the tunnel abruptly widened and they found themselves in a natural arena-like cavern, the walls and ceiling sloping away on all sides, giving a sudden disorientating sense of space. Once again, Mr. Hardacre eased back on the brake and the engine groaned to a halt.

"Right," he said, "who fancies a bit of mining?"

This time the response was not quite as enthusiastic. Tess and Yvonne ushered the children out of the train and ordered them to follow Mr. Hardacre, who led them across to what looked like a huge, squared-off well, surrounded by a metre-high wall. The shaft of the "well", a raft-sized square of impenetrable blackness, had been overlaid with a sheet of thick but rusty wire mesh.

"This is the secondary shaft I was telling you about," he said.

"The one that the boy fell down?" one of the girls asked.

"That's right. This shaft has been unused since the mine closed a hundred years ago. Even before then it was prone to floods and cave-ins."

"Are there any plans to open the shaft up again?" asked Yvonne.

Hardacre shook his head. "It would cost too much money. And there's nothing to see down there that you can't see up here." He raised a finger. "Now, remember I told you that children often used to sit down here for hours in the darkness, waiting for their fathers to finish work? Well, when I said darkness, I *meant* darkness. I was talking about the kind we don't usually experience in this modern age. The kind where you literally can't see your hand in front of your face. How many of you want to know what that kind of darkness is like?"

Tess glanced around. Most of the hands were going up, though some of the children looked nervous.

"All right then," Mr. Hardacre said. "But when the lights go off, I want you all to stand absolutely still. We don't want any accidents. Okay?"

There was a murmur of assent.

Mr. Hardacre crossed to a chunky plastic box on the wall, which had once been white but was now grimed and smeared with black fingerprints. The box had a single switch in its centre, and thick black wires snaked out of the top of it, leading to the ceiling of the tunnel, along the length of which, Tess noticed, were a series of dimly illuminated light bulbs. Mr. Hardacre switched off the lamp on his miner's helmet and then looked around at the group and smiled, evidently relishing the moment.

"Ready?" he said, and before anyone could answer he pressed his finger down on the switch.

There was a loud click, like a bone snapping, and the world vanished. Around her, Tess heard a brief, shrill chorus of alarmed squeals, which then seemed to abruptly cut off, leaving a silence and a darkness that felt skin-tight, constrictive. For a few seconds Tess was convinced that she could no longer move; she felt her throat closing up, her chest tightening. She couldn't shake the notion that she was all at once utterly alone. With an effort she raised her hand in front of her face, but she couldn't see it, she couldn't see anything.

She didn't realise she was holding her breath, waiting for something to happen, until she heard a scuffle of movement to her left. Then, for the third time in twenty minutes, Matthew Bellings cried out, his familiar, teeth-grating mewl of protest echoing jaggedly in the confined space. Immediately the light clicked back on and the world was restored. Blinking, somewhat dazed, Tess looked around her.

The children were standing in little groups, all except for Matthew. He was standing alone, in their midst but isolated. Tess focused on him, and her heart gave a sudden lurch. Matthew's face was scored with streaks of blackness. It was as if the darkness had not allowed him fully to return, as if it had eaten part of him away.

But of course that was nonsense. The black streaks were not darkness; they were simply dirt. Clearly someone had stepped up behind Matthew when the lights were out and had smeared begrimed hands across his cheeks. The question was—

"Who did this?" Yvonne snapped, stepping forward.

Tess's colleague was quivering with rage, pointing at Matthew but sweeping her burning gaze around the rest of the class. The children stared back at her silently or looked down at the floor.

"What did Mr. Hardacre tell you?" she continued. And when again she was met with silence, she shouted, "Well?"

"He told us to stand still so there wouldn't be any accidents, miss," replied Julie Steele, whose dark fringe half-obscured her chubby face.

"Yes he did, Julie. So why did one of you decide to be an idiot and do the exact opposite?"

Again, silence. Angrily Yvonne said, "Right, well there's only one way to resolve this. Everyone hold out your hands."

There was a shuffling, a collective glancing around, and then hands appeared, palms up, for inspection. Tess looked from one pair to the next, her gaze skittering. As far as she could see, they were all white, unsullied.

But not all the children had complied with Yvonne's instructions. At the back of the largest group, partly concealed by their classmates, were two crouching, whispering figures. They appeared to be facing each other, holding hands. And then Tess realised that they were not *holding* hands, but that one was *cleaning* the hands of the other.

"You two," she shouted, pointing, striding across.

Two guilty heads snapped up. Beneath the yellow bulbs of their hard hats, Tess recognised the faces of Jason Hayes and Francesca Parks.

Yvonne had joined her now. With her curly red hair streaming from beneath her own hard hat, she looked faintly ridiculous, but no one was laughing.

"Come here!" she hissed, her furiously sibilant voice echoing around the cavern.

Jason and Francesca shuffled forward. Francesca was holding a begrimed Wet Wipe.

"Jason Hayes, show me your hands," Yvonne ordered.

Jason hesitated, but the expression on his face was almost resigned. Slowly he turned over his hands, revealing his palms. Despite Francesca's ministrations they were still mostly black.

And so, a split-second later, was everything else.

Just as they had a couple of minutes before, the lights in the tunnel suddenly went out. This time, caught unawares, the screams from some of the children were louder, edged with panic. There was shuffling movement and someone called out; from the sounds they made, either they or someone else appeared to stumble and fall.

Yvonne's furious voice rose above the melee. "Everyone just *stand still!* Mr. Hardacre, what's going on?"

Tess heard the click-click, click-click of their guide testing the light switch.

"Must be a power cut," he said. "Hang on a sec."

There was a smaller click and suddenly a thin beam of white light cut through the blackness. It was the lamp on Mr. Hardacre's helmet. The beam bobbed and shivered, playing across the walls and the faces of the children as he moved his head.

"No need to panic," he said. "We'll just get back on the train. I'll soon have us out of here."

"Miss?" said a voice in the darkness.

Tess turned, but the children were little more than shadowy shapes.

"What is it?" she asked.

"Jason's gone, miss," the voice said, and now Tess recognised it as belonging to Francesca Parks. "He's not here."

"What do you mean—gone?" snapped Yvonne.

"I don't know, miss," said Francesca. "He was standing right next to me. But when the light came back on, he'd . . . disappeared."

Yvonne huffed. "Oh, this is ridiculous. What is that little idiot playing at?"

"Matthew Bellings has gone too, miss," one of the boys said.

Tess felt as though the situation was spiralling out of control. "What?" she said. "Are you sure?"

"Yes, miss. He was right there." A shadowy shape raised an arm, pointing at the spot where Matthew had been standing a few seconds before.

"Matthew?" Tess called, looking around. "Jason?"

There was no response. Tess and Yvonne looked at each other. Tess saw a flicker of fear in her colleague's eyes.

"Let's get the other children on the train," Yvonne said. "Count them to make sure we haven't lost anyone else."

They did it as quickly as the darkness would allow, while Mr. Hardacre did a quick recce of the tunnels leading off from the central cavern, shining his helmet-mounted light down each one and calling the boys' names.

Finally he returned, shaking his head. "I'll put a call through to the main office," he said. "Find out what—"

"*Listen*," said Tess.

"What—" Yvonne began, but Tess held up a hand for silence.

"I heard something . . . There it is again!"

They all listened now. From somewhere ahead of them and to their left came a scraping, a shuffling, as if someone or something was emerging from a burrow, scrabbling towards the light. Mr. Hardacre walked slowly forwards, placing his feet with care on the uneven ground, the beam of light from his helmet sweeping across the cavern walls.

Several of the children gasped as something suddenly tumbled out of one of the side tunnels. Tess saw white hands clawing at the ground, eyes flashing as a face turned towards them.

"Matthew!" she shouted and ran forward, ignoring Mr. Hardacre's warning about minding her footing.

Matthew was on his hands and knees, shivering with fear, his eyes wide and staring. His face was black with dirt. His mouth was hanging open, and as Tess approached him a string of drool fell from his lips and spattered on the ground.

She dropped to her knees, gathered him up in her arms. He flinched and then relaxed, clutching at her as though craving her warmth.

"Matthew," she said softly. "What happened? Do you know where Jason is?"

Matthew looked up at her. He was clearly dazed, confused.

"He called me Michael," he whispered.

"Who did?" asked Tess. "Jason, you mean?"

Matthew shook his head. "He called me Michael. He thought . . . he said. . . ."

Suddenly his face crumpled and he began to sob.

As Tess hugged him tight, trying to comfort him, Hardacre slipped past her, into the tunnel. Yvonne, bringing up the rear, panting a little, crouched down beside her. Before Yvonne could say anything, Tess gently transferred Matthew into her colleague's arms and muttered, "Look after him."

She stood up shakily. She could still see the white light from Hardacre's lamp shimmering across the walls of the side tunnel—and then he turned a corner and all at once they were plunged into blackness again.

Tess stepped forward, feeling her way into the tunnel. She moved sideways, crab-like, her hands sliding along the rocky walls, her feet probing ahead. With every step she couldn't help but imagine a precipice in front of her, a gaping abyss. She told herself she was being foolish, but she couldn't shake the idea from her mind.

Then she rounded a corner and suddenly saw thin slivers of ice-white light limning the jags and crevices of the tunnel ahead.

"Mr. Hardacre, wait!" she called and hurried towards him.

She flinched as he turned towards her, the light from his lamp flashing across her vision, blinding her.

"What are you doing here?" he said almost angrily. "You should have stayed in the cavern with the children."

"Yvonne's with them," Tess said. "Jason is one of my pupils. I couldn't just wait around in the darkness, doing nothing."

Hardacre made an exasperated sound, but he said, "Come on then. But be careful."

They moved on down the tunnel, Hardacre leading the way, his lamp light sliding across the glossy walls. Down here the world was stark and primal. A world of rock and silence, of harsh white and deep black, nothing in between.

"How deep does this tunnel go?" Tess whispered.

Hardacre's shoulders hunched in a shrug. "A mile maybe."

"Will it—" Tess began, but then she stopped.

There was a figure crouching in the tunnel ahead.

It was on its haunches, bent forward, its back to them. It was naked, its forehead resting against the rocky wall. It reminded Tess of a child playing hide-and-seek, counting to a hundred before standing up and shouting, "Coming, ready or not."

Hardacre had halted too. Tess stepped up beside him.

"Jason?" she said.

The figure didn't respond. Tess slipped by Hardacre, moving towards it.

"Be careful, miss," Hardacre said.

"It's all right," Tess replied, though her stomach was crawling with nerves. "There's nothing to be frightened of."

She was within arm's reach of the figure now. She could see the nubs of its vertebrae, the white skin streaked blackly with grime.

"Jason," she said again, and reached out to touch the figure's shoulder. It was freezing cold.

Unbalanced by her touch, the figure rocked backwards. It tumbled over like a turtle on to its back, still in a crouching position, its hands crossed in front of its belly, its knees drawn up.

When she saw what had been done to Jason's face, Tess screamed. She screamed and screamed, the sound echoing off the walls. For ever afterwards she would see the image in her mind. She would see black dirt spilling from the gaping cavern of Jason's mouth and tumbling from his empty eye sockets like thick dark tears.

BITERS

The guard on the gate stared at Mrs. Keppler's pass for a long time. He stared at it for *so* long, his face stern beneath his peaked cap, that Fleur began to get nervous. When he went back into his little hut, Fleur felt sure it was to call for reinforcements. She knew she'd done nothing wrong, and she was pretty sure that neither her friends nor Mrs. Keppler had done anything wrong either, but the sense of guilt and crawling dread persisted just the same.

Maybe it was the research facility that gave her these feelings. It was like a prison, all high steel fences and barbed wire and clanging gates. In that sense, it was only like a smaller version of the Compound in which they all lived. But the difference with the Compound was that you couldn't *see* the fences, not on a day to day basis anyway. And the guard uniforms were different here, grey and more formal than the faded brown combat fatigues that her brother Elliott and the rest of the perimeter security team wore. She saw the guard in the grey uniform speaking into a telephone and casting glances in their direction. Finally he put the phone down and marched stiffly across to the open door of the yellow school bus, where Mrs. Keppler was patiently waiting. Fleur was so relieved to see a smile break across the guard's face that her breath emerged in a gasp.

"That's all fine, madam," he said. "You have clearance to proceed."

Mrs. Keppler thanked him and the doors of the school bus concertinaed shut. The huge gates creaked slowly inwards and Mr. Medcalf, their driver, drove through the widening gap. Inside the facility, which looked to Fleur like nothing more than a mass of giant concrete building blocks stuck haphazardly together, more grey-uniformed men were pointing and waving their arms. Following their directions, Mr. Medcalf drove around to a car park at the back, where a squat, bald man whose brown suit matched the colour of his bristling moustache directed them with fussy hand movements into a designated space.

"Welcome to the Moorbank Research Facility," the man said when they had disembarked. "I understand you're here to participate in the Infant Care Program?"

Mrs. Keppler, a tiny, owlish woman, who to Fleur and her friends seemed ageless, said, "Yes, that's right."

"Excellent." Raising his voice slightly to address the class, the man said, "My name is Mr. Letts. I'm the assigned facilitator for your visit here today. I'll be escorting you to the Crèche, explaining the procedure and answering any questions you may have. Can I ask that you stick close together at all times and follow my instructions? We don't want anyone getting lost now, do we?"

He bared his small white teeth in a grin, which instantly tightened to an exasperated grimace when a hand shot up.

"Yes, Joseph," Mrs. Keppler said.

"Sir, Miss, I was wondering, are the betweeners allowed to walk around inside?"

A few of his classmates sniggered at the babyish phrase. In her sweet and patient voice, Mrs. Keppler said, "Of course not, Joseph. We won't be in any danger. Isn't that right, Mr. Letts?"

"Oh, absolutely," Mr. Letts agreed. "Security is paramount here at Moorbank."

He led them across the car park, towards a pair of large glass doors beneath a curved metal awning. Next to the doors, inset into a recess in the wall, was a dark glass panel. The pressure of Mr. Letts' hand on the panel activated a criss-crossing network of glowing red lasers, which drew murmurs of appreciation from the children. After the lasers had scanned Mr. Letts' handprint, a series of clunks announced that the locks sealing the doors had disengaged, allowing their guide to lead them inside.

"It smells funny," whispered Millie to Fleur, before clenching her teeth as her words echoed around the high-ceilinged lobby.

Her voice clearly didn't carry as far as the girls had thought, because the only person who answered was Alistair Knott, who stooped to push his freckled face between the girls' heads to murmur, "That's the chemicals they use to keep the biters fresh."

Millie pulled an "eeew" face and shuddered violently enough to rattle her beaded dreadlocks, but Fleur just rolled her eyes. As Mr. Letts led them along a series of featureless corridors and up numerous flights of stairs, Fleur recalled Mrs. Keppler telling them in their history lessons that although people had started turning into what Alistair had called "biters" before Fleur and her classmates were born, it wasn't really all *that* long ago—only thirty or forty years. It was long enough, Mrs. Keppler had said, for the world to have changed from the way it had been at the beginning of the twenty-first century, and for the living to have become sufficiently organised that their lives weren't a daily battle for survival. However it was not *really* long enough for the older generations, who remembered how things used to be, to have fully come to terms with the situation, or for scientists to have found a cure for the R1 virus.

The R in R1 stood for Reanimation. Mrs. Keppler had told them that too, though Fleur, like most kids, had known that since she could remember. It was a word she heard almost daily. It was what politicians and newsreaders called those with the virus: the Reanimated. Most people, like Elliott and Fleur's mum, Jacqui, just called them R1s, though sometimes Elliott called them "reamers." Jacqui didn't like him using that word, though; she said it was "derogatory," which Fleur thought meant that it was kind of a swearword, though she wasn't sure why. Most little kids called the R1s "betweeners" because they were neither one thing nor the other. And there were other words for them too, slang words like "biters" and "decoms" and loads of others.

What people never seemed to say, though, not directly anyway, was that the R1s were *dead*. It was like it was a taboo subject. It was like admitting something that was dark and forbidden. On the TV R1s were always described as "sufferers" or "victims" or "the infected." Fleur knew that scientists had been searching for a cure for the R1 virus for years, and she thought the reason no one ever actually said the R1s were dead was because you couldn't cure death, and that therefore that would mean the scientists had been wasting their time. When Fleur had asked Jacqui what the Reanimated were reanimated *from*, her mum had mumbled something about it being a "grey area." And when Fleur had pushed her to explain further, Jacqui had gotten angry and said she didn't want to talk about it.

The Facility was such a maze of corridors, staircases and numbered doors that the novelty of being inside it quickly paled. Fleur tried to imagine what might lie behind the doors. Offices? Laboratories? Cells for the inmates? If so, they must be empty or soundproofed, because, despite walking for what seemed like miles, she and her classmates did not encounter another soul, living or otherwise, on their journey. Plus they heard nothing but their own clomping feet and Mr. Letts' occasional barked orders to stay together.

When their guide finally turned and held up a hand, Fleur initially thought it was to reprimand those children who had begun to moan about their aching feet. Then Mr. Letts turned to a key pad and tapped in a code, whereupon the door beside it unsealed with a magnified wheeze. He marched inside without explanation, leaving Mrs. Keppler to usher the children after him.

Entering shoulder to shoulder with Millie, Fleur found herself in a white oblong room twice as big as her sitting-room at home. Despite its size, however, it was spartan, but for a desk, chair and computer tucked into an alcove in the left-hand wall. The most notable thing about the room was that almost the entire wall behind Mr. Letts, who had turned to face the children filing through the door, was composed of black glass. It reminded Fleur so much of a cinema screen that she half-expected Mr. Letts to tell them to sit down in cross-legged rows to watch a film about the history and function of the Facility.

He didn't, however. He simply stood, hands clasped in front of him, until they were all quiet. Then he said, "This is the observation and monitoring room for the Crèche here at Moorlands. Behind me is the Crèche itself, which I'm sure you are all eager to see. However, before I reveal it, I need to prepare you as much as I'm able for what you're about to experience. I also want to talk for a few minutes about the Infant Care Program in general. Before I start, can I ask how many of you have seen photographs or news footage of the Reanimated?"

Almost all the children raised their hands.

"And how many of you have seen the Reanimated in the flesh?"

All but two of the hands went down.

Mr. Letts fixed Ray Downey, who still had his hand up, with a penetrating stare. "Would you care to tell us about your experience?"

Now that he had been put on the spot, Ray's smug expression slipped into nervousness. As if justifying himself, he said, "I was with my friend, Jim Brewster. We were on our bikes one day and we heard all this shouting round the back of Hampson's store, so we went down to take a look. The biter was this old guy who must have gotten sick somewhere nearby and hadn't been reported in time. Mr. Hampson and some other men were holding him off with poles. Then the cops . . . er, the police came and they caught the biter in a net and took him away in a van." Almost reluctantly he added, "It was pretty cool."

"Cool," repeated Mr. Letts tersely. "Is that what you really thought?"

Ray Downey shrugged.

Pursing his lips disapprovingly, Mr. Letts turned to John Caine, the other boy with his hand up. "What about you?"

John's blond fringe twitched as he blinked it out of his eyes. His voice was so low and muffled it sounded as if his throat was trying to hold it back. "My dad took me to see the perimeter when I was six. We didn't go very close. We parked on a hill looking down on it. When we were there we saw an R1 come up to the fence. A woman."

"And how did that make you feel?"

John frowned in embarrassment or resentment. "Scared," he admitted.

"Why?"

"Because she made a horrible noise. And her skin was all sort of . . . blue and purple." As if the memory had enlivened him, the rest of his words emerged in a rush that threatened to descend into incoherence. "There was this look on her face. Blank, but like something had taken her over, as if she was a person but not really a person, as if she had turned into something *awful.* . . ." He ended with a coughing gasp, as if he'd run out of breath, and then in the same low, muffled voice with which he'd started his account he added, "It gave me nightmares."

Mr. Letts nodded as if in approval. "Thank you. That is closer to the response I was looking for." Clasping his hands again, he said, "The point is that a first hand encounter with an R1 is far more debilitating and disturbing than any amount of photographs or news footage can ever convey. The reason for this is that the Reanimated don't give off the subtle human signals we're used to, and which we subconsciously pick up on all the time, and so denied of that input, and coupled with their alarming appearance, our minds automatically recoil from them. It finds them repugnant, it finds them *wrong*, and therefore something to be avoided."

He paused, allowing his words to sink in. Then he said, "That, I'm afraid, is something that you're all going to have to accept and put aside in this instance. As I'm sure you have been informed, the Infant Care Program has been designed and formulated with a number of objectives in mind. First, it is to give young people like yourselves prolonged exposure to R1 sufferers—but exposure which, if you behave responsibly, will not result in either the slightest risk or injury to yourselves or those around you.

"Now, some of you may be wondering *why* exposure to the Reanimated is considered such a valid and valuable exercise. The simple answer is that it will both enable you to understand and come to terms with those afflicted by the virus, and also hopefully allay some of the fears and prejudices you perhaps have about them. R1 is part of our world now, and despite ongoing research it is unlikely to disappear in any of our immediate futures. The more understanding and acceptance we therefore have of its effects and of those afflicted by it, the better it will be for all concerned in the long term. After all, it is likely that some of you will be working with, or in close proximity to, R1 sufferers once you leave school and venture into the world of employment. It is therefore best to be prepared—and the Infant Care Program is an invaluable step towards that state of preparation."

Warming to his subject, he continued, "A further reason why the Program itself has been implemented is to give young people a chance to temporarily assume what is in effect a considerable amount of personal responsibility. This may seem daunting, even frightening, at first, but we in the Program hope that ultimately you will come to look upon this next week as both a challenge and an opportunity to show just *how* mature and resourceful you can be. Before I talk about the specifics of your assignments, let me dispel some of the rumours about R1."

He raised a finger, as if about to accuse them of starting the rumours themselves. And then, as forcefully as if resuming an argument, he said, "Yes, R1 *is* a virus, but it could only be contracted by living beings such as yourselves if your blood and/or other bodily fluids were to become mingled with that of an R1 sufferer. R1 is not—I repeat *not*—an airborne virus. Neither can it be contracted simply by touching the flesh of a sufferer—however, we will issue you with a plentiful supply of disposable gloves as an extra precaution against physical contact.

"In the unlikely event that you *should* get scratched or bitten by your assigned R1 infant during the course of the Program, the important thing to remember is, firstly, not to panic, and secondly, to seek immediate medical attention. Although we are still some way from finding a cure for the virus, we have discovered a vaccine that can eradicate R1 cells in the early stages of infection. Evidence has shown that patients treated with this vaccine within the first ninety minutes of infectious contact have a 98.7% recovery rate. However, there is *no need whatsoever* for you to become involved in any situation where there is even the remotest risk of infection. The R1 infant assigned to you should remain muzzled at all times, and as long as you adhere to the necessary precautions you will be fine."

Alastair Knott raised a hand. Mr. Letts frowned. "Yes?"

"What about feeding time?" Alastair asked. "Won't we have to take the muzzles off then?"

"Not at all," Mr. Letts replied curtly. "We will issue you with more than enough disposable feeding tubes, which you attach to the front of the muzzle. I will demonstrate how in a few minutes."

As if Alastair's question had emboldened the rest of the class, Millie now raised her hand. "What about the smell?" she said. "My mum says she doesn't want an R1 in the house because they stink."

Mr. Letts looked momentarily outraged, but a huff of exasperation downgraded the expression into a scowl. Acidly he said, "The Facility's inmates do not smell. Like all R1 sufferers, it's true that their bodies have succumbed to a limited amount of physical corruption—a process which is subsequently arrested by what we call the 'R1 barrier', which incidentally we still do not fully understand—but all of our test subjects have been treated with a combination of chemicals which negates the more unpleasant effects of bodily decomposition." He glanced at Mrs. Keppler. "Well, if there are no more questions, I think it's time for you to become acquainted with your charges."

For the first time Fleur felt jittery with nerves as the class lined up to each be presented with a metal tag bearing a four-digit number. When that was done, Mr. Letts crossed unhurriedly to a narrow door tucked between the edge of the glass screen and the adjoining wall and tapped out a code on a key pad. The effect of his action, as he stepped back, was two-fold. The lights flickered on in the Crèche, transforming the black screen into a viewing window, and the door unlocked with a series of clicks.

As she shuffled forward behind a dozen of her classmates, Fleur glanced almost unwillingly at the room beyond the glass. She was just in time to see rows of evenly-spaced incubators made of opaque plastic the colour of sour milk before she was through the door and among them.

The first thing that struck her about the Crèche was its stillness. The incubators were so silent that they might have been occupied by dead meat, or nothing at all. The stillness seemed to reach out and stifle the combined sound of almost thirty thirteen-year-olds—the rustle of clothing, the squeak of rubber soles on vinyl flooring, the soft rasp of respiration that was trying not to escalate beyond nervousness. When Mr. Letts, who had slipped into the room at the back of the group, spoke, it made them all jump.

"Some of you may be experiencing a sense of disquiet, perhaps even anxiety or distress, about now. Am I right?"

As if on cue, one of the girls—Fleur thought it might have been Lottie Travis—failed to curtail a sob. Around her she became aware of heads nodding slowly, and then of her own joining in.

"That's a perfectly natural reaction," Mr. Letts said in an almost kindly voice. "Living babies are a bundle of instincts. As human beings we're used to them moving almost constantly, even in repose—but the R1 infants, as you will see, are a different case entirely. Their only instinct is to feed, but they seem to know—or at least their bodies do—that there is little point transferring energy and resources into limbs that do not respond in an efficient manner. Therefore they remain motionless as they wait to be fed. Having lived almost all their short lives in the Facility they have become creatures of habit. They feed three times a day and they expel waste products once a day. The advantage of this for you is that as long as you administer to these routine requirements you will find the R1 infants simple to maintain. If, however, you deny them their sustenance for any length of time then they will do what normal infants do. Can you guess what that is?"

Fleur put up her hand. "Cry?"

"Exactly," replied Mr. Letts. "Though it is a cry you will never have heard before, and almost certainly will never want to hear again."

Behind her, Fleur heard another sob tear itself loose from Lottie. There was a prolonged shuffle and bump as Mrs. Keppler led the girl through the crowd and out of the room, and then Mr. Letts said, "Time to match you up, I think."

Gesturing towards the incubators, he told them to search for the one that matched the number on their tag. Fleur looked at hers as her classmates shifted around her like restless cattle. After a few seconds several of her peers—Ray Downey, Alastair Knott, Tina Payne—broke away from the huddled group and began to move tentatively among the rows of tiny plastic boxes.

"What's *your* number?" Millie asked almost fearfully, as if one of the tags might prove the equivalent of a short straw.

"4206," Fleur replied.

"Mine's 9733. Let's look together, shall we?"

The numbers on the incubators seemed random, as if this was a treasure hunt or a puzzle, but Fleur supposed they must adhere to *some* system somewhere. Like Millie she tried to focus on the numbers stamped on the ends of the plastic boxes rather than on their contents, which remained nothing but darkish blurs on the periphery of her vision. It took her several minutes, but at last she spotted the number that matched the one on her tag.

"It's here," she said, suddenly breathless.

"What have you got?" asked Millie. "A girl or a boy?"

"I daren't look," Fleur replied.

"I'll look for you then, shall I?" Millie moved up beside her. After a few seconds, she quietly said, "It's a boy."

Fleur felt as though she was having to override a physical restraint in order to raise her head. She managed it at last, blinking to focus her gaze. The baby in the incubator was lying on its back with its arms spread in a crucifix position. It looked not dead but as if it was pretending to be, which was somehow worse. Its eyes were dark glints in its mottled, bluish face, and its chest, which should have been rising and falling, was as still as a lump of clay and not dissimilar in texture.

"He's cute," Millie said, not at all convincingly. "What are you going to call him?"

Fleur's thoughts felt heavy as wet cement. She blurted out the first and only thing that came to mind.

"Andrew," she said. "After my dad."

"So this is it, is it?"

Elliott peered into the portable crib, which Fleur had put on the kitchen table. As always he looked tired and grubby after a long shift spent patrolling the perimeter, his hair peppered with the dust that kicked up from the scrubland. He was twenty, lean and muscular, often difficult to predict emotionally. Sometimes he was broody, uncommunicative; other times he was easy-going, quick to smile. Fleur loved her brother, but she couldn't say that she fully understood his quicksilver personality. Needless to say, most of her friends found him mysterious, and so had a massive crush on him.

"He's a he, not an it," she said.

Elliott snorted. "Has Mum seen it?"

"Not yet. She's at Aunty Valerie's."

"Course," said Elliott, raising his eyebrows. "It's Friday. I lose track in my job." He opened the fridge, took out a bottle of soda and opened it with a crack and a hiss. Dropping his weight into a wooden chair with a groan, he took a swig, then gave her a shrewd, sidelong look. "She won't like having it in the house, you know. She hates those things."

Fleur felt irritably defensive. "He can't help how he is."

Elliott shrugged. "Even so."

As Fleur prepared the baby's feed, the silence stretched between them. It was a silence redolent with bad memories and unspoken grief. The reason Elliott was a perimeter guard was because their father had been one before him. Seven years ago, when Fleur was six and Elliott thirteen, Andy McMillan had been on patrol when a section of faulty fencing in his quadrant had collapsed, allowing a group of at least two dozen R1s to swarm into the Compound. In the ensuing melee, Andy had suffered multiple bites—so many that the virus had taken hold quickly. Jacqui was the only one who had seen her husband in the hospital, raging and inhuman. And it was she, alone and traumatised, who had had to make the terrible decision which faced every R1 sufferer's next of kin—to allow their loved one to live on in a contained, controlled environment, or to give the order to bring their suffering to a swift and humane end.

Fleur had been too young to fully appreciate Jacqui's anguish over the decision, but Elliott's reaction and the subsequent screeching arguments between Fleur's mother and brother were scarred onto her memory. Elliott had accused Jacqui of murdering their father. Jacqui had retaliated by saying that she had only been carrying out Andy's wishes, that he had made it abundantly clear that if the worst ever happened the last thing he would want would be for his family to see him reduced to the state of a slavering, mindless animal.

Eventually, of course, the raw wounds had closed up and the arguments had subsided. But they had never properly healed. There had been so much venom released during the endless round of accusations and counter-accusations, so much anger and hatred and hurt expelled and absorbed by both sides, that there would always be a tenderness there, a weak spot. Jacqui and Elliott loved one another, relied on one another, looked out for one another—but there still existed an underlying tension between them, a sense that if, for whatever reason, circumstances should ever force the wound to re-open, then all the old venom and more besides would come gushing out anew.

It was Elliott who eventually broke the silence. "That stuff smells disgusting."

Fleur couldn't disagree. She had emptied one of the sachets of powdered meal, which they had each been given before leaving the Facility, into a bowl and was now adding hot water, as instructed. The stench that rose from the reddish paste was like the most rancid dog food imaginable. Holding her breath and screwing up her eyes, she nodded at a silvery rucksack emblazoned with the Moorlands logo, which was leaning against a table leg. "Get a feeding tube out of the pack, will you?"

Elliott stretched out a leg, hooked the pack with his foot and pulled it towards him. He rummaged through its contents and extracted a short length of corrugated tubing with a metal screw attachment at one end and a funnel at the other.

"I'm guessing you mean one of these," he said, handing it to her.

She took it from him. "Thanks."

He watched as she screwed the tube into a circular aperture at the front of the visor-like muzzle that was fastened securely around the lower half of the baby's face.

"Fucking grotesque," Elliott said with a bleak laugh. "Now it looks like an elephant foetus."

Ignoring her brother, Fleur mixed cold water into the thick, foul-smelling gruel and then began to spoon it into the funnel-like end of the feeding tube. After a moment the baby's black eyes widened, its limbs began to twitch and squirm, and it began to eat with a muffled, wet, gnashing sound.

"Oh, that is totally gross," Elliott said almost delightedly, rocking back in his chair.

Fleur shot him a disapproving look. "He needs to eat, Elliott."

Elliott sat forward again abruptly, his eyes narrowing. "Why does he? I mean, why does *it*?"

"Because it's a school project," Fleur said. "I have to look after him. Do you want me to fail for being a bad mother?"

Elliott shrugged. "Who's going to know?"

Fleur pointed at a thin metal bracelet around the baby's right wrist. "That monitors his physical state—his metabolism and stuff. They'd know if I didn't look after him properly."

Elliott peered at the bracelet. "I could probably fix that."

"Don't you dare!" said Fleur. "I want to do this properly."

"Why?"

"I just do, that's all."

Elliott pulled a face. "Well, I think it's sick. Looking after those things, keeping them alive. . . ."

"They're test subjects," said Fleur. "Without live subjects we'd never find a cure for the R1 virus."

"That's what you're doing now, is it?" taunted Elliott. "Vital medical research?"

Before Fleur could reply there was the rattle of a key in the lock and the front door along the hall opened, admitting a brief roar of traffic noise.

Fleur tensed as her mother's footsteps approached the kitchen. She'd wanted to get the first feed over and done with before Jacqui arrived home. As it was, her mother appeared in the kitchen doorway with her face screwed into an expression of repugnance.

"What's that awful smell?" she said.

"It's the baby's feed," said Fleur nervously. "Sorry, Mum. It does pong a bit."

Jacqui put down her bags and sloughed off her threadbare coat as she walked across the room. She'd become thinner over the last few years, though not in a healthy way. She looked haggard and pale, her green eyes too large for her once elfin face, her almost-black hair tied back in a lifeless ponytail. Fleur felt her guts squirm as her mother examined the feeding infant, the repugnance on her face hardening into something more deep-rooted.

"How was Aunt Valerie?" Fleur asked to break the silence.

"Same as always." With barely a pause, Jacqui asked, "Where are you going to keep it?"

"In my room," Fleur said.

"It'll stink the place out."

"It doesn't smell. Only its food does. It'll be finished in a minute." She avoided Elliott's eye as she spoke, aware that she too was now referring to the baby not as "he" but "it"—compromising her principles to avoid conflict.

To her surprise her mum said, "Poor creature."

Elliott made a non-committal sound that could have been an acknowledgement of her comment or a rebuttal of it.

"I thought you hated the R1s," Fleur said tentatively.

"I hate the virus," Jacqui said. "And when people get infected the virus is all they become." She nodded at the baby. "It doesn't mean I don't grieve for the people the virus wipes out, the ones who once occupied the flesh—or in this case the one who never even got a chance to become a person."

"You don't think the real person is still in there somewhere then?" said Fleur. "And that if they find a cure those people will come back?"

All sorts of emotions chased themselves across Jacqui's face. "I want to believe," she said eventually. "But I don't know if I can."

"Ricky Jackson's dad took his back. Said he and Ricky's mum couldn't stand having it in the house. So did Lottie Travis's mum—she said it was giving Lottie nightmares. But did you hear about Tina Payne?" Millie's brown eyes were wide.

Fleur shook her head.

"Get this," Millie said, and lowered her voice to a dramatic murmur. "Her dad came home drunk, and the baby was crying 'cos Tina wasn't feeding it properly. So he took it outside and dumped it head-first in the bin and buried it under some rubbish and didn't tell anyone. It was there two days before Tina went out and heard it crying."

"That's awful," said Fleur. "Was it all right?"

Millie's shrug sent her dreadlocks swaying and clinking. "S'pose. They don't die, do they, even if you don't feed them? You have to cut off their heads or burn them to kill them."

Fleur tried to imagine being upside-down in a bin full of stinking rubbish for two days. The thought of it made her feel sick. "Do they feel pain or distress, do you think?"

Millie pulled a face. "Don't think so. Don't think they feel anything really."

"Must be awful," said Fleur.

Millie nodded. "Yeah, I'd rather be dead than. . . ." Then she realised what she was saying and clenched her teeth in apology. "Hey, sorry, I didn't mean. . . ."

Fleur waved a hand as though wafting a fly. "It's okay. So how did you find out all this stuff anyway?"

Millie dipped her hand into the pocket of her shorts and extracted a wafer-thin rectangle with a burnished steel finish. "Smartfone 4.5," she said. "Gossip Central. You should get one. Then we could talk all the time."

"I wish," said Fleur, trying not to look envious. "But we can't afford it. We've only got Elliott's wage coming in. Mum's got a 2.5, but she doesn't let me use it."

"Bummer," said Millie, then her eyes brightened. "Hey, I might be getting a new 5.1 for Christmas. If I do, you can have this one."

"Thanks," said Fleur, but she knew that even with the best network deal she could find she would still never be able to afford to actually use the damn thing.

That was the only drawback about coming to Millie's—sometimes her best friend forgot, or simply didn't realise, how tight money was for Fleur and her family. That was why she hadn't seen Millie for the whole of the half-term holiday—she couldn't afford the bus fare and it was too far to walk. Ordinarily Fleur might have cycled round on her rickety old bone-shaker, but with "Andrew" to look after she hadn't been able to. So she had been stuck at home all week with nothing to do except feed and change the baby, read books and do household chores for Mum.

Now, however, it was Friday, which Mum always spent with Dad's sister, Aunt Valerie. Jacqui passed Millie's house on the way to Valerie's, so Fleur had persuaded Mum to drop her off en route and pick her up again on the way home.

The house Millie lived in was big, with apple trees in the front garden and a huge backyard with a swimming pool. Beyond the yard was a meadow, and beyond that was woodland. If you walked straight through the woods for about four hours, Millie's fifteen-year-old brother Will had told them, you would come to the perimeter. He had been there with his friends several times, and said it was "jazz" and that they should do it sometime. However, the girls preferred to stay close to civilisation—to the pool and the computer and Millie's mum's home-made peanut cookies.

Today had been the warmest day of the holiday. The girls had been for a swim and were now sitting on the wooden seat which encircled the largest of the ancient fruit trees in the front garden. Their backs were resting against gnarled bark which had been worn smooth by the pressure of many such backs over the years. Sunlight winking through the leaves overhead formed a moving pattern of light and dark on their bare legs.

"Can't wait to give the stupid thing back," Millie said. "Only three days to go now." She waved her clenched fists in the air and made a muted cheering sound.

Fleur glanced at Andrew, lying like a dead weight in his portable crib a few metres away. He seemed unaffected by the sunlight shining directly onto his tiny, mottled, blue-grey body.

"It hasn't been so bad," Fleur said. "In fact, it's been quite easy."

"Yeah, but I dread waiting for mine to shit every day," said Millie. "It stinks like . . . rotting fish or something. Doesn't it make you gag?"

"I've gotten used to it," Fleur said. "I hold my breath."

"But it's the look of it," said Millie, pulling a face. "It's *green*. And *slimy*."

Fleur grinned and was about to reply when a howl of pain from behind the house sliced through the drowsy afternoon air. This was followed by several people all shouting at once, their voices shrill with panic.

"That's Will," Millie said, jumping to her feet.

She ran towards the path that led round the side of the house. Fleur glanced at Andrew lying motionless in his crib, decided he'd be fine, and went after her.

The backyard was full of boys in swimming shorts. They were crowding round Will, whose dark-skinned shoulders were gleaming with water or sweat. Will was holding up his right hand, and so shocked was Fleur to see his bottom lip trembling and tears pouring down his face that she didn't notice the blood at first. Then she saw the cut on the pad of his upraised index finger, from which blood was trickling into his clenched fist. Fleur was confused. It didn't look bad enough to warrant all this fuss.

"What happened?" Millie shouted. "What happened?"

One of the boys glanced behind him and Fleur followed his gaze. On the stone flags a couple of metres from the edge of the pool was the portable crib which she assumed contained the R1 baby assigned to Millie, a girl who Millie had named "Rose."

"We were playing chicken," the boy said, his voice tight and high with the knowledge that they had made a terrible decision, a decision from which there was no going back. "It was Ryan's idea."

"It wasn't my fault!" a boy who must have been Ryan protested.

"Never mind whose fault it was," Millie shouted. "What's chicken? What do you mean?"

All at once Fleur knew exactly what they meant. Calmly but urgently she said, "They were daring each other to stick their fingers in Rose's feeding hole. Only Will didn't pull his finger out quickly enough and he got bit."

Millie's eyes widened in horror. "You idiot!" she screeched at her brother. "You stupid idiot!"

Will was blubbing like a baby, tears and snot pouring down his face. "I'm gonna get the virus," he wailed. "I'm gonna become a biter."

"No you're not," Fleur said firmly. "If you get treatment within the first ninety minutes they can stop the infection."

"Really?" Will said, his teary eyes stretched wide with desperate hope.

Turning to Millie, Fleur said, "He needs to go to hospital. Is your mum—"

But Millie was already wheeling towards the house. "Mum!" she screamed. "Mum!"

"He'll be fine, Mum," Millie said softly. "You'll see."

Millie's mum, Clara, had once been a model. To Fleur, her mahogany-coloured skin seemed to glow, as if with some inner light. She had thickened a little around the waist since her modelling days, but even now, in her forties, she was a breathtakingly beautiful woman. At this moment, however, she looked wretched, her finely-boned face taut with worry, her hands quivering as they twisted a tear-dampened handkerchief into smaller and smaller knots.

Fleur was sitting on the other side of Clara, in a plastic chair against the wall of the waiting area outside a pair of sealed grey double doors. Above the doors was a sign which read:

R1 INFECTION AREA
RESEARCH AND TREATMENT
AUTHORIZED PERSONNEL ONLY

"Millie's right, Mrs. Hawkes," Fleur said reassuringly. "The man at the Moorlands Facility told us they have these drugs called—" she wrinkled her nose as she struggled to remember "—anti-necrotics, which block and kill off the R1 cells. They're, like, virtually a hundred per cent effective."

Clara Hawkes nodded vaguely, but she shot a venomous glance towards Andrew, who was lying silent and still in his crib on the seat next to Fleur. "I don't know why they let you girls *have* those damn things in the first place. I always said this project was a bad idea."

Fleur stayed silent. She knew it wasn't the right time to say that the babies weren't to blame, and that the situation had occurred purely as a result of Will's stupidity. Clara had insisted that Millie leave Rose behind at the house, even though she would need feeding again in an hour or so. At first Fleur thought Clara was going to tell her that she couldn't bring Andrew either, but Millie's mum had been so preoccupied with her panic-stricken son that she had made no comment when Fleur had placed Andrew's crib on the middle seat in the back of the car.

They had been at the hospital now for over an hour, waiting for news. The bearded doctor who had spoken to them when they had first arrived had told them that Will would be treated immediately, but that they would have to monitor him for a while until they were sure that all traces of the infection had been eradicated.

"How long will it be before you know for sure?" Clara had asked.

"It depends entirely on Will's response to treatment," the doctor had replied smoothly. "Based on past experience it could be anything between one and six hours."

In the seventy minutes or so since their arrival, a couple of white-coated doctors had entered the Infection area, having first tapped entry codes into a key pad on the wall, but no one had come out. Fleur looked at her watch. It was almost 3:50 PM. Her mum wasn't due to pick her up until six, but if nothing happened within the next hour she'd have to call her and tell her what was happening. She looked at Andrew lying in his crib. She couldn't say she felt any particular affection for the boy, but she no longer felt the anxiety and repugnance she had experienced in the presence of the R1 infants a week ago. In that respect, she supposed, the project *had* been a success, whatever Millie's mum thought. She looked round as the double doors to the Infection area hummed, clicked and then began to open as someone pushed them from the other side. The person who emerged was the last one she expected to see.

"Mum!" she gasped.

Jacqui froze, a look of horror on her face. It was the expression of someone who had been caught red-handed, someone who had nowhere to hide. As if reading her daughter's mind, Jacqui blurted out the question that was on Fleur's lips: "What are *you* doing here?"

"We were . . ." Fleur said, trying to pull her jumbled thoughts together. "I mean . . . Will got bit . . . Millie's brother, I mean." She frowned. "Why aren't you at Aunt Valerie's?"

For a moment Jacqui looked trapped—then her shoulders slumped. "Oh well, I suppose it had to come out sooner or later," she said.

"What did?" asked Fleur.

Jacqui gave her a strange look—a sad, resigned look that made Fleur's stomach clench.

Then, quietly, she said, "We need to talk."

Sitting hunched over, as if weighed down by a burden of unspoken revelations, Jacqui reached out and took Fleur's hands. She drew a long breath into her lungs and slowly expelled it, and then she said, "I lied. Your father's not dead."

The instant Jacqui said the words, Fleur knew she should have been expecting them. Yet they hit her like a bolt of lightning. She jerked in her seat; her mind reeled; her world flipped upside-down. She gripped hard on to her mother's hands to stop herself from falling, and from somewhere far away she heard her own small voice asking, "So why did you say that he was?"

Jacqui sighed and her body slumped lower in her seat, as if she had been inflated by nothing but secrets and regret for the past seven years, and it was all now leaking out of her.

"Because he wanted me to. Because he couldn't bear the thought of you seeing him like . . . like that." Her voice dropped to a whisper. "But *I* couldn't bear to let him go. I knew there was research going on. I knew that scientists and doctors were trying to find a cure for the virus. And if I'd given the order for your dad to . . . to be despatched and then they'd found a cure . . ." She shook her head. "I would never have forgiven myself."

Fleur didn't know how to feel. Didn't know whether to be angry or happy, horrified or betrayed. "We could have helped you," she said, "Elliott and me."

Jacqui shook her head. "It wouldn't have been fair on you. You were just a little girl. I thought a clean break. . . ."

Her voice tailed off. Fleur said quietly, "But you let Elliott think . . . you let him *say* all those terrible things to you."

"It was the best way," insisted Jacqui. "The *only* way."

Another short silence, as if the conversation was too big or too painful to be handled in anything other than bite-sized chunks.

Eventually Fleur said, "And what about now? Will you tell Elliott now?"

"Will you?" countered Jacqui.

Fleur shook her head. "I don't know. I don't know what to do. I don't know what to *think*."

"You don't have to decide anything yet. Why don't you just . . . get used to the idea first?"

Fleur let her gaze slide past Millie and Clara, sitting a dozen or so metres away, to the grey doors beyond them. "Is Dad in there?"

Jacqui nodded.

"So you come here every Friday? You don't go to Aunt Valerie's at all?"

"I see your Aunt Valerie in the mornings," said Jacqui. "We have lunch and then I come here. Valerie used to come with me at first, but she found it too upsetting. Now it's just me."

"What do they do to him in there?" Fleur asked. Anger sparked in her and she welcomed it, grasped it. It was a real emotion, something to anchor herself to. "Do they *experiment* on him?"

"No!" Jacqui's denial was loud enough to make Millie and Clara turn their heads. Controlling herself she said, "No, I wouldn't allow that. They try to cure him, that's all. Anything new they discover, any breakthroughs they make, your dad's one of the first to benefit from it."

"So he's a test subject," said Fleur.

"You make it sound bad. It's not bad. They're trying to make him better. They're not hurting him. I make sure of that. He has a good life . . . for what it is."

Another silence. Fleur felt sick and hollow. She was finding it all hard to digest. Finally she said, "Have they made any progress?"

Jacqui didn't answer immediately. And then hesitantly she said, "I think so . . . yes."

"I want to see him," said Fleur.

Jacqui looked alarmed. "I don't know if that's a good idea."

"He's my dad. I want to see him. You can't tell me he's alive and then not let me see him."

Now Jacqui looked anguished, torn. "I'm not being mean," she said. "I just . . . I don't want you upset, that's all."

"I can handle it," said Fleur stubbornly. "I'm old enough." She paused and then said with quiet conviction, "I want to see my dad."

Jacqui stared at her for what seemed to Fleur like a long time. She stared at her as if she had never seen Fleur properly before, as if she had not noticed until now how quickly her little girl had grown up.

Then she gave a short decisive nod. "Okay," she said. "Come with me."

She stood up and walked back towards the grey doors. Fleur picked up Andrew's crib and followed her. As they passed Millie and Clara, Millie half-reached out. "Hey, you okay?"

"Fine," said Fleur, giving Millie no more than a glance. She could see that her best friend was brimming with questions, but she averted her gaze, unwilling to give Millie any encouragement to ask them right now. Instead Fleur watched Jacqui stab a code number into the key pad on the wall, and then she followed her through the grey doors.

Dr. Beesley had hair growing out of his nose. Fleur couldn't stop staring at it. She felt not quite real. She felt as if this was a dream, or as if her thoughts were floating like balloons a few metres above her head. She shifted her gaze to Dr. Beesley's plump wet lips in the hope that if she saw the shape of the words he was forming, she would find it easier to concentrate on them.

"We think there has been some definite progress," he was saying to Jacqui. "Thanks to the new drug treatment, Andy's aggression levels are considerably reduced, and he seems far more responsive to his surroundings and to both auditory and visual stimuli. Dr. Craig informs me that you were there when they played the music this morning?"

Jacqui nodded. "Yes. It seemed to me as if Andy was listening to it. Aware of it, at least."

Dr. Beesley nodded. "And he's the same with voices. He no longer automatically identifies a human voice as simply the location of a potential food source. When we talk to him he appears to listen. Sometimes I swear he understands every word I'm saying." He chuckled at his own joke, and then asked, "Did he establish eye contact with you this morning?"

"No, I . . . no," Jacqui said.

"Well, hopefully that will come. There have been brief indications of it already. Nothing conclusive, but we remain cautiously optimistic—as ever." Finally Dr. Beesley turned his attention to Fleur. "So you've come to see your father, little lady?"

Fleur frowned and for a fleeting moment considered telling the doctor that she was thirteen, not six. Instead she nodded.

"Very good. First contact with an infected loved one is never anything less than an emotional experience, but if you're prepared for that, I'm sure Andy will benefit from your visit."

"He might not," muttered Jacqui.

Dr. Beesley frowned. "I'm sorry?"

"Fleur found out about Andy by accident. Until twenty minutes ago she thought he was dead." Jacqui took a deep breath. "Now she insists on seeing him, though personally I'm worried how Andy might react. He never wanted his children to see him . . . well, you know. . . ."

"I see," said Dr. Beesley slowly. "Well, the decision is yours to make. I would offer advice, but such encounters are entirely unpredictable. All I can recommend is that if Andy *does* start to show signs of distress, it might be best to beat a hasty retreat."

"We will," said Jacqui decisively.

"Could I see my dad now, please?" said Fleur.

A little taken aback at her directness, Dr. Beesley said, "Er . . . yes of course. This way."

He led Fleur and Jacqui along several corridors until they came to one which had a gate stretching wall to wall and floor to ceiling. A six-digit code punched into yet another wall-mounted key pad opened the gate. Beyond were closed, numbered doors not unlike the ones at the Moorlands Facility. Dr. Beesley led them around the corner and halted outside a door numbered 5.13. Another key pad, another entry code, and the door clicked open.

With a sweep of his arm, Dr. Beesley invited Jacqui and Fleur to precede him into the room. Not knowing quite what to expect, Fleur allowed Jacqui to go first, and then followed, moving with a lop-sided lurch because Andrew's crib, which she was carrying by the handles, kept bumping against her thigh.

She found herself in what amounted to a smaller version of the Crèche at the Moorlands Facility. The ante-room was narrow, rectangular. A nurse's monitoring station, currently unoccupied, was tucked up against the left-hand wall. Directly before them, opposite the door through which they had entered, was another wall made of what appeared to be thick transparent Perspex. The white-walled room beyond that was twice the size of this one, simply furnished with a bed and a chair, both of which were bolted to the floor. There was a man lying on the bed, arms by his sides, unmoving. Fleur could only see him in profile, but she gasped in recognition.

"Dad!"

He was thinner than she remembered him, and his skin had the same mottled, blue-grey hue of all R1 sufferers. Beesley appeared from behind her and indicated a small metal grille on the wall above a pair of buttons. "You can speak to him if you like. Just press this button here."

Fleur didn't move. All at once she felt uncertain, a little overwhelmed by the situation. Unable to tear her eyes from the motionless figure, she was only half-aware of her mum stepping across to the grille and thumbing the button.

"Andy." Jacqui's amplified voice made Fleur jump. "There's someone here to see you."

To Fleur's consternation the figure on the bed stirred. Her father's leg twitched slightly; his fingers moved like worms probing blindly for the light.

He looked like Frankenstein's monster coming alive in some of the old movies she'd seen.

"Say hello to your dad, Fleur," Jacqui said softly. "Don't be shy."

Fleur licked her lips. She put down Andrew's crib and moved across to stand beside her mum. She felt as if she were floating, drifting. Jacqui, her thumb still on the talk button, smiled encouragingly.

Fleur bent her head towards the grille. Her mouth was dry. She licked her lips again. Finally she croaked, "Hello, Dad. It's me. It's Fleur."

Slowly, like an old man waking from a deep sleep, her father rose from the bed. First of all he sat up, and then he turned, his legs swinging clumsily over the side of the mattress, his feet brushing the floor.

Fleur stepped back, unable to stifle a small, involuntary bleat of distress. Viewing her dad full-on for the first time, she saw that his face was slack, expressionless, his mouth hanging open, his eyes blank and staring. There seemed to be nothing of the father she remembered in there at all. No life, no personality. He seemed nothing but a walking lump of dead flesh, a receptacle for the virus that animated him. He dropped his weight forward on to his feet, swayed a moment, and then clumped heavily towards them.

Fleur took another step back, and then felt a hand—her mum's—in the small of her back.

"It's all right," Jacqui said soothingly. "Don't be scared."

Fleur braced herself, and then stepped forward. Her dad shuffled right up to the Perspex wall, so close that if he had been breathing a mist of condensation would have formed on its transparent surface.

"Talk to him," Jacqui whispered. "Go on."

Fleur didn't know what to say. Then, hesitantly, she muttered, "I know you didn't want me to come here, Dad, but it isn't Mum's fault, so don't blame her. I kind of found out about you by accident, and I made her bring me. I'm thirteen now and . . . and I've missed you, Dad. I've missed you a lot." Suddenly she felt emotion welling inside her and did her best to swallow it down. After a few seconds she continued, "I know you're sick, but it isn't your fault, and you shouldn't be ashamed. The people here are trying to make you better. They say you're doing really well."

She wasn't sure her words were getting through. Certainly there was no change of expression on her dad's face. But suddenly his eyes flickered and slid to the left, making Jacqui gasp.

"He's looking at the baby," she hissed. "Show it to him."

Fleur turned, to find that Dr. Beesley had already picked up the crib and was handing it to her. She took it from him and turned with it in her arms, presenting it to her dad like an offering.

"He's not mine," she said. "I'm looking after him for a week, as part of a school project. He's sick like you, Dad, but everyone's working really hard to come up with a cure to make you both better."

Her dad continued to stare at the baby. He seemed mesmerised by it. Then, slowly, his gaze shifted. His pale, bloodshot eyes rolled up and all at once he was staring at Fleur. Staring *right* at her.

Behind her, Fleur heard Jacqui whisper, "I don't believe it. He's looking at you. Oh, Fleur, *he knows who you are.*"

Fleur continued to stare into her father's eyes, their faces—separated by the Perspex wall—less than a metre apart. She smiled. "Hello, Dad," she said softly. "Remember me?"

As if moving in slow motion, Andy raised his right hand and pressed it, palm down, against the transparent wall. Lowering the crib to the ground, Fleur echoed his action, raising her left hand and placing it against his, so that they were separated by nothing more than the thickness of the barrier between them.

Suddenly Jacqui let out a gasp, and Dr. Beesley, his voice hushed with wonder, said, "Oh my God. Would you look at that?"

Fleur *was* looking at it. She couldn't tear her gaze away from it, in fact. As the single tear brimmed from her father's eye and trickled slowly down his mottled cheek, she didn't know whether to laugh or cry.

THE NAME GAME

ƎMAƆ ƎMAИ ƎHT

"Oh, look," said Phyllis, brandishing a cream-coloured card with writing on it, "our new neighbours have invited us round for dinner this evening. Isn't that nice?"

Len had unpacked the telly and was trying to tune it in. "Do we *have* to go?" he said. "I'm knackered after lugging boxes around all day. I was really looking forward to a takeaway and a DVD tonight."

"Don't be such a misery guts," Phyllis said. "I think it's a really nice gesture."

But Len, who was less gregarious than his wife, scowled. "You know what I'm like with new people, Phyll. They make me nervous."

"Don't be so pathetic," Phyllis said, her face hardening. "We're going, and that's that."

Three hours later Phyllis was ringing the doorbell of number 14 while Len stood glumly behind her.

She barely had time to tell him to make an effort before the door was plucked open.

"Hi, come in, come in," said their host. "I'm Paul and this is my wife, Jayne."

Len felt his already low spirits plummeting further. The man who had answered their knock was about forty, tall and tanned and fit-looking, and so immaculately groomed in his crisp green shirt and beige slacks that Len felt like a dishevelled schoolboy in comparison. He hung back as Phyllis stepped forward, a dazzling smile on her face.

"Lovely to meet you," she said. "I'm Phyllis and this is Len. Thank you *so* much for inviting us."

"Not at all," Paul replied, kissing her cheek and taking her proffered bottle of wine. "What can I get you to drink?"

"Gin and tonic would be lovely," Phyllis said.

"Ice and lime?"

"Ooh, yes, please."

As Phyllis stepped past Paul to greet a smiling Jayne—who looked, thought Len, like a Spanish aristocrat with her refined features framed by tumbling curls of dark hair—Paul reached out to shake Len's hand.

It was a warm May evening, and Len had been on the go all day, sweating and toiling. Even a shower and a change of clothes hadn't helped, and his own hand—like the rest of him—felt warm and limp. By contrast, Paul's hand was cool and dry and steely, and Len tried not to wince as it enfolded his with bone-crushing force.

After what seemed an unnecessarily long time, Paul relinquished his grip. "What can I get *you* to drink, Len?" he enquired affably.

"Er . . . beer?" Len said, and immediately wondered whether he ought to have asked for something more sophisticated.

Paul, however, exclaimed, "Beer it is!" And then he formed a question out of the name of a foreign beer which Len didn't catch, and which he thought he probably wouldn't have heard of anyway.

"Fine," Len said, forcing a smile.

As Paul strode off to make the drinks, Jayne lightly took Phyllis's arm. "Come through to the conservatory," she said. "Meet the gang."

Len didn't like the sound of that, but he dutifully followed the two women through the house and into the conservatory. There were four other couples in there, sitting around on pale-coloured furniture, sipping drinks. All the men were taller and slimmer than Len, and despite the sun pouring in through the glass walls and ceiling there was not a red face or sweat-patch to be seen. Len noted too that not a single one of them was drinking beer.

The wives of the men were willowy and elegant, and made Len feel like an ugly, blotchy troll. Jayne made the introductions, and for the next minute or so, he and Phyllis were bombarded with names, all of which Len repeated, nodding and smiling, as he shook hands and kissed cheeks, and none of which he remembered five seconds later.

"Isn't your garden lovely?" Phyllis said to Jayne, and just for a second Len both hated and admired her for seeming unfazed by all these intimidatingly self-possessed people. "I'm really looking forward to making something of ours. We've never had a decent-sized garden before."

"Where have you come from?" asked a blonde woman, whose name, Len vaguely remembered, had sounded European—Rula or Inga. Katya maybe.

He gritted his teeth in a rictus grin as Phyllis explained how they had moved here from a small terraced house in the inner-city.

"Just two up, two down. But we wanted more space. We wanted a house that would be big enough for a *family*," she explained, and she smiled shyly at Len in such a way that in an instant his resentment dissolved and he loved her as much as ever.

"Oh? Are you . . . ?" asked another of the women (Len had no idea what *her* name was) and lightly patted her own enviably flat stomach.

"Oh *no*," said Phyllis, as if the idea was preposterous. But then she smiled shyly again, though this time for the benefit of everyone. "But we're working on it. Aren't we, Len?"

"Um . . . yeah," said Len, whose face now felt so hot that he wondered whether his cheeks were about to rupture.

At that moment Paul returned with the drinks, which saved him further embarrassment. The beer which he handed to Len in a frosted glass shaped like a giant light bulb was dark and peaty, but refreshing. Len gulped at it too quickly, and felt his head swim. A trickle ran out of the side of the glass and down his chin. He swiped it quickly away with the back of his hand, though not quickly enough to prevent a drip landing on his mostly white shirt and creating a brown, teardrop-shaped stain.

The women twittered around Phyllis, talking about nurseries and local schools. Len heard one of them say that her son Sebastian just *loved* Montessori, but Len had no idea whether she was referring to the name of a school, a holiday destination or even the family goldfish.

He didn't have time to find out either, because by this time the men were rising from their seats and moving into a vague circle around him. Len guessed that their intention was friendly rather than threatening, but he couldn't help being reminded of the time he'd been ambushed after school by a group of older boys and robbed of his money and sweets.

"So Len," said a white-haired man with pale blue eyes, "what is it that you do?"

Len had always thought this a strange question. It insinuated that everything you needed to know about a person—their personality, their attitudes, their social standing, their inner desires—could be gleaned just from ascertaining how they made a living.

"I sell golf equipment," he said, and then, when this was met mostly by silence, "or rather I'm a projects manager at a company that sells golf equipment. I develop sales strategies and . . . er . . . things."

A couple of the men nodded sagely.

"Great game, golf," said Paul. "So what's your handicap, Len?"

It was a common misconception that just because Len sold the equipment he was an enthusiast of the game himself. However, the truth was, he had no interest in golf whatsoever. It—or rather the equipment he sold—were merely commodities. He could just as easily have been selling fizzy drinks or disposable razors or fitted kitchens. "Um...I don't have one," he said. "I don't actually play."

"*Really*?" Paul raised a disbelieving eyebrow.

"So what *is* your sport then, Len?" asked a man with a squarish head and very short dark hair.

"Well, I don't know really," Len admitted, and again felt from the silence as though he ought to qualify the statement. "I . . . er . . . used to play five-a-side, but I got a groin tear a few years ago and had to have an operation. I'm more of an armchair sportsman these days . . . though I do go to the company gym when I can."

This wasn't quite true. Len went to the company gym probably about once every couple of months, and his visits were usually prompted by guilt rather than a genuine desire to get fit, often coming in the aftermath of a period of gluttonous self-indulgence.

The man with the squarish head said, "There's a great gym about a mile down the road. You should join. The two of us could be fitness buddies."

"Is that a euphemism?" Len said, inviting the other men to chuckle along by injecting a note of jocularity into his voice. No one did.

"What do you mean?" the squarish-headed man said.

"Nothing, I just. . . ."

"Just what?"

"Nothing. It was a joke, that's all."

Len noticed the men all glance at one another, though whether out of genuine bafflement or because they were silently judging him in some way he had no idea. He gulped at his beer, then raised his glass as though toasting them. "This beer is really nice," he said to change the subject.

"It's from Belgium," said Paul.

"Oh," said Len.

There was a bit more general men-talk—cars, jobs, the appalling state of the economy—and then it was time for dinner. As starters were brought to the table and wine was being poured, Len stole a glance at his watch. He was dismayed to see it was not even eight thirty. He'd hoped it was at least nine, maybe later. He decided to just get pissed and make the best of it. Maybe he'd relax into it a bit more with a few glasses of red inside him.

He didn't though. He felt uptight and awkward throughout the meal, and clumsy with his cutlery in a way he never was at home. He slopped wine down his shirt and dropped a gobbet of duck, smeared with honey and oyster sauce, into his lap. Phyllis, who seemed to be enjoying herself immensely, made a joke about having to get him a bib. It wasn't meant nastily, but it made Len feel more like a child than ever. He drank so much wine that he started to slur his words—not that he was saying much. The conversation flowed around him like a flock of brightly-coloured birds that he kept reaching for but never quite managed to catch.

After the main course was finished and the plates were cleared away, Paul carefully wiped his lips with his napkin and said, "Right then. Shall we get down to business?"

Len saw everyone except Phyllis nod. He caught his wife's eye and raised his eyebrows. He could see that Phyllis was just as mystified as he was. She pursed her lips and gave a little shrug in reply.

"Your names," Paul said, and looked directly at Len.

Len wasn't sure how to respond. He glanced around the table and saw that everyone was looking at him. He licked his lips nervously and made a supreme effort not to slur his words.

"What about them?" he asked.

"What are they?" asked Paul, not exactly in an interrogative way but with a definite hint of irritation in his voice, as if Len was being deliberately obtuse.

Len looked to Phyllis for guidance, but there was none to be had from that quarter. He licked his lips again.

"Len and Phyllis," he said.

Paul closed his eyes in exasperation.

One of the women—Helda, Inga, whatever—said gently, "We know that. But what is your surname?"

"Jackson," said Len. "Why?"

Nobody answered. They were now all looking at the squarish-headed man, who had produced a BlackBerry or a Palm Pilot or something (Len wasn't very good at technology) and was tapping his fingers on it, frowning in concentration as he peered at the screen.

Finally the squarish-headed man shrugged. "Nothing of consequence," he said.

"Ah," said Paul, and steepled his fingers beneath his lips. "Well, well. We appear to have a problem."

The other dinner guests—all except Len and Phyllis—shook their heads sadly.

Len belched a nervous laugh. "Look, what's going on?" he asked. "Is this some sort of. . . ."

"Some sort of . . . ?" prompted Paul.

"I don't know. Test? Game? Initiation?"

"If only it *were* a game," Paul said. "But no. It's rather more than that. It's a requirement. A requirement of residency."

Len looked at Phyllis again. She looked back at him, blank-faced. "What do you mean?" he asked.

"Your names," Jayne said. "I'm afraid they just won't do."

"Won't do?" Len said. "What are you on about? What's wrong with our names?"

"I would have thought that was obvious," said Paul. "They don't *mean* anything. They don't *resonate*. I'm sure you're both perfectly acceptable people, but with names like yours . . . well, frankly, you're a couple of nobodies. And we can't have nobodies living on the Avenue."

Len was not a forthright man. He didn't like being the centre of attention. He would never complain about bad service in a restaurant, or turn round in a cinema to tell a group of noisy teenagers to shush. But being called a nobody by someone he barely knew . . . well, that was going too far. He had had enough (he had also had far too much to drink). He pushed his chair back with an over-loud screech and stood up.

"I don't have to listen to this," he said. "I'm going home. *We're* going home, I mean. Aren't we, Phyllis?"

Phyllis nodded and put down her napkin, which she'd been unconsciously clutching in her hand. Before she could stand up, however, the squarish-headed man said, "You're going nowhere."

His voice was quiet, but it sent a sudden horrible chill through Len. His guts quivered like the onset of food poisoning and all at once his legs felt so hollow that he had to grab the edge of the table for support.

He tried to speak, but his mouth was so dry, his throat so tight, that he could make no sound at all.

"Sit down, Mr. Jackson," said the white-haired man.

When Len didn't immediately comply, the man's voice became a whip-crack.

"*Sit down!*"

Len sat, feeling small and humiliated. His gaze skittered around the table and saw nothing but cold eyes set in stern faces gazing back at him.

"Thank you," Paul said calmly. "As I'm sure you understand, Len, it's important that we get this sorted out as soon as possible."

For the first time since the evening had taken its strange turn, Phyllis spoke. Her voice high and flinty, she asked, "Get *what* sorted out? We don't know what you mean."

Paul sighed. His wife Jayne said conciliatorily, "It's obvious they haven't been told, Paul."

Paul turned on Jayne with a scowl. "How can they not have been told? Why the hell didn't the Mirrens—"

"I don't know," Jayne said, placing a hand on his arm. "Perhaps they forgot."

"*Forgot?*" Paul snarled. "You can't just *forget*. The contract clearly states—"

"A couple of weeks before the sale, Helen told me that Bob was getting desperate," interrupted one of the other wives. "With the state of the housing market, and having to stick to the contract, and with the job offer in Dubai hanging in the balance. . . ."

"You should have said something," said Paul angrily. "We would have taken steps."

"Don't blame Kathy," said Jayne. "It's not her fault. What's done is done. We're just going to have to deal with it."

Paul blew out a long, growling sigh and nodded. "All right," he said, "all right."

He stared at Len, still scowling, accusatory. Len tried not to flinch.

"My name," said Paul, "is Paul Newman."

Len cleared his throat, and though it still felt tight he found he could speak again. "Like the actor," he said.

"Exactly," said Paul sourly. "Like the actor."

Further along the table, the white-haired man said, "I'm Sean Connery."

Len barked a laugh, and then realised it wasn't a joke. "Oh," he said.

The squarish-headed man pointed at his wife. "My name's Frank Taylor," he said, "but my wife's name is Elizabeth."

"And I'm David Beckham," said a bespectacled man at the end of the table who had been fairly quiet all evening.

Paul spread his hands. "So you see," he said, "where the problem lies?"

"Not really," said Len.

Paul looked exasperated again. "But you can see what we're telling you?"

"That you've all got the names of famous people," said Len.

Paul nodded sagely.

Len looked around the table. "So?" he said.

"So what are you going to do about it?" Sean Connery demanded.

Len blinked. "What do you mean, what am I going to do about it? I'm not going to do anything."

"You'll have to do *something*," said the wife of David Beckham.

Len shook his head. "Will I? Why?"

"Because it's the rules," said Jayne.

"Whose rules?"

"Our rules. The rules of the Avenue."

Len still wasn't sure whether there was a big joke at the heart of this. "So you're telling us," he said slowly, "that you've made up a set of rules which say that to live on the Avenue one of you has to have a famous name?"

Everyone nodded as if this was the most sensible thing in the world.

Len smiled. "That's just stupid," he said.

Paul's face tightened.

"You're really serious about this, aren't you?" said Len.

"It's the rules," said Jayne again.

Len looked at Phyllis. She looked a bit scared, as if she'd been accused of a crime she hadn't committed.

"But no one told us anything about these rules," said Len.

"Well, they should have," said Elizabeth Taylor.

"Well, they didn't! So there's nothing much you can do about it, is there? I mean, we're here now, so you're just going to have to make the best of it, aren't you?"

Paul shook his head. "I'm afraid that won't be possible."

"What do you mean, it won't be possible?" exclaimed Len. His voice had gone high and chalky, mostly with anger now, though there was still an undercurrent of fear in there too.

"You'll have to leave," Paul said.

Phyllis burst into tears.

"*Leave?*" repeated Len, feeling the heat of anger rising up through his body, reddening his neck and ears. "Excuse me, but . . . well, fuck off. We're not leaving. We've only just moved in."

"You'll have to leave," Paul repeated obstinately.

"Didn't you hear what I said? I said we're *not* leaving. *You* fucking leave if you're so bothered."

"You have no choice," said Paul. "It's the rules."

"*Fuck the rules!*" shouted Len, and jumped to his feet again. "You're a bunch of nutters, you lot. Come on, Phyllis, we're going."

He reached out towards his wife, as if he expected her to scramble across the table to join him. Before she could move, however, Frank Taylor said, "We can *make* you leave."

Len looked at him. He was shaking badly, but even he wasn't sure now whether it was mostly through fear or anger. "What did you say?"

"I said we can make you leave. And we will. Don't doubt it."

"Are you threatening us?" asked Len incredulously.

Frank Taylor nodded. "We can make you leave. Everyone in the Avenue will turn against you. We can make your life hell."

Len swallowed. Once again for a few seconds he couldn't speak. He forced the words out of his tightening throat. "I'll tell the police."

Frank Taylor smirked and pointed at the bespectacled man. "He *is* the police. Chief Superintendant David Beckham."

"Then I'll . . . I'll go to the papers," said Len. "I'll tell them everything. I'll—"

"You try that and you'll disappear," Frank Taylor said quietly. "No one will ever find you."

The room thrummed with silence. Len looked around at all the faces looking back at him. They were spinning, blurring. He felt hot and ill. His heart was pounding much too fast. He thought he was going to faint.

He forced himself to take a deep breath, and then another. He felt better. Not much, but a little.

"You heard him," he said, pointing at Frank, and then swinging his hand from left to right to implicate them all. "You just heard him threaten to kill us."

Chief Superintendant David Beckham stared back at Len unblinkingly. "I'm afraid you're mistaken, Mr. Jackson," he said. "No one heard anything of the sort."

Len felt his legs giving way. He plumped back down on his chair. His breath was shuddering now, wheezing. "You can't do this," he said. "You can't do this to us."

Paul shrugged. David Beckham's wife took a sip of white wine.

Jayne Newman said almost kindly, "There are several alternatives."

Paul frowned. "No, Jayne. We talked about this before and—"

"Give these people a chance, Paul," Jayne said. "It's hardly their fault that they're in this position, is it? Bob and Helen Mirren should be the ones who—"

"Oh, they'll get what's coming to them, believe me," Frank Taylor said. "If Bob thinks he's safe in Dubai—"

"All right, Frank, thank you!" Jayne snapped, raising a hand.

Suddenly she seemed to be the one in charge. Everyone was looking to her. Even Len couldn't help thinking of her as a sort of ally—or at least, as someone who was prepared to be flexible.

"What alternatives?" he asked.

"You could change your name," she said brightly. "You could change it by deed poll. I know it would be bending the rules," she added quickly before her husband could protest, "but at least it would show a certain level of commitment."

Everyone was nodding now, the women happily, the men grudgingly, to show that, yes, they'd be prepared to accept that.

"You could be Michael Jackson," Elizabeth Taylor suggested.

"Or Samuel L," put in Sean Connery. "Actually, you'd be better off being Samuel L. If you were Michael Jackson people would only—"

"I'm not changing my name," said Len.

There was another shocked silence. David Beckham's wife was the first to speak. "Why ever not?"

Len had never felt so forthright and so passionate about anything in his life before, and even though he was still scared out of his wits he found that he quite liked the sensation.

"I like my name," he said. "Why *should* I change it just because of you people and your stupid rules?"

Paul shook his head, albeit with an expression of grim satisfaction on his face. Frank Taylor cracked his knuckles like an East End gangster in a bad movie.

Jayne shot Len an exasperated look, a look that clearly stated: *Can't you see I'm trying to do my best for you here?* She turned to Phyllis.

"It'll have to be you then, Phyllis—though the options are a bit more limited. Off the top of my head I can only think of Millie. Can anyone else—"

"Phyllis isn't changing her name either," said Len.

This time there was not silence but uproar.

"Oh, for Christ's sake!" snapped Sean Connery. Frank Taylor slammed his fist down hard on the table.

Sitting opposite Len, Phyllis looked like a sparrow surrounded by a cluster of hungry cats.

"I don't mind," she said, her shrill voice barely rising above the clamour. "Honestly I don't. If it'll make everything—"

"No, Phyllis!" said Len. "I won't allow it. We're not pandering to these people, and that's that."

Phyllis looked stricken. "But I want to stay here, Len. I want to live on the Avenue."

"Not on these terms," said Len grimly.

Paul shook his head. "We're wasting our time here," he muttered.

Frank Taylor looked suddenly eager. He glanced around the table. "Do you want me to get rid of them?"

Before anyone could respond, Len snatched up a dessert fork and jumped to his feet once again. "Don't you dare touch us!" he cried.

Frank Taylor leaped to his feet too, shoving his chair back so violently that it fell over with a clatter.

Phyllis screamed.

"Oh, for God's *sake*!" yelled Jayne, her voice rising above everyone else's. "Will you all just *calm down*!"

She had a certain authority, Len had to admit. Even Frank Taylor looked momentarily cowed.

"There is one final option," Jayne said.

Paul shook his head. "No, Jayne, we've never had cause to—"

"It's the rules," Jayne insisted, her voice steely. "We offer the Jacksons this one final option, and if they *still* refuse. . . ." She threw up her hands in a clear gesture: *Then that will be that*.

"What *is* the option?" asked Phyllis nervously.

"Deferment."

Phyllis looked baffled. "Deferment? What's that?"

Sean Connery's wife regarded her pityingly. "You said you wanted a family, dear. Well, now's your chance."

"The rules state that a 'nameless' couple can still qualify for residency if either a) one of their children has a recognised name, or b) they have a child within twelve months of taking up probationary residency on the Avenue, and give said child a recognised name," explained Jayne.

Len's reply was caustic. "So you're saying we'd be on probation?"

"Effectively, yes."

"We'll take it," said Phyllis quickly. "I mean . . . we agree."

"We most certainly do not," replied Len.

"Yes, Len. We *do*," said Phyllis with a flash of her old fire. "We worked hard to get here, and I for one want to stay. There are two of us in this relationship, you know. And it's not such a difficult sacrifice to make, is it?"

"That's not the point," said Len. "It's the principle of the thing."

"Oh, sod your principles!" exclaimed Phyllis, and she turned deliberately away from her husband to look at Jayne. "We accept your terms."

"Excellent," said Jayne. She looked pleased, even if some of the men—most notably Frank Taylor—didn't. "Then let's complete the paperwork."

Forms were duly produced and signed and witnessed. As Len scrawled his name, he told himself that although he was doing this under protest, maybe things wouldn't turn out so badly. As luck would have it, Millie had been one of the names he and Phyllis had discussed giving their first child if it happened to be a girl. However he was damned if he was going to name any son of his Michael or even Samuel L; Adam was *his* preferred option. Ah well, no doubt they'd cross that bridge when they came to it.

When the last form had been signed and put away, and the Jacksons had been given their own copy, Jayne Newman let out a great sigh and sat down.

"Well, I'm glad that's resolved," she said, and she smiled around the table, the perfect hostess. "Now then, who's for dessert?"

THE RED DOOR

ЯOOD DƎЯ ƎHT

"Let us pray."

Although Chloe closed her eyes and clasped her hands together, she barely heard the words that her brother Luke was intoning. She had never had a panic attack, but as she stood among her family and her parents' friends she felt light-headed and jittery; felt her heart-rate increase and sweat break out on her body.

"Amen," Luke said finally, and although Chloe murmured the word along with everyone else it seemed like a husk in her throat, hollow and dry and hard to expel.

Her problem—if such a cataclysmic life-shift could be termed so mildly—had started even before her mother had been diagnosed with the liver cancer, which had taken most of the last year to kill her. Although her mother's unbearable suffering had made it even more difficult for Chloe to rediscover the path from which she had strayed, she firmly believed that her London life had been the true catalyst—or more precisely the fact that she had finally moved away from home two years ago, thus distancing herself, both geographically and ideologically, from her devout parents.

Not that her mother and father had been fire and brimstone types, intent on indoctrinating Chloe and her siblings with the notion of a vengeful and belligerent God. On the contrary, the God that Chloe had grown up with had been a merciful and loving one; a God that gave comfort and succour. As a small child she had thought of Him as a seventh member of the family—a kindly grandfather figure, whose influence was overwhelmingly benign. He was someone to whom she felt she could pour out her problems, someone who could always be relied upon to make things better.

It distressed her greatly, therefore, that she had recently begun to have doubts, not simply about the nature of God, but about His very existence. Back home in Buckinghamshire for her mother's funeral, she decided to confide in Joanna, her older sister.

On the night following the funeral the two girls found themselves sleeping in the bedroom which they had shared as children, the bedroom in which they had swapped secrets and gossip, and in which they had done so much of their growing up. Chloe found it nostalgic and yet at the same time, now that their mother was gone, desperately sad to be sleeping in her old bed, with Joanna in *her* old bed, just a few metres away. When the two girls had been small their mother had tucked them in every night after listening to their prayers. She had kissed them on the forehead and whispered, "Sleep well, sleep tight, may God protect you through the night."

The only thing whispering to Chloe now was the harsh wind in the branches of the denuded apple trees in the back garden. She listened to them scraping and rustling as she worked up the courage to speak, and then finally she whispered, "Jo? Are you awake?"

"Yes," Jo said immediately, as if she had been expecting the question.

"Can I ask you something?"

"If you like."

She was only two years older than Chloe, but Jo, who had always been considered the practical, pragmatic one, often acted as if the gap between them was much wider.

"Have your views changed at all since you left home?" Chloe asked.

"About what?"

"Well . . . about anything? God, for instance."

"No. Have yours?"

The response was blunt, and threw Chloe for a moment. Finally she admitted, "I think they have."

"In what way?"

"I don't know. I suppose I'm not as . . . certain as I used to be."

"You mean you don't believe any more?"

"It's not that, it's . . . well, I'm not sure."

Jo paused for less than a second, and then she said almost crossly, "Well, either you do believe or you don't. Which is it?"

Chloe felt dismay seize her, felt herself shrivelling inside. I'm not going to cry, she told herself. But when she again said, "I don't know," her voice cracked on the last word, and all at once she was sobbing.

Lying in the dark, she half-expected Jo to move across to her bed, to offer comfort, but the older girl remained so still that Chloe might have believed she was suddenly alone in the room. Eventually Jo asked, "Have you spoken to Dad about this?"

With an effort Chloe swallowed her tears. "No. I don't want to worry him. Especially not now, when he's got so much to contend with."

"Probably wise," said Jo. Silence settled between them again, albeit one filled with the frenzied scraping of the tree branches outside. Then Jo asked, "What's made you have doubts?"

Chloe struggled to put it into words. "It's not one thing. It's an accumulation. I suppose when I was at home I saw evil as . . . I don't know . . . the Devil's work. Something separate from humanity. I knew it existed, I knew people did terrible things to one another, but it was as if it was this separate thing that bubbled up every now and again like . . . like lava from a volcano."

"And now?" said Jo.

"Now I realise that it isn't like that. Living in the city I suppose it's made me realise that evil isn't always big and grand and uncontrollable. It's petty and vicious and banal. It's there in everybody. Every day, in one way or another, I come up against cruelty or cynicism or selfishness or envy or indifference. I was sitting on the tube the other day, and the day before there'd been delays on the District Line because a girl had thrown herself under a train, and this couple were griping about her, saying what a selfish bitch she was because she'd made them late for the pub."

"Welcome to the real world," Jo murmured.

"But why is the world like that?" protested Chloe. "Why, if God exists, has he let things get in such a state? A girl where I work was mugged the other week by two guys outside Ladbroke Grove tube station. People just walked past while one of the guys held a knife to her throat. And I read in the paper that a fifteen-year-old girl at the local school had been beaten up, and that even while she was lying on the pavement unconscious her attackers had carried on punching and kicking and stamping on her while other children laughed and filmed it on their phones."

She subsided into silence, aware that her voice had become stretched and almost whiny. Jo's response was as cool and considered as ever.

"God gave us free will," she said. "How we choose to live in this life will determine our role in the next one."

"But why?" Chloe asked. "Why give us free will if so many innocent people suffer for it?"

"We all need to be tested," said Jo.

"But why? That's what I don't understand. If God is all-good and all-powerful why does he need to make us suffer? Why put us through this at all?"

"To test our faith, of course. If we can suffer the hardships of life and still have faith in God, then we will prove ourselves worthy of sitting at His right hand. We have to earn our place in the Kingdom of Heaven, Chloe. If we didn't suffer the hardship and misery of our earthly lives we wouldn't appreciate the ultimate glory of life everlasting. We would be complacent, selfish beings, with no concept of good and evil, no perspective."

"But what about good people who don't have faith in God?" Chloe said. "What about people who don't believe in Him, but who are still kind and generous and loving to their fellow men? Don't they deserve their place in the Kingdom of Heaven?"

"Without God there is no Kingdom of Heaven," said Jo firmly.

Chloe spent the train journey back to London the next day gazing bleakly out of the window. How easy it would be to abandon her career and return home. She imagined herself withdrawing from the stress and responsibility of city life, of giving up her independence and becoming an unofficial housekeeper to her father. She could grow stout and spinsterish in the bucolic tranquillity of the village where she had grown up. And once there, surrounded by God's love, perhaps she would rediscover her faith, even if only by default.

These thoughts dismayed her even while they comforted her. Was her faith really so fragile that the merest test was enough to rattle it to its foundations? Jo had told Chloe that the real test of faith was to remain steadfast in the face of challenge and adversity, but it was easier said than done. Jo was tough, inflexible. Was it Chloe's fault that she was less robust than her sister? Was it a sin to be sensitive, to be lacking in confidence?

As the train drew closer to London, and the surrounding fields and villages were gradually superseded by urban sprawl, Chloe felt her spirits sinking still further. In recent weeks she had become obsessed with the notion that the very fabric of the city had become imbued with the decades of wickedness perpetrated within its confines, that the stones and bricks and timber of its buildings had soaked up every bad deed, every foul thought.

The walls and roofs of houses and factories and apartment blocks flashed by the grimy window, many of them old and crumbling and dirty, their facades stacked and angled haphazardly, as if the buildings they supported had been crammed in wherever there was space. Lost in her thoughts, Chloe barely registered them, and yet all at once something snagged her eye—something so fleeting that it was nothing but an impression, gone before she could focus upon it.

Nevertheless, whatever she had seen was unusual enough to lodge in her mind, as irritating as a sharp morsel of food stuck between her back teeth. As she disembarked at Euston her mind was probing at it, trying to bring it into the light, but it wasn't until she had sat on the rattling Northern Line tube to Tufnell Park, and had trudged the maze of streets back to the Victorian house containing her third-floor flat, and was fitting her key into the lock of the front door as the daylight faded into smoky dusk, that it suddenly popped into her mind.

It was a door. That was what she had seen. A door in a wall. The door had been painted a deep, shimmering red, though what had been odd about it—what had snagged her attention—was that it had been not at ground level but half-way up the wall. And furthermore, it had been upside-down.

That, at least, was how she remembered it. That was the image that had lodged in her mind. A bright red, upside-down door, half-way up a wall.

It was ridiculous, of course. That can't have been what she'd seen. And even if it was, there must have been some reason for it. It must have been a contrivance, an architectural gimmick, perhaps even part of some obscure advertising campaign. London was full of oddities, of things that didn't make sense. Some people loved that about the city—its quirkiness, its hidden corners, the fact that it was crammed with bizarre sights and bizarre stories.

By the time Nick called, Chloe had put the red door to the back of her mind. She ate some pasta and was washing up her plate, pan and cutlery in her tiny kitchen when her mobile rang. Thinking it might be her dad calling to make sure she'd got home okay, she went through to the main room, drying her hands on a tea towel, and retrieved her burring phone from her jacket pocket. Seeing Nick's name she almost didn't answer. But then she reluctantly pressed the "Accept" button and said, "Hi."

"Chloe?"

"Yeah."

"Oh, it *is* you. I wasn't sure. You sounded weird."

"I'm just tired."

His voice grew soft, concerned. "Are you okay? How was it?"

"It was fine. As far as these things go."

There was a silence, as though he expected her to elaborate. When she didn't he said, "You're not all right, are you? Do you want me to come over?"

The thought wearied her. "Not tonight, Nick. I really am tired. I'm going to have an early night."

"Tomorrow then. Let's do something tomorrow. Take your mind off things."

She knew he was only trying to be kind, but she wanted to snap at him, *Do you think I can just forget as easily as that? Do you think I'm that shallow?* But instead she said, "Yeah, okay, I'll see you tomorrow."

"This used to be a power station," Nick said, the wind whipping at his wispy blond hair and twitching the scarf at his throat. "It's pretty impressive, don't you think?"

Chloe gazed at the imposing edifice of the Tate Modern, the chimney stack high above her stabbing at the grim sky as if mockingly pointing the way to Heaven. Troubled, she turned her attention to the wide slope leading down to the entrance doors.

"I think it's ugly," she said.

"Really?" Nick looked half-surprised, half-offended, as if he was personally responsible for the building's design and construction. "Well, just wait till you see inside. It's amazing. Like a cathedral."

It had been Nick's idea to come here. He had wanted Chloe to see an installation in what he called, with a sense of ominous grandeur, "The Tanks". Since they had met two months ago, after Chloe's friend and work colleague Christine had all but bullied her into trying online dating, he had made it his mission to take her to all the places in London where she hadn't been that he thought were worth visiting. In recent weeks he had introduced her to the South Bank, to Highgate Cemetery, to Camden Market, and to several of his favourite restaurants. Chloe had tried to match his enthusiasm as he unveiled each new treasure, but she had thought the South Bank hideous, Highgate Cemetery depressing, Camden Market gaudily pretentious, and most of the restaurants too expensive.

Nick was a nice guy, and had been nothing but supportive throughout the last days of her mother's illness, but Chloe had begun to wonder whether their relationship was really going anywhere. They had little in common—he loved London, she didn't—and she had so much to contend with right now that she couldn't help thinking the timing was all wrong. A year hence things might have been different, but currently Nick was less a pleasant distraction than simply one more thing to worry about.

"Isn't this amazing?" he said as they passed through the entrance doors and entered the vast, echoing space inside. Shivering, she tugged her coat tighter around her. In truth she felt nothing but dwarfed and daunted, and further away from God than ever.

"It's certainly big," she admitted.

"Come on," Nick said, taking her hand. "What I want to show you is this way."

The Tanks, located on level 0, had originally been a trio of huge underground oil tanks, and were accessed via a series of side doors arranged either side of a wide, dank, low-ceilinged corridor. The sign outside the door that Nick led her to bore the name of a Japanese artist—all spiky, sharp syllables, like jags of broken glass—and a long explanation about dreams and shifting states of consciousness which Chloe's eyes skimmed over without taking in.

The interior was dark, though not pitch black. However the lighting, such as it was, had been angled in such a way that it played with Chloe's perceptions, disorientating her, making her unable to tell where the floor met the walls, and the walls the ceiling. As a result she felt unsteady and uncertain, even a little sick.

"I'm not sure I like this," she whispered.

"It does take a bit of getting used to," Nick murmured. "But it's worth it. There's nothing here that can hurt you."

Ahead of her, Chloe could see shadows blundering about—other visitors tentatively picking their way forward. The room was full of ambient noise— slow, soft booms and the continuous echo of wordless whispers—and undercutting that, as though coming from a nearby but as-yet-unseen room, she could hear the drone of a voice speaking in a foreign language, its tinny quality suggesting that it was a radio or TV broadcast of some kind.

Edging forward, she was distracted by movement to her left, and turning she saw a number of figures, blacker than the darkness around them, standing in silhouette, their arms upraised. They looked to be pleading for their lives, or begging for help, but drifting closer Chloe realised that they were simply visitors like herself, standing on the other side of a thick glass wall which she had assumed, until she was close enough to touch it, was a continuous dark space. These people had their faces pressed to the glass and were peering through; Chloe could see the glint of their eyes in the gloom. From their blank expressions she guessed that the glass was one-way, that she could see them, but that they couldn't see her. The thought unsettled her, and she shivered and moved away.

It was only now, with a jolt of surprise, that she realised Nick was no longer holding her hand. When had the two of them disengaged? It must have been when she had stepped to her left, but she couldn't for the life of her consciously remember tugging her hand free of his grip. She peered into the gloom, but could not distinguish him from any of the other shadows bobbing ahead of her.

"Nick?" she said softly, but her voice was instantly swallowed up, incorporated into the ambient soundscape. She tried again, raising her voice a little, though oddly reluctant to draw attention to herself. "Nick?"

None of the shadows responded.

For a moment Chloe considered retracing her steps, waiting for him outside, but then she moved forward. He couldn't be more than a few metres ahead. He was probably waiting for her to catch up. She held her hands out like a blind woman as she tentatively placed one foot in front of the other. Remembering how the glass wall had been invisible until she was standing right next to it, she felt vulnerable, certain she was about to walk into or trip over something.

The shadows ahead seemed to be bearing left, like fish following the course of a stream, and so she moved with them, going with the flow. She realised she must have rounded a corner, for all at once the space in front of her opened up, and she could see the source of the droning voice, which had abruptly become louder. It was a television, icy blue in the gloom. It seemed to be suspended in mid-air, hovering like a ghost. On the screen a bespectacled Japanese man—possibly the artist—was giving what appeared to be a lecture direct to camera. However, as he spoke, white circular scribbles jittered constantly around his eyes and mouth, giving him a monstrous, corpse-like appearance. Chloe knew that the effect had been achieved simply by scratching circles around the man's features on each individual frame of film, yet in this environment the sight was unsettlingly nightmarish. A huddle of dark shapes was clustered around the TV, motionless as mannequins; they seemed to be hanging on the man's every word. Did they really understand what he was saying? Or could they see something in the overall work that she couldn't—something fascinating, even profound?

Feeling isolated, she peered into the shadows beyond the droning man on the screen, and her eyes were instantly tantalised by a shimmer of red in the distance. Drifting away from the throng around the TV, she moved deeper into the darkness. She wondered if what she was seeing was an illusion, whether it was even possible to pick out colour when there was no discernible light source. Certainly at first the redness seemed to shift both in and out of her vision, and in and out of the darkness, causing her to constantly adjust her eyesight. Then as she moved closer it seemed to rise from the gloom around it, to become more solid, and she realised that it was a door.

She halted in astonishment. Not only was it a door, but it was the door she had glimpsed yesterday from the train—or at least, like that door, it was upside-down, and positioned not at ground level but a metre or so above it. All at once Chloe felt frightened, as if she had stumbled across something very wrong, possibly even dangerous. Instead of backing away, however, she instinctively stepped forward, overwhelmed by a compulsion to touch the door, to check whether it was real. But before she could raise a hand, something hard slammed into her forehead, rocking her backwards and filling her head with sudden, unexpected pain.

Almost abstractedly, as if the shock had jerked her consciousness from her body, she became aware of her legs giving way, of her surroundings dissolving into black static. The only thing that prevented her from passing out was the sensation of surprisingly strong arms curling around her body, holding her upright. A particularly strident burst of static close to her right ear gradually resolved itself into a voice.

"Chloe? Chloe, can you hear me?"

Ten minutes later she was sitting in the café with a handkerchief which Nick had soaked in cold water pressed to her forehead. She could feel a lump forming there, the blood pulsing in thick, soupy waves just above her right eye. There was a clatter of crockery and Nick was back with tea and cake. She looked up to see his concerned face, and then turned her attention to the cup and saucer which he was pushing across the table towards her.

"Here you go," he said. "How are you feeling now?"

"Like an idiot," she admitted.

"How's the head?"

"Throbs a bit, but I'll be fine."

"Oh God, I feel so responsible," he said. "They ought to warn people about those glass walls. They're dangerous."

Chloe sipped her tea and said nothing.

"Maybe we should complain," he continued.

Chloe squinted at him. The electric light hurt her eyes. "Did you see anything through the wall?"

"Like what?"

She took a deep breath. "A red door."

"No. But then I was more worried about you." He looked at her curiously. "Maybe we ought to get you checked out. You might have concussion or something."

"I'm fine," she said firmly. "I just need a couple of paracetamols and a lie-down." She finished her tea and replaced the cup in the saucer with a clatter. "Sorry to be a party pooper," she said, "but I think I'd like to go home now."

"Hi, Dad, it's me."

"Chloe, my darling. How are you?"

"Oh . . . fine. A bit sad."

"Well, that's understandable. How was your journey back yesterday? I'm sorry I didn't ring. I felt exhausted once everyone had gone. These last few weeks have taken it out of me rather."

Chloe felt tears prick her eyes. She pictured her stout, bespectacled father, the wispy white hair receding from the pink dome of his head. Trying to keep the waver from her voice, she said, "Will you be all right in that big house on your own?"

"Oh, I'll be fine," he said with a confidence she suspected was entirely for her benefit. "My parishioners are spoiling me rotten. You should see how many fruit pies and lasagnes and goodness knows what else I've got in the freezer. And of course none of us are ever truly alone, are we? Not with God to see us through."

At first Chloe was unsure whether she could respond, but finally whispered, "No."

Her father's voice was suddenly full of concern. "Chloe, my love? Are you all right?"

She sniffed and swallowed. The tears which had been threatening to come brimmed up and out of her eyes, forming dark coins on the leg of her jeans as she leaned forward. Forcing out the words, she said, "It's just . . . Mum. I miss her, Dad."

"I know," he said softly. "We all miss her, my love. But isn't it a great comfort to know that her suffering is finally over, and that she's now at one with God?"

"That boyfriend of yours been knocking you about?" said Christine cheerfully.

Chloe blinked at her. "What?"

Christine gestured at her forehead. "That lovely bruise on your bonce. Get a bit carried away in the bedroom, did we?"

Chloe hoped she wasn't blushing, though she rather suspected she was. Chris was the best of only a handful of friends Chloe had made since moving to London, but that didn't prevent her fellow copy editor from taking a perverse delight in poking fun at what she regarded as Chloe's naiveté.

"Believe it or not, I bumped it on a glass wall," Chloe said.

Chris's false eyelashes gave her widening eyes the appearance of Venus fly traps sensing prey. "I'm intrigued. Tell me more."

Ironically, for a magazine with a relentless publishing schedule and a strict remit to keep its finger firmly on the rapidly beating pulse of city life, the atmosphere in the *London Listings* editorial office was mostly relaxed and easy-going. Chloe would have preferred to have worked slowly and steadily through the week, but so much of what she did was reliant on the output of her colleagues that she had little choice but to adapt herself to the long-established regime and culture of the workplace. What this effectively meant was that for eighty per cent of the time she was either making or drinking coffee, exchanging gossip and twiddling her thumbs, and for the other twenty per cent she was engaged in a grim, feverish, to-the-wire race to meet her weekly deadlines.

Chloe told Chris about her and Nick's less than successful visit to the Tate Modern, though she felt oddly reluctant to mention the red door. Already it was adopting the texture of a dream-memory in her mind, of something that, paradoxically, was both vivid and unreal. It disturbed her to think that the door might be a figment of her imagination, though the alternative was more disturbing still. She tried to console herself with the assertion that she had been under stress, that grief could play funny tricks with the mind, and that this was subsequently only a temporary aberration. She had even been trying to convince herself that "seeing" a door was a sign of hope and optimism, that it was a symbol of new beginnings.

"I take it you still haven't shagged him then?" said Christine.

Chloe grimaced. "No, and I'm not planning to."

"You want to watch it, girl," Christine warned. "Even the nicest bloke in the world won't stick around forever if you don't give him a bit of what he needs."

Chloe looked away, trying to appear casual, though in truth she felt uncomfortable, out of her depth. If Christine ever found out that she was still a virgin, Chloe thought she might shrivel up and die of humiliation.

"I'm not sure if I'm really that into him," she said. "I don't think he's the man for me."

Christine rolled her eyes. "I'm not saying you should marry him, for God's sake. Just have a bit of fun while you can."

"But I don't think I even fancy him that much," Chloe said, trying not to sound defensive.

Now Christine looked pained. She shook her head slowly. "You know what your problem is?"

"I'm sure you're going to tell me."

"You're too picky. Ten years from now you'll be desperate to get a man into bed. And you won't be so fussy then, believe me."

Chloe shrugged, a dismissive gesture to hide the tightening in her stomach, and wandered over to the window. From up here on the third floor she could look down on the bustle of Tottenham Court Road, the continuous flow of people and traffic, and kid herself that she was removed from it all, that for the moment, at least, her world was an oasis of calm amid the chaos.

Directly across from the *London Listings* office was a row of unprepossessing retail outlets—a printer's, an office equipment suppliers, shops selling mobile phones, white goods, music and electronics equipment. Gazing out at the familiar view, Chloe suddenly gasped, as if someone had placed a cold hand on the back of her neck. On an anonymous patch of wall, between a sandwich shop and a display window packed with second-hand TVs, was the red door.

As before, it was upside-down, and was situated not at ground level, but about half-way up the wall. People were walking to and fro past it, partially obscuring it at times, but despite its unusual aspect no one appeared to be giving it so much as a second glance. Chloe stared at it unblinkingly for several seconds, her heart beating hard. Then she closed her eyes, and kept them closed for a count of five, before opening them again.

The door was still there. Immediately a thrill went through her, though whether it was a thrill of fear or excitement she wasn't sure. She shuddered, her arms bristling with goose bumps, but in her head she was thinking, *It is there. It is real.*

"Chris," she said, hoping her voice didn't sound odd.

"Yeah?"

"Come over here a sec."

"What for?"

"I want to show you something."

"What?"

"Just come here. It's easier to show you than to explain."

Behind her she heard Christine sigh in exasperation, but she didn't turn round. Now that she had established that the door was there, Chloe didn't want to take her eyes off it even for a second. After a moment she was rewarded with the sound of Christine's chair scraping back and her footsteps crossing the wooden floor.

"Okay. So what's so amazing?"

"Look across the road at that wall between the sandwich place and the TV shop and tell me what you see."

Christine was almost shoulder to shoulder with Chloe now, which brought her into Chloe's peripheral vision. Just as she was tilting her head to look where Chloe had indicated, a high-sided delivery van drove past on the opposite side of the road, temporarily obscuring their view of the red door.

When the van had passed, Christine shrugged. "I see a wall. What am I supposed to see?"

Chloe felt sick. "No," she moaned.

"What's the matter?"

"It's gone."

"What has?"

"What I wanted you to see."

Christine looked at her in exasperation. "Well, what was it?"

Chloe shook her head. "It doesn't matter now."

Christine's expression became an angry scowl. "Are you taking the piss?"

Miserably Chloe shook her head. "No I'm not. I swear I'm not."

"So what was it then?"

Chloe took a deep breath. "A door."

"A door?"

"Yes. A door in the wall." She groped for an explanation. "It must have been an optical illusion."

Christine's eyes bored into her. She looked as though she wasn't sure whether to respond with pity, anger or contempt. Finally she shook her head and turned away. "You're fucking weird," she said.

"Thanks for taking this so well," said Chloe.

Nick gave her a wry look and rubbed absently at the chipped veneer of the circular table. The pub was so cavernous that it seemed relatively empty, though they still had to raise their voices above the buzz of chatter which echoed off the high ceiling.

"I've never been one for screaming and shouting," Nick said, "though that doesn't mean I don't care. To be honest with you, I'm crying inside."

Chloe wasn't sure how to respond. Was he joking? "Really?"

"Well, maybe not crying, but . . . I can't pretend I'm not disappointed. I thought we had something. I thought we were getting on pretty well."

"We do get on well," Chloe said. She was briefly tempted to reach out and take his hand, but in the end she kept them folded in her lap. "And you're a nice guy, Nick, a really nice guy. You're good-looking, funny, interesting, kind. . . ."

"Please don't tell me you're about to say 'it's not you, it's me'?"

The remark could have been cutting, sarcastic, but he said it gently, with a faint, sad smile. Chloe matched his smile with her own. "I suppose I am in a way. I'm just . . . not ready for a relationship. I'm cut up about Mum, I'm confused . . . to be honest, I don't know what I want right now. I've lived in London for two years, but I don't actually like it that much. I might even go home . . . or does that sound too much like giving up, admitting defeat?"

He shrugged. "It's entirely up to you. Ultimately you have to do what you think is best."

"I know." She sighed. "But the trouble is I don't know what that is."

He smiled, a warmer smile this time, and leaned forward. "You're a sweet girl, Chloe, and I understand about you not wanting a relationship right now, what with your mum and everything—but that doesn't mean we can't still be friends, does it? We can meet for drinks, days out; perhaps we can go to the cinema or the theatre now and again. What say we jettison the romantic baggage and just be mates?"

She looked at him sceptically. "And you'd be happy with that?"

"Yeah, why not? I do have girls who are just friends, you know. I'm not so desperate that I see every woman as a potential partner."

He looked sincere. "I'd like that," she said. "But what about the whole online dating thing?"

"I'll try again. If nothing else, it's a way to make friends—and you can never have enough of those. What about you?"

She wrinkled her nose. "I think I'll give it a miss. Not that this hasn't been nice, but it's not really my thing. My friend Chris kind of bullied me into it in the first place."

He gestured at her empty wine glass. "Well, now that we've got that sorted, fancy another?"

She hesitated. "Why don't we go back to mine for a cup of tea instead? It's on the way to the tube station."

He raised his eyebrows slightly. "Well, I don't know. Are you sure you'll be able to contain yourself once we're alone together?"

She laughed. "It'll be tough, but I have a will of iron."

It was a cold night, windy enough to propel leaves and litter along the street in loops and spirals. They walked briskly up Tufnell Park Road, turning left by the theatre on the corner. The illumination from the street lamps was splintered by a row of wind-blasted trees lining the edge of the pavement, casting a jittering kaleidoscope of vivid orange light and deep black shadow upon the ground. As they walked up Carleton Road, Chloe leaned in to Nick and surprised him by taking his arm. Ironically, now that there was no longer the pressure to become romantically linked with him, she felt more affectionate towards him, more at ease in his company. They were about half-way between the pub and Chloe's flat when a series of elongated shadows detached themselves from the darkness ahead.

Chloe tensed, unconsciously tugging on Nick's arm, but he said, "It's all right, come on."

"Let's cross the road," she whispered.

"There's no need. We'll be fine."

His confidence was reassuring, but Chloe still felt nervous. As she and Nick approached the hovering shadows, they began to move, sliding forward out of the darkness with a series of soft, snake-like rustles.

There were four of them, boys in bulky jackets and baggy jeans, hoods pulled up around their faces. One of them spoke, his voice both conversational and threatening.

"What you doin', man?"

Nick's reply was friendly. "We're just walking home."

Another voice came out of the darkness: "Oh yeah? Where you live?"

"Not far from here."

"Where exactly?"

Nick barely missed a beat. "I'd rather not say if you don't mind."

"Why not? What you think we gonna do?"

"I don't think you're going to do anything."

"You got a phone?" said the first boy.

"Yes."

"Can I borrow it?"

"What for?"

"Wanna make a call."

"Haven't you got a phone?" Nick asked.

The boy made a clicking sound with his teeth. "All out o' charge, innit?"

"What about your friends?"

The boys moved forward en masse. The one who had first spoken, the tallest of them, suddenly had a knife in his hand. "Never mind about them. Give me your fucking phone, man," he said.

"No," said Nick.

"Fucking give it, or I stab your fucking eyes out."

Chloe's throat was dry with terror, but she managed to croak, "Just give it to him, Nick. It's only a phone, for goodness sake."

Nick glanced at her, as if about to say something. As he did so, like a weaving snake sensing a chance to attack, the tall boy sprang forward.

Chloe screamed as Nick and the boy came together. There was a clash of bodies, a grunt, and then Chloe became aware of a dragging weight on her arm and realised that Nick was sliding slowly and silently to the pavement, his legs folding beneath him.

She clutched him for a moment, trying to hold him upright, but eventually had to let him go to prevent herself being dragged down with him. As Nick fell, the tall boy stepped forward and shoved Chloe in the chest hard. She staggered back, certain for a moment that she'd been stabbed and that the shock and the pain would kick in later. As she put a hand to her chest, expecting to feel the wetness of blood, the tall boy crouched over Nick like a hawk over a rabbit, picking at his coat and the pockets of his trousers, pulling out a phone, a wallet, keys. Then the boys were slipping away into the night, not hurrying, crowing over their booty, their victims forgotten.

Chloe scrambled forward, legs like water, heart and head pounding, lips gummed together with saliva that had dried to glue in her mouth. She reached out, touched Nick's body.

"Nick," she whispered, "Nick."

She touched something wet. She lifted her hand. It was black under the street light.

Nick's parents were Jean and Brian. His sister, who was in the second year of her "A" levels, was called Liz. They arrived around four AM, having driven down from Durham.

When they walked into the intensive care unit, Chloe rose from the chair beside Nick's bed and said, "Hello, I'm Chloe. I'm a friend of Nick's. I was with him when it happened."

Nick's sister looked down at her brother, white-faced; his mum burst into tears. Only Brian acknowledged her.

"How is he?"

"They think he's going to be fine," Chloe told them. "The knife punctured his lung, but he's had an operation, and they've patched him up. As you can see he's breathing on a respirator at the moment, but they . . . they think he's going to be fine."

Her voice petered out. She was exhausted, emotionally and physically. She swayed on her feet, had to sit down again. Then Jean was stepping forward, grasping her hands.

"Look at you, pet," she said. "You're just about done in. Thank God you were with him. You saved his life."

Her eyes were wet with tears, but she was smiling shakily now, beaming with gratitude. Like Brian she was portly, her hair chestnut brown and worn in a way that made Chloe think of Shirley Bassey.

"I don't know about that," Chloe said. "I just called for an ambulance. Anyone would've."

"He'd have bled to death without you," Jean insisted. "Little life-saver you are."

Chloe didn't have the courage to tell her the truth—couldn't bring herself to say that if she hadn't arranged to meet Nick in the pub to tell him their relationship wasn't working out, and if she hadn't refused that final drink, and if she hadn't suggested he walk her home, then her son would never have been stabbed in the first place. Sitting beside Nick's unconscious form, staring at the transparent plastic mask covering his nose and mouth, and listening to the machines that were monitoring his life signs, Chloe couldn't help but think that this was all her fault, that if she hadn't been so selfish this would never have happened.

Suddenly, surrounded by Nick's family, she felt stifled, and pushed herself to her feet.

"I'll leave you to it," she said. "I'm sure you'd like to spend some time with Nick on your own."

Ignoring their protests she stumbled from the room. By the time she had pushed through the swinging double doors and was out in the corridor she was all but hyperventilating. She staggered to a chair with a pale blue vinyl seat and dropped heavily into it. The corridor outside the ICU was quiet, the only sound a faint buzz from the fluorescent strip lights overhead. Chloe slumped forward, closed her eyes, clasped her hands together. She didn't realise she was readying herself to pray until she actually started to speak.

"Lord, if you're there, and if you're listening, please help me. Give me the strength to overcome my doubts and believe in you again. I can't tell you how much the thought of losing my faith terrifies and upsets me. Without it I feel . . . cast adrift. But I can't pretend that I believe if I don't, I can't say I have faith if I don't feel it on the inside. Help me, Lord, please. If this is a test, or even a punishment, then believe me when I tell you that I want to overcome it, that I want my faith in you to be restored more than anything else in the world. But I can't live a lie, Lord. I need your strength, I need you to help set me back on the right path. Perhaps that's selfish of me, or weak, but that's how it is. I'm only human, after all."

Her voice trailed off. She didn't know what she expected to happen, but she felt just the same inside. Empty, lost. It was like a kind of darkness gnawing at her, devouring the light. Groggily she raised her head, her eyelids peeling apart.

The red door was on the other side of the corridor, directly opposite her, no more than half a dozen metres away.

Something rushed through her then—not faith, but a kind of tingling heat that was part awe, part wonder, and part raw, primal terror. For a split-second she wondered if this was it, the sign she had been praying for, but the notion had barely formed in her head before she was dismissing it.

No. This door was something different. Something wrong. Something unholy. She could sense it. She could feel it in her blood, in her nerve endings, in her very essence.

And yet she felt ensnared by the door too. Tempted. Tantalised. Repelled though she was, she had to know what was on the other side. Had to.

Almost unwillingly she rose to her feet. Took a step forward. The door seemed to throb like a heart, to call to her. As before it was half-way up the wall, upside-down. And now, up close, she could see that its paint was peeling and scabrous, that its wooden panels were cracked, its brass knob scratched and tarnished.

She took another step. She felt stuffed with heat, her eyes and throat pulsing, her heart like a drum whose vibrations shuddered through her body. Slowly she raised a hand, readying herself to knock.

"Our Nick's awake, if you want to see him."

The voice was like a slap, snapping her head round. Chloe gasped, blinking and swaying. For a moment her vision swam, and she thought she was about to pass out. Then the blur of colours and shapes tightened into focus, and she was looking at Jean, whose cheeks were flushed, and whose eyes were alive with excitement and curiosity.

Before Chloe could respond, Jean said, "Sorry, pet, did I startle you? What were you doing?"

"Nothing, I. . . ." Chloe stammered, and turned her head back towards the red door. It was gone.

She sighed. She felt partly relieved, partly bereft.

"Nothing," she repeated.

When she woke it was dark. For ten or fifteen seconds she lay in bed, her mind almost comfortingly blank, trying to remember where she was, what had happened. Was it night-time? The early hours? For some reason that didn't feel right. Massaging her hot forehead with a cool hand, she sat up, groping with her other hand for her phone on the bedside table. She brought it up to her face, peered at the time: 7:13. Time to get up, time to go to work—but that didn't feel right either. It was only when she looked again and realised that it was PM and not AM that the memories came flooding back.

She had got back from the hospital around twelve hours ago, with barely enough strength left to stagger into her bedroom and collapse into bed, peeling off clothes and leaving them in her wake as she went. The adrenaline crash after the trauma of the previous evening had caused her to sleep solidly and dreamlessly for the past twelve hours. Checking her phone again Chloe saw that she had a couple of missed calls and several texts, mostly from work, wanting to know where the hell she was. There was also a message from Nick, who sounded tired but okay, asking her if she was all right, and a text from Jo which said: *How are you? Feeling better after our talk?*

Still sitting in the dark, Chloe scrolled through her address book until she came to "Home." She selected "Dial" from the Options menu and snuggled down into bed as the cricket-like burr at the other end of the line broke the silence.

"Hello?" Her father's voice was like honey. Emotionally raw after waking up, Chloe was shocked to feel tears springing instantly to her eyes.

"Dad, it's me. Can I come home?"

A moment of surprised silence. Then her father said, "Chloe, my love? Are you all right?"

"Not really," she said. "I'm not doing so well at the moment. Can I come home?"

"Well . . . of course. At the weekend, do you mean?"

"No, I was thinking now. Well, tomorrow. I thought I'd catch an early train."

"I see."

"Is that all right?"

"Well, yes. But what about your work?"

"They'll be fine about it," she said, not caring whether it was true or not. "They know about Mum. They said if I needed any time off. . . ."

There was another moment's silence, and then her father said. "Right, well I shall expect you tomorrow. I'll look forward to it."

"Me too, Dad. And . . . Dad?"

"Yes."

"I need to talk to you about something. Something important."

"Right. Well, I shall look forward to that too."

Chloe rang off, feeling as though she had taken a step in the right direction, as though she had achieved something. Perhaps it was naïve to think her dad would solve all her problems, but talking to him would help, she felt sure of it. His was the voice of reason and compassion. He would untangle her muddled thoughts and put everything into perspective.

"I'm trying, Lord," she whispered. She threw back the duvet, crossed the room and switched on the light.

The door was back.

Chloe almost dropped her mug when she saw it. As it was, she jerked back from the window, slopping hot coffee over the back of her hand. "Ow!" she yelled, gritting her teeth as she ran through to the kitchen to douse the reddening skin in cold water. Once she'd patted her stinging hand dry with a tea towel she returned to the main room, sidling round the edge of the kitchen doorframe and keeping low, like someone targeted by a sniper. It was ridiculous to think she was being stalked by a door, and yet she couldn't help but feel that she was under scrutiny. She crept along the wall on bent knees until she was underneath the light switch, then reached up and snapped it off. With the flat in darkness, illuminated only by the glow of the street lamp outside, she felt marginally less exposed, though her heart was still thumping hard as she scrambled across to the window and jerked the curtains across, shutting out the night.

She rose, parted the curtains a chink with her finger and peered through the gap. She half-expected the door to have vanished, but it was still there, the peeling red gloss that coated it shimmering in the lamplight. It was on a section of wall that was part of the frontage of a second-hand furniture warehouse directly across the road from her apartment block. It was several metres to the left of the rolling metal shutter that was both wide enough and high enough to admit a sizeable truck, and that served as the warehouse's main entrance. As ever, the door was half-way up the wall and upside-down, and to Chloe it seemed to be flaunting its wrongness.

"You're not there," she muttered, and then, when that was not enough to dispel the image, "Go away, go away."

She let the curtain drop back into place, telling herself that if she ignored it, it would disappear, that next time she looked it would be gone.

She turned on the TV, checked her emails, made herself another cup of coffee, flicked through yesterday's *Metro*, even though she'd already read it. Try as she might, however, she couldn't put the door out of her mind; it was like an itch she was desperate to scratch.

Her flat was full of clocks—there was one on her kitchen wall, one on her computer, one on her phone, one on her DVD player tucked neatly beneath the TV—and every few moments she found her eyes straying to one or another, whereupon she would catch herself mentally calculating how many minutes had passed since she had last looked out of the window. She moved restlessly from room to room, sitting down for no more than two or three minutes at a time before feeling compelled to jump up and prowl again. Finally she tried to lie on her bed and close her eyes, but her mind was buzzing with anxiety, her stomach churning, and in the end she jumped to her feet, marched into the main room and twitched the curtain aside again.

The door was still there. Chloe gasped, feeling something between despair and fear curl inside her. She wondered whether, ultimately, she would be able to outrun the door, whether it was confined to London, and whether if she left the city and returned home it would somehow be unable to follow her.

She tried to glean comfort from that thought, though she couldn't help but be aware that she was only speculating, and that sometimes the only way to overcome a fear was to confront it. Allowing the curtain to drop she made herself a promise: if the door was still there in an hour she would attempt to discover what lay behind it.

For the next hour she forced herself to sit in front of the TV, to stare at the screen, even though her mind was elsewhere and she had no idea what she was watching. For the last ten minutes her eyes kept flicking to the digital clock on the DVD player, and with a minute to go, she shuffled to the edge of the settee, hands braced either side of her. As soon as the green numerals changed, completing the hour, she shoved herself to her feet and rushed across to the window. Jerking aside the curtain she cried out, as though at a sharp stabbing pain, and felt her legs begin to shake.

The door was still there.

"Oh God," she breathed, unsure whether her words were an oath or an appeal for strength, "oh God." As she pulled on a jacket and gloves, the shaking spread from her legs, into her hands and belly.

"Come on, Chloe," she told herself, "you can do this."

She walked out of her flat and down the stairs, gripping the banister as though it was her only connection with reality, as though without it she would drift away and become lost. At the bottom of the stairs she hesitated a moment, then plunged towards the front door. As she twisted the Yale lock and pulled the door open, her heart was pounding so much it hurt.

Please be gone, she thought, *please be gone*.

She stepped outside.

And there was the red door, across the road, waiting for her.

Chloe descended the steps at the front of the house and moved down the path towards the gate. There were several seconds when the red door was hidden from view by the high hedge bordering the front of the property. *When I step through the gate, it will be gone*, she thought.

But it wasn't. She crossed the road towards it as though in a dream. She wanted it to flicker and vanish, wanted something to distract her so that when she looked back she would see only a blank wall. She reached the opposite pavement and the door was metres away. It looked as real and as solid as everything around it.

"One more chance," she whispered, and closed her eyes. She kept them closed for a count of ten, breathing hard and fast. When she opened them again there was the door, its surface red and peeling like burnt skin.

"Okay," she said, crossing the pavement in four strides. The door was directly above her now, its lowest point level with her chin. She reached out, forming her hand into a tight fist. When she knocked what would she feel beneath her knuckles? Wood or solid brick? If brick, perhaps it would break the illusion, snap her out of whatever was causing this.

She knocked. Knuckles on wood. The sound echoed away from her, as though carried along some unseen, impossible corridor.

Three, four seconds slipped by. Then she heard something beyond the door. Slow, approaching footsteps. She wanted to turn and run, forced herself to stand still. The footsteps stopped. The door opened.

Light spilled out. Chloe took a step back, screwing up her eyes. Through the door she saw a corridor, almost as narrow as the door itself. A cylinder on a thin pole jutted from a white floor about half-way along; much closer to her, just beyond the door, something large hung from what appeared to be a carpeted ceiling. She couldn't make sense of it at first, and then she realised that what she was seeing was upside-down. The cylinder on the pole was a lamp hanging from a ceiling flex. And the large, dark shape drooping from what appeared to be a carpeted ceiling like an over-sized bat was a figure, its feet planted firmly on a carpeted floor, to which upside-down furniture clung as if glued or nailed into place.

With the light behind it the figure was mostly in silhouette, though Chloe got the impression that it was a woman—small and hunched and wizened.

"Mum?" she said before she was even consciously aware that she had made the connection. "Mum, is that you?"

The figure remained silent. Chloe could not even hear her—if it was a her—breathing.

"What's happening?" Chloe whispered. "What do you want from me? Why are you upside-down? How can you defy gravity like that?"

The figure leaned forward. It creaked and rustled, as though made of parchment, as though it was nothing but a dried-up husk.

Its voice, too, was papery. "Gravity is an act of faith," it whispered.

"What do you . . . ?" Chloe began, and then her eyes widened in horror. "No!" she cried. "No!"

And all at once her feet were leaving the ground, she was kicking at the air, she was falling. As she plummeted helplessly towards the infinite blackness of space, the night sky rushed up to engulf her.

WHITE WINGS

WHITE WINGS

So consciousness hits me, and despite the numbness, I get the immediate impression that I'm in an enclosed space. I feel strange, like I've been given a shot of something, like I've been drugged.

And then I remember. Linsey and the Black Russian. Her peculiar insistence that I drink it. It seems so obvious now that I feel a bit of a twat for falling for it, but at the time I just assumed that she was trying to loosen me up.

Why? Because she wanted to tell me about *him*. About *Michel*. Because once again she was ashamed of her voracious appetites and felt a need to unburden herself. That's what I thought, at least. Only this time I'd vowed that I was going to stand firm, draw the line. This time I was going to tell her that she'd fucked me about once too often, and that no matter how much she begged I wouldn't take her back. That it was over between us. Finished. Kaput. A man has his pride, after all, and mine had not only been dented over the past twenty-odd years of marriage, but screwed up and stamped on. And not just once, but again and again.

Ironic then that just when I was on the verge of getting rid of *her*, she'd decided to get rid of *me*, albeit in a more permanent way. Least, that's what I assumed. I mean why else would she have slipped me a mickey finn if not to bump me off? She'd drugged my drink and now here I was waking up . . . where?

In a car boot, mate, my mind informed me, as if the thoughts weren't my own, but those of some friendly, helpful bloke I carried around in my head. You're in a car boot, you know you are; you knew it as soon as you woke up. You can tell by the faint waft of petrol fumes and the smell of leather seats. You can tell by the wiry texture of the vinyl matting beneath the side of your face, and the occasional gentle tinking of metal as the engine cools down.

A car boot. My *own* car boot, most likely. Cheeky fucking bastards. I listen, expecting to hear the mush of muffled voices from the front of the car, but all is silent. From the lack of engine noise, and the fact that I'm not being bumped and jostled about, I've already worked out that the car is stationary. Which presumably means that we've already arrived at wherever my wife and her lover were taking me.

Unless we've just stopped off en route, of course. For all I know we could be in a service station car park. Linsey and *Michel* might be sitting in Costa now, sipping matching lattes, smug in the knowledge that I'm still out for the count, and that nothing can possibly go wrong with their murderous plan.

Well, excuse me for pissing on your bonfire, bitch, but I'm fucked if you think I'm going to go gentle into that good night. You might have spent almost our entire married life fucking me about, but it stops right here, right now. This time you've gone too fucking far.

So I start to punch and kick the padded metal ceiling above me, and I start to yell for someone to let me out. Not in a scared, panicked way, though. I don't want to sound like some frightened little kid. No, I make myself sound angry, outraged. Trussed up and incarcerated though I am, I make myself sound like I'm in charge of the situation.

Hang on, though. I'm *not* trussed up, am I? Funnily enough—probably because I'm trying to process so much information in one go—I only properly realise that fact once I've punched and kicked the inside of the boot a few times.

Despite my predicament I grin. Useless bastards. Total fucking amateurs. Linsey might have caught me off guard with the drink, but there's no way she'll do so again. In my twenty-eight years in the construction industry I've chewed up and spat out bigger, harder bastards than that poncey *Michel*, and plenty of them too. Linsey might always have been able to twist me round her little finger when it came to our marriage, but if she thinks she can do the same when my life is at stake then she can fucking think again. What she doesn't realise is that when it comes right down to it, I'm not the soft touch she thinks I am. Like a lot of blokes in my position, that conniving bitch has been my *only* blind spot, my *only* weakness, over the past three decades.

But no more. No fucking more.

There's no response to all my kicking and thumping and shouting, which leads me to conclude that we're in some isolated spot somewhere. The fact that Linsey and *Michel* don't respond either seems to indicate that they've buggered off for the moment—though it's also possible that they might just want me to *think* that, and that in reality they're actually close by, perhaps with their hands over their mouths to stifle their laughter.

That particular thought *really* pisses me off, and I start to kick at the underside of the boot with increased fervour. I know I shouldn't, I know I should conserve my energy and my air, but I can't help it. I kick and I kick, my teeth gritted in fury, my head hot and pounding.

And suddenly something gives and the boot pops open. Just like that.

For a split-second I assume *Michel* must have opened it, and I brace myself, ready to fight the narrow-hipped little cunt, to tear his fucking head off with my bare hands. But there's no one there. As the boot yawns I see silvery light sketching in the outlines of trees—lots of trees—standing as close together as punters at a music festival. The upper branches of the trees are all tangled together, forming a canopy, which in the summer must be an impenetrable ceiling of green, but which now, at the arse-end of January, is more like the mangled, twisted spars of a collapsed roof, through which moonlight leaks and dribbles like milk laced with mercury.

I sit up, look around, alert for a broadside attack. I don't expect the little cunt to have a gun, or even a knife—he hasn't got the guts to use a real weapon—but he might have picked up a branch, and he might whack me with it out of panic.

But there's nothing. The woods—'cos that's almost definitely where we are; in a woodland clearing somewhere—are as still and as quiet as you can reasonably expect. I hear the faint scratching of branches overhead as the wind bullies its way through them. And I hear insects chirruping softly in the undergrowth. Grasshoppers or something. I don't know; I'm not a fucking zoologist.

But there's nothing else. Just a deadening cold, which numbs me a bit—though to be honest, that feeling could just as easily have come from whatever shit Linsey slipped into the Black Russian. I get out of the car and stand up, opening and closing my hands, rubbing my arms and legs to massage some life into them. And then I glimpse movement in the silvery-black mass of trees up ahead, and my eyes snap towards it.

A white, disembodied face, glimmering faintly, is staring at me from out of the tangle of branches.

I don't mind admitting it; my body jerks in shock. That face gives me the creeps. It's just hanging there, and all I can see of it are two round black eyes and the suggestion of a small, puckered mouth.

"Who the fuck are you?" I say, sounding bolder and more aggressive than I feel.

The face doesn't answer. It just hangs there, bone-white in the moonlight. I narrow my eyes, trying to make out the impression of a body underneath it, thinking that it must be some bloke in dark clothes standing half-hidden in the trees. But I can't see anything. There's just the face staring at me.

Then something fucking weird happens. Great white wings unfold and stretch out on either side of the face, and then fold themselves back in again. For a moment my whole world turns inside out. It's like I've had reality pulled from under my feet like a rug. I experience a moment of total disorientation, undercut with what I can only admit is a sudden sharp punch of primal fear. My mouth goes dry, and my instinct is to turn and run. Then my logical mind kicks in, and I suddenly realise what I'm really looking at.

It's not a white, winged, disembodied face at all.

No. It's a fucking owl.

I feel so relieved and so stupid that I bark out a dry laugh before I can help myself. Immediately I slap a hand over my mouth to stifle any other sound I might make, but beneath the hand I'm grinning.

What the hell was I thinking? It's an owl. A fucking owl. Of *course* it is! Now that I can see it, it's so fucking obvious. It just sits there on a branch, cool as you like, looking at me. It's eerie and beautiful, like some kind of forest spirit. Silent and serene, totally in its element.

"All right, old son?" I whisper. The owl stares at me. Despite the situation, I feel a moment of . . . I dunno. Awe, I suppose. Wonder. Like I'm being allowed a glimpse into something that's denied to most people. Like I'm privileged.

I hesitate a moment or two, then I walk towards the owl. I expect it to spread its wings and swoop silently away. But it doesn't. It just sits there on its branch, calm and unimpressed. Three metres from it I stop. Then I take a careful step forward. Another. Another. Every moment I expect those great white wings to unfurl, but now I'm only a metre away from it, and still it sits there. I take one more step, looking into its face. It stares back at me, unblinking. I raise my arm, stretch out my hand, wondering if it'll let me touch it. My fingers are inches from its downy white chest when I hear a sound from deeper in the forest.

Low voices, accompanied by the scrape of metal on dry earth. I listen hard. My hand still hovers in the air, a few inches in front of the owl.

Then slowly, reluctantly, I lower my hand. I give the owl a little nod. We understand each other, me and him. I back up a couple of steps, and then I edge my way around the tree he's perched on, and I push my way deeper into the woods.

The talking gets louder. I pick out individual words, get close enough to differentiate between the two voices—a man's and a woman's. The woman sounds nervous. She's telling the man to hurry up, and he, his voice wavery, irritable, brittle as flint, is telling her it's easy for her, just standing there, doling out instructions.

The woman is Linsey, of course. That elastic-snap voice of hers has never sounded so hateful. And the bloke, of course, is *Michel*. Spineless little bastard. It's not hard to see who wears the fucking trousers in *that* relationship.

I smell the smoke from Linsey's cigarette before I see the orange glow from its tip. There's a brighter glow too. It comes from the torch she's directing down into the hole that *Michel*'s been digging. He's standing beside it, his grey T-shirt dark with sweat around the collar and armpits, despite the cold night. The torchlight shows his breath as a white ghostly vapour wreathing his head. His dark, bushy hair looks shiny and his forehead is beaded with little jewels of sweat.

As I realise what they've been doing, my stomach clamps, not with fear but with outrage. It's a grave. The little fucker has been digging me a grave! Well, they're going to get more than they bargained for when their intended victim comes up behind them and bangs their fucking heads together!

Michel's got a shovel in his hand, but that doesn't bother me. Even if I gave him a free swing, I doubt he'd have the strength to do any real damage. Using the trees as cover, I sneak forward, hoping the crackle and rustle of my approach, stealthy though it is, will be drowned out by their bickering. Then the Dambusters march, tinny and incredibly loud in the relative stillness of the forest, jangles out like some fucking idiot alarm, and I realise my cover is blown.

It's my fucking mobile. Jesus fucking wept. Talk about bad timing. Knowing the damage is already done, I instinctively grope for my pocket. Then I realise that my biggest problem is not to turn the fucking thing off, but to deal with the consequences of being discovered, and my head snaps back up again. I expect Linsey and *Michel* to be looking at me, probably with shock and a bit of fear on their faces, but they're not.

They're looking down into the hole.

It's only then that I realise that's where the noise is coming from. What the fuck? Why bother taking my mobile out of my pocket and chucking it into the grave?

"For fuck's sake!" Linsey snaps. "Turn that fucking thing off!"

Like an obedient puppy, *Michel* drops down into the hole and scrabbles about, and a few seconds later the phone stops. He holds it up and Linsey snatches it off him and drops it on the ground and grinds her heel into it.

"There," she says. "Now fucking hurry up and get this over with, so we can get out of here."

But—and here's a funny thing—my hand's still in my pocket, and it's currently wrapped around a smooth, cool slab of plastic and metal. Slowly I take the thing out and look at it. It's my mobile phone. The same one that Linsey's just ground into the dirt.

That weird, tilting, inside out feeling overwhelms me again. It's like vertigo; I almost stagger. I watch, a bit dazed, as *Michel* climbs out of the hole and starts filling it in, the muscles in his scrawny arms tightening as he shovels quickly. Linsey watches him silently. She finishes her cigarette and tosses it into the hole.

Silly bitch, I think. DNA. Do you *want* to get caught?

Then *Michel*'s finished, and scraping dead leaves and shit over the grave with the side of his foot to conceal it.

"All done," he says.

"Right then," says Linsey. "Let's fuck off out of here."

They turn away from the hole, facing in my direction. And that's when I step out from behind a tree, directly into their path.

I expect to see them gasp and tremble, to cry out in shock. But they don't. They fucking don't. They don't break their stride; their muscles don't tense; their eyes don't even flicker. And at that moment I know—I just *know*—that it's not that they're playing it cool. No, it's much, much more than that.

The truth is, they don't even know I'm there. They can't see me. To them I'm invisible.

The thought terrifies me. Fucking *terrifies* me. I watch them walk towards me, and I wonder what'll happen if I stand in their way. I even raise a hand to stop them, but at the last moment a horrible feeling of dread overwhelms me, and I step aside. I feel and hear the crunch of leaves beneath my feet as I move out of their way, but it's clear that they don't hear anything. They just walk on, oblivious.

I stand there, facing the grave, listening to them behind me, moving away. Eventually the rustle-crunch of their footsteps fades into silence, which is broken a minute or so later by the cough of ignition. This then settles into the growling purr of a car engine. *My* car engine. Then I hear the sound of that too moving away, growing fainter and fainter, until eventually silence swallows it up.

Now it's just me. I'm alone in the forest. I walk slowly to the grave and drop to my knees beside it.

I'm not alone for long, though. After a while I hear something at my back, something moving through the trees towards me. At first I don't know what it is. It sounds like whispering. Then it gets closer, and all at once I recognise it.

It's the steady, slow beating of wings.

THE COMPLICIT

TIJIJ9MO J HT

"Where she's coming from is Jesus Christ . . . and his life . . . and the fact that he rose from the dead," I hear a woman several seats in front of me say. Some of her words are blurred by the creaking rush of the train, so I don't grasp the full meaning, but she speaks with enough glib arrogance for me to feel quietly furious.

He didn't rise from the dead, I want to tell her. *No one does*. But I stay in my seat, hands clamped between my thighs. Am I angry because it's death that's bringing me back, or is it the idea of resurrection I find appalling?

Certainly the resurrection of my memories is every bit as unwelcome as I'd feared it might be. My heart is beating so rapidly it feels close to palpitating as I stand on the station platform, staring at the grime-blackened wall and the grubby sign bearing the name of the town in which I grew up.

I remain motionless for so long that eventually a guard asks me, "Are you all right?" He makes it sound as though I'm preventing him from doing his job as efficiently as he'd like.

I force my unwilling lips into a smile. "I haven't been back for a long time."

"Emotional reunion, is it?" he asks in a manner which might be construed as sarcasm.

I merely grunt, and will my body towards the station exit. The swing doors beyond the ticket barrier are closing on the smattering of passengers from the train. The wheels of my suitcase squeal as I drag it in my wake, beneath which I fancy I can discern the uneven hobble of footsteps. I halt and the footsteps stop when the squealing does. I glance back and am met by a hint of stale cigarette smoke, but there's no one there. No one except the guard, who is mournfully wafting the train out of the station with his flag.

The sights through the cab window during the ride to my parents' and latterly my mother's house have changed so little in the past two decades that I can't help feeling I'm being reeled back in. I close my eyes as we pass the school gates where my Uncle Terry used to meet me after his half-day on Wednesdays, even though I was old enough to walk home on my own— or at least with my friend Joe.

Even in winter his brown-stained fingers as he grasped my hand were damp and fat, and so warm my arm would tingle. By the time we reached home I'd be feeling feverish, though not only from his body heat and the stale fug that clung to him. I gag, as if at the memory of that, and use my own fingers to bar the way to my lips. The taxi driver glances at me in the rear view mirror and I alter the gesture as casually as I can, rubbing my hands over my stubbled cheeks as if massaging life back into my tired skin.

As the school recedes into the distance I glance again at the rear view mirror to see if the cab driver is still watching me. He isn't, but through the back window of the car, or at least its reflection, I glimpse a figure lurching lopsidedly out of the school gate and on to the pavement. I twist so quickly my neck makes a gristly, wet sound, but the only thing that resembles a figure is the grey metal pole of the bus stop. Less than two minutes later the cab pulls up at the kerb outside the house where I grew up.

I expect it to look smaller or shabbier to how I remember it, but it doesn't. If anything I'm startled by how precisely it matches my memory. It's almost as if the building has jumped out of my head to occupy a space in the real world. For this reason it initially seems almost hyper real. Even after the cab's engine has faded to silence I stand on the pavement outside the gate, afraid to enter. My gaze skitters across the two downstairs windows and the pair above them, fearful both of glimpsing movement in the house's dark interior and of missing it. Abruptly I shudder, spooked by the stillness—the *watchfulness*—of the building, but at least it gives me the impetus to push open the gate and march up the compacted gravel path to the front door. As I near the house I recollect standing at the window of my parents' bedroom and watching my Uncle Terry limping up this same path. The way my stomach tightens is like a muscle memory of how it used to when he got so close to the house that I'd lose sight of him.

The key is under the blue plant pot by the front door, exactly where Mrs. Forbes told me it would be. When she rang last week I had no conscious memory of her at first, such were the barriers I'd erected to keep out the past. My subconscious knew, though. The instant I heard her voice, cracked and shrill with age, say, "Is that Matt?" I felt vertiginous, as if I was something small targeted by a bird of prey, plucked without warning into the air.

Gripping the receiver to ground myself, I replied, "It is. Who's this?"

"It's Mrs. Forbes, love. I've lived across the road from yer mam since before you were born. Do you remember me?"

"I'm . . . not sure."

"Well, that's to be expected. It *was* a long time ago. I used to be the lollipop lady at yer school when you were a nipper. I bet yer remember that, don't yer?"

"Yes," I said, "of course." Though all I reluctantly remember is her bright yellow coat and black peaked cap and her metal lollipop, whose words I always thought meant she didn't like kids until I realised that STOP CHILDREN was an instruction for oncoming drivers, along with the reason why they should.

"I'm afraid I've some bad news for yer, love," she said. "Yer mam's passed on. I thought it better yer heard it from me than the police."

It makes no odds to me, I wanted to tell her, but all that emerged was, "Oh."

"You'll be coming back for the funeral?" she only just managed to turn into a question.

Will I? "When is it?"

"Week on Thursday. Have yer a pen? I'll give yer the details."

Even now, a week later, I still don't know why I'm here; I didn't come back for my dad's funeral eight years ago. Closure maybe. A wrapping up of our family's affairs. Perhaps when Mam's in the ground and the house that's now mine has been sold I can truly move on instead of trying to convince myself I have. When I unlock the front door and step inside, the stench of cigarette smoke hits me at once.

I recoil, almost stumbling backwards over the front step. By the time I recover my balance the smell has gone. *Fuck you*, I think savagely, propelling myself over the threshold and shutting the door so forcefully behind me that its glass panels shudder.

The past closes around me as I cross the hallway and step into the front room. It's just as I remember it. Cream walls, lace curtains which blur the light, floral-patterned suite faded by age, a mirror above the wooden mantelpiece shaped like a fan or an open clam shell with scalloped edges.

My startled reflection in the mirror makes me realise I'm more or less the same age as Uncle Terry was when he first came to live with us. I loved Mam back then. She had never given me reason not to. Dad too probably, though he's a more distant figure. I have to concentrate hard to bring his face into focus even if I want to.

Leaving my suitcase in the front room, where it perches beside the settee like a guard dog awaiting orders, I prowl through the rest of the ground floor rooms. Narrow kitchen with a corner pantry and wall-mounted melamine cupboards; tiny toilet I'd sometimes pretend was my secret log cabin in the woods where no one could find me, because of its faux-wood walls; draughty extension on the back of the house, which Mam always called the 'snug', even though it was anything but.

When I hear a creak from above my head, as if someone upstairs is attempting to be stealthy, I look up, as if hopeful the ceiling might suddenly become transparent. Exiting the snug, I move swiftly across the hallway and pause at the bottom of the stairs. Shadows gather at the top, though they're insipid rather than ominous. I think about announcing my presence, but what if it's an intruder? Perhaps I should arm myself. Take a knife from the kitchen or a rolling pin. Almost immediately I balk at the idea—it might instigate violence rather than prevent it—and ascend swiftly, mindful of the fact that I'm vulnerable to attack from anyone who might lean over the upper balcony.

It annoys me that my heart is beating so hard when I reach the top of the stairs. But perhaps my anxiety is understandable, considering the circumstances under which I last stood on this spot twenty years ago. Then, of course, I was facing the other way, about to descend the stairs and leave my life behind. Now I stand and listen, and I sniff the air too—though I hear nothing, smell nothing. Am I relieved? I should be, though I feel such a mix of emotions—including anxiety and fear and even guilt—that it's hard to pick out the positive from the negative.

There are five doors on this landing. Closest is the bathroom, then what was once my bedroom, then a storage cupboard, then the spare room, then at the far end, overlooking the front garden, my parents' bedroom.

Determined to be methodical, I open the bathroom door. The avocado toilet suite is so familiar I might have been here only yesterday. As the door opens a flash of movement from inside the room startles me, then immediately I feel embarrassed, even though I'm alone, as I realise that what spooked me was my own reflection in a free-standing circular mirror on the shelf above the sink.

Curling my hand around the door handle of what was once my bedroom I wonder whether to enter stealthily or quickly. Before I'm even aware I've made a decision I've twisted the handle and shoved the door savagely open.

What shocks me is not that the room is exactly as I left it, but that it isn't. Indeed, it's so empty the sound of my movements echo off the bare walls. There's my old wardrobe with its doors hanging open and a mattress stripped of bedding on my familiar wood-framed bed, but everything else has gone: the clothes and shoes I left behind, the posters which adorned the walls, the curtains, the lampshade, my books and CDs, the stack of board games on top of the wardrobe.

Even the carpet has been pulled up and removed, leaving brown underlay edged with wooden carpet strips bristling with the spikes of nails. Did Mam carefully store my stuff somewhere in the hope I would one day return, or donate it all to charity? Maybe my parents threw it away, discarded my life like a failed experiment, like something they'd rather forget. I feel my resentment growing, my stomach cramping with anger, and I exit the room quickly, perhaps hoping to trap my negative feelings inside.

I glance in the storage cupboard, which contains a vacuum cleaner, a mop and bucket and a high shelf cluttered with cleaning fluids, then move on. Despite my vow to be methodical, I hesitate at the door to the next room, then bypass it and decide to first check out the room at the end of the landing.

My dad's presence was clearly phased out of my parents' bedroom in the years after he died. The furnishings consist of flowery fabrics and lace-edged cushions; the dressing table is home to hair products, bottles of perfume, a sequinned jewellery box, another box whose central slit sprouts pink tissues. The air smells sweetly of talcum powder, which catches in my throat. I cough and try to stifle it, as if afraid of giving away my position. Despite myself I glance over my shoulder at the door I haven't opened yet. This is the spare room, which for the last six years of my life here was occupied by my Uncle Terry.

Last time I entered this room . . . I stifle the thought. I'm an adult now. I'm thirty-five. But the instant I grip the door handle it's as if the last twenty years have been a fantasy, and that this is the only reality. This house. This moment.

I open the door. The room beyond is dark. Something comes flapping out of the shadows towards me, but only in my imagination. I reach to my left, slap my hand on the light switch. Nothing happens. The darkness thickens. I blink.

No. The darkness doesn't thicken. It *doesn't*. The curtains on the far side of the room are closed, but it's daylight outside. The room is dim, but it's not too dark to see that it's unoccupied. Even so I stride quickly across the grey carpet, giving the bottom of the bed a wide berth, so that nothing can slide out from beneath it and grab me. I yank open the curtains so violently they make a sound like ripping paper. Late afternoon daylight tumbles into the room, highlighting its drabness.

Nothing remains of Uncle Terry, of course. The place has been redecorated. None of this furniture was here when he was. There is nothing that he once owned, or even used. He has been expunged as effectively as I have. I think of Mam getting rid of the men who once outnumbered her, kicking over their traces, moving on.

Gathering rain clouds make the walls look as if they're marbled with grey veins. Everything looks old, tired. The furnishings are non-descript, the bedding a washed-out blue, the pillow lumpy.

There's something on the pillow. A shadow? No, it's too dark, too hard-edged. I move closer to the bed, glancing at the gap filled with darkness between the floor and its underside, which, although narrow, is still wide enough to conceal a body.

I haven't checked under the bed since I was a kid—and surely doing so, putting your face to the gap, will make you even more vulnerable—but I do it all the same, knowing it will nag at me if I don't, especially at night when the house is dark and quiet. I step back from the bed before dropping to my knees, then dip and peer quickly, my cheek brushing the coarse grey weave of the carpet, a stale, dusty smell filling my nostrils.

There's nothing under the bed. Of *course* there isn't. I rise to my hands and knees. My face is level with the pillow. The black thing that was on it, the fleck, is gone. *Could* it have been a shadow, after all?

But the bedding is moving. No, not moving exactly. There's the faintest flicker, the faintest suggestion of life, from beneath the thin blue coverlet that lies loosely over the elasticated white sheet stretched tightly over the mattress. I rise quickly, a pulse jumping in my throat. I pull back the blue sheet.

The bed is full of charred flesh. Shreds and scabs of it. More substantial than ashes, though not much.

And some of them are moving. Twitching.

I stagger back, stifling a cry with my hand. My mind races, struggling to make sense of what I'm seeing. Then my perception adjusts, and I realise that what I'm looking at isn't animated flesh, it's moths. Dozens of them.

An infestation. More and more of them fluttering feebly as I watch, as if reacting to the light. But they're too weak to fly. They must have crawled between the sheets for warmth, for darkness, or perhaps they hatched out under there. I don't know if that's possible, whether moths do that, but it's the only explanation I can think of.

Should I bundle up the sheet, shake it out of the window, release them into the light? Or maybe even grab the vacuum cleaner from the storage cupboard and hoover them up? But I do neither. Their feeble fluttering, their desperate bid for life, for escape, sickens me. So I retreat, stumbling out the door, slamming it behind me. I'm gasping, sweating. I can't bear to be in this house a moment longer, I need a break. I hurry along the landing, down the stairs, and it's only when I've slammed the front door behind me that I wonder whether I've locked myself out. But no, the key is in my pocket, where I must have put it after letting myself in, even though I have no recollection of doing so.

Ten minutes later I'm in a pub, The Fountainhead, which is halfway between my parents' house and my old primary school. I had a vague memory of there being a pub on this route, and here it is, a forbidding place of sooty red brick perched like an island in a grey flat lake of mostly empty car park.

Odd to think that once upon a time I used to pass this building twice a day, yet this is the first time I've ever stepped inside. It's a soulless place, high-ceilinged, echoey. The few drinkers, surrounded by swirling dust-motes trapped in shafts of late afternoon light angling in through the windows, look isolated, sad. They gaze into their beer as if remembering better times.

Soon I'm one of them. Although it's not my intention I feel as if I'm blending in so as not to be noticed. I sit at a corner table sipping my pint of bitter. After a while I half-close my eyes, feel myself drifting, which is why I'm unaware that someone has approached my table until they say, "Bloody hell! It's you!"

I look up, startled. The man looming over me is big and red faced with short sandy hair. He's grinning expectantly. But then the expression slips, whereupon his doughy jowls drag the rest of his features down.

"You don't recognise me, do you? Have I really changed that much?"

I look through the weight and the age, and all at once recognition glimmers like a faint light in the darkness. Is it something in the eyes, the set of the mouth, the inflection of the voice?

"Joe?"

The grin reappears and he eases himself on to the empty stool opposite me. The circular table creaks as he rests his elbows, and then the entirety of his upper body weight, on it. His hands are so big—twice as big as mine—that the pint glass he's clutching looks dwarfed.

"One and the same," he says. Then his tone becomes almost accusatory. "So what brings you back here? I thought you'd escaped the clutches of this shithole for good."

"Mam died," I say. "I'm back for the funeral."

"But no longer?"

"What?"

"I mean that's all you're here for? Straight after you'll be heading back to . . . wherever it is you live?"

"London," I say. "Ealing."

"Yeah, right. You don't want to hang around in this dump any longer than you need to."

His attitude is unfathomable. Not only the fact that he didn't bat an eyelid when I told him about Mam (not that I care; at least that means I don't have to pretend to be upset), but also that he seems simultaneously pleased to see me, yet eager that I up sticks and move on again as quickly as possible.

"You have," I say.

He looks blank. "Have what?"

"Hung around in this dump."

His eyes drop to his pint. "Yeah, well. Haven't got your adventurous spirit, have I? Your strength of character."

"Is that what I've got?"

"I always thought so."

I snort a laugh. "I'm a drifter, Joe. I've got no ties, no one to . . ." *Come home to? Care about me?* I shrug. "Anyway, you know what I mean. At least you've got roots here. And you look well."

"Fat, you mean?"

"Settled. So—what are you up to now? Where are you living?" I nod at the wedding ring on his left hand. "And who with?"

He shrugs. "I work at Whitworth's over Green Vale way—the confectionary firm, you know?"

"You make gobstoppers?"

He looks rueful. "I maintain the machinery. Joined them straight from school. I wasn't clever like you. Didn't go to university."

"Neither did I."

"No, but you could've done. If things had been different."

I see him struggling with himself, wondering what to say, what to ask. Before he can decide I jump in with my own questions. "So what about the rest of it? Who's the unlucky woman?"

"Oi," he says, but although he takes it as a joke I can see he's not in the mood for banter. "You probably won't remember her? Charlotte Foster? She was in the year below us at school."

"Was she the blind one?"

"I'll swing for you in a minute. She was the pretty one. Too pretty for you. Still is. Reddish hair."

I have no idea who he's talking about. "Any kids?"

"No fear."

"Don't you want kids?"

His eyes meet mine. "Would you have kids round here?"

Do you mean because it's a dump? I want to ask him. But I don't. I also want to ask him what he knows about me, about why I left, but in the end I just say, "I wouldn't do anything around here. Not anymore. I'm done with this place. No offence, but once Mam's in the ground I'll be out of here for good."

"You make sure you are," Joe says, and I glance at him sharply, but there's no threat in his words. He looks around again, as if afraid of being overheard. "Don't let it suck you back in, Matt. Promise me you won't."

"I promise," I say.

I'm not a big drinker, but by the time I crawl into bed that night I'm drunk. It's the only way I can face going back to the house where I grew up, the only way I can face closing my eyes in there and letting unconsciousness claim me.

I sleep, fully-clothed, on the bare mattress in my old room, even though there's no bedding. I use my bundled up jacket as a pillow. I drag a thick sweater out of my suitcase, which I pull across my upper body as a blanket.

The alcohol fug encases me like a shell that seems impervious to outside influences like temperature, and internal influences like fear and imagination.

When I lower my head to the pillow my mind spins like a roundabout in a children's playground. I feel sick, but it's a distant feeling and not entirely unwelcome, because at least it stops me thinking about the dark, and the house, and the fact that I'm alone in it. I lie on my side, bunching my hands under my chin as though praying, drawing my knees up to my belly. I'm protected by the velvety blackness inside my head. I'm invincible and invisible.

My hope is that I'll wake with daylight streaming through the thin curtains and birds singing in the trees, but when I open my eyes again it's still dark. I feel as though I've clawed myself into consciousness from a place defined by discomfort, but when the shreds of sleep fall away I realise that the opposite is true, that it's my discomfort which has prodded me awake. My head is pounding, my stomach rolling, my bladder achingly full. I'm shivering too. I'm freezing. The cold has penetrated my defences and settled inside me, bone-deep.

I need to piss. I need to be sick. I need to get warm. But moving, I feel sure, will upset the delicate balance between containing my woes and losing control of them. I breathe slowly, evenly. I smell cigarette smoke, faint at first, but growing stronger. Then I feel the mattress dip beneath my feet as someone sits on the end of my bed.

Despite how wretched I feel, I scramble upright, jerking my feet out of the intruder's reach, pressing myself back against the headboard. The terror that engulfs me is raw, primal. My skin tingles as if burned; my shivers turn to shudders, violent and uncontrollable. I glare into the darkness.

Perched on the end of my bed, blacker than the blackness around it, is a shape.

Is it a human figure? It's hard to tell. If so, it's a misshapen one, or at least unfinished. It looks like a figure that's tried to stitch itself a form using the deepest clots of shadow in the room. It reeks of cigarette smoke and something else; something I tell myself can't be singed hair, can't be charred meat.

Waves of nausea roll through me. I will the figure to disappear. I tell myself I'm dreaming, or at least half-dreaming, that I need to wake up.

The figure stirs; the bed creaks. The dark mass above the figure's neck changes shape, and I realise it's turning its black ruin of a face towards me.

I try to scream, but when I open my mouth vomit surges from my stomach and into my throat. I twist my head just in time, so that instead of throwing up over the bed and myself, I'm sick on the floor.

The vomit reeks of whisky, and I remember the whisky chasers that Joe and I started to drink to supplement our pints of beer. The memory makes my stomach cramp again, and a second wave of sickness rushes up and out of me, causing my body to jerk and stretch and go taut.

Tears pour from my eyes as I puke. I feel as if every drop of liquid is being squeezed out of me. I don't know if the figure means me harm, but even if it did there would be nothing I could do about it; the sickness has me in its grip. As if to illustrate the point my body convulses again, my limbs going rigid as I throw up for a third time.

Then, at last, the sickness ebbs, my muscles relax. I turn my head to where the figure was sitting, but my vision is still too blurred to differentiate between the different gradations of darkness. I scramble, slither from the bed, feet kicking and hands pawing the bare underlay, trying to avoid the spatters of vomit. I imagine the figure coming after me, scuttling like an insect, and that gives me the impetus to propel myself to my feet, lurch across the room, slap my hand down on the light switch.

I spin around so quickly that only the wall at my back stops me from falling. The room is illuminated by merciless white light from the unshaded bulb dangling from the ceiling.

If there *was* a figure there it has gone now, extinguished like the shadows, like the darkness. It has left no residue, no lingering odour—or at least, not one I can detect beneath the high, acrid, whisky stench of my own vomit.

The hard reality of the brightly lit room instantly makes the previous few minutes seem like a bad dream. The way we think changes in the darkness. With nothing to contain them our imaginations blossom. Within seconds of staring, wide-eyed and panting, at the ordinary, even sordid space in front of me, my fear begins to deflate. Almost defiantly I yank open the bedroom door, stomp down the hall to the bathroom, switching lights on as I go, and take a long, satisfying piss. I spend the next hour scraping up the vomit in the bedroom, scrubbing the underlay with hot, soapy water. I open the window and prop the door ajar to allow a through circulation of fresh air, and then I go downstairs and spend the rest of the night dozing on the settee in the front room.

"You remember your Uncle Terry?" Dad says. "He'll be staying with us for a little while."

How do I feel when I first hear those words? Excited at the novelty of someone new joining our household? Resentful at the thought of having to share my parents with someone else? Wary of the stranger?

In all honesty, I don't remember, though whenever I think of Uncle Terry (not that I do; I have studiously *avoided* thinking of him these past twenty years) I associate him with seediness, grime, dissolution. I think of bad skin, unwashed hair, teeth and fingers yellowed by cigarettes. I think of doughy flesh, sagging jowls, dark bags under colourless eyes. I think of his sly grins, the way he used to stare at me, the way he used to grunt in the darkness.

"Why?" I ask when Dad tells me Uncle Terry will be staying with us. Not hostile, just curious.

Dad frowns. "Because he will. Because he's been having a hard time. And because families stick together."

Uncle Terry smiles at me. His skin is shiny and wet as if he's been running, though his lips are dry and cracked. "Is that all right with you, little man?"

I shrug. I have no opinion one way or the other.

"We're going to be great friends, you and I, aren't we?" he says.

I stare at him. Can a man and a boy *be* friends? Does that mean Uncle Terry will play football with us? Come out on bikes with us?

Uncle Terry looks at Dad and laughs. "He doesn't know what to make of me."

"He'll come round," Dad says. "Fancy a cup of tea?"

Uncle Terry jumps up from his chair. "You stay there. I'll do it. Got to earn my keep."

When he walks across the living room, one of his legs stays straight instead of bending and swings out with each step, making him hobble.

"Why do you walk like that?" I ask, earning a scowl from Dad, who also snaps my name.

But Uncle Terry doesn't mind. "It's all right, our Eric. The lad's curious, that's all." His gaze slides across to me, the movement of his eyes making me think of something slick and greasy.

"I hurt my leg," he says. "It got broken."

"How?"

"I had an accident. At work, like."

He looks at Dad, and Dad looks at him. Then he turns and hobbles out of the room.

It's only when I hear the clamour from the school playground that I wish I'd taken an alternate route. My mind is so preoccupied that it simply hadn't occurred to me I'd be passing the school during morning break. I slow for a moment, wondering whether to turn back, then tell myself I'm being foolish and pick up my pace. What am I afraid of, apart from old memories?

In spite of my defiance, the sight of dozens of children, running, screaming, laughing, unnerves me. The school uniform might be less formal now—sweatshirts instead of V-neck jumpers over shirts and ties—but the school colours of vivid purple edged with grey haven't changed, and it's this that takes me back. I don't realise I've come to a halt, that I'm staring through the railings that encircle the school grounds, until a voice says, "Excuse me, can I ask who you are?"

I blink. The diminutive woman on the inside of the railings has black hair glossy as a raven's, the bottom edge of her perfectly straight fringe like a ruler line a bare millimetre above her almost equally dark eyes. Her angular face with its square, almost masculine jaw looks pale by comparison. A scarf splotched with autumnal colours froths at her throat and her hands are encased in multi-coloured mittens.

"I'm . . ." I feel reluctant to give my name. "I used to come here. When I was younger. I haven't been back for a long time."

The tightly suspicious set of her lips doesn't alter. "Is there someone you've specifically come to see?"

She makes it sound like a challenge. I'm about to admit there isn't, then I'm struck by inspiration. "Does Mrs. Sykes still teach here?"

"Doris Sykes?"

"I don't know her first name."

Her eyes narrow as her lips purse. "She retired a few years ago. She's not well, I'm told."

"Oh dear. What's wrong with her?"

"Dementia, I think. I'm not sure how bad. She's pretty old now."

"Does she still live round here?" Before the woman can answer I add, "She was a good teacher. I liked her. We got on well. It would be nice to see her again."

She looks curious. I expect her to ask where I've come from, where I live now, but instead she says, "She's in a home. I'm not sure where. Someone at the school might know. You could ring."

"I will," I say. "Thanks." I turn away from the railings.

"What's your name?" she asks. "Just so I can tell them in the office to expect a call."

I hesitate, then force a smile. "Matthew Fuller."

"I'll pass that on," she says, and turns away from me without another word.

"Mr. Fuller, please come in."

When the grey-bearded man in the crisp black suit reaches out I half-expect him to clutch my jacket and tug me into the wood-panelled office behind him, but instead he leaves his extended palm hovering in the space between us. I clasp his proffered hand and try to match the firmness of his grip as I shake it; then I follow him through the blue door flanked by display windows filled with lavish flower arrangements and samples of engraved tombstones, which have been polished until they gleam.

I had imagined the funeral director's office would smell of flowers or chemicals, but it smells of nothing at all. There's a low table to the left on which a stack of brochures are guarded by scentless flower displays. Steel-framed chairs surround a pine-topped desk, and a trio of brass chandeliers ringed with electric candles hang in an equidistant line across the centre of the ceiling. As I sit on the customer side of the desk I feel scrutinised by generations of Bewleys in black suits and top hats, who gaze out of dozens of framed photographs on every wall.

"Would you like a tea or a coffee?" the latest Mr. Bewley asks.

"No thank you. I'd just like to. . . ." I'm about to say "get on with it" before I realise how mercenary that might sound.

With practised ease, Mr. Bewley says, "Of course, I quite understand. But if we could get a few formalities out of the way first?"

No doubt worried that no one else would bother if she didn't do it herself, Mam has made all of her own funeral arrangements. All I have to do is sign a few forms as her next of kin, and then I'm led through a door and along a corridor to the chapel of rest.

It's darker in this part of the building, but not excessively so. The lighting is soothing rather than sombre, and the music, a murmur drifting from hidden speakers, whilst not exactly jaunty, is at least more uplifting than funereal.

Mam's coffin is illuminated by a discreetly placed standard lamp, the glow of which bestows a healthy bloom to her surprisingly sunken cheeks. In fact, the generous padding which once encased her bones has diminished in the years since I've seen her. Her skin is now stretched so taut it's eradicated her wrinkles.

The woman nestled among plump frills of cream silk is still recognisably her, though. I've never seen a dead person before, but it's not the visceral experience I was expecting; if anything it's an anti-climax. I feel as though I'm looking at a shell, a cocoon. I feel that if I were to press Mam's cheek with my thumb it would collapse like papier mâché, revealing but a cavity, like the inside of an Easter egg.

Behind me Bewley murmurs, "I'll give you some privacy, Mr. Fuller," and withdraws so silently that the next thing I hear aside from the music is the door bumping shut behind him.

His departure seems to be the cue for my anger to emerge. Although I realise the bland, shuttered face I'm gazing at is a mask at best, the anger fills my chest and throat like heartburn and causes my head to throb.

"How could you, Mam?" I hiss, addressing not only the mortal remains in the box, but the air around it, the ether. "If you're there, if you're listening to me, you ought to be fucking ashamed. You ought to be . . . well, I hope you're in fucking Hell, that's all."

The words, though I mean them, seem inadequate, melodramatic. I picture myself punching the still face, or spitting into it. I could do it too, or at least something less obvious to show my contempt. The woman who gave birth to me and then betrayed me, abandoned me, is entirely at my mercy.

I'm engulfed by a savage, almost sadistic fury, but as it reaches its peak it abruptly crumbles, leaving me sickened, ashamed. All at once I feel dizzy, and then I shock myself by starting to cry. They're tears not of grief, but bitterness, yet they're just as enervating. I feel no less wretched for hating Mam instead of mourning her.

There's a quartet of steel-framed chairs against the wall at the foot of the coffin. I grab one, drag it towards me and sit down. I slump forward, my head level with the side of the elevated box. Propping my elbows on my thighs, I sob into my hands. After a while I hear the soft pad of approaching footsteps and then I feel Bewley's hand on my shoulder.

He must see this every day, but even so I feel resentful he's caught me crying. I want to tell him I don't need his sympathy, that I didn't love Mam, that I don't care she's dead, but wouldn't that sound disingenuous, churlish even?

Then Bewley begins to knead my shoulder, the movement of his fingers almost seductive, and I tense, my tears drying abruptly. I raise my head and smell cigarette smoke. Jerking my shoulder from the hand that's gripping it, I spin round so violently that the chair legs judder over the carpet, and I see that the room behind me is empty, that there is no one there.

I can't face sleeping in my old room again, and not only because it still smells faintly of vomit, so tonight I make up a bed for myself on the floral-patterned settee in the front room. It's a little short, so I have to lie with my knees bent, and because I can't abide the thought of using the duvet and pillows from Mam's bed, I again drape my thickest jumper over my upper body and my jacket over my legs to keep warm. Although I'm not drunk I sleep fully-clothed, appalled by the idea of stripping off, making myself vulnerable. I feel like a vagrant, but I tell myself it won't be for much longer. It's Mam's funeral the day after tomorrow. In forty-eight hours I'll be back in London.

To discourage nocturnal visitations I leave the red-shaded table lamp next to the TV switched on, and I lie there staring at it until I fall asleep. When I wake up, though, it's dark and I don't know where I am. I'm still trying to work out what's woken me when a large, damp, smoky hand clamps over my mouth and I feel myself being hauled out of bed.

No, this can't be right, it *can't*. I'm not *in* bed—and yet I distinctly feel the weight of blankets sliding away from me, hear the springs in the mattress creak as my weight is lifted from them.

I struggle against my attacker, I thrash, but he must be a giant, and so *strong*, and he clamps my limbs beneath his weight and I can't move. Then it occurs to me that it's not that my attacker's abnormally large; it's that *I'm* small. Somehow I've shrunk like my mother must have done in her final illness. I've regressed.

I'm a child.

This is a dream. It must be. All I have to do is wake up. I feel fat, damp fingers pressing against my mouth, crushing my lips, reeking of stale sweat and cigarettes. My attacker is grunting like a pig as he fumbles at me, and my feet as I try in vain to kick at him are bare and cold, and he forces me onto my knees, bears down inexorably with his weight on my spine and neck until I'm bent forward over the mattress. He shifts his hand to the back of my head, and pushes my face down into the mattress until I can't breathe, until I think I'm going to suffocate. I'm wearing pyjama bottoms, and I feel them yanked down, and hear them rip, and he grunts as he thrusts himself against me, and I feel his wetness slithering across my buttocks, and I can't scream.

With an effort born of panic, terror and desperation, I wrench myself from my attacker's grip, and this time I *do* wake up. I come to thrashing on the floor, having fallen or hurled myself from the settee, my jacket half-tangled around my legs. I get the impression not that I've snapped from a nightmare, but that I've barely escaped from a situation into which it's all too possible to once again become ensnared. It's as if the past has remained here all these years, a real and living entity, waiting for me to let my guard down, waiting to swallow me whole.

The room stinks of cigarette smoke. I smell it on my clothes, in my hair. As my heart pounds and I gasp for breath, it catches in my throat like iron filings, making me cough. I yank the jacket from around my legs, clamber to my feet and stagger to the window. Wrenching back the curtains, I fumble at the catch on the left-hand of the three windows that overlook the front garden. The lawn is black as tarmac, the gravel path that bisects it speckled with glints of orange from the street lamps whose bulbous heads seemed wreathed in mist. The only light I can see aside from these is a white square in the black façade of the house directly opposite. The light shines from an upstairs window, in which a figure stands in silhouette. Although I can't see the figure's face I feel sure it's looking directly at me.

It's time to speak to Mrs. Forbes.

The tea is weak and tasteless and there isn't enough sugar in it. Mrs. Forbes' house smells mustily of cats, though I can't see any. Her crimson carpet is threadbare at the edges, her furniture dark and heavy. The mantelpiece is cluttered with porcelain figurines—milkmaids, women in ball gowns, dandies in powdered wigs—and the French dresser against the opposite wall is dominated by framed photographs of a dowdy couple wearing clothes (albeit not especially fashionable ones) I associate with the 1960s.

My perusal of the photos is fleeting, but it prompts Mrs. Forbes to confide, "That's my Angus. Lovely man he was. A real charmer. Died in 1969 from an infection after kneeling on a bit of broken glass. Stupid way to go. They could put a man on the moon, but they couldn't stop my Angus from dying of a bloody knee."

She speaks lightly, but even now I can hear the resentment underpinning her words. It's as if she believes the doctors and scientists of the time didn't save her Angus because they were too preoccupied with their space adventure to care.

"That must have been terrible," I say.

She narrows her eyes as if she suspects me of insincerity.

"Well, it *was* a long time ago." She says this with a brusqueness that suggests *I'm* the one pursuing the matter.

She must have seen me coming. When I knocked on her door a few minutes earlier she plucked it open immediately.

"I wondered when I'd be seeing you," she said. "You'd better come in."

She's a tall, angular woman with big hands and a sharp-boned face. I was almost relieved when she answered the door in her nightgown. It would have been disconcerting to discover her fully-dressed at 3:15 AM.

Now she asks, "Have you settled in?"

"I'm not staying," I tell her hastily. When she frowns I clarify, "I'll be leaving straight after the funeral."

"Aren't you taking the time to see old friends? Visit old haunts?"

I wonder whether she's choosing her words deliberately. Shaking my head I say, "There's nothing for me here."

"Your Mam. . . ." Then she appears to think better of what she's about to say and sips her tea.

"What?" I feel compelled to prompt.

"Well, far be it from me to interfere, but the way I see it . . . she missed you. In her last years, I mean. She didn't say so, but I think it broke her heart that you never visited."

My grip becomes so tight around the handle of the mug that I hear it or my skin creak. "She should have thought of that before."

"Oh, come on now, love. Was she really the one to blame?"

Her response is so ambiguous that I narrow my eyes at her. "Don't tell me you knew what was going on?"

She sighs and leans back. "I know that brother of your dad's was a bad lot."

"That doesn't answer my question. *Did* you know? Exactly, I mean?"

This time she stays silent. The air thickens between us. Slowly I shake my head.

"You did, didn't you? You knew what was happening and you did nothing to stop it."

She tuts as if I'm being unreasonable. "It was a long time ago. Things were different back then."

"Different how?" I'm struggling to keep my temper. "I was just a boy, and that man . . . that *cunt*. . . ."

She winces at the word, and I feel both ashamed and savagely gleeful.

"Why didn't you call the police?" I say. "Why didn't you tell someone?"

Her reply is almost sullen. "It wouldn't have done any good." Then, as if that reply is only partly satisfactory, she adds, "It weren't my place."

I'm ten years old. I'm sitting in my bed, trying not to shake, trying not to cry. I'm hurting inside, and the seat of my pyjamas, and the mattress beneath me, feels wet, and I wonder if I'm bleeding, I wonder if I'm *dying*.

My mind is so full of fear, so full of misery, that I can't think, can't speak. I'm cold, and the coldness seems to come from inside me, from the pit of my stomach. I clench my fists and my teeth so tightly that my bones ache.

My room is in semi-darkness, just a thin band of light from the landing seeping through the door, which is barely ajar. The only other light source is Uncle Terry's cigarette, which glows orange as he draws on it. Uncle Terry looks relaxed. He's sitting on the end of my bed, half-hunched forward, one leg crossed over the other. He always smokes afterwards, always sits with me for a few minutes as if we're pals chewing the fat. Sometimes he talks about when he was a boy, irrelevant things. "When I were your age they used to have a ha'penny tray at our local shop," he'll say. "You could get two chews for a penny. Black Jacks were my favourites. The liquorice ones. Do they do them any more?" Or, apropos of nothing, he'll tell me, "Even fifteen, twenty years after the war, you'd still find shrapnel here and there. Bits of bombs and that. It was just something you were used to, part of life."

But then always at some point he'll say, "Remember, this is nobody's business but ours. You don't want to get your family into trouble, do yer?" Or: "You're all right, lad, there's no real harm done." Or: "Nobody likes a liar, and that's what they'd think you were if you said owt."

One night Mam comes in when Uncle Terry's sitting there. I don't know if he hears her or not. She pushes open the door and she sees him sitting smoking on the end of my bed and she freezes.

"It's getting late," she says, and Uncle Terry smiles.

"The lad and I were just having a chat, that's all? Weren't we, Matt?"

I say nothing. I look at Mam, a mute appeal. I don't want to get into trouble, I don't want to be accused of lying, but I will her to look into my eyes and see what's wrong and make everything right.

But she does nothing more than glance at me, and then her gaze skitters away, as if she doesn't want to see what's there, as if she's scared or ashamed to face it.

In a tight voice she says, "He needs his sleep. He's got school in the morning."

Uncle Terry says nothing. He just stands up from the bed, taking his time, making the springs creak. There's a little foil ashtray on my bedside table that he brought in with him. It's sitting on top of the book I'm reading—*The Castle of Adventure* by Enid Blyton.

Uncle Terry stubs his cigarette out in the ashtray, crushing it down with his fat, brown fingers.

After he's gone, after Mam has whispered goodnight and pulled my door shut, trapping the after-stink of Uncle Terry and his cigarettes in the room with me, I lie on my side, staring at the crushed butt in the ashtray. Even though it's dark I can see a thin, seemingly never ending thread of blue-grey smoke curling sinuously up from it and merging with the blackness.

Mrs. Sykes looks like she's wilting. She's slumped in a wicker armchair facing the glass wall that overlooks the narrow, neatly tended back garden screened by fir trees. From the side, daylight bleaches her wispy white bouffant into a dazzling nimbus and seems to expose the skull beneath the thinning flesh of her face. Her chin rests on her chest, and her hands and feet, which look over-large, dangle from rope-like limbs.

As I approach I'm dismayed to see that her eyes are milk-white orbs and her mouth is open and drooling. Then I step closer and the light shifts and I realise my mistake. She's merely asleep.

"Ooh, here's a live one," croons a voice to my right, and looking across I see a mostly toothless octogenarian with pink-framed spectacles and lilac hair flapping an arthritic claw at me. I smile vaguely and avert my gaze, hoping her words won't awaken a ripple of interest among her fellow residents. Fortunately they don't, and by the time I reach Mrs. Sykes's side my admirer has sunk back into a torpor that seems to inhabit the room like the soupy, warm air of a tropical jungle.

When I was a child Mrs. Sykes seemed formidable, so it's sobering to now see her so reduced. She has biscuit crumbs on her ice-blue cardigan, and the line of drool that stretches from the side of her yawning mouth to the bony point of her bristly chin gleams like a slug trail as it catches the light.

I pull up a moulded black plastic chair and sit down. Should I speak to her, attempt to wake her, or would that only confuse her? I don't even fully know why I'm here. Why do I feel compelled to pick at this particular scab? Is it because, deep down, I came back expecting an apology, a show of remorse? But from whom and where? Perhaps I'm driven by a desire for justice that I wasn't even aware I craved before coming here? Or is it simply that my return has given me a last opportunity to rant and rave, to accuse, before I fuck off forever?

I'm still wondering when Mrs. Sykes opens her eyes and looks at me. The teacher at the school had said she was suffering from dementia, but her gaze is every bit as penetrating as I remember it. Her voice, though, is shriller, more brittle.

"Who are you?"

"Hello, Mrs. Sykes," I begin, "you probably don't remem—"

"You're the Fuller boy, aren't you? Martin. No, Matthew."

I'm shocked into momentary silence. Then I say, "You've got an incredible memory."

Mrs. Sykes attempts to pull herself a little more upright, but her muscles aren't up to the job; I wonder if I should help her. "The mind is a fickle beast. I expect they told you I was demented?"

I grimace and unconvincingly mumble, "No, not really."

"I expect they also told you this was one of my good days?"

Still feeling uncomfortable, even a little intimidated, I shrug.

"Yes, well, they weren't wrong. I'm forgetful. I have lapses. And they're getting worse. Sometimes I wander about in a fog for days." She squints at me. "From your expression I suspect I look a fright. The ravages of age are never pretty."

"You look fine," I say automatically. "Quite well, in fact."

"Rubbish. I'm a decrepit old bat." She reaches out, her hand trembling with age, and paws at my sleeve. "You are real then? I thought you might be a figment of my imagination." She sighs. "Pity. I thought you were one of the lucky ones."

"Lucky? What do you mean?"

"I thought you got away. Did a moonlight flit, never to return."

"I did," I say. "I have. I came back for Mam's funeral. She died."

"Should hope so. Be terrible to put her in the furnace if she hadn't."

I'm so startled I bark out a laugh, which echoes in the high-ceilinged room. No one responds, not even my admirer with the lilac hair.

"Once, when I was young," I say, "nine or ten, you asked me to stay behind after class because you wanted to talk to me. Do you remember?"

She looks momentarily troubled. She shakes her head. "I told you, my mind's a fog. My memory's very selective these days."

"You asked me if I was all right, if everything was okay at home. I can't remember what I said, but I'm pretty sure I gave the impression that it wasn't, that I needed help. I remember thinking that someone had finally recognised what I was going through and was going to help me . . . but nothing happened. After speaking to me once you never did so again. In fact, I have the impression you deliberately avoided me." I drew in a breath. "So what happened, Mrs. Sykes? Why *didn't* you help me? If not directly, then why didn't you at least tell someone you had concerns about my welfare?"

She frowns, her eyes drifting away from me. Her hands, which have returned to her lap, are trembling more violently than before.

Suddenly I'm aware how quiet it has become in the room. The creak of chairs, the papery ripple of newspaper and magazine pages, the click of counters and chess pieces and knitting needles—it's all stopped.

I feel the hairs prickling on the back of my neck. Slowly I turn round. No one's looking at me, though I get the impression that's only because they've all just looked away. I scan the residents, but they studiously avoid meeting my eyes. I turn back to Mrs. Sykes, who shakes her head.

"I'm sorry I can't help you, love. I really am. But the past is a foreign country to me now."

I sigh. "Never mind."

I'm about to stand up, but then Mrs. Sykes says quietly, "You had a friend."

"What?"

"Joe something. Something to do with fish."

"Pike," I say. "Joe Pike."

Thoughtfully she stares out the window. "Perhaps he's still around. Perhaps he can help you. He *was* your friend, wasn't he?"

Though her words seem laden with meaning, her winter-blue eyes give nothing away.

"Yes," I say, "he was. Goodbye Mrs. Sykes."

"Goodbye, Matthew."

Joe's house is nondescript. Like Mam's. Like all the houses in this town. It gives me the feeling that everyone's hiding, keeping their heads down, hoping not to be noticed.

His face changes when he sees me on his doorstep. "Matt," he says warily, his eyes flickering beyond me as if to check none of his neighbours have seen me arrive.

"I need to talk to you," I tell him.

A quick grimace, which he smothers in a grin. "Fine. Meet you at The Fountainhead in an hour?"

I'm about to concur, but then I shake my head. "No. I want to talk to you now."

He sighs, slumps. "Fine. Come in."

He turns and trudges into the house, leaving me to follow him.

Somewhere a washing machine is grinding and whooshing. The house smells of bacon. My stomach rumbles.

"Excuse the mess," Joe says, leading me into the front room. "We tend to veg out on a Sunday morning."

The room isn't actually all that messy. There's an empty wine bottle and two glasses on a coffee table, which I presume are from the night before, and a newspaper and its supplements spread across the settee, which Joe gathers into a pile and dumps on the floor so we can sit down. He's wearing a baggy blue T-shirt so faded that the logo on it is unreadable, and pyjama bottoms in green and black tartan. His feet are bare.

"Charlotte's having a lie-in," he says as if I've suggested she's avoiding me. "Fancy a coffee?"

I shake my head. "I've just been to see Mrs. Sykes."

"Who?"

"From school. Our old history teacher. You remember."

His eyes slide towards the TV screen, even though it's blank. "Vaguely."

"She said I should talk to you."

"Why?"

"You tell me."

His head snaps round and he glares at me. "How can I tell you when I don't fucking know?"

"You must know something," I say calmly.

"How do you work that out?"

"Because Mrs. Sykes told me you did. Or hinted at it anyway."

"So that makes it true, does it? The word of some mad old bat in an old folks' home?"

"I thought you could hardly remember her. How do you know she's in a home?"

He looks momentarily caught out, then the scowl reasserts itself. "Someone said something about it. It was you mentioning her that reminded me."

"Right."

He's silent for a moment. His fist clenches and I wonder if he's about to hit me. If he does I'll bleed all over his carpet. I'll make sure of it.

But he doesn't hit me. In fact, when he next speaks his voice is soft. "Look, Matt, what's your problem? Why are you stirring all this old shit up again? Why not just leave it be?"

Maybe he's right. Maybe I should book myself into a hotel tonight, fuck off after I've laid Mam to rest tomorrow and never look back, never even think of this place again.

But Joe misinterprets my silence for stubbornness. Fiercely he says, "It's easy for you, raking up the past. But you're not the one who has to live here."

I blink, surprised. "What do you mean?"

"It wasn't just you, you know. It was all of us. But some of us can't get away so easily."

"All of us?" I say. "All of who? What are you telling me, Joe?"

But he looks alarmed now. Clearly he feels he's said too much.

There's a noise in the doorway. We both look up. A woman stands there. Pretty. Glasses. Reddish hair. She looks vaguely familiar.

In a tight voice, without even looking at me, she says, "Can I have a word, Joe?"

She turns and marches away. He flashes me a look, then follows. He's gone maybe two minutes. When he comes back he looks forlorn. Scared. There's something almost manic about his eyes.

"Look, Matt," he says, his voice low, "just go now. Get out and never come back. Leave this minute if you can."

I lean away from him, as if afraid his mania will infect me. "Don't be daft. I've got Mam's funeral tomorrow."

He reaches across, grips my knee briefly in his huge hand, then lets his hand drop. "Never mind that. Just go. Get out. We keep it contained, we do all right, but with you here . . ." he shakes his head. "Why do you think no one came after you after . . . after what happened to your uncle?"

I jerk as if he's jabbed me with a stick. "That was an accident."

"Yeah, right." His voice drops to a hiss. "Look, we're on your side, mate. Charlotte and me. But you've got to go. For all our sakes. You've got to fuck off *right now*."

It sounds odd to say I'd had enough after six years, when in truth I'd lived in terror and despair from the first time it happened. I would say it had been unendurable, aside from the fact that I endured it. Quite *how* I did it, I don't know. I simply kept on living, kept on breathing, from day to day, hour to hour, minute to minute, second to second.

I told no one. I was abused by my uncle, raped by my uncle, on a regular basis, and yet I told no one. I kept my mouth shut.

Why? Why didn't I seek help? Is it because my uncle told me not to? Is it because I was afraid people wouldn't believe me or that I'd bring shame on my family?

Not entirely. It was more than that. It was this town. It poisons and it devours. It's taken me twenty years to realise it, but I see it now. The scales have been removed from my eyes.

This town where I grew up. My uncle was its limb, its appendage, and perhaps in time I would have become the same. Some do, some don't. But those that don't are overwhelmed, struck dumb, gripped by fear. They want to leave, but most of them can't. And the tragedy is they don't know *why* they can't.

But I do. It's because this town feeds them even as it feeds *on* them. My friend Joe knows this, but he won't do anything about it. He's too scared to break free, too weak. But he's strong too. Strong enough not to have children, not to perpetuate the misery, not to pass it on.

It's twenty years ago. I'm fifteen again and I've had enough. I'm sickly, small in stature. I think *I'm* the weak one. I think I'm nothing. I think I'm worthless. But the irony is, I'm strong without even knowing it.

I think about the deed for some time before doing it. I fantasise about it. And then one day, when the shame and the terror outweighs my fear of the consequences, I think: *this is it*.

The town tries to stop me, of course. Hush, it says, hush. You are mine. You are not going anywhere. You are going to take what I give you, without complaint, without retaliation, and I am going to take from you in return, as I always have and I always will.

But I refuse to listen. I'm a rogue element, a fly in the ointment. I'm not unique, I'm sure, but I'm unusual.

I wait until they're all asleep. I wait until my uncle is snoring. It's Friday, so he's been to the pub and he's drunk himself so insensible that I know he won't wake up even if I were to try my very hardest to rouse him.

I get dressed. I put on my warmest clothes. I open the drawer where Mam puts my underpants and socks after she's washed them and I find what I stole from my uncle—a cigarette and one of his cheap lighters, which he buys in packs of five.

I go to his room. I open the door a crack and slip inside. He's sprawled in a star-shape on his bed, his mouth open, his fat belly rising and falling beneath the sheet that he's half-dragged over himself. His clothes, which he removed drunkenly and in haste, are strewn on the floor. His room stinks of cigarette smoke and unwashed flesh.

Despite the stench I stand there for a while, breathing shallowly, watching him sleep. At last I put the cigarette in my mouth and light it, sucking in the smoke so that the tip glows orange. I don't inhale the smoke. I hold it in my mouth for a moment, then blow it out. I step right up to the bed, stretching out my arms until I'm holding the Bic lighter in both hands directly over my uncle's fat belly. I look down at his yawning mouth for a moment and then I clench my teeth in a silent snarl and snap the lighter in half. A few glittering drops of fuel spill out and over the sheet. I toss the shattered lighter aside, then suck the cigarette in my mouth as hard as I can. When the tip flares orange. I take it out of my mouth and drop it on to the fuel-spattered sheet.

I don't know if he'll die. I don't know if he'll burn. I turn and walk out of my uncle's bedroom, closing the door behind me. Out on the landing I keep walking. I go down the stairs, across the short hallway and out the front door. I walk down the garden path, through the gate, along the road.

I walk away from my house, away from my life.
I don't look back.

As soon as I step into the house the stench of cigarette smoke engulfs me. Putting my hand over my mouth, I blunder into the front room.

He's angry. He wants to hurt me. I sense it as clearly as if he's standing in front of me, eyes blazing, hands clenched into fists. I gather together my few belongings and stuff them into my suitcase. As I zip it up and pull out the extendable handle so that I can wheel it behind me, I hear sounds from upstairs.

The creak of bedsprings. The double-thump of feet planting themselves heavily on the floor.

"Fuck you," I mutter, and then I'm on my way. Across the hallway I go, hand already reaching for the front door.

I sense rather than see it at the top of the stairs. A thickening, an agglomeration, as if darkness, or perhaps smoke, is drawing itself together, trying to gain substance. I don't look at it. I don't give it that satisfaction. I leave the house, shut the door behind me and walk away. I don't look back.

The streets on this Sunday morning are silent. I walk through them unmolested, though I feel them pressing around me. I try to ignore the gnawing guilt, the voice telling me I'm abandoning Mam, I'm being ridiculous, that it wouldn't hurt me to stay one more day, just to see her off.

It takes me the best part of an hour to walk to the train station. By the time I arrive the sky has compressed itself down to the colour of cigarette smoke. The air around me is grainy, dense; I'm finding it difficult to draw breath. I'm sweating and my head throbs and my eyes are sore. All I want is to sit down, close my eyes. Perhaps there'll be a café in the station, or a bench where I can rest.

But no. This is what the town wants. I half-expect to be obstructed as I enter the station, but there's no one around; even the ticket window beside the turnstile is deserted. Proceeding on to the empty platform, the only sound that accompanies me is the clatter-rumble of my suitcase wheels. I look up at the digital display board, across which train information scrolls in red. There is a train in eleven minutes.

I don't care where it goes. Anywhere will do. I'll pick up my return journey from wherever the next train takes me. I look up the track, focusing on the spot where it bends out of sight, where the train will appear. The seconds tick by, each one nudging me closer to salvation. Abruptly the air around me grows darker, thicker.

Even when black spots begin to speckle the grey platform, I don't move. As the rain grows heavier it begins to patter, and then to hiss. It taps on my head with cold fingers, leaving patches of wetness. The wetness accumulates, forms rivulets, which scurry through my hair like insects and trickle down my face.

I blink water from my eyes, but still I don't seek shelter. I continue to stare at the bend in the track as the seconds tick by.

Behind me, faintly, I hear the wet crackle of footsteps as someone passes through the ticket barrier and emerges on to the platform. The footsteps are uneven, as if whoever is making them is hobbling.

Slowly I hear the footsteps approach. They get closer and closer.

But I don't turn round. Not even when they're right at my back. Not even when a drift of cigarette smoke prickles my nostrils.

VICIOUS

VICIOUS

There was this bird. John said she was bad news. But then John thinks everyone's bad news. He's just fucking paranoid.

Not as bad as Malcolm, though. Malcolm thinks the CIA and the FBI and fuck knows who else is following us. He thinks they're waiting for the chance to blow us all away. Wipe the Sex Pistols off the face of the earth.

Well, ha fucking ha. They won't get me. I'm Sid Vicious. I'm fucking indestructible. I'm gonna live for ever.

This bird, though. Came on to me after the gig. These American birds love me. "Sid, Sid, fuck me." "Yeah, alright, darlin'. Anything to oblige."

John says I'm disgusting. He says I'm turning into a Rolling Stone. But he's just uptight and jealous. He ain't as pretty as me. Ain't got no anarchy in his soul no more. I'm the only one with any anarchy left. Steve and Paul. What a couple of cunts. They're just the backing band. After the gig tonight Steve went mental. Said I was out of control. Said I was dragging them all down.

"We're *supposed* to be out of control, you fucker," I told him. "We're the Sex Pistols."

He told me if I didn't sort myself out I'd be out of the band.

"You can't throw me out," I said. "You'd be nothing without me. People don't come to see you. They come to see me."

"Yeah," said John. He was sitting in the corner on his own, with a can of beer in his hand like an old man in a pub. "But that's 'cos most of the morons who go to the circus prefer the clowns to the artistes."

He don't know what he's talking about. He's so full of shit. He's a miserable bastard. They're all miserable bastards. Not me, though. I'm having a great time. I ain't got no gear, and that's fucking killing me, but at least I'm making an effort.

Thing is, I hurt all over from not having any stuff, and I can't sleep, and every time I eat something I throw it back up. And I fucking itch. Itch, itch, itch. All over. My arm, where I cut myself, and my chest, where I carved "Gimme A Fix" (and I don't even remember doing that), and my fucking bollocks. My bollocks most of all.

I thought I had some disease. I thought I was dying. Our tour manager, Noel Monk. He's a fucking hippy, with a moustache like a fucking faggot cowboy, but he's all right.

"Noel," I said. "There's something wrong with me. I fucked some bitch before I come here and I fucking itch like crazy."

He laughed. "Don't worry, Sid. You got crabs, that's all," he said.

So yeah. I hurt and I itch and I'm sick and I need some stuff so bad and I'm missing Nancy, but that don't stop me enjoying myself. Fucking America. It's great.

So this bird. She come up and she wanted to fuck me. We were hanging out after the show. We're in this place. Baton Rouge. Louisiana. The Kingfish Club.

I was feeling alright. I was drinking peppermint schnapps 'cos it stops the hurting, and Noel had given me some of his valiums, and I was floating. Everything soft and mellow. And this bird said, "Sid, you're beautiful. I want to fuck you."

And so we fucked. Right there on the bar. Animal magnetism. People were watching and taking photos, but I didn't care. Let 'em. It's their problem if they wanna be perverts, not mine.

She was going down on me, and I was lying back, thinking of England (ha ha ha) and then there was all this shouting, and I opened my eyes, and there was Noel and Glen, one of the security blokes, and some other geezers, and everyone was going apeshit. Glen was trying to grab someone's camera and Noel was pulling the bird off me, and so I took a swing at him with my bottle, but I missed.

"What the fuck are you doing, Noel?" I said. "You said I could shag who I wanted."

It's true. He wouldn't get me no smack, but he said any time I saw a bird I liked he'd bring her to me.

"And so you can, Sid," he said. "But not here. Here is a bit too . . . public."

I saw John out of the corner of my eye. He curled his lip and sneered at me. He looked disgusted.

"Where then?" I said.

"We'll find somewhere. Come on."

They took us away. Me and the bird. It was like being arrested. Surrounded by all these bodies. Big guys. Like a fucking moving wall. I saw faces through the wall. A blur of faces, looking at me. I spat at them. "Fuck off." They were like demons. Grinning. Eyes shining. "Fuck off, fuck off." I wanted to slash them all open.

We didn't have a hotel. When the equipment was packed we were all getting back on the bus and driving through the snow and the dark and the shit. Endless fucking black roads. Driving and driving.

I don't mind the driving, to be honest. It's a bit boring, but it's alright. I like that we stop at roadside diners. Steak and eggs. I love my steak and eggs. Steak rare, eggs runny. But I can never keep it down. Eat it all up, yum yum, lovely. But then my guts cramp and I have to run for the bog and throw it back up again. All over the wall. In the sink. Everywhere. Blood and puke all over America. Sid was here.

"Oi, Glen," I said.

Glen looked at me. He's a big fucking guy. Big fucking beard. I told him only hippies and arseholes have beards, but he's all right. Glen's tough.

"Yeah, Sid?"

"Where we going tonight?"

"When we've finished here, you mean?"

"Yeah."

"We're going to Dallas, Sid."

"Oh yeah," I said.

Dallas. That's where that President got shot. I remember my mum telling me about that when I was a kid. Big deal. Big news. Maybe we'll get shot in Dallas too. Maybe we'll be as famous as that President.

"Dallas," I said. "Yeah, brilliant."

Noel and Glen found us this place backstage. Fucking broom cupboard. Sink in the corner.

"We'll be right outside, Sid," Noel said, "so don't get any smart ideas about running out on us."

"I won't, Noel. No way."

He shut the door. It was fucking dark in there, but me and the bird fucked on the floor. I was knackered. I felt sick. I puked in the sink. My head was pounding.

"You okay, Sid?" the bird asked. She tried to touch me, but my skin was sore. Her touch was like needles. I shrugged her off.

"Don't fucking touch me," I said.

"Jeez," she said. "What's your problem?"

"You," I said. "You're my fucking problem."

She went all whiny. "What have I done wrong, Sid? Tell me what I've done wrong and I'll put it right."

"I need smack," I said. "You got any smack?"

"No," she said.

"Then you're no fucking good to me," I said. "Why don't you fuck off?"

She started to cry. Black lines trickling down her face. I felt bad. "Fucking hell," I said, "don't cry."

"I can't help it. You're mad at me."

"No, I'm not," I said. "I'm not mad at you. I just need some stuff. Noel and that lot, they won't let me out. They won't let me go anywhere. They think if I go off somewhere I'll end up killing myself."

"And will you?" said the bird. Little squeaky voice.

I laughed. I was hurting again. Sweats and chills. Body cramps. "Yeah, probably," I said. "Or some fucking cowboy will shoot me. They hate us here. Fucking America hates the Sex Pistols."

"I don't," said the bird. "I love the Sex Pistols."

"Yeah, well, you're one of the smart ones," I said. "Most people are scared of us. They think we're gonna destroy America."

"You should," said the bird. "You should destroy America. It's a dump. I hate it."

"Yeah," I said. "It's a fucking dump."

"Maybe I'll come to England," the bird said.

"Don't bother," I said. "It's a dump there too."

I didn't wanna talk no more. I finished the schnapps and curled up on the floor and closed my eyes. I hurt all over. I just wanted everything to go black.

"Do you want me to go?" the bird asked.

"I'm not bothered," I said. "Stay or go. I don't care."

I went to sleep. I had these dreams. Bad dreams. Faces looking at me. All these fucking faces. Shouting and laughing. Twisting out of shape. Turning into something bad. I was trying to push them away, but I was trapped. I couldn't get out. I couldn't breathe. I was a kid again. I was crying for my mum. I was cutting myself. Slash slash, across my arms, across my chest. I wanted the pain and the blood. But there was no pain, no blood. I couldn't make myself bleed. I couldn't feel anything. I cried out, but I couldn't make any noise.

"Shh, mon petit."

The voice was in my head. It went through me like a cold breeze on a hot day. It blew all the shit and fear away. Made me feel calm.

I opened my eyes. Big brown eyes looking down at me.

"Who are you?" I said.

This wasn't the bird I'd fucked earlier. This was someone different. Light brown skin. Smooth, like toffee. Big brown eyes and big red lips. Black hair in little twisty dreads. She was fucking beautiful. She was so beautiful I couldn't breathe.

"You want to be saved?" she said.

I was shivering. My leather jacket was over me like a blanket, but the floor was cold underneath me and I felt like there was nothing left of me but bones.

"Saved from what?" I said.

"From yourself."

"Dunno what you mean."

I tried to sit up. I felt so weak. She had to help me. She jangled when she moved. She was wearing all these bracelets and necklaces. She smelled like flowers and spice and dark forests.

"How did you get in here?" I asked her.

"I go where I please," she said.

She put her hand under the tap in the sink and turned it on. She held her dripping fingers over my face. I opened my mouth and the water ran over my lips and tongue and down my throat. It tasted sweet, made me feel like a kid again. Everything new and bright.

"You want to be saved?" she asked again.

I shrugged. "I dunno. Are you one of those Jesus nutjobs?"

She laughed. "I believe in spirits, mon petit. Do *you* believe in spirits?"

"Yeah," I said. "Whisky and vodka."

She didn't laugh this time. She reached out and touched a badge on my jacket. "Is this true?"

"What?"

"'I'm A Mess'. Is it true, mon petit? *Are* you a mess?"

I looked into her big brown eyes. They held me. They were fucking hypnotic. It was like just by looking at me she was clearing all the shit out of my brain. I wanted to cry. I felt it all rushing up through me like puke. I nodded, but I couldn't speak.

"Tell me," she said.

I still wanted to cry, but I swallowed it back down again. "I'm a junkie," I said. "I'm fucked up. I don't wanna be, but I can't help it. People offer me stuff and I can't say no. But I'm gonna get straight. I am. I'm gonna get straight and pull this band back together. I'll be a better bassist than that art school cunt, Matlock. We'll conquer the fucking world. We're the best fucking band there's ever been."

I stopped. It sounded like someone else talking. After a minute I said, "My head is fucked up. I don't know what's true and what isn't any more. I don't know who I am."

"Who do you *think* you are?" she said. "Tell me everything. Let it all out."

"I'm Sid Vicious," I told her. "I'm a Sex Pistol. I'm a fucking star. I'm the bass player who can't play. I'm a joke. A pathetic junkie. I'm gonna live forever. I'm gonna be dead before I'm twenty-five. I fucking love Nancy. I can't live without her. She's fucked up my life. She's the worst thing that ever happened to me. John's my best mate. He looks out for me. I hate him and he hates me. He's got no future. I want him to fuck off. I love him. I don't wanna lose him. Everything's falling apart. Everything's turning to shit. We're gonna rule the fucking world. We're gonna be heroes. We're gonna destroy America. Malcolm's a fucking genius. Malcolm's a cunt who doesn't care about us. I'm gonna be a legend. I'm gonna be forgotten."

I couldn't stop. It was like cutting my arm and watching the blood spurt. I put a hand over my mouth to stop it pouring out of me. What I was saying was all true and all lies. It was everything and nothing, the good and the bad, the dream and the nightmare. They were different, but they were the same. It was all happening together, all at once, and I was stuck in the middle.

"You are at the crossroads, mon petit," the girl said.

"The crossroads, yeah," I said.

"Which way do you go from here?"

"I dunno."

She was staring at me, like she could see the thoughts fighting in my head. What was I? The bassist in the best fucking band in the world? Or a walking fucking cliché, press fodder, Malcolm's fucking puppet? If I cleaned myself up, got myself together, we could be fucking huge, we could go down in fucking history as the band that changed music forever. But did I really want that? Did I wanna be a legend? Did I wanna be Elvis Presley twenty years from now, fat and ugly and useless, dying of a heart attack on a fucking toilet? Did I wanna be a dinosaur, like Led Zep and Pink Floyd and all that hippy shit? Did I wanna be a fucking *rock* star?

Fuck that. Fuck it all. I'd never be fucking *establishment*. But I'd find a way. My way.

The girl was still staring. Her eyes were glittering. At that moment she could've been an angel or a demon.

"It is your decision," she said.

"Is it?"

"Of course. If you want it to be."

"Can you help me?" I asked her.

Instead of answering, she stood up and held out her hand. "Come with me."

"Where we going?"

"To get you what you need."

I took her hand and she pulled me up like I weighed nothing.

"Noel and Glen are outside," I said. "They won't let me go."

She smiled. "Like I say, mon petit, I go where I please."

She pushed open the door and led me outside. Noel and Glen were sitting in the corridor playing cards. They didn't even look at us.

"Come," she said, and she gave me a little tug. I kept thinking that any second Noel would look up and say, "Where do you think you're going, Sid?"

But he didn't. Him and Glen just kept playing cards.

"What's wrong with 'em?" I whispered.

"They cannot see us," she said. "To them we are like the wind."

"Yeah?" I said. I walked right up and leaned over them. "Oi," I said.

They ignored me.

I laughed. It was like being a fucking super hero. The fucking invisible man. Noel had a can of beer on the floor by his chair. I picked it up and spat in it. He didn't respond.

"Oi, Noel," I said. "You're a fucking cunt."

He kept on playing cards.

I laughed again. And then suddenly I felt scared. I looked at the girl.

"Am I dead," I said. "Am I a ghost?"

She smiled. "No, mon petit."

"But no one can see me," I said. "I don't like it that no one can see me. I don't wanna be ignored."

The girl was still holding my hand. She leaned in and whispered in my ear, like it was a secret. "Trust me, mon petit."

I felt calm again. "Yeah," I said, "alright."

"Come," she said.

We went down the corridor and out through the stage door, into the main hall. There were still a lot of people around. Roadies, journalists, some fucking groupies and fans. I thought they'd turn round and look at us, but no one did. It was weird. It was good not being hassled, but I like it when people look at me. I like seeing their faces when they recognise me. Specially the birds.

There was no sign of Steve and Paul and Malcolm. I knew Steve and Paul were sick of all the driving, and earlier Steve had said he was gonna tell Malcolm that from now on he and Paul wanted to fly to the gigs like proper fucking pop stars, otherwise he'd fuck off home, so maybe that's what had happened.

John was still there though. Still hunched over in the same place with his can of beer and his fag. He was surrounded by cunts hanging on his every fucking word, but as usual he looked bored and pissed off. He always took the piss out of me for being a "Daily Mirror punk," but he was just as bad. He was alright on the bus, then soon as he went out in public he turned into a moody, hostile cunt. Johnny Rotten, the punk rock star.

I was glad he was there, though. Glad he'd decided to stay with me and not fuck off with the others. Maybe it'd be easier with the others gone. Maybe we could be mates again. I hope so. Me and him, we're the real Sex Pistols. The others are just fucking wankers.

Me and the bird walked right across the room and no one even looked at us. We walked out of the room and out of the door and into the night.

It was fucking cold. Raining. Downtown Baton Rouge was a dump. The whole of America was a fucking dump. That bird had been right.

"Where we going?" I said. "I'm not fucking walking nowhere."

"Didn't I tell you to trust me?" the girl said and she tugged on my hand again. "Come."

I don't like being told what to do, but with this girl it was alright. I didn't even wanna fuck her. Well, I did, but it would've been wrong. It would've been like fucking an angel or something.

She had a pick-up truck parked round the side of the club. An angel with a knackered fucking shitmobile of a pick-up truck. Ha fucking ha.

She opened the passenger door and told me to get in. I did. I was cold, shivering. She started the engine. It sounded like an old man coughing his guts up. I put the heater on, but I was still cold. But at least I didn't feel sick any more. At least I didn't have stomach cramps. At least I wasn't itching.

"What's that smell?" I said.

"Crawfish. My brother is a fisherman. He supplies restaurants here in town and out in the bayou."

There was a fucked-up music system with a tape hanging out of it. I pushed the tape in and turned it on.

"What's this music?" I said.

"It's zydeco."

"Zydeco? What the fuck's that?"

"Roots music. You like it?"

"Yeah," I said. "It's good. It's like reggae, but faster."

"It's the music of the land," she said. "The music of the blood and the soul."

"Like the Sex Pistols," I said.

She smiled. "You think your Sex Pistols will play zydeco music?"

I grinned. "Yeah," I said. "Why fucking not?"

We drove out of town. It was just traffic lights and rain. The world looked like it was melting. The roads turned to dirt tracks. The truck bounced in and out of pot holes. Trees and swamps all around us. Shacks at the side of the road.

Then there weren't even any shacks. Just trees tangled together. Bent over and covered in slime. No stars, no moon, just darkness. I didn't know where we were and I didn't care.

The girl pulled over at the side of the track and turned off the engine. When the engine stopped the music did too. That's when I knew the sound of rusty violins weren't part of the music. They were insects screaming in the darkness.

She looked at me. Big brown eyes glowing.

"We're here," she said.

"Where?"

"At the crossroads."

"So where do we go now?"

"That's your decision, mon petit."

I got out of the truck. It had stopped raining. The trees dripped. The world still looked like it was melting. There was a smell of something old and rotting. I liked it here. It was dead, but it was away from the madness. Away from everything.

Something slithered in the darkness nearby and splashed into the water. I thought of the mayhem behind me. The blood and puke and shit and fights. The first sweet rush of smack through my veins and into my brain. I thought of all the people and the noise. The faces crowding me. Demon eyes and hungry mouths. Sucking my life away. Feeding on my corpse.

"I wanna stay here forever," I said.

"Which way, mon petit?" said the girl.

I turned round. Round and round on the spot. I didn't know what I was looking for, but then I saw it. A light through the trees. An orange glow. Like the moon had fallen out of the sky and was sinking into the swamp.

"There," I said. "Let's go there."

We walked towards the light. Insects made a noise like a thousand rusty doors creaking all at once. Things moved around us. I remembered Glen telling me on the bus about the animals they get here. Alligators and snakes and poisonous spiders. He told me hoping it would scare me. So I wouldn't run off to find some smack.

Well fuck you. I'm Sid Vicious. I ain't gonna get eaten by no fucking alligator. I ain't scared of nothing. I'm the most dangerous fucking animal in America.

The light was further away than it looked. We walked for ages, my boots splatting through mud and water. The girl walked next to me. She seemed to blend in, like she was part of the land. She moved silently, like she was floating.

The track got narrow. Water lapped on both sides of us. Things moved in the trees. Things splashed in the water. I thought of thousands of demon eyes watching us. Thousands of grinning mouths full of sharp teeth. I had no smack, no booze, nothing to keep the pain away. But I felt alright. The girl was my drug. My fucking angel.

Then the track widened into a clearing. In front of us was a wooden shack. It was raised up off the ground with a porch at the front. Orange light was shining out the front windows. Something flapped on the roof. Tarpaulin or plastic. When we got closer I saw the windows were covered in wire mesh. Big fucking moths were bouncing off them, desperate to get to the light.

I looked at the girl. The light was shining in her eyes, making them glow in the dark. She looked like a cat. A fucking leopard walking on two legs.

"Where are we?" I said. "Who lives here?"

"Why don't you find out, mon petit?"

I walked up the steps and knocked on the door. There was a sound from inside. A rusty old creak that might have been a voice. I pushed the door open. "Hello?"

The place was gloomy. Candles burning. Flickering shadows. Ratty old furniture. Wooden floor. It smelled old. Like old people. Dead and stale. There was no one here.

"Hello?" I shouted again. "Anyone home?"

There was a doorway at the back of the room. A big black opening. The shadows made it move and sway. It made me think of a mouth. An old man's mouth. No teeth. Yawning, struggling for breath. A voice came out of the mouth. Small and tired and creaky. It said something in a foreign language. French or something, I dunno.

I walked across to the door. Boots clomping on the wooden floor. I stuck my head through the opening, looked into the room. Couldn't see a fucking thing. Pitch black. I heard something moving, rustling.

"Who's there?" I said.

The scrape of a match. A flame. Behind the flame a yellow face, hanging in the darkness. The flame moved across, lit a candle. Light jumped into the room, surrounded by black moving shadows. The light was orangey-brown. There was a big bed and an old woman lying on it. She was fat and saggy. The light made her brown skin look shiny, like polished wood. She had bulging eyes. A big fuzz of black hair. The candle-light made the ends of her hair twitch like snakes.

"Hello," I said and grinned at her. "Who the fuck are you then?"

She said something else in a foreign language. I didn't know if it was her name or what.

"I ain't got a fucking clue what you're talking about," I said.

The girl spoke. I didn't even know she was behind me until I heard her voice. She said something foreign to the old woman and the old woman said something back. They spoke quickly. Jabba jabba jabba.

"What's she say?" I said.

"Her name is Madame Picou," said the girl. "She says she will help you."

"Madam what?" I said.

The girl spelled the old lady's name for me.

"Hello, Mrs. Picou," I said to the old lady. "I'm Sid."

The old lady said something. I shrugged.

"Madame Picou says take a seat," said the girl.

"All right, thanks," I said. There was a wooden chair under an old dressing table against the wall. I went over to it, and just for a second, when I looked in the mirror, I saw a skull looking back at me. I jumped and looked again. It was just me. In the candle-light my skin was white and my eyes were full of black shadows. I noticed things hanging off the sides of the mirror. Beads. Snake skins. I dragged the chair over to the bed and sat down.

The old lady jabbered again. She leaned towards me. She was so fat that she grunted like a pig as she rolled on to her side. A big fucking fart ripped out of her. I nearly pissed myself laughing. I was still laughing when she took my hands and looked at them, turning them over. Suddenly she shoved up the sleeves of my leather jacket and ran her fat thumbs up the insides of my arms.

I stopped laughing when I felt her stab something into my arm. Right into the fucking vein near my elbow. I was used to needles, but I wasn't expecting it and it made me jump.

"Ow!" I shouted and pulled my arm back. "What did you do that for, you cunt?"

I was angry. I wanted to smash something. Her face or her fucking furniture. I stood up and then I felt a hand on my shoulder, warm breath that smelt of spice and perfume against the side of my face.

"Hush, mon petit."

"She fucking stabbed me," I said.

"It is nothing," the girl said. "Relax."

My anger went away. Just like that. I sat down again. Suddenly I felt tired. Really tired. I couldn't move. I felt so relaxed that I couldn't even lift my hand from my leg.

"What's going on?" I said.

"It is nothing, mon petit," said the girl. "You are fine."

"I can't fucking move," I said.

"Madame Picou has paralysed you. But it is only temporary. Do not worry."

"What's she paralysed me for?"

"It is necessary."

"Why?"

Instead of answering me, the girl and the old bird jabbered at each other again. It seemed like the girl was asking questions and the old bird was giving her instructions, waving her arms about.

The girl went away. The old bird stared at me. Her face didn't move. She didn't blink.

"What you staring at?" I said.

She didn't answer.

Then the girl came back. She had some stuff in her hands. She put it on the bed.

There was a little doll made of string and cloth and twigs. A pair of scissors. A pin cushion. A little cloth bag. A bottle with some sort of liquid in it.

"What's going on?" I said.

The old bird put her finger to her lips and hissed at me.

"Shush yourself, you cunt," I said. "What's that? A fucking voodoo doll? You gonna put a curse on me or something?"

"It is a gris-gris," said the girl.

"What the fuck's that then?"

"It is to bind us together," she said.

"What do you mean?"

The girl took my hands and knelt in front of me. Usually when she touched me she made me feel calm. But I was getting scared and that made me angry. I'm a Sex Pistol. I ain't supposed to be scared of nothing.

"I need you, mon petit," the girl said. "I need you to save me."

"I thought *you* were gonna save *me*," I said.

"I would if I could, mon petit," said the girl. "But you are beyond redemption. I am sorry."

"Fuck off," I said. If I could've moved I would've smacked her one. But I couldn't, so I spat on her instead. My gob hit the side of her face. A big greeny. She just stayed where she was. Looked at me sadly and let it trickle down. Then she stood up.

She and the old bird jabbered some more. The old bird was waving her arms about, telling her what to do. The girl picked up the little doll. She got something out of her pocket and showed it to me. It was a picture of me, cut out of a newspaper. I was up on stage playing my guitar. The girl pinned the picture of me to the little doll and gave it to the old woman. Then she picked up the scissors from the bed and came towards me.

"Fuck off," I said. "Get away from me." I spat at her again. It hit the front of her dress, but she ignored it.

I tried to move, but I was still fucking paralysed.

"You cut me and I'll fucking kill you," I said.

She reached out towards me. She made a sound through her teeth like she was trying to calm a fucking wild animal. When her hand got close enough I tried to bite it, but she was too quick. Her hand shot up and grabbed my hair.

"Fucking get off," I said.

She brought up the other hand with the scissors and cut a bit of my hair off.

"*Fuck off!*" I screamed at her. "*I'll fucking kill you, you bitch!*"

She held up the tuft of black hairs. Like she was showing me I didn't need to worry 'cos she'd only cut off a few. The old bird held up the doll and the girl stuck the hairs to it. There was so much Vaseline on them that she didn't need glue or nothing. The old woman put the doll down on the bed and then picked up the little cloth bag and opened it. There was some sort of powder in it. I wasn't sure what it was, but it looked like smack. The old bird sprinkled some of the powder over the doll and started to jabber something in a foreign language. She closed her eyes and started to sway from side to side.

"What the fuck's she doing?" I said.

"Offering your image to the spirit," said the girl.

"What for?"

"So that we can seal the bond."

I shook my head. "What is this fucking bond? What are you doing to me? I ain't done nothing to you."

The girl looked at me. "I was like you, mon petit," she said.

"What do you mean?"

She pointed at the badge on my jacket. "I was a mess. I was. . . ." She mimed injecting a syringe into her arm.

"A junkie?"

She nodded. Behind her the old bird was still swaying and jabbering.

"And now you're clean?" I said.

The girl pulled a weird face. Like: not really. "You will *keep* me clean," she said.

"Oh yeah?" I said. "And how am I gonna do that?"

"By accepting my desire as your own."

I asked her what she meant, but she just smiled and turned round and went into the other room.

"Oi!" I shouted. "Don't fucking walk away from me! Come back here, you cunt!"

But she was gone. The old bird was still swaying and muttering. I could see her bulging eyes moving under her eyelids.

"And you can shut the fuck up as well," I said.

But she didn't. She just kept on and on. Jabba jabba jabba.

A few minutes later the girl came back. She'd taken all her clothes off. She was naked. Gorgeous. The most beautiful girl I had ever seen.

"Fuck," I said. "Are we gonna shag? Is that part of this voodoo shit?"

The girl smiled, but she didn't say anything. She came towards me. The light slid across her naked flesh. It was like she was made of golden oil. I didn't think it was possible for anyone to be so beautiful. I loved Nancy, but this girl made Nancy look like a skanky old slag. I didn't know whether I had a hard-on 'cos I couldn't feel anything from the neck down. But in my brain I had a hard-on. The biggest fucking hard-on in the world.

I sat there staring at her with my mouth open as the girl came over. My eyes couldn't get enough of her. I wanted to touch her so bad. Fuck all that angel stuff from before.

I was staring at her tits and cunt, so I didn't notice the tattoo at first. It was only when she started to pull my leather jacket off that I saw she had a tattoo of a thin black snake around her right arm.

"What's that?" I said.

"Le Grand Zombi," she replied.

"You what?"

"It is the serpent. It protects me from harm."

"Bollocks," I said. "Oi, what you doing with my jacket?"

She had my jacket off me now. She threw it on the bed at the old bird's fat ugly feet and looked at my arms.

"So many scratches, so many bruises," she said. She sounded sad. "Why do you hate yourself, mon petit?"

"I don't hate myself," I said. "I fucking love myself. I'm fucking brilliant, me."

I grinned at her, but she just looked sad. She turned away from me. Beautiful arse.

She picked up the little bottle and pulled the cork out of it. Then she started to shake out the liquid inside, spraying drops of it over the old bird and the voodoo doll.

The old bird didn't seem to mind. Didn't even notice.

The girl closed her eyes and started to jabber like the old woman. She started to dance too, her body rippling like a snake, her tits jiggling. She really got into it, went into a kind of trance. She shook more of the liquid over herself. Poured it over the snake tattoo on her arm, making it shine. Then she sprinkled the liquid over me, over *my* arm, the one I'd cut open. The wound had gone septic, but I couldn't feel it, not now. I looked at the arm as the liquid splashed over it, but only for a second. Looking at the girl's jiggling tits was much more fun.

Both of the fucking women were totally out of it now. Jiggling and jabbering. All that ju-ju voodoo bollocks. The girl kept splashing liquid around. All over me, over her, over the old bird holding the doll.

"I'm fucking bored of this," I said loudly, but neither of them heard me.

The girl kept splashing water until the bottle was empty. Then she threw the bottle away.

The jabbering changed. It was creepy. It was like the two of them were linked together or something. Suddenly their voices got deeper. Slower. They started saying the same words. The old bird held out the doll and the girl grabbed it. They both clung to it like a couple of kids fighting over a toy. The girl reached out with her other arm and grabbed my hand. I couldn't do nothing about it. We were like a human chain. The old bird and the girl still swaying and jiggling like nutters.

"What is this? Ring a ring of fucking roses?" I said.

Then the snake tattoo on the girl's arm started to move. I thought it was just the light at first, or my eyes, or that fucking stuff the old bird had injected into me fucking up my head.

"Fucking hell," I said. I squeezed my eyes shut, then opened them again. The snake tattoo was still moving. The thin black snake was curling down the girl's arm like a stripe on a fucking barber's pole. Down towards her wrist. Towards her hand. Towards *my* hand.

I tried to break free, but I couldn't move. I shouted and spat at her, but it made no difference.

The snake tattoo wasn't a tattoo no more. It was a real snake. It made a rustling sound when it moved. Its tongue flickered in and out. Its little yellow eyes fucking stared at me.

I yelled out when it moved from the girl's hand on to my hand. Then it was coiling up my arm. Taking its time. I couldn't feel it, but I could see it. I moved my head back as far as I could, terrified it was going to come all the way up my arm and bite me in the neck like a fucking vampire. Maybe it'd eat my eyes. Or crawl down my fucking throat and choke me. Maybe it'd go inside me and lay eggs and loads of baby snakes would hatch out and eat their way out of my stomach. I screamed at them to get the fucking thing off me, but they were still out of it, jiggling and chanting.

The snake moved up my arm to just above my elbow. Then it stopped. It gathered in its coils, bunched up. Now it looked like the belt I wrapped round my arm when I wanted to find a vein. The snake tightened round my arm until a big blue vein popped up in my elbow. I could see the vein pulsing away. Slowly the snake lifted its head. Then it struck. It opened its mouth wide and sank its fucking fangs right into the vein.

I screamed. I couldn't feel nothing, but I screamed.

"Get it off, you bitches! Get this fucking thing off me!"

My voice sounded weird in my own head. Rough and echoing. Like it was someone else's voice shouting from down the end of a long metal tunnel. My body was still paralysed, but my arm felt hot. I thought of the snake's venom mixing with my blood. Rushing through my body, travelling to my heart and my brain. I wondered if I was gonna die. The thought of dying didn't seem too bad. If I died on tour I'd get in the papers. I'd be on the front page. Yeah, that'd be all right.

My thoughts were falling apart. The room pulsed in and out, getting small then big, bright then dim. I didn't know the two birds had stopped their voodoo bollocks until the girl knelt in front of me. She took my hands. She smiled at me. Face shiny with sweat. Big brown eyes glowing. Even now she was beautiful. She'd fucking killed me, but she was beautiful.

"The snake is my desire, mon petit," she said. "You must feed my desire as well as your own. This way only one of us will die."

I could hardly keep my eyes open. My head was like a heavy rock. I tried to speak. I heard the words in my head, but I don't know if she did.

"Fuck you," I said.

Then it all went black. When I woke up it was dark and I was shivering. There was a hammering sound. Voices.

"Sid! Sid!"

I didn't realise I could move until I sat up. I felt like shit. Body aching, full of cramps. Covered in cold sweat. Arm, chest and bollocks itching like crazy.

I looked around. My head felt full of broken glass. I was in the broom cupboard in the Kingfish Club. The cupboard where I'd shagged the bird. The cupboard where the girl had come to me.

There was no one here now. Just me.

"Sid! Sid!"

"What?" I shouted.

The door opened. It was Noel.

"We're all packed up, Sid. Ready to move on."

"Where we fucking going?" I said.

"Dallas, Sid. We're going to Dallas. Come on, man. You want a hand?"

Noel came into the room and helped me up. I rushed over to the sink and puked my guts out.

"You okay, Sid," Noel said.

"No, I feel fucking terrible," I said. "I need some stuff, Noel. I need it now."

"No stuff, Sid. You know that. Soon as we get on the bus you can have some valium. How's that sound?"

I wasn't listening. I remembered what the girl had said. "You must feed my desire as well as your own."

I took my leather jacket off. Curled around my arm was the little black snake. It lifted its head and flicked its tongue at me. I screamed.

"Jesus, Sid," Noel said. "What's wrong?"

"*Get it off me, Noel!*" I yelled. "*Fucking get it off me!*"

"Get what off you, Sid?" Noel asked.

I held my arm out. "*The snake! Get the fucking snake off!*"

Noel looked at my arm. "There's no snake, Sid," he said. "You're hallucinating, man. Come on."

He walked out of the room. I looked at the snake wrapped around my arm. The snake only I could see. I looked at the blue vein pulsing in the crook of my elbow, and in that second I knew.

I was lost. Lost for good. There was no way back.

Feed the snake, I thought. *Feed the fucking snake.*

I put my leather jacket on and followed Noel out of the room.

BAD CALL

BAD CALL

My boss, Rik, has got a Chinese dragon tattooed on the side of his bald head. It's one of the things I like about my job. Other things I like, in no particular order, are: the bakery next door, which makes the best egg custards in the world; the shrink-wrap machine, because it's so satisfying to turn the hot-air blower on to the cellophane and watch it seal itself tightly around whatever it's covering like a second skin; the fresh, inky smell of new comics and/or the fresh, plasticky smell of new bubble-packed action figures, which envelops you every time you open a delivery box; Laura Stevens.

Okay, I lied. The other stuff I like in no particular order, but I deliberately left Laura till last because she's the best. She's been working at Planet X for six months now, and she's been my girlfriend for three. She's the coolest girl I've ever met, and the only one I know who can sit through my entire collection of Takashi Miike movies without throwing up or bursting into tears. Lately we've been talking about getting a place together. Trouble is, we've both got so many comics and stuff, it'd have to be a *big* place. Another problem is that our collections overlap in some areas and we're not sure what to do about that. We *could* sell the overlap on eBay and make some money, but I know she thinks the same as me on that subject, even though neither of us wants to say it: what would happen to our joint stuff if we split up?

But that's our problem. It's nothing to do with this story. I guess that started when Rik came out of the back office this morning and up to the counter, where I was talking to one of our regulars about the Iron Man movie.

"Hey, Als," Rik said, "there's a call for you. It's your mum."

"'Kay," I said, trying to sound casual, though to be honest I felt a bit embarrassed. Getting a call from your mum at work *always* makes it seem as if you're a mummy's boy, even when you're not. It gives people the idea that you still live at home, and that your mum's ringing to check you've brushed your teeth or are wearing clean underpants.

To be fair, Mum didn't ring me at work that often. In fact, I couldn't remember when she'd *ever* rung me at work before. I'd given her the number, but had issued strict instructions that she should use it only in an emergency. Suddenly remembering this meant that by the time I picked up the phone in the cluttered back office I was feeling queasy and nervous.

"Hi, Mum, what's up?" I said.

"It's your dad," she said, "he's had a heart attack."

There was an Incredible Hulk poster on the opposite wall. I wasn't looking at it as such, but it was in my eyeline, and as soon as Mum said those words the room seemed to stretch like elastic, then to shrink back again, and the acid green that was the predominant colour in that poster seemed to bleed out and engulf my senses, like a spreading ink stain on a sheet of blotting paper. And all at once I knew that whenever I saw the Incredible Hulk from now on it would remind me of this moment. I had a split-second to feel sad, and even a bit resentful, about that, and then without thinking I said, "Shit. Is he all right?"

I never swore in front of Mum. Never. I expected her to pull me up on it, but she said, "No, Alan, he isn't. He's very ill. The doctors say he might not last out the night. I think you should come—"

Her voice choked off, and suddenly I realised how hard this was for her, how desperately she was trying to hold herself together.

"Course I'll come, Mum," I said. "I'll come straight away." And then I did that thing people always do in adversity, which is to try and sound cheerful. As if a bit of cheer can stave off the darkness somehow.

"You hang in there, Mum. And tell Dad he'd better do the same or he'll have me to deal with."

I set my face and went back out on to the shop floor. There must have been something about my expression, though, because Rik took one look at me and said, "You okay, dude?"

I told him what had happened, and asked if it was okay to have the rest of the day off. He pulled a doubtful expression, hissing through his teeth.

"I dunno, mate. We're expecting a big delivery of Manga later." Then he widened his eyes to show he was joking. "Well, *duh*, course it is. Take as much time as you need." I turned away and he too did that cheerful-in-adversity thing: "I doubt we'll even notice you're gone."

I went into the back office to grab my rucksack and get my head together. Five minutes ago I'd been looking forward to my lunchtime veggie pasty and tonight's episode of *Heroes*; now my whole world had been tipped on its head.

Laura came in just as I was shrugging my rucksack on to my back.

"Thought you'd try and sneak off without saying goodbye, did you?" she said.

I was too preoccupied to realise she was also joking. "No, I was just going to—" I began, but she put a hand on my arm. Her fingernails were painted green with little gold suns in the centre of each one.

"Rik told me what happened. Do you want me to come too? Offer a bit of support?"

I shook my head. "No, it's okay."

"I don't mind."

"It's probably not the best time to meet my parents."

It struck me that this might be Laura's *only* opportunity to meet my dad, but I didn't say it.

"You're probably right," she said. "But you drive carefully, okay? Keep yourself safe. I'll be watching over you from afar."

"I will." I kissed her, and she responded so tenderly that for a moment I wanted to cry.

Ten minutes later I was on the motorway.

My car's shit. It's a clapped-out, fifteen-year-old Mazda 323, which could boast half a dozen reckless owners before me. The bodywork's dented, the front passenger side door won't shut properly, the interior lights flicker, the engine sounds like an asthmatic old man, and the radio reception gives the impression all stations are broadcasting from Siberia. But it's all I can afford, and at least it gets me from A to B *fairly* reliably. Laura calls it 'The Bastard', due to the fact that I encourage it with cries of, "Come on, you bastard!" whenever it's straining to get uphill.

Mum and Dad live in a little village not far from Cirencester in the Cotswolds. I live in Leeds, which is a couple of hundred miles away, give or take. It's a four-hour drive on a good day, and it had never struck me before what a fucking long way that is. Because when things are ticking along nicely, it's fine. I talk to Mum and Dad on the phone whenever I want, and when I go to see them (which admittedly isn't that often—maybe three or four times a year) it becomes a proper *event*, which I've always thought was quite nice. I've always liked the fact that seeing Mum and Dad is special, but at the same I'm glad that I don't see them that often.

I mean, don't get me wrong—I love my parents. But I also love the space and freedom to live my life as I *want* to live it, and I know that if I was nearer to them we'd end up falling out more. Dad always wanted me to be a solicitor or a doctor or something, and if I lived close to him he'd become more aware of my lifestyle, and would view it with disappointment and disapproval. I know he'd only do it out of concern and love, but that doesn't mean it wouldn't piss me off and lead to massive rows between us.

So yeah, I'd always been happy that I lived a couple of hundred miles away. I'd never seen it as a problem. But it was a problem now, now that the doctors had told Mum that Dad might not last out the night. I mean, what did that actually *mean*? That Dad had about twelve hours left before his ailing ticker finally wound down? Or that he might go at any moment? That he might die while I was half-way home, and I'd end up missing his last moments?

I'd never expected it to be like this. I know that sounds really naive, but I'd honestly always thought that when it came to my parents' deaths, I'd get plenty of warning, plenty of time to prepare. Of course, I'm aware that people die "suddenly" all the time. You see it in the obituary columns every day—"Suddenly, at home" (and by the way, have you noticed how it never says, "Suddenly—in a massage parlour" or "Suddenly—while out shopping at Sainsbury's?"). Even so, I'd always envisaged Mum and Dad living to a grand old age, and ending their days fading away in a nice old peoples' home. I'd imagined I'd be there by their bedsides, holding their hands and listening to their peaceful breaths getting slower and slower. It had never occurred to me that Dad might wake up one day feeling fine, and be dead by teatime. Not that he *was* dead, of course, not yet—or at least, I hoped he wasn't—but you know what I mean.

Traffic on the motorway was slow. All stop/start, with lanes narrowing due to non-existent road works, and bloody bollards everywhere. And there were loads of lorries, and rain, and by the time I got off at the junction that would take me onto the A-road, that would then lead to several B-roads, and finally to the winding country lanes of my childhood, I was fraught and frazzled and calling God a twat for throwing a bunch of obstacles in my way just when I needed them least.

And *that* was when I hit the worst traffic of all. It was about 4 PM by this time, but because it was January, and a shitty day weather-wise, it was already starting to get dark. All the cars had their lights on, and all the lights, surrounded by misty haloes of rain, were reflected in jagged, gleaming strips on the wet road. It struck me that this was the perfect weather to die by—murky, cold and slipping towards premature darkness. It would have depressed me if I hadn't been so angry. What *made* me angry was seeing the stationary line of traffic ahead, just when I thought I'd finally managed to escape the worst of it. I slowed down and gave the top of the steering wheel a hefty whack with the flat of my palm.

"Fuck!" I shouted. "Fuck! Fuck! Fuck! This is *so* fucking unfair!"

Then it occurred to me that this might be God's punishment for calling him a twat, and so I apologised and promised never to do it again. But nothing happened, which I could only conclude meant that either he didn't exist or that he was still hacked off with me.

I sat there in traffic, my stomach tying itself into knots, for the next fifteen minutes, and in that time the traffic crawled forward a grand total of fifty yards. The urge to throw open the door, jump out and run along the row of cars ahead of me, screaming that my dad was dying and that they all had to get out of my way, was superseded only by my natural reluctance to draw attention to myself. And so I just sat, listening to the windscreen wipers swishing back and forth, and thinking that that was probably what the respirator in my dad's hospital bedroom sounded like. I was so stressed that I thought if I didn't calm down soon, Dad wouldn't be the only member of the family having a heart attack that day.

Eventually I gritted my teeth and turned on the radio. I tried to do this as little as possible, because no matter how low the volume, the surges of static you'd get whenever you tried to tune the damn thing in were so sudden and loud that they'd sometimes make your fillings ache.

Sure enough, as soon as I clicked the dial to "on" I was met with a rush of white noise akin to being engulfed in an avalanche of gravel.

"Fuck off!" I screamed in such a hysterical voice that I frightened myself. Squinting and clenching my teeth, I began to twist the dial, searching for a local station that might have some traffic news. It took a while, but eventually, through the mess of interference, I heard a female voice say, ". . . local . . . affic. . . ."

I listened closer and heard: ". . . outbound A . . . oad closed . . . van fire . . . police . . . ternative route . . . lays are expec. . . ."

There wasn't much else. Or at least, I could only pick out the odd meaningless word. Then eventually some music started, which—because of the crap reception—it took me a good thirty seconds to recognise as a little-remembered 80s hit by the little-remembered JoBoxers.

I switched the radio off. I didn't even know if what I'd heard applied to the queue I was in, but I assumed it did, simply because I had nothing better to go on. It sounded as if a van had caught fire (how, in this weather, I had no idea, but no doubt it had done it just to spite me) and police had closed off the road and were now encouraging motorists to find an alternative route. Which was all well and good, but how could you find an alternative route when you were stuck in a fucking gridlock? I had a good mind to drive up the banking, smash through the fence at the top and career across a farmer's field simply to prove my point.

But I didn't.

Instead I got my map book out and considered the alternatives. I wished I could call Mum to let her know what was happening, but of course neither she nor Dad had mobiles. They had always been proud of this fact, just as they were proud that they had neither internet access nor Sky TV. Before today I'd found their attitude towards the modern world partly irritating and partly endearing, but right at this moment I found it wholly irritating. With a capital I.

I tried to stay calm and saw that if I got off at the next junction and took the first exit at the roundabout I could work my way home via the back roads. It was a circuitous route, and would add a good forty minutes to my journey, but it was better than sitting in traffic for the next hundred years.

By the time I finally reached the junction, I'd been on the road nearly six hours. It was after 5 PM, but it was so dark it might as well have been midnight. No doubt Mum would be wondering where I was by now. I just hoped she wasn't in a private hospital room, sobbing over the death of the man she had spent most of her life with and thinking that everyone had abandoned her. I wondered whether my sister, Josie, was on her way up from London, and whether she was having as horrendous a time of it as I was.

When I got to the top of the slip road I saw that the police had closed off the exit I wanted to take. There were red plastic barriers stretched across the road, cutting it off completely, and a police car parked on the verge, presumably to prevent desperate fuckers like me from lifting the barriers aside and driving through. As I gaped at the barriers in disbelief, the two police officers sitting in the car stared back at me implacably. I thought about stopping and asking them what was going on, but I was flustered, and I always feel a bit nervous around authority figures. Besides which, I didn't want them looking too closely at the Bastard. I had a suspicion that it was probably unroadworthy in several different ways.

So I drove on and got off at the next exit. As soon as I spotted a lay-by I pulled over and consulted the map book again. I saw that if I drove up this way for a bit, then turned left, and left again, I could still work my way back to where I wanted to go. I felt as if I was in a maze by now, trying to reach the tower in the centre, but being forced further and further afield by dead ends.

At least there wasn't much traffic on this road, though as I sat there in the lay-by with the windscreen wipers swiping back and forth and the heater struggling manfully to keep the temperature above zero, I was vaguely aware of a silver Mazzerati cruising gracefully by. I probably wouldn't have registered it if I hadn't seen the same car coming back in the opposite direction a few minutes later. The driver, a shaven-headed guy in a black suit who looked like a nightclub bouncer, was scowling. Alarm bells immediately started ringing in my head.

Sure enough, I rounded a corner a couple of minutes later to find another police barrier. As I slowed down, staring at it in despair, a policeman got out of a panda car parked on the verge, put his hat on (probably just to protect himself from the rain, though it made me think of a judge putting his wig on to pass sentence) and strolled over to me.

I didn't particularly want to speak to him, but I couldn't just drive away. So I wound down my window and said, "Hi."

The policeman was young, probably even younger than me, which reassured me a bit. He talked just like any other policeman, though. "I'm afraid the road ahead is closed, sir."

"Yeah, so I see," I said. "What's going on?"

"There's been an incident, sir," he said, in a way which suggested either that he didn't know or that he wasn't allowed to say.

"Right," I said, and wondered whether I should ask him what sort of incident. Instead I said, "Any idea how I can get to Melcham?"

Stony-faced, the policeman said, "You'll have to find an alternative route, sir."

"This *was* my alternative route," I said, trying to sound light-hearted rather than confrontational.

"Sorry, sir," he said bluntly.

I got the feeling he wanted me to finish the conversation there, to say something like, "Oh well, can't be helped," and then to turn round and drive away. But instead I said, "The thing is, my dad's had a serious heart attack and I really need to get home. I might already be too late."

I don't honestly know what I expected him to do. Open up the barrier and let me through? Escort me to the hospital? Call up a police helicopter and have me airlifted in? He didn't do any of these things. Instead he just adopted a slightly more sympathetic look than before, and said, "Very sorry to hear that, sir, but these restrictions are in place for your own safety. I'm afraid I can't make any exceptions."

Anger rose in me suddenly, which surprised me a bit. It wasn't directed at the policeman, but simply born of frustration. Even so, I had to bite back a sarcastic retort. I took a deep breath and felt my head sink. For a moment I felt dizzy and tired; I just wanted to give up, go home, go to sleep. I heard the policeman say, "I hope you manage to get where you want to go, sir. And I hope your dad's okay."

I looked up at him, and suddenly I saw his youth and inexperience and humanity. I nodded. "Cheers." Then I wound up my window, turned the Bastard round on the wet road, and drove back the way I had come.

Looking back, I feel as though I didn't know what I was going to do until I actually did it, that it was just a spur of the moment thing. I drove back down the road for a mile or so until I reached the lay-by on the opposite verge where I had stopped earlier, and without even pausing to think I pulled over and cut the engine.

For a minute I sat there, looking at the rain slithering down the windows and at the black fields over the low hedge to my left. Then I grabbed my rucksack and got out of the car. I walked round to the back and opened the boot, hoping that my memory wasn't cheating me. It wasn't. There was a dusty, crumpled-up cagoule squashed into the back corner, next to my hiking boots, left there from the last time I had gone walking.

I pulled the cagoule over my head, flipped up the hood and put my boots on. Rain pattered on the plastic hood as I hunched over to tie my laces. It was a soothing sound. It made me think of camping trips as a kid, curled up warm and snug in my sleeping bag while it pissed it down outside. On one trip Dad and I had gone fishing, and a duckling had somehow got a fishhook stuck in its throat. I have no idea how Dad caught the duckling (did he reel it in like a fish?), but I have a vivid memory of him tenderly and painstakingly removing the hook before placing the tiny bird carefully back into the river, whereupon it swam happily away, seemingly none the worse for its ordeal.

The memory abruptly made me well up. Stupid, I thought, swiping at my eyes. What I was planning was probably stupid too, but I couldn't see any alternative. If I was going to have any chance of seeing my parents today, I had to strike out on foot, head back home across the fields, in the dark and the rain.

I thought about calling Laura, just to let her know what was happening, but decided not to. She'd only persuade me it was a really dumb idea and then I'd be stuck, not knowing what to do. I wasn't exactly looking forward to tramping through the pitch black, and knew that sooner or later I'd almost certainly freak out and start imagining all sorts of creepy stuff. But what was *really* the worst that could happen, I asked myself. This was rural England, not some freaky American backwoods, full of grizzly bears and inbred cannibals. Probably the scariest thing I'd come across would be a stray sheep, looming out of the darkness like a dozy-looking ghost. Just the same, I could have done with a map of the local area and a torch to light my way. But I had neither. I hadn't exactly envisaged this little jaunt when I set out earlier.

I climbed over a rickety stile which led in to the field behind the hedge and started walking away from my car, boots squelching through the waterlogged grass. After twenty yards or so I felt as if I had already left civilisation behind. Despite everything, my thoughts were more active in the darkness than I would have liked. It wasn't long before I was imagining a newspaper bearing the headline: CAR OF MISSING MAN FOUND. Then I found myself picturing another, and on the front page of this one the headline read: MUTILATED REMAINS DISCOVERED IN WOODS. It would be a dog-walker, I thought. That or children playing. It was *always* either one or the other. I saw the story spooling out before me, almost as though it was written on the rain-lashed darkness: *A dog walker today made a grim discovery in woods close to the village of Melcham, near Cirencester. The dismembered remains of a man were found in a shallow grave, not far from the spot where the car of missing Leeds man, Alan—*

Stop it, I told myself firmly. Stop it *now*.

I wished I had a better sense of direction, but I was rubbish when it came to instinctively knowing which way to go. I can read maps okay, but put me down in the middle of somewhere without one and I'm fucked. My mum says that you're either born with a pigeon in your head or you're not, and I guess I'm one of those people who's not. Oh well, at least that means I don't have to put up with a crap-eating winged rodent in my skull, fluttering about and shitting everywhere (har de har har).

The thing is, I didn't have much of an idea where Melcham was from here, but I knew it couldn't be more than about five miles away. I reckoned all I had to do was keep walking, and eventually I'd come to a road within the cordoned-off area, where there'd be signposts.

As I walked it struck me for the first time how odd it was that the police had closed off all these roads just because a van had caught fire. You could understand one or two roads being out of action, but a simple vehicle fire couldn't be causing this much disruption, surely? I started to wonder whether something else was going on. Maybe terrorists were using germ warfare, and had decided to test it out on this sleepy little corner of the Cotswolds. This whole scenario reminded me of that film, *Village of the Damned*, where everyone within a certain area fell asleep for twenty-four hours, and everyone who went into that area instantly fell asleep too, and in the end the police and the army put a cordon around the place, until eventually, a day later, everyone magically woke up again, only to find that all the women were pregnant.

It took me about ten minutes to walk across the field, my feet squelching and the rain drumming on my hood all the way. At last I came to a tough, prickly hedge. I walked along it for a couple of hundred yards until I arrived at a gate. The mud around the gate oozed up over my boots, and each step I took made a sound like a sink plunger unlocking a toilet, but at least my feet stayed dry.

I was half-way across the next field, with the black bulk of the woods looming up, several hundred yards in front of me, when I saw the lights.

They were over to my right, a string of bobbing yellow circles, maybe a dozen or more. In the dark it was hard to judge how far away they were, but I'd say about half a mile, maybe less. My initial, ridiculous thought was that they were fireflies; then I realised, a split-second later, that they were the beams of torches. As far as I could see, that could mean only one of two things. Either this was a group of boy scouts out on a camping trip, or it was a police search.

But if the latter, what were they searching for? A missing child? An escaped criminal? And what would they do if they found *me*? Before I could help myself, I was picturing a frenzied mob from an old Frankenstein film, so fuelled by anger and alcohol that they would shoot first and ask questions later.

Whoever the torch-bearers were, I decided that I wanted to avoid them. So I veered off to my left, in a direction that would take me away from the search party, but towards the thickest part of the wood.

I wasn't exactly scared, but I was a bit nervous, and anxious to press on, to put this awful day behind me, despite what would be waiting for me at home. I reached the edge of the wood and plunged into it without hesitation, the trees and bushes around me coalescing into an impenetrable tangle of blackness. However, even at this point I didn't feel any fear—at least, not until I heard the growling.

It came from somewhere ahead of me and to my right, and it immediately stopped me dead. Coldness washed over me that had nothing to do with the rain. Feeling constricted within my hood, I pulled it down, and at once several fat drips of rain splatted on my head as if they had been waiting for just this opportunity. In the wood the rain was a soft sound, like the distant drumming of tiny hoof beats.

Had I really heard something growling? Maybe it was what the police were looking for—a savage dog, or a big cat, like a puma or a panther. Maybe the animal had already attacked and killed several people. Surely I wasn't about to become a "shreddie," the real-life equivalent of one of those unnamed victims from a million horror movies?

The experts say that if you're ever confronted by a large predator you should stay still—but I was fucked if I was going to stand around here all night. So I started walking, slowly and deliberately, feeling my way ahead with the toes of my boots, alert for the slightest sound or movement. I suppose I must have taken around a couple of dozen steps when I heard the growling again.

It was behind me this time, and it almost made me piss my pants. "Fuck," I muttered in a rusty croak, "fuck, fuck, fuck." As potential last words go, they weren't exactly earth-shattering, but as there was no one around to hear them, I guess it didn't much matter.

I think it was at this point that I came to the conclusion I had watched too many movies. I could almost picture the scene shot for shot: close-up on my face, eyes widening, as the "beast" slowly rises, slightly out of focus, over my right shoulder; slow camera pan, the tension building, as I turn to confront whatever is behind me; brief, almost subliminal, close-up of burning red eyes and slavering jaws full of long sharp teeth; and then. . . .

I whirled round, unable to prevent air escaping my throat in a thin squeal.

There was nothing there.

Except there was. It may not have been *right* behind me, but it was there somewhere, in the darkness. Watching me. Stalking me.

"Fuck," I whispered again, and resumed walking. It was all I could do. Put one foot in front of the other, and tell myself that each step was a step closer to safety.

My legs felt tight and I could feel my muscles bunching in my back. I walked in a semi-stoop, head hunched into my shoulders. I felt flimsy and vulnerable, my body a fragile cage around my pummelling heart. I considered dialling 999, but then thought that if the animal heard how scared I was, it might just gain the extra bit of encouragement it needed to attack. I clung to the hope that at present it was still sizing me up, wary of tangling with such a sizeable opponent. Maybe the rain was damping down my terror, which I guessed must be pulsing from my body like radio waves.

The next ten minutes were the longest of my life. I just kept walking, all the time imagining that something large and fast, with hooked claws and pointed teeth, was about to leap out of the darkness. I saw it a dozen times out of the corner of my eye—a sudden flash of movement—but whenever I whirled to confront it, there was never anything there.

At last I realised I was nearing the other side of the wood. The mass of blackness began to break apart into the jagged, though blurry shapes of individual tree branches, through which I could see darkness that wasn't *quite* as dark as the darkness in the wood—if that makes any sense. What I mean is, by any normal definition the darkness was still dark, but it was no longer *black*. The sky was full of deep blues and dense greys, which meant that the land visible beyond the trees had a kind of murky definition. I could certainly see enough to tell that there was another field ahead of me, bordered on the far side by a black thread that must have been a stone wall. And just beyond that was a straight-angled block of blackness that could only have been a building.

I trudged on, the sound of rain becoming harder as I moved out from under the cover of the trees. I hadn't heard the growling since it had seemed to be right behind me, ten or fifteen minutes earlier. I didn't know whether to feel encouraged by that or apprehensive. One thing I definitely wasn't was complacent. I decided that the building was a good place to head for, and that once I got there (*if* I got there) I would re-assess my situation.

I wondered what I'd do if I saw the bobbing lights of the search party again now, and thought that I'd almost certainly decide there was safety in numbers and head straight for them. Hearing the growling had put a whole new complexion on things. Suddenly the chance of speaking to other human beings was something I'd welcome with open arms. But the string of torch lights was now nowhere to be seen. I, and possibly the creature that the searchers were looking for, seemed, without too much difficulty, to have slipped through the net.

Since I'd started walking again after my last scare I hadn't looked behind me. Partly that was because I hadn't *heard* anything behind me, and partly it was because a kind of fatalism had set in. Terrified though I still was, I'd decided that if the thing was going to attack it was going to attack, and there would be nothing I could do about it. However, once I left the oppressiveness of the wood, with its many potential hiding places, and started trudging across open ground again, I started to think differently. Suddenly I *wanted* to turn round, if only to reassure myself that the animal wasn't right behind me. If I could get half-way across the field, and turn in a circle to see nothing but open ground around me, then I might allow myself to start believing that things would turn out okay, after all.

And so I turned round.

And there it was.

It was standing at the edge of the trees, almost but not quite blending into them. It was as big as a Great Dane, but shaggier, with a pointed snout.

Wolf, I thought. *It's a fucking wolf.* And it wasn't *just* a wolf, it was a *big* wolf, its head almost on a level with mine.

I started to back away slowly. The wolf padded forward, keeping pace with me. It looked relaxed and casual, but I couldn't help thinking it was letting me know that it could close the distance between us in a matter of seconds if it wanted to. Even though the creature showed no immediate signs of attacking, I honestly don't think I could have been more terrified than I was at that moment. I was out in the open with a wild animal, for fuck's sake! People generally think of wolves as being like big dogs, but I was so scared that as far as I was concerned, it might as well have been a tiger or a grizzly bear standing by the trees. I might as well have been treading water with a Great White Shark circling me.

I'd like to say that I acted sensibly, that I carefully assessed the situation and how best to handle it. But that's not what happened. *Some* people might have had the presence of mind to think things through, but all that happened with me was that my brain locked, and my body responded by doing exactly what every instinct was screaming at it to do, which was to turn and run like hell.

It's weird. Even as my body chose the flight over fight option, even though my thoughts felt frozen with terror, there was a part of me that knew I was doing a very, very stupid thing. More than that, there was a part of me that was comparing my actions to the movies once again, even to the point of callously informing me that if I was a character in a film, then I'd *deserve* to die, simply for being such a moron.

Something else: I was dream running. Or at least, that was what it felt like. You know in dreams, when you're trying to get away from something and you feel as though you're wading through sludge? Well, all I was aware of as I fled was how stiff and heavy and slow I was, and of how the mud and grass absorbed my footsteps, draining my energy and making me feel as though I was about to stumble and pitch headlong any moment.

And yet I made it. It sounds impossible, I know, but I did. Don't get me wrong—I don't for a second think I *outran* the wolf. If it had wanted to catch me, it would have done so, no problem. All I can tell you is that I ran and ran and kept on running. I reached the wall and scrambled over it, and then thirty seconds later I reached the building, which I could now see was a rickety and abandoned old barn. I threw myself against the door, desperate for some kind of sanctuary, however flimsy. I had a horrible few seconds when I realised that the door opened outwards, and that it was stuck through lack of use. I hauled on the edge of it, screaming and swearing, and at last it gave a little, creating just enough of a gap for me to slip inside. Once there, I curled my wet fingers around the saturated wood and yanked the door shut again. It was a big door, warped and spongy, and there was no way of locking it. All I could hope was that the wolf, unable to find a gap big enough to fit through, would lose whatever interest it had in me and bugger off.

Once I was inside and had shut the door, I assessed my surroundings. Not that there was much *to* assess, to be honest. The barn was old and empty, and obviously hadn't been used for some time. It smelled of manure and wet mould, and it was so dark that I couldn't even see the ceiling above me. I had a quick scout around, mainly to check the walls, and realised—because I kept walking through the bloody things—that the place was full of spider webs. At one point, after the sticky strands of a web had stretched across my face, I'm sure I felt its owner scuttle across my cheek and through my hair. That was only slightly less alarming than stumbling across what I at first thought was a slumped body, only to realise that it was a heap of old sacking.

By this time my ordeal was catching up with me. I was starting to feel weak, sick and shaky, and all at once I had a desperate need to sit down. I stumbled over to what I thought was roughly the middle of the floor and sank into a cross-legged squat, my upper body slumping forward. I was aching and exhausted, and soaked with rain and sweat. I was starting to shake badly now with cold and reaction; I felt as though I was coming down with flu. Suddenly even sitting down wasn't enough. I needed to *lie* down. The ground was damp and earthy, but at that moment I didn't care. I stretched out, put my wet rucksack beneath my head as a pillow, and closed my eyes.

I had never felt so lonely, so scared and so far from civilisation. I couldn't believe that an hour ago I had been in my car on the motorway. The rain continued to patter down outside, like an echo of my chattering teeth. I felt my thoughts breaking up, drifting away. For a few seconds I resisted, thinking that I ought to stay awake and alert, be ready to run or fight. Then I thought: fuck it. And I allowed sleep to take me.

I have no idea how long I was out for. It could have been a couple of minutes or a couple of hours. However long it was, the sleep I had was deep and black and total. Being jerked out of it felt like being born, propelled into a world of stress and clamour. I experienced an instant of profound and heartfelt regret before realising that someone was hammering on the barn door.

Feeling like an old man, I unfolded myself into a sitting position and stared in the direction of the banging. For a few seconds I didn't speak or do anything. All I could think was that this was it, that the wolf had finally decided it was hungry and was coming to get me. In my confused state of mind, it didn't occur to me that wolves didn't tend to knock on doors—except maybe in fairy tales. It was only when I heard a girl's voice shouting, "Help me, please!" that my thoughts snapped fully back to reality.

Pushing myself to my feet, I walked on shaky legs to the door. I was almost there when the banging came again, accompanied by the girl's voice, which was even more desperate this time. "Is there anyone in there? Oh God, please help me! *Please!*"

"Hello?" I said, too dozy to think of anything else *to* say.

"Oh, thank God," said the girl. "Please, will you let me in? There's something out here."

"The door's not locked," I said.

"I can't open it," she said. "Can you do it for me?"

So I shoved the door, which opened with a wet, gritty scrape. The girl bobbed into view, and even in the darkness I saw that she was pretty and blonde and terrified. She looked behind her, and then at me.

"There's something out here," she said. "It's been following me."

"I think it's a wolf," I said. "It followed me too."

"Can I come in?" she asked.

"Yeah, course you can," I said.

So she slipped through the gap and I closed the door behind her.

"Sorry it's so dark," I said. "I haven't got a torch."

"That's all right," she said from about twelve feet away. "I've got some candles. Hang on."

I heard some rummaging about, then the scrape of a match, and suddenly we had light. The girl had lit a fat white candle, which was standing in a copper candle-holder on the floor. As our grungy, cobwebby surroundings came alive, the rotting and rain-sodden wooden walls lapped by warm, buttery light, the girl moved across to another white candle in another candle-holder a few metres away and lit that too. Now the light was quite homely. Or spooky, depending on how you looked at it.

The girl looked at me and gave me a smile that, if I didn't know any better, I'd say was a bit seductive. "Thanks for inviting me in," she said.

"That's all right," I said, though I have to admit I felt slightly nervous. The girl was really pretty, and I'd been desperate for someone to talk to, but all the same I couldn't help feeling that something was . . . well, *wrong* somehow.

It was the girl's manner for one thing, the way she had gone from terrified to flirty in a matter of seconds. And another thing was that she wasn't really dressed for a night-time trudge through the countryside in the rain. She was wearing a thin sweater—a *tight*, thin sweater, which proudly showed off her considerable attributes—a pair of jeans, a pair of trainers, and that was it. Her clothes were drenched and her blonde hair hung down her back in dripping wet ropes, but she didn't seem to care.

"Were you with the search party?" I asked.

She shook her head, as if she was amused by the question.

"Where've you come from then?" I persisted.

She walked towards me, light and lithe like a ballet dancer, water dripping off her. She stopped a metre or so away and tilted her head slightly, looking at me as if I was something new and interesting.

"Do you know what the search party were looking for?" she said.

I shook my head. Then I said, "The wolf, I suppose."

She laughed and the sound was disturbingly deep and guttural. "I suppose . . ." she murmured, as if mimicking me. Then she looked at me again, *examined* me again. "Have you really not heard the rumours? The *silly* rumours? They've been on the local radio all day."

"I've been busy," I said. "I'm not from around here."

I took a step back as she took another step towards me. She was close enough to kiss.

"When sheep are found with their throats torn out," she said, "folk don't pay much attention. But when a *person* is found in the same condition. . . ."

She grinned, showing all her teeth, revealing long pointed canines.

And suddenly I thought back to that radio broadcast I'd only partly heard in the car, and it struck me that maybe the newsreader hadn't been saying "van fire," after all.

I'd like to say I fought bravely, but the truth is, she was so fast I didn't even have time to blink.

When I woke up, she was gone, leaving nothing but the still-burning candles to show she had ever been there. I sat bolt upright and then leaped to my feet, feeling stronger, faster and more alert than I had ever felt when I was alive.

I knew what I was, of course. I knew it immediately and instinctively. I thought of Mum and Dad and Laura.

I had such a gift to bestow upon them.

And I had such a *thirst*.

FEEDING FRENZY

"Satan's Beast," sneered Oliver. "You'd think the people they employed here would be at least semi-literate."

"Don't be a snob, Olly," said Jacinta. "At least it shows the owner reads something. Too many people don't these days."

Adam overheard the exchange as he crossed the gap between the fire door at the top of the concrete stairs and the staff break room. All but his first two steps were hesitant, because he had quickly realised they were talking about him. Well, not him specifically, but the paperback he'd left on the long table strewn with thumbed newspapers, unwanted promotional freebies and discarded coffee mugs. When he entered, Oliver was pinching *Satan's Beast* between his thumb and forefinger, holding it at arm's length as though it was a dead mouse he was transferring from trap to bin.

"Better to read nothing," Oliver began before Adam, who had decided to brazen it out, stepped forward with a confidence he didn't feel and said, "I think that's mine."

"Are you sure you want to admit it?" Oliver said, who looked peevish at having had his flow interrupted, and nothing else.

"Of course I am. I mean I do," said Adam.

At least Jacinta had the decency to look contrite. "We didn't mean anything by it. We were only mucking about."

"You've nothing to apologise for," Adam said, wishing he'd emphasised the first word before being glad he hadn't. It wouldn't do to be making enemies on all their first days. He took the book, whose cover depicted a horned demon making a messy meal of a man with glossy entrails spilling from the bite in his stomach, and trying not to make it sound like an excuse, said, "I read this stuff because it's as far enough away from reality as I want to be."

Oliver's thin, bespectacled face looked disdainfully unconvinced. "Pornography for sadists, I'd call it."

"If you think I'm a sadist you'd best not get on the wrong side of me," said Adam, and curled his lips in as much of a smile as he could muster. "Really, though—Oliver is it? —if you ever read any of this guy's books you'd laugh. They're too daft to be taken seriously."

"Why read them at all then?" said Jacinta. When Oliver began to look triumphant she added, "I'm not taking sides, I'm just interested."

"For entertainment," said Adam.

"You find entertainment in things like what's on that cover?"

"Well, it's hardly real life, is it? And you must admit, most human beings have a taste for the macabre."

"Speak for yourself," said Jacinta.

"Not just for myself. I mean, granted, most of us are disturbed by the horrible things that can happen to people, but you can't deny that we're fascinated by them too. And evil, we're all fascinated by evil, by what it is and how it works. It's to do with being aware of our own mortality, I suppose, and by trying to understand what makes one another tick."

"Hang on," said Oliver, "so on the one hand you're saying these books are brainless entertainment and on the other you're saying they provide an insight into the dark side of the human psyche?"

Adam pressed the top of his head as if to keep his thoughts in place. "No, I didn't say that. Or I didn't mean to. God, I only came up for a coffee."

Jacinta laughed. "Leave him alone, Olly. Your first day and you're already giving everyone the third degree." To Adam she said, "He's been my book buddy all day and not only has he wheedled my life story out of me, he's plotted my future so I don't make the mistakes he thinks are inevitable."

Oliver rolled his eyes and said, "It's for your own good, dear." A perfunctory glance at his watch prompted him to drawl, "Well, I can't stand here talking to you peasants all day. I've Thackeray and Wilkie Collins awaiting my attention."

After they had listened to him clattering down the stairs towards the chaos that would be a high street store open to the public by this time next week, Jacinta poured them both a coffee from the percolator whose dark brown smell filled the room. As they sipped, she told Adam she had worked in a cinema and a vegetarian café and had been part of a co-operative that found accommodation for the homeless before getting the job at Hanson's. He thought it made what he'd done sound dull, especially since his business had dragged his marriage down with it, but her pale blue eyes, startling in conjunction with her raven-black hair and thick eyebrows and especially her long lashes, widened.

"That's a hell of a skill. How did you get into that?"

"I played violin in an orchestra. But I never thought the sound of it was quite right, so I decided to have a go at making my own. It turned out okay, and so eventually I started making and selling instruments for a living."

"That's amazing. It must be very satisfying to create something beautiful."

"Time-consuming and unprofitable, more like," he said, then noticed how uncomfortable she looked at his sudden bitterness and tried to smile. "It didn't work out, that's all. It's a shame, but there you go, that's life."

Her silence made him certain she was building up to excusing herself, when she said, "What you said before about the story you were reading being far away from reality. . . ."

"What of it?"

"Well, with me it'd be the opposite. I'd find the blood and guts too real."

Might she be testing him because she wanted to get to know him better? It was heartening to imagine so. Choosing his words as carefully as he was able, he said, "Yeah, but it's so over the top it feels anything *but* real. I mean, it's not as though I'm reading about car crashes and terminal illness. What happens to the people in these books and others like it is so extreme that you can't take it seriously. And the thing is, the characters don't have real emotions, so you feel cushioned from real life. And the goodies always win in the end, the evil gets vanquished, and the heroes go off happily because of that—they're never traumatised by what they've been through." He laughed. "In a way it's comfort reading."

"Strange way to find comfort," she said. "I think I'll stick to my Alice Hoffman and Iris Murdoch."

"You're joking, aren't you? That's the stuff that's too real for me."

For most of the bus journey back to the grim flat he couldn't bring himself to call home, Adam's mind seesawed between wishing he'd taken up the invitation to celebrate his and everyone else's first day with a drink and being glad he hadn't. It might have been fun to socialise with a bunch of strangers he hoped would become friends. Then again, most of his work mates were younger than he was by a decade or more, and he was worried that the age gap, which he (if no one else) had been conscious of at work, might have become even more evident in a social situation. There was nothing more dismal than feeling alone in a crowd of people who were enjoying themselves.

Even so, his dilemma over whether he had made the right decision made the beans on toast, the smell of which couldn't quite mask the odour of damp in his flat, hard to swallow.

His dissatisfaction continued to distract him through a police drama in which he tried to immerse himself. When he found his gaze straying more frequently from the screen to the bulging, fleshy patches in the wallpaper above the TV, he gave up and went to bed. Reaching for his book, he told himself that this was the life, that having no one but himself to worry about could only be a good thing. The clammy duvet and the muffled but insistent thud of music from the flat below, however, felt like ways in which life was taunting him. With nothing else to do except face the prospect of continuing to feed his own negative thoughts, he opened his book so vigorously the spine cracked and forced himself to focus on the words. For a moment he saw nothing but Oliver's sneer, then the sheer simplicity of the story pulled him in. The words began to feel like rungs he was using to drag himself up and out of the murky, complex stew of his life. He lost himself in the prolonged account of a sacrifice carried out by the Brotherhood of Demnos, in which the victim was disembowelled and facially mutilated with a pair of scissors. Despite the subject matter—or perhaps because of it—by the end of the chapter his eyes were drooping in response to his rapidly fragmenting thoughts. He was barely aware of putting his book aside before falling asleep.

"There's nothing wrong with escapism, but when it comes in the form of death and destruction it's setting a dangerous example."

"For whom, may I ask?"

"For whoever might be influenced by it. Children primarily."

"Ah, but my film's not *for* children, you see. It has a 15 certificate."

"That seems to count for nothing in this video age—or dee vee dee, as I believe it is now. Sadly films like yours are all too readily available these days."

Adam turned the radio off, and not only because it was time to go to work. The headache he'd woken up with, which seemed to clog his nasal passages with an exaggerated odour of ink and paper, was bad enough for the shrillness of the complainant's voice to feel like a sharp implement probing a nerve. Thankfully the pain, which may have been building all day yesterday, stuffing his head with the smell of books like deadly, odourless gas, lasted for less than the length of his bus journey. By the time the abandoned, graffiti-tattooed cinema came into sight just before his stop, the headache had dwindled to nothing more than a tightness above his eyes—expunged, no doubt, by the Nurofen he'd swallowed with his tea.

It was still early, not yet 7:15. Between the still-shadowed buildings of the city the trapped sky was struggling to widen its paler streaks. He liked the city like this; its somnolence soothed him. The illusion of tranquillity did not last long, however. When he turned the corner into Edward Street, where Hanson's was, he had to halt a moment to take everything in.

Three panda cars were parked on double yellows outside Starbucks across the road. Uniformed police were erecting an incident barrier around the entrance of the alleyway that cut between Hanson's and its neighbour, Muji. A group of Adam's work colleagues were standing around, looking shocked or dazed, some clustered around the assistant manager, Rachel, who was weeping. Adam walked forward until he was in earshot of a plump curly-haired guy smoking a cigarette, whose name he tried but failed to remember.

"What's going on?" he asked.

The curly-haired guy looked at him without expression. "Some bloke's been murdered in the alley," he said. "Rachel found him."

"You're kidding."

"You reckon so, do you?"

"No, I just meant . . . I'm shocked, that's all. What happened?"

Curly shrugged. He would have seemed lethargic if it hadn't been for the way his hand kept jerking his cigarette to his mouth. "Dunno. Sounds like the guy was stabbed and dumped."

"Jesus. So what's going to happen now? Are they going to let us in?"

"Not yet. They're going to cordon off this part of the street until they've searched it. They want us to wait in Starbucks until they decide whether to question us or not."

Clutching his cappucino twenty minutes later, Adam observed the police activity through the window, which seemed to consist of various people rushing in and out of the alleyway. Though he was sitting at a table with five others, he still felt out on a limb until Jacinta came over and knelt beside him. "Hi," she said.

"Hi. How are you?"

"Well, I *was* hungover, but this seems to have cured it—not that that's a good thing. It's terrible, isn't it?"

Adam nodded. "It seems unreal."

"I've been looking after Rachel. She's in a terrible state."

"I bet she is. Has she said much?"

"More than I'd want to hear."

Her voice had been getting quieter, and his with it, as if each in turn had been taking a cue from the other. Despite the circumstances Adam liked the fact that she had chosen him to confide in, if that was what she was doing, or about to. "Do you want to talk about it?"

"Unburden myself, you mean?"

"If that's what you feel you need."

She shuddered. "What Rachel saw sounds like something out of one of your books."

Adam tried not to grimace. "The books I read aren't anything like real. This is."

Briefly she closed her eyes, as if that might deny the reality. "It's horrible."

"You don't have to talk about it if you don't want to."

"No, I need to. I need to get it out of me." She leaned close enough for him to feel the warmth of her breath on his face. "The guy Rachel found had been killed by a pair of scissors, but that's not all. Whoever had killed him had cut his stomach open and pulled out his intestines. But Rachel said that even worse than that was that the guy had had his lips and eyelids and ears cut off. She said they were scattered round his head like. . . ." She made a sound that was not quite a groan and not quite a gag, but that released a rush of breath that smelled of stale coffee.

"Don't go on," Adam said, less as a plea for Jacinta to be spared than himself. His head felt suddenly stuffed with a darkness that seemed to pulse in tandem with his heart, and that threatened to drag him into an even darker place within itself. Jacinta looked taken aback at his abruptness, but Adam couldn't bring himself to explain his reaction—not even to the police, who let them all return to work just before mid-day.

Although the police had spoken to Rachel at some length, they hadn't felt a need to question anyone else. Adam was grateful, but he felt guilty for not having shared his insight with them. The problem was that he couldn't see how he could and not be regarded as the main suspect. On the other hand, if someone were to stumble across the passage in *Satan's Beast*, which was in his jacket pocket, wouldn't his silence be viewed with even greater suspicion?

As soon as he got into work, he locked himself in a toilet cubicle and transferred the book from his jacket to his trousers. For the rest of the afternoon he carried it around with him, aware of its weight and shape, fearing that its very presence would incriminate him. It wasn't the murder weapon, but Adam found himself regarding it as though it was. His mind was on anything but his work, though he was toiling mechanically and efficiently enough, when he felt a hand on his arm. He spun round to confront the store manager, Nigel, who asked if he might have a word.

Adam followed Nigel up to the first floor, where outside contractors were transforming an area as wide as two tennis courts into a café. At the top of a set of stepladders stood the bottom half of a man whose backside was swelling out of a pair of dusty jeans. The red and grey loops depending from the square hole in the ceiling through which he had thrust his top half were not intestines, but electrical wires sheathed in plastic. Adam tried to swallow the lump in his throat as Nigel led him to a pair of plump leather armchairs clad in polythene.

"Might as well sit in comfort," he said, lowering himself with a crackle.

Adam had to adjust the rectangular bulge in his pocket to follow suit. Nigel's sharp, bird-like features on his balding, disconcertingly scaly head remained deadpan as he remarked, "I hope you're not relieving us of stock."

Adam laughed, though he felt certain his voice was thick with guilt. "It's just a book I've brought from home."

"Oh? What are you reading?"

Was Nigel asking him to produce the book to prove he hadn't stolen it, or did he know more than he was letting on? "It's just a trashy thing. A bit of easy reading. Oliver's already made me feel embarrassed about it."

"Has he? That's not the sort of thing I want to hear. I'd rather we all pulled together, especially after this morning."

Adam couldn't help feeling he'd avoided one trap only to step into another. "He was only messing about."

"There's nothing wrong with a bit of that," said Nigel, "as long as it doesn't go too far." The polythene crackled as he leaned forward. "Team spirit's important to me, Adam. That's why I wanted us to have this chat."

"It's important to me too," said Adam, "to get on with the people I work with, I mean. If you're wondering why I didn't come out last night it's just that I couldn't afford it. I'm getting divorced from my wife and my finances are a bit tight."

Nigel raised a hand as scaly as the dome of his head, which Adam at first took to mean that he didn't want to hear any excuses. The corner of *Satan's Beast* was pressing into his thigh. He shifted position, but the crackle of polythene felt like an attempt to draw attention to the book.

"I'm not interested what you do outside of work. Or rather, I am, but what I mean is, your time there is your own. The only commitment I'll ask from you is to the store."

"I am committed," said Adam.

"Or should be, you mean."

"Sorry?"

"Just my little joke."

Each time Nigel moved, Adam couldn't help thinking that the crackle came from him and not the chair, that his dry skin was a brittle sheath he might be in the process of emerging from. The wires drooping from the ceiling suddenly drew in with a muffled clatter, making Adam jump.

"Don't think I'm singling you out, Adam," Nigel was saying. "I'm having these chats with everyone, only sooner than I might have done after what happened today. How has the incident affected you, do you think?"

Adam shrugged. "Well, it was a shock obviously, but I guess you just have to put it out of your mind, get on with your job."

"That's the kind of attitude I'm hoping everybody shares."

"I'm sure they will."

"I'm sure so too. I think we've got a good team here."

On the bus on the way home, Adam felt encased in a cloud composed of minute flakes of cardboard. He'd been disembowelling boxes all afternoon, scooping out their innards of books to fill the ranks of scrupulously-dusted new shelves, *Satan's Beast* still pressed against his thigh like a lover's hand. As he had left the store he had expected his stiffly nervous walk to arouse the suspicions of at least one of the policemen guarding the entrance to the murder site, but he had walked past them unchallenged. When he stepped off the bus he waited for it to round the corner, then plucked *Satan's Beast* from his pocket. Folding at the knees, he posted the paperback through two of the bars of a drain beside the kerb, and was already walking away when he heard the faint plop below.

Twenty minutes later, a mug of tea in his hand and Debussy on his portable CD player, Adam felt not only calmer but able to think more clearly than he had all day. Of course the murder had nothing to do with him. It was an appalling coincidence; the killer had probably read *Satan's Beast* and sought to imitate it. There was even the possibility that the killer could be one of his work mates who had got the idea from browsing through the book that Adam had left in the break room. After all, he had only known them for a couple of days; some of them he had barely exchanged a word with. Who was to say that one of them wasn't capable of murder?

Oughtn't he to be telling the police all this? He might be putting himself and all but one of his colleagues at risk by not doing so. But what excuse could he give for not having come forward earlier? And what reason could he offer for having got rid of the book when they asked to see it? He could say it had been stolen, he supposed, gone missing from the break room. He wasn't much good at lying, but suddenly he knew what to do. He would write an anonymous letter, give the police what information he could, but explain that he didn't want to get involved.

The letter was harder to compose than he'd thought. It took several attempts before he was satisfied, after which he spent a laborious hour writing it out in block capitals. The exercise made him feel oddly depressed, and he sat staring at the sealed envelope in the stealthily darkening flat before the effort of leaning forward to reach for the telephone produced a sigh that was more like a groan. On a whim he dialled a number and listened to four distant rings before a weary voice said, "Hello?"

"Ange, it's me."

"Adam. Why are you ringing so late? I was just about to go to bed."

"Is it late?" Adam said, and angled his watch under the desk lamp whose light was all that held back the darkness. "It's only quarter past ten."

"I go to bed earlier these days. It was only your influence that kept me up till midnight."

My sparkling personality, you mean, he wanted to joke, but didn't think he'd be able to cope with the silence that might provoke.

"Sorry," he said. "I just thought you might have rung to find out how my job was going."

"The bookshop thing, you mean. Yeah, sorry, it's just been full on here, you know what it's like. Laura had gym yesterday, then swimming today, then I took her to the Pasta Parlour for tea."

"Very nice," he said, trying to swallow his bitterness. "How is my gorgeous girl?"

"Which one of us do you mean?"

The darkness in the corners seemed to swell and thicken as sourness rose in him. He couldn't help blurting, "Well, you've made it clear you're not my girl any more, so of course I mean Laura."

There was a silence, then a thin sigh. "Don't get like this, Adam."

"Like what?"

"I can do without you going off on one just before I go to bed."

He closed his eyes for a moment, then said, "Sorry, I'm just feeling a bit lonely, that's all. It's been a tough day. Someone was murdered in the alley by the shop last night."

"Oh, how awful. Do they know who it was?"

"If they do they haven't told us. Anyway I don't want to talk about that. I just want to know how Laura is."

"She's fine. Doing well at school and gym. Lively as ever."

"Is she looking forward to seeing me on Saturday?"

"I'm sure she is. She hasn't said so."

"Okay. Well, I'll be there at the usual time. Give her a kiss from me, won't you?"

"Of course I will. Good night, Adam."

"Night."

To stave off the despair that he knew would anchor him to the sagging armchair all night if he allowed it to, Adam forced himself to the light switch and then the bookcase. Despite what had happened that day, he still found the gratuitous titles on the lurid spines of his paperbacks oddly comforting. Here was *Cannibal Vampire*, here *Revenge of the Face-Eater*, here *The Demon Rapist*. Adam ran his finger along the spines until it came to rest, seemingly of its own accord, on *Night of the Blood Fiend*. He hooked the top of the spine and liberated the book from the shelf. The cover depicted a figure, whose face was in shadow aside from its pointed teeth, reaching for the reader with hooked, blood-coated talons.

Angela had never been able to understand Adam's fondness for books she'd described as having no literary merit. Or more specifically, she had been unable to understand why a man who preferred classical music to more modern styles could demean himself by choosing to read trash. As far as Adam was concerned, her inability to comprehend what made him tick was ultimately responsible for their split. Not that the decision to part had been his, or even mutual. Despite his and Angela's failure to connect he had been content with his lot. They had (had had) a nice house, a car, a lovely, happy, well-adjusted daughter, good friends. The failure of his business had been a blow, but it was something they could have overcome, if they had only tightened their belts and pulled together. But Angela had not been prepared to do that. She had used the collapse of Strings as a catalyst to confess she didn't love him, was no longer happy in their relationship, and that she saw no future for them together. And so it had ended, and despite the fact that she was the one who had rocked the boat, he had been the one out on his ear.

He didn't realise he was clutching *Night of the Blood Fiend* so tightly until he heard it creak. He turned away from the bookcase, and as soon as his eye lighted on the letter he had written to the police, he realised why he could never send it. Even if they didn't identify who the fingerprints which must be all over it belonged to, they would carry out a hand-writing analysis of everyone who worked at Hanson's, or perhaps simply question the store's employees. Jacinta and Oliver knew he'd been reading *Satan's Beast* and that would be enough. By the end of the week he would be in a police interview room, desperately trying to convince a cynical audience he was innocent of murder.

In a rage bordering on self-loathing, he crossed to the armchair, snatched up the letter and ripped it to shreds. After that there was nothing to do except go to bed, which he did, taking *Night of the Blood Fiend* for company. He read with a feverish intensity, until the fiend in question had eviscerated a young mother and fed her baby to the family Alsatian, handcuffed a girl to a railway track and listened to her screaming for mercy until a train dismembered her, and ripped the face off a pizza delivery boy with his bare hands. The series of killings, which seemed as distant from reality as the stories about a teenage witch and her talking cat which Laura liked, served to soak up the anger in his gut and allow sleep to take its place.

He could think of several reasons why the previous day's headache was waiting for him with added intensity when the alarm roused him on Wednesday. Perhaps he had strained his eyes from reading; perhaps spores from the lumps of damp in his flat were slowly poisoning him; perhaps his stress had coagulated into a knot of pain in his skull. The headache smelled of ink and paper, which made him dread getting to work where the odour, and perhaps therefore the pain too, would be doubled. In lieu of breakfast he swallowed four Nurofen which he sluiced down with several pints of water, and by the time he arrived at work he was grateful to be left with nothing but a vague buzzing in his ears, like the fading aftermath of a pop concert.

He was more aware than ever on this third morning at Hanson's of the growing familiarity between his work mates. Bizarrely it seemed that yesterday's terrible events had encouraged his colleagues to seek solace and unity with one another—or at least the ones who had gone out drinking last night as a remedy for what they had been through that day, which seemed to be everybody except him. Because of his eagerness to rid himself of *Satan's Beast*, he had sneaked away before Jacinta, or anyone else, could put him in the awkward position of having to refuse her (their) invitation a second time. He had no doubt he *would* have been invited along, even though Jacinta was barely acknowledging him this morning. She was chatting away with a round-faced, bespectacled girl called Ellie, who reminded Adam of Penfold from the Danger Mouse cartoons.

He had no reason to feel like a pariah, he told himself, but at the shift meeting before work he felt as though he might as well have been invisible. No one asked for his contribution, nor left a gap into which he might add one—not that he had anything to say. He was glad when the meeting was over and it was time to work, though he felt so anonymous that he was almost surprised when Gordon, the "leader" of the day, turned to him and told him he would be spending the morning in the Book Sorting room.

The "Sort" room was cavernous and maze-like, filled with rows of metal shelves, each labelled with an index number, on to which books and magazines were stacked. In one corner was a desk and computer terminal. On the far side of the room a ramp led down to a loading bay where the deliveries came in. Unlike the shop floor, the Sort room was drab and dusty, the concrete floor littered with shreds of cardboard, bits of polystyrene packing, screwed up chunks of brown tape. There was a large table in a gap between two of the shelves and a heavy fire door between the Sort room and the shop floor, which could only be opened by tapping in the four-digit combination on the locking panel by the handle. For the most part Adam worked alone, though occasionally someone would come in to fill a trolley with books or fetch a box that had been pre-consigned to a particular section. Each time the fire door opened he would hear chatter and music from the shop floor as if there was a party going on out there.

At first he felt envious and lonely, but after a while he began to enjoy his solitude. The work was undemanding and he liked not having to make conversation with people he hardly knew. He found that after the first half-hour he got into a routine that became mesmerising, almost soporific. Over and over again he would slit open a box, sort out the haphazard mixture of books inside and place them in the correct sections on the shelves. Eventually he reached a state where he felt irritated each time he was interrupted, though he did his best to hide it. He had been in the Sort room for just over an hour when Ellie came in.

"How you doing?" she said brightly.

"Okay," he replied, trying to smile.

He hoped that would be sufficient, but she stood and looked at him thoughtfully for a moment. Adam was aware of her eyes on him, but didn't acknowledge them in the hope it would discourage her. However a few seconds later she said, "You don't have to work in silence, you know."

When he looked at her blankly she said, "There's a CD player and a bunch of CDs in the desk drawer."

"I'm fine," he said. "I like the quiet."

She looked at him as though he'd told her he liked having needles pushed under his fingernails, then she shrugged. "All right, please yourself."

"Just because I'm not like you doesn't mean I'm weird," he muttered, but not until she had gone. He tried to get back to work, re-establish his routine, but he was unsettled now, distracted. Maybe it was time for a break. He'd been working in here for over two hours and nobody had come to relieve him. He was bracing himself to step out into the over-bright clamour of the shop when he heard a sound behind him.

Shoulder-blades tingling, he spun round, then stood perfectly still as his gaze scuttled over the metal shelves, the piles of boxes, the stack of cardboard, the plastic bin full of rubbish. The sound he had heard had put him in mind of the dry slither of a snake. It had lasted for only a second or less, but he had heard it clearly. Could it be possible that a snake had got in here? Did they even *have* snakes in the city? Of course, he may simply have heard the quick scuttle of a mouse, or even the sound of a book sliding from an unstable pile.

He thought about telling someone, then immediately decided against it. He felt isolated enough as it was; he certainly didn't want to become known as the loony who thought there was a snake in the Sort room. Pulling his sleeves over his hands, as though that would make a difference, he edged around the table towards the place where the sound had come from. When he reached the waist-high pile of flattened cardboard boxes he'd been adding to all morning, he gave it a swift kick. He imagined something shooting out from behind it, perhaps flying at him with wide-open jaws, but nothing did.

The metal shelves along the back wall towered above him, and his head jerked on his neck as he looked up, down, left, right. He knew it was either ridiculous or foolhardy even as he wheeled the metal steps from the corner and clumped up them to take a closer look at the upper shelves, which were a foot or more apart and stacked with piles of books. As he leaned forward it occurred to him that he was acting like a character in one of his books, like the kind of character whose actions seemed too stupid to be real. But if he was a character in a horror story, would his behaviour *seem* stupid to a reader? If so, it would surely only be because the reader would know they were reading a horror story and therefore had an idea what to expect. As a character he couldn't be expected to expect the unexpected, because what happened in horror stories didn't happen in real life.

At once he felt dizzy and clutched his head with his left hand a split second before his right curled around the hand-rail of the metal steps. With the dizziness came the merest whiff of ink and paper, which was the smell of his earlier headache. At the same moment he had the oddest impression not only that his previous thoughts had not been his, but also that he was being toyed with or mocked in some way. Perhaps continuously breathing in the smell of chemicals involved in the manufacture of books was like a mild form of glue-sniffing. Whatever the reason, he needed to clear his head.

His legs felt like lead as he clumped to the bottom of the metal steps and pushed them back into the corner of the room. The instant the steps ceased their clattering he heard the sound again, or something like it. For a second time he whirled round, but just as before saw no indication of movement. The sound had been so brief that he had to recreate it in his mind to realise how it had differed from the first sound he had heard. Rather than a slithering, this had been more of a shifting, as though something much larger than a human being was turning over in its sleep. He might almost have believed that a number of the boxes were haphazardly stacked and were moving against one another, perhaps prior to toppling, if the sound had not appeared to come from floor level.

Go get a coffee, he thought. *Forget about it. This is not your problem.* He would do that very thing just as soon as he'd pulled aside a couple of the boxes that had been stacked on the floor beneath the bottom shelf, to satisfy his curiosity. He gave the boxes he was intending to move an experimental kick first, promising himself that if he heard movement from behind them he wouldn't touch them. He remembered Ellie telling him that he didn't have to work in silence, that he could listen to music if he liked. Perhaps that was why no one had heard the sounds before, because they'd always had their row blasting out.

He bent down, grabbed the corners of one of the cardboard boxes that was protruding from beneath the bottom shelf, and heaved. Christ, it was heavy! Nevertheless, by using all his strength he was able to shift the box an inch at a time. Eventually the widening chunk of darkness behind it grew lighter, as if it was the box's crumpled, sticky shadow thinning as it stretched. Sweating, Adam bent more than double to peer into the still-dim gap, and his eyes widened.

Set into the floor was a wooden trap door, inset with an iron ring he could have fitted his clenched fist through. It was obviously ancient; over the years the roughly-hewn block of wood had been worn so smooth that it now more resembled stone. The ring was knobbly with rust, and Adam was stretching his hand towards it when a voice behind him said, "Found something?"

Adam jerked forward, cracking his head on the sharp edge of the metal shelf. The cold sheet of pain that spread across his skull made him think for a moment that his scalp was cut and flowing with blood, but a quick examination proved otherwise. Even so, he felt dizzy enough, when he looked round, to think for a moment that he was being confronted by a snake in human form shedding its skin. Then he realised it was Nigel, whose peeling head seemed to bulge as he loomed forward.

"Sorry, Adam, I didn't mean to make you jump. Are you all right?"

"I didn't hear you come in," Adam said, then wondered whether he had. He imagined Nigel's dry skin scraping against his clothes, flakes of it drifting from his shirt and trouser cuffs, leaving a trail. He shuddered and closed his eyes briefly.

"Can you stand?"

"I think so."

"Up you come then."

Adam scrambled to his feet before Nigel's hand could clamp tight as jaws around his arm.

"Been exploring?" Nigel said. Adam was not sure whether he detected a hint of disapproval in the manager's voice.

"I heard a noise. I thought I'd better check in case it was rats."

"I'm not sure how wise that was to do alone. I take it you didn't find any?"

"No. This is interesting, though."

Nigel barely gave the trap door a glance. "I understand this building used to be a theatre. Perhaps this was the stage."

"And this was the trap door that magician's assistants and whatnot used to disappear down, you mean? Shall we have a look?"

"Absolutely not. There'll be nothing down there now except rubble and dirt and God knows what."

"Maybe whatever I heard moving is down there."

"Then it'll stay there. Give me a hand pushing this box back and then you can go for your break."

He's the only man I've ever known who has more dandruff than hair. Adam sat in the break room, trying the line out in his head. It was lunchtime and he was hoping that Jacinta would come in. Perhaps it was the bang on the head, but he'd decided to try to be more outgoing, and to start by asking Jacinta to have lunch with him.

Oliver sauntered into the break room, wearing a white shirt, waistcoat and tight black breeches.

"Hi, Oliver," said Adam cheerfully. "You haven't seen Jacinta, have you?"

Oliver had barely acknowledged him before he turned languidly away and busied himself with the contents of his locker. "Within what time span do you mean?"

"Now. I mean, do you know where she *is* now?"

"Out to lunch, I expect."

"Whereabouts? Would you know?"

Oliver banged his locker shut and fixed Adam with a pitiless stare. "Why the desperation? Do you need someone to hold your lead?"

"Fuck off," Adam said, laughing to show he intended taking the comment as a joke. "I need to see her about something, that's all."

Oliver raised his eyebrows. "I can't say for certain, but she usually goes to the bagel shop."

"The one down the side-street by the theatre?"

"I know of no other."

"Thanks, Olly, you're a pal."

"I sincerely hope not."

The mutilated body of the still-nameless young man had been found only the day before, yet it appeared that fresher crimes were already demanding the attentions of the police. As Adam slipped out into the insipid October sunshine, the sole indication that anything out of the ordinary had occurred were the strips of yellow and black tape criss-crossing the entrance to the alleyway.

The Big Bagel Company, less than five minutes walk from Hanson's, was small, loud and always busy. A third of the floor space, which was tiled in gleaming black and white, was taken up by a stainless steel serving counter and kitchenette area where bagels were warmed, sliced and stuffed with various fillings—spicy sausage, hummus n' crunchy vegetable, ham n' coleslaw, cajun chicken—by hot-faced staff in white aprons and hats. When Adam arrived the place was so full of office workers scowling at their fellows for daring to have the same idea that he decided to hover in the doorway rather than joining the queue. He raised himself on tiptoe and for several minutes scanned the crowd, but saw no sign of Jacinta. He was on the verge of deciding to grab a sandwich from somewhere less congested and wait for her back at Hanson's when someone screamed.

It was an ear-splitting, nerve-shredding sound, and it came tearing its way out of the shop with almost physical force. The crowd seemed to flinch then freeze as one, Adam included. There followed a second, or perhaps less, of almost eerie motionlessness, during which the scream seemed to be overlapped by its own echo. Then all hell broke loose.

It started as a ripple, and quickly became a surge. The people in front of Adam at the back of the queue were barged by whoever was in front of *them* and forced to take a stumbling step, or more, backwards. Then further screams punched the air and the crowd heaved as a wave of panic rushed through it.

Adam jumped back as a chubby woman in a coral-coloured dress was knocked sprawling on to the pavement, followed by a skinny man in a grey suit who fell on top of her. Within seconds other people were spilling into the street, many tumbling over, others staggering before regaining their balance. Some looked sick, others wide-eyed with horror. One girl, who had spots of blood (hers or somebody else's?) on her white blouse, was dragged out almost in hysterics. Close behind her a well-built man of around twenty wearing a Nickelback T-shirt staggered out ashen-faced spattered with considerably more blood. Adam thought he had been stabbed, then saw a few stragglers behind him, fighting to get through the door, who were equally stained. One of them, a girl, dashed into the street and was sick.

Once they were out, most people didn't seem to know what to do. Some hurried away (a few running as though wild dogs were after them); several produced mobile phones and jabbed at buttons with trembling fingers; most simply stood around like sleepwalkers who had woken up in a strange place.

Adam approached the man with the Nickelback T-shirt, who was pressing a hand to his face (and unconsciously leaving bloody fingerprints on his cheeks), looking dazed.

"Are you all right?"

The man looked at Adam a moment as though it was the most astonishing question he had ever heard, then his glazed eyes seemed to focus.

"Uh . . . *I* am, yeah."

"So who isn't? I mean . . . what happened?"

Because of the out-flood of customers from the shop, Adam was now standing some way from the entrance and couldn't see inside. The Nickelback man shook his head slowly from side to side. "It was . . . unbelievable, man."

"What was?"

"There was this . . ." A flicker went across the man's face, as though he didn't know how to express what he had seen. Then he said, ". . . guy, and he got into an argument with one of the guys serving bagels. And suddenly this guy reached across the counter and he shoved his fingers into the bagel guy's mouth, and next thing he'd just . . . ripped the guy's face off."

He looked stunned by the memory, his eyes glazed over again, and his voice went very quiet. "Just ripped it off," he repeated, "like it was a . . . a rubber mask or something."

For a few moments the thin sunlight seemed suddenly too bright; Adam thought he was going to faint. Unconsciously aping the actions of the Nickelback man, he began to shake his head. "No, that's . . . that's impossible."

The Nickelback man looked almost sympathetic. "Yeah, but it happened, man." Then he seemed to register the blood on his clothes for the first time and spread his red-stained hands. "Aw, man, look at me . . . aw, man . . . aw, man. . . ." Suddenly he began to cry.

Awkwardly Adam patted his shoulder, mumbled something reassuring and wheeled back around to face the shop. Before he had time to think about it, he began to lurch towards the entrance, pushing through the ever-expanding crowd, who seemed compliant as sheep. Most people were standing well back on the pavement, though two men were hovering close to the shop doorway as though trying to pluck up the courage to enter. As Adam approached, one of the men raised a hand, splaying his fingers as though warding off evil.

"Careful, mate, there's a bloke with a knife in there."

"I don't think there is," said Adam.

The man waggled his narrow balding head on his long neck and said petulantly, "Well, no one's seen him come out."

"No, I mean I don't think he's got a knife."

The other man pursed his lips as though brandishing his moustache. "Were you here when it happened?"

"I was standing just outside."

"Well, word is, this nutter stabbed someone in the face."

"I was told he used his bare hands by someone who was standing just behind him," Adam said.

"His *hands*," said the first man incredulously.

"Either way," said the man with the moustache, "I think we should wait till the police get here. Me and Stan are hanging around in case he makes a break for it, like."

"But the staff are still in there," Adam said. "Someone might be bleeding to death. I think we should help."

Stan and the moustached man glanced at each other, as though gauging how courageous the other was prepared to be. Adam took a step forward. "Well, I'm going in," he said. "You can't stop me."

Stan's Adam's apple bobbed as if he was swallowing a gobstopper. "I'm with you, mate," he said, though it sounded as if he wished he wasn't.

"Me too," said the man with the moustache.

Adam took the lead, the two men tucking themselves in behind him. Stan muttered something about watching his back, but Adam knew their real intention was to make sure he was first in the firing line. Even now he wasn't entirely sure why he was doing this, apart from the fact that he felt involved in what was going on, even—awful though the prospect was— partly responsible for it. It surely couldn't be coincidence that firstly the murder and now this appalling attack had been almost identical to fictional passages he had read, but on the other hand what else *could* it be? Was he somehow breathing life into words on a page? The notion was ludicrous. All Adam knew was that he had to find answers. Indeed, his need for them at that moment was great enough to supersede his instinct for self-preservation.

He stepped over the threshold into the shop. The first thing he saw was a pool of shockingly red blood drooling from the stainless steel serving counter to the black and white checked floor below. The blood on the floor had been stepped and slid in. Gory overlapping footprints led out of the shop, on to the pavement outside.

"Jesus wept," murmured one of the men behind Adam. The other said something too, but Adam didn't hear it, because as soon as he saw the blood his head started buzzing.

At first he thought the sound came from some unattended piece of equipment, or was perhaps some kind of low-level alarm. Then he wondered whether it was simply inside his own head; certainly it filled his skull like the reverberations of a dentist's drill, made the bone beneath his skin tingle. He began to feel woozy, detached from his surroundings. Darkness gathered at the edge of his vision like encroaching dusk. Something seemed to move in the dimming corner of the room. He had to make an effort to focus upon it. Emerging from the thickening shadows he saw a figure whose face was in darkness apart from its grinning display of jagged teeth. It seemed to glide forward, and as it did so it reached out long bloody talons towards him.

"You all right, mate?"

Adam had no sense of time passing, but suddenly he was opening his eyes and immediately having to close them again against the harshness of the light. Little by little he realised he was lying on the pavement, something soft and bulky, a bundled-up blanket perhaps, behind his head. The man who had spoken was kneeling beside him, his head charred by the light pouring from his corroded skull. He shifted position, blotting out all but a shimmering corona of sunlight, and suddenly his features formed from the receding murk of his face.

Before Adam could work out that he was expected to answer the man's question, an acrid smell propelled spikes of itself into his head. He jerked away from the smelling salts, tears springing to his eyes.

"What happened?" he asked, his words mashed by a tongue that felt twice the size it should be.

"You passed out, mate, that's all. The sight of blood takes a lot of people that way."

"No." Adam struggled to sit up. The man—a paramedic, Adam realised, from his jacket—told him to take it easy, but supported him with strong hands nevertheless. "There was a man in there. The one who did it. I saw him."

The paramedic shrugged. "Well, he'd scarpered by the time we got here, probably legged it out the back. If you reckon you saw him, you'd better speak to the police. Do you feel up to it?"

It was over an hour before Adam arrived back at work. Nigel, who Adam had phoned to explain his lateness, met him at the door and tugged him aside, though only to ask whether he'd prefer to take the rest of the day off.

"No, I'm fine," Adam said. "I'll only dwell on it if I go home."

"Good lad," Nigel said, despite Adam being older by several years. "Well, if you find it a bit much, I'll let you slip away quietly."

"Thanks," said Adam, but despite his ordeal he spent most of the rest of the afternoon surprised at how okay he was feeling. Okay, but . . . strange, as though he was observing himself from afar, watching and waiting, with an almost academic detachment, for the reaction to kick in.

Perhaps side-stepping reality, or feeling as though he was, *was* his way of reacting. Certainly, when he tried to conjure up an image of the figure he had seen in the bagel shop, it was like trying to grasp a slippery bar of soap with wet hands. Instead of recalling details, his mind kept substituting the image on the cover of *Night of the Blood Fiend*. The reality, such as it was, of the figure, remained elusive, unformed as a half-forgotten dream.

It wasn't until he took a break at four PM that Adam realised he had had nothing to eat all day. Perhaps that was part of the reason why he was feeling so light-headed; perhaps lack of food was making him hypoglycaemic, which was what his mum always claimed to be when she needed a cup of tea.

The earlier sunshine was spread thinly across a sky like hard white marble when he hurried down the street towards the newsagent's several doors from Starbucks. Despite not having eaten for almost twenty four hours, the thought of a "proper" meal, even a sandwich, made Adam feel slightly nauseous, but he was not averse to filling up on empty calories—crisps, chocolate bars, maybe a packet of biscuits. His stomach began to growl the instant he entered the shop, which was stuffed so full of displays of confectionery, magazines, drinks and cigarettes it gave the impression it was being squeezed narrow by its more muscle-bound neighbours. Adam selected a Crunchie, a Yorkie, a tub of Pringles and a cellophane-wrapped packet of chocolate chip cookies, then waited impatiently as a barrel-shaped man in a football shirt that smelled of stale sweat took his time buying cigarettes from the turbanned proprietor.

Eventually the man rolled out of the shop and it was Adam's turn. He had placed his selection on the topmost copy of a stack of local newspapers on the counter, and was delving into his pocket for coins, when he noticed the headline that his Yorkie bar seemed purposely placed to underline.

Instantly he froze, then snatched at a breath to quell the sense that his thoughts were beginning to spiral lazily in his skull. The old Sikh man, face the colour and texture of used teabags, wild, peppery beard tamed within a fine black net, watched him serenely.

As carefully as a bomb disposal expert dealing with a volatile device, Adam dragged three pound coins out of his pocket and placed them on the newspaper. He felt as though he was dredging his voice up from deep within himself, and so was surprised at how normal it sounded when he said, "I'll take a paper too."

The old man scooped up the coins with a hand made of too many knuckles and gave Adam his change. In a daze, Adam stuffed the food into several of his pockets and folded the newspaper towards himself as he peeled it from a pile of its clones, then lurched out of the shop, wondering whether the sensation that his knees were no longer connected properly was apparent to anyone but himself.

Half-way back to Hanson's he unfolded the paper to look at the headline again, hoping for one brief moment he had misread it. But no, there it was, in bold black letters: HORRIFIC TRAIN MURDER. And beneath that the strapline: 14-Year-Old Girl Tied To Railway Track.

Three times, he thought. Three times it had happened now. Three deaths. Three's a crowd. Third time lucky. The Three Stooges—Father, Son, Unholy Ghost.

He thumped to a halt in the street, closing his eyes, pressing his hands to his throbbing head. Ink and paper. He could smell ink and paper.

"Are you all right, Adam? You look white as a sheet."

He could barely remember getting back to Hanson's, thumping up the motionless escalator, then up the concrete stairs beyond the door in the café, to the break room. His outward persona was a pre-programmed robot, not him. He was cowering inside himself, his thoughts twisting like snakes in a pit. He was a murderer, though he had never killed anyone. He had the power to destroy, though he felt helpless and inadequate.

He made himself read the article, though he knew what it would contain. The girl's body had been found by the earliest of that morning's commuters. She had been tied to the railway track and dismembered by a train. Police were not yet naming her, though the detective leading the inquiry said it was the most appalling crime he had ever had to deal with.

Alone in the break room, Adam made a crumpled tent of the newspaper and placed his head inside it. It smelled of ink and paper, or his headache did. He lowered his head to the table until he felt the coolness of formica against his brow. Squeezing his eyes shut, he whispered over and over, "It's not real, it's not real." He crumpled the newspaper around his head, filling his ears with the sound of its crackling.

It was Jacinta's voice that roused him. It wasn't until he looked up at her blearily that he realised he had been asleep.

"Was it a dream?" he asked.

"Was what a dream?"

Instead of answering he snatched the newspaper off his head, smoothed it out, read the headline, groaned.

"What's wrong?"

"Nothing, it's just . . . I'm confused. I've got a headache. I've had nothing to eat all day."

Jacinta made them both coffee while Adam, after his first bite of chocolate, tried not to eat as quickly as his body wanted him to. "How long have I been up here?" he asked.

"I don't know. What time did you come up? It's quarter to five now."

"Soon be home time."

"You don't sound too happy about it."

He shrugged. "It's just . . . I don't want to sound like a whinger, but it's been hard recently finding anything to look forward to. I split up with my wife a couple of months ago and now I live in a dump. I'm sure once I've been here a while and we start getting paid, things'll start to look up."

It came out in a rush, and was surprisingly easy to say, and although it was all true, Adam was aware that it was no longer at the heart of his problems, that he was merely peeling off the outer layers. He had reached the stage where he needed someone to help shoulder his burden, someone who could put things into perspective and suggest a practical solution. He couldn't deal with what was happening to him on his own any more. He felt engulfed by it. He didn't know what was real and what wasn't, whether he was sane or barking mad.

Managing to restrain himself from clutching at Jacinta's sleeve, he said, "I don't suppose you fancy a drink tonight?"

Before she could reply, Nigel's voice boomed over the intercom. "Hi everyone. Could you all drop what you're doing and meet me in the café in five?"

Jacinta gave him a resigned look. "Better see what our esteemed leader wants, I suppose."

Adam followed her out of the room. Not wanting to sound too needy, he left it until they were half-way down the stairs before saying, "About that drink..."

"I suppose we'll all end up in the pub at some stage," Jacinta said airily. "We usually do."

Adam could picture it—a big group of them crammed around a couple of tables, the loud ones hogging the limelight, no chance to be intimate or discreet. He had no choice but to make the best of it, though, would simply have to tag along and hope for the best.

Looking scalier than ever, wearing flakes of himself on the shoulders of his black U2 T-shirt, Nigel started the meeting by thanking them for coming. "You've all been working bloody hard these past few days. I couldn't be prouder of the effort you've put in. Having said that, because of what happened yesterday morning, and because the dozy prats at head office have under-estimated the amount of work that still needs doing to get us up and running by next week, we're falling behind schedule. What I'm therefore proposing—and head office have given the okay—is that instead of locking up at six we make tonight an all-nighter. You don't have to stay, of course, it's strictly volunteers only, but those that do will get double-pay for the extra hours they work, plus we'll order in pizza and beer and make a bit of a party of it. A working party." He grinned so widely at his own weak joke that Adam thought his face would split. "So let's have a show of hands. Who's for the graveyard shift?"

Adam was going to keep his hand down until he realised he would be the only one who did. Jacinta's hand shot up so quickly he instinctively felt it had been the excuse she'd been looking for not to have to listen to his problems, before telling himself he was being paranoid. There was no way she could know what he was going through, and how much he needed a friend.

"Incredible," Nigel said, looking overwhelmed. "You guys are just stunning. I don't know how to thank you enough."

"Make it triple pay instead of double," someone said, and Adam tried to join in with the laughter.

"Believe me, if it was my decision, I would," Nigel said, then clapped his hands with enough force to expel a puff of skin particles. "Right, gang, let's get to work. Beer and pizza at nine. Let's see how much we can do before then."

"Do you need a hand in Kids'?" Adam asked Jacinta as everyone filtered back to their designated sections.

"What about Gardening?" said Jacinta.

"Looking at all those book covers with flowers on them is giving me hay fever. I need a change of scene."

The furthermost quarter of the basement was in the process of being transformed into Book Planet, an area which a welcoming arch stretching between the backs of two sets of shelves claimed was 'Out Of This World!' The uprights between the shelves were thin wooden cut-outs of space rockets, the carpet was an inky sky a-swirl with planets. From the ceiling, three-dimensional counterparts of the exotic worlds underfoot dangled from wires like over-sized Christmas baubles.

For a while Adam worked almost silently alongside Jacinta, opening boxes, sorting books, labelling shelves, constructing displays. To an outsider he might have looked diligent, absorbed in his work, but in fact he was in turmoil. He wanted to tell Jacinta everything, but how could he without sounding like a lunatic? He felt it building inside him, and with each second that passed came an increasingly greater pressure to unburden himself. But paradoxically the longer it went on the harder it became to say anything at all.

He might have remained in an agony of silence all night if Jacinta hadn't suddenly said, "Adam, are you okay?"

He looked at her wildly, and could only blurt, "Why?"

"It's just that you look like a chicken trying to lay a bowling ball."

Instead of matching her smile, he said quickly, before the opportunity could pass, "I have to tell you something."

Immediately she looked wary. Pausing with a pile of Pullmans in her hands, she asked, "What is it?"

Now that he'd plunged in he had to maintain his impetus. But he was equally aware that he should take his time, not start babbling like a mad man. "Something's been happening to me," he said. "Something which sounds really crazy, and which I don't understand, but which I can't keep to myself any longer."

"Go on."

"Okay. But before I start, can I say that I've never had any mental problems, I've never had treatment for depression, I've never thought of myself as gullible or easily led, I don't particularly believe in God or the Devil or ghosts or UFOs or any of that stuff."

"Okay."

"Oh, and I'm not on any sort of medication. I mean, don't get me wrong, I've had a bad time of it lately, what with my marriage breaking up and everything, but I'm getting by, I'm doing okay, I've not had to go into therapy or anything."

"Just get on with it, Adam."

"All right, I will. Sorry." He paused briefly. "I suppose the best place to start would be with that book of mine—you know, the one that Oliver was waving around the first time we met?"

He took it from there, told it as simply and matter-of-factly as he could, re-building the events of the last two days incident by incident. He fought to keep his voice steady, to clamp in the nervousness that made his limbs want to jitter and twitch. When he had finished, Jacinta said, "So what do *you* think is making all these things happen?"

Adam spread his hands. "I don't know. But it's got to be something to do with me, hasn't it?"

A little too calmly she said, "You don't think you're attacking these people without knowing it, do you?"

"*No!*"

She jumped as if he'd snapped at her like a dog, and instantly Adam raised a hand. "Sorry. I have considered that possibility, believe me, but I'm sure it's not the case. I've had headaches, but I haven't had blackouts. There are no blank spots in the last few days. Everything I've done I can remember."

"So what then?"

"I don't know. I really don't know." He turned to the shelf to slot in a couple of Alan Garners, and then said, "Everything I've thought of sounds as crazy as what's happening."

"Such as?"

"Such as the possibility that something is plundering my thoughts, taking what I've read and making it real."

"What kind of something?"

"I don't know. Some force. Some . . . some entity. *I don't know.* I told you it sounded mad."

"It sounds like a plot of one of the books you read."

"Except much more horrible. The books I read are just escapism. They don't try to be anything else. But this is the opposite. I *want* to escape, but I can't."

"Perhaps you're not the person who's supposed to escape."

"What do you mean?"

Jacinta held up the books she was holding. "I sometimes think, what if we're just characters in someone else's story? We *feel* real to ourselves, but maybe that's only because we've been given life by whoever's reading about us. And what if the stuff you've been reading about leaks into our story, and then the stuff in our story leaks into the story of whoever's reading about us, and so on?"

"Cosmic, man," Adam said.

Jacinta grinned. "I know it sounds silly. But is it any more silly than what's happening to you?"

Adam sighed. "I don't know. I feel as if I don't know anything any more. There must be a reasonable explanation for all this."

"Why?"

"Because everything has a reasonable explanation."

"Does it?"

"Yes. Or at least it should do."

"Maybe it would be easier for you if you stopped looking for one."

"But what if it just carries on? What if people keep dying?"

"You'll have to think of a way to stop it."

"But how do I do that?"

Jacinta shrugged. "Stop reading. Burn your books. If this whatever it is has got nothing to feed on, maybe it'll die."

Adam blinked, puffed out air, like a man emerging from a nightmare. "I can't believe we're having this conversation." He reached out and gently squeezed her shoulder. "Thanks, Jacinta."

"What for?"

"For listening to me. For not running away screaming."

"I'm not a running away screaming kind of girl."

"I feel better for having talked to you," he said. "Even if nothing's been resolved, it's still a weight off my shoulders."

They got back to work. Adam wondered whether the solution really *was* as simple as Jacinta had suggested. If he stopped reading books would the killings stop? But what if the thing that was plundering his mind didn't limit itself solely to what he had read? Should he also refrain from watching movies and TV programmes that might contain the kind of material it could imitate? Did he have to spend the rest of his life starving his imagination? How would he cope without his fix of harmless fantasy that had proved itself to be not quite so harmless, after all?

"This is the last of the boxes," Jacinta said, ripping it open. "We need some more from the sort room."

"I'll get them," said Adam. He grabbed a V-cart and dragged it on squeaky wheels to the lift. After less than a minute of waiting, the lift opened with a sigh and raised Adam to the next floor. The sort room was silent and deserted when he stepped out into it; evidently the onus tonight was on making the shop floor look as presentable as possible. Adam dragged the V-cart, its wheels clanking over bits of cardboard and chunks of polystyrene, to the shelf containing the stock for Book Planet. He was almost there when he heard a scurrying sound.

It made him think of rats in the walls; not one, but several, perhaps dozens. He twisted his head, half-expecting to see furry bodies flowing over and between the stacks of books, but as soon as his eyes focused on the place where the sound had come from, they stopped.

It was as abrupt as that; as though someone had pressed Mute on a TV remote control. "Hello?" he called. "Is someone there?" The only response was the papery echo of his voice, ebbing towards the high ceiling.

He hesitated a moment, then marched to the desk in the corner and picked up the phone. Pressing the intercom button, he said, "Could Jacinta call 312, please? That's Jacinta, 312."

Almost immediately the phone buzzed and he snatched it up. "Hi, Jacinta, would you mind coming to the sort room?"

"What for?"

"There's something I want to check out. But I don't want to do it on my own."

"Is it something to do with what's been happening?"

"Maybe. I'm not sure."

She barely hesitated before saying, "Okay, I'll be there in a minute."

Adam put the phone down and waited. Less than a minute later the lift doors wheezed open and Jacinta stepped out. She looked round, a little warily, Adam thought, until she spotted him, whereupon she smiled. "So what is it you want me to see?"

"There's something I didn't tell you before," he said. "It wasn't deliberate. It's just that it didn't seem relevant."

"And now it does?"

"I'm not sure." Quickly he told her about the sounds he had heard, and about the trap door in the stone floor.

Jacinta hunched her shoulders. "So what do you want to do?"

"I want to get the trap door open, see what's inside."

"Do you think that's a good idea?"

"Probably not. But I don't think I'll rest until I know."

Jacinta's pale blue eyes stared into his for a moment, then she walked over to where Adam had told her the trap door was and gazed down at the pile of boxes covering it. Finally she said, "I must be mad, but . . . okay."

"You're sure?"

"No, I'm not bloody sure. But let's just do it before I change my mind."

Adam stepped forward and began to tug at the nearest box. "Help me with this then."

A few minutes later the boxes had been hauled aside and the trap door uncovered. Panting, Jacinta said, "Doesn't look as though it's been opened for a long time. It's probably fused solid with the floor."

Adam palmed sweat from his forehead. "Let's see, shall we?"

He bent down, grasped the iron ring and tugged. "Bloody hell, it feels like it's been super-glued flat."

"You need something to lever it up." Jacinta looked round, then crossed to the desk and grabbed a claw hammer from the miscellany cluttering it. "Try this."

Adam forced the twin claws of the hammer as far under the edge of the iron ring as he could and heaved on the handle. For long seconds nothing happened, and then suddenly, with a teeth-grating screech of metal, the ring shifted. A few heaves later Adam and Jacinta were able to curl their fingers around it. They stood side by side, their shoulders pressed together, and tugged until the ring was standing vertical.

"What now?" Jacinta said, straightening up and slapping her rust-smeared hands together.

Adam knelt beside the trap door. "Pass me one of those Stanley knives and I'll try to scrape some of this gunk out from around it."

For the next ten minutes the two of them worked on loosening the compacted dust and dirt which all but cemented the thick wooden door to the stone floor in which it was set. By the time they had finished they were both sweaty and dishevelled.

Still on hands and knees, Jacinta raised her head. "That's weird."

"What is?"

"Listen."

Adam tilted his head as if that would make his hearing more acute. "I can't hear anything."

"Exactly. There's no music."

It was true. For the past three days, the staff in the music department on the second floor had provided themselves and their fellow workers with an incessant soundtrack to accompany their labours. Adam had found much of the music execrable, which was another reason why he had enjoyed working in the sort room—at least before the slithering, scurrying sounds had started. However, although there were no speakers in the sort room, the music from the shop had still filtered through as a dull murmur invariably accompanied by a muffled beat. Now, though, there was nothing. The silence seemed laden, like a dramatic pause.

"Maybe whatever was on has finished and they're too busy to replace it," Adam said.

Jacinta shook her head. "It's a loop system. When one CD finishes, the next one automatically starts. When the last one ends, the first one starts again. The only way there'd be silence would be if someone took all the CDs out or switched the power off."

"Well, maybe that's what's happened," Adam said. "Maybe they're swapping the CDs over."

"Seems strange, that's all. It makes me feel as though we're the only ones here."

Be nice if we were, Adam didn't dare say. "It *is* quiet, isn't it?"

Before Jacinta could reply the lights went out.

She screamed and clutched at him. He might have enjoyed it if she hadn't dug her nails into his skin.

"Ow!" he cried, the darkness making the cavernous room seem suddenly full of echoes. "That hurts!"

"Sorry," she muttered, though released her grip only marginally. "What's happened?"

"Power cut, that's all. The leckies have probably shorted something."

"It's pitch black. I can't even see my hand in front of my face."

"Hang on, I've got something in my pocket. Here we go."

A thin beam of light cut through the blackness. Adam turned it on to his own face and grinned reassuringly. "Torch key-ring," he said. "Stocking filler from my mum last Christmas."

"Thanks Adam's mum," said Jacinta weakly.

She was still holding on to him, though not as fiercely. *Now* Adam was enjoying it. He shone the torch around. Shadows bulged and dipped like soft dark shapes shying away from the light. "It would have been a nightmare trying to find our way out of this place in the dark. Sharp edges everywhere, boxes all over the floor. We'd have been black and blue by the time we got to the door."

"You don't still want to get this open, do you?" Jacinta said, giving the trap door, beside which they were still kneeling, a couple of gentle taps.

"I think we'll leave it until—" Adam said before Jacinta squeezed his hand hard.

It wasn't that which caused him to leave his sentence unfinished. It was the sound of movement from all around them. Adam shone his torch above their heads, half-expecting to see the ceiling alive with snakes.

"What the fuck is *that*?" Jacinta said, her voice glassy with panic.

"It's what I heard before. What does it sound like to you?"

Her eyes were wide, her skin the colour of porridge. "Who cares? It's a bloody infestation. Let's get out of here, Adam."

They scrambled to their feet and ran hand in hand to the door. While Adam shone the pencil-thin beam behind them, sweeping it from side to side like a sword, Jacinta punched the four-digit code into the access panel.

"*Shit!*" she shouted as her jittering finger hit the wrong button and she was forced to start again.

"Stay calm," Adam told her. "They're only noises. We haven't actually *seen* anything yet."

"Don't tempt fate," she muttered. "There, done it." She pushed down the handle and they all but tumbled on to the shop floor, the torch-beam slicing wildly through the darkness.

"If it's any consolation, I think someone's fucking with us," Adam said after they had slammed the door behind them.

"What do you mean?"

"Well, listen at the door now. The sounds have stopped, cut off like a recording. I know this door's thick, but you'd be able to hear *something* through it, wouldn't you?"

Jacinta looked puzzled, and now that they were out of the sort room her fear was turning to anger. "But who'd do a stupid thing like that?"

Adam shrugged. "Maybe this whole thing is just some big set-up. Maybe someone's fucking with my head."

It was almost reassuring to think that. What he tried *not* to think about were the flaws in his reasoning. If this *was* some elaborate plan, then what was its purpose? To frame him for murder? Drive him mad? Adam couldn't think of any reason why anyone would want to do either of those things. But even if it *was* a set-up, there still remained the question of how its protagonist knew what he'd been reading, not to mention how, for God's sake, he had managed to execute the attack in the bagel shop?

Adam shoved the flurry of questions to the back of his mind and tried to concentrate on the here and now. If similar questions had occurred to Jacinta, she was keeping quiet too. "Let's just find the others," she said. "Nothing'll happen to us if we're all together."

Adam shone the torch ahead of them. To their right was the stationary aisle, to their left the magazine section. Directly ahead, bookshelves marched down to the front of the store in ever-darkening rows until the blackness swallowed them up. There was not a soul in sight, nor any sound of movement or voices in the darkness.

"Hello?" he called. "Anyone here?"

The answering silence seemed like the deepest he had ever known.

"I don't like this," Jacinta said, pressing herself against him.

"They probably just congregated upstairs when the lights went out, and because we were in the sort room nobody thought to tell us. Either that or the pizza's arrived."

Jacinta shot him a look that made it clear she wasn't fooled, but said, "Let's go and see then."

Sticking close to one another, moving slowly as though to avoid unseen pitfalls, they crossed the shop floor. The range of the torch beam was limited and Adam couldn't help thinking of a primitive man attempting to keep unseen night-creatures at bay with a burning brand. They passed History and Genre, and then the lance of torchlight was reflected back at them from the metal steps of the motionless escalator.

"If they're in the café we should be hearing something by now," Jacinta whispered.

"Maybe they went to the break room. Maybe there's more light up there. We'll probably find them having a candle-lit supper."

"What time is it?"

Adam directed the torchlight on to his watch. "Twenty to eight."

"Pizza's not being delivered until nine."

"All right, a candle-lit cup of tea then."

They ascended the escalator, treading as quietly as they could, though there was no particular reason not to draw attention to themselves. The first floor, in actuality the third if basement and ground were taken into account, was as silent and deserted as the one below. Neither Adam nor Jacinta felt inclined to call out, but Adam performed a perfunctory sweep with his torch. Blocks of light that were the plastic sleeves of videos, CDs and DVDs winked at them; shadows that were only suggestions of shapes solidified momentarily into shelves, a central information desk, a table stacked with movie books. Cardboard boxes stood open on the floor, books and CDs, which had been in the process of being sorted, piled around them.

"Upstairs?" Adam said.

Jacinta nodded, but said, "What if there's nobody there?"

"There will be."

"But what if there *isn't*?"

"If there isn't . . . I guess we'll just have to assume that everyone's gone home without telling us."

Jacinta was silent for a moment, then in a small voice she said, "And what if they've not gone home? What if something's happened to them?"

"Like what?"

"I don't know." Jacinta said it so firmly that Adam knew what she really meant was: *I don't want to say it in case it's true.*

"If something had happened there'd be . . . evidence," Adam said.

She sighed. "I suppose you're right."

"Come on." He turned away from the top of the escalator, towards the café area whose windows overlooked the street outside. They had taken several steps when he stopped abruptly enough for Jacinta to walk into him. "What's wrong?"

He hardly dared say it. Trying to keep his voice casual he said, "I've just noticed that there are no street lamps on outside. The power cut must be more widespread than we thought."

He made to move off again, but before he could do so Jacinta grabbed his arm. "Adam, you haven't read a book recently where everyone in a shop disappears without trace, have you?"

He tried to smile. "No."

"Good. Listen, if there's no one in the break room let's call it a night and get out of here. Let's find a pub and get hammered."

"You're on," he said.

They moved through the café, torchlight slithering on furniture shrouded in plastic. Adam punched in the four-digit code on the panel outside the door that was labelled STAFF ONLY and Jacinta pushed it open with a click. Light spilled on to the floor beyond and zigzagged up the first few concrete steps. The two of them stood and listened.

"I can't hear anything," said Jacinta.

"Come on."

Light preceded them up the stairs, which turned back on themselves at the half-way point. The silence seemed to thicken as they climbed. By the time they reached the fire door at the top, Adam felt as though it was clogging his ears like a change of air pressure. Neither of them commented on the continuing silence; it was as though they were both too intimidated by it to speak. Grimly resolved to confirm what they were sure they already knew, Adam once again punched in the four-digit code and Jacinta shoved the door open.

As soon as they were over the threshold, Adam directed his torch towards the break room door. It was propped open by a folded-over wedge of cardboard. Light spread itself thinly over the wall of grey metal lockers in the room beyond, murkily picked out the central table and the wooden chairs surrounding it, all but one of which was unoccupied. Adam had taken four steps towards the room, the light intensifying with each one, when what he had thought was a crumpled coat propped on a chair on the opposite side of the table rustled and leaned forward.

Light lurched away from the chair's occupant as Adam jumped. Behind him Jacinta uttered a wordless cry. With a twitch of his wrist, Adam caused torchlight to swoop from the ceiling and fall like a net upon the feebly moving collection of what appeared to be bones and rags. Jacinta groaned and sagged against him, but it wasn't until the withered mass raised its peeling, hairless head that Adam recognised it for what—or rather, who—it was.

"Oliver." The word emerged as the faintest breath. Yet the figure, diminutive, emaciated, but still somehow recognisable, seemed to hear it. It turned its head slowly in his direction, causing its spectacles, dangling grotesquely from one shrivelled ear, to sway and flash in the light. Adam did not know whether Oliver could see him, because his eyes, if he still had any, were so deeply sunken that his sockets were merely puckered hollows crammed with shadow.

So was his mouth. As the lipless slit widened, darkness seemed to bloom out of it rather than rush in, making Adam wonder whether that was all his stick-thin body contained. A moment later a papery-white sliver that had once been a tongue, followed by the brittle, breathy remains of a human voice, emerged from the darkness.

"Nearly . . . gone," Oliver whispered, each word drawn-out, tortuous. "Not . . . real . . . enough . . . you . . . alone. . . ." The effort seemed too much and his head drooped forward as if it had finally become too heavy for the impossibly thin neck to bear. There was a hollow clunk as the almost fleshless skull hit the table, a final rattling sigh.

"What's happened to him?" Jacinta said, her voice almost as fragile as Oliver's had been.

Adam's thoughts felt numbed, as if his mind was shielding him from a terrible dawning truth. "I don't know."

"We've got to help him."

"He's beyond help."

"No!" Her cry was raw and shrill, and seemed to have been torn out of her. "He *can't* be dead! He just . . . *he can't be!"*

"He is," Adam said, amazed at his own calmness. "Come on, we need to leave."

"But what killed him? What killed him, Adam?"

"I don't know."

She glared at him, then her face twisted with fury. "Yes you do. It was you, wasn't it? You're making this happen!"

"If I am I don't know how or why. I'm as much in the dark as you are."

As though she hadn't heard him she sobbed, "Make it stop! Make it stop!" She began to pummel him with her fists.

He caught her wrists in his hands. "I don't know how," he said.

Her sobbing intensified. He released her wrists and pulled her to him, holding her tight. "Come on," he said, "don't give in to it. You're not a running away screaming kind of girl, remember. You've got to stay strong."

He held her until she stopped crying and shaking, until she gently disengaged herself from him. Her face was red and blotchy, her lips pale. "Okay," she said, "I'm all right now."

"I think we should get out of here."

"And go where?"

"I don't know. Anywhere where stuff like this isn't happening. Let's think about that later."

Hand in hand they went back down the concrete stairs, across the dark and silent shop floor and down the escalator to ground level. From here it was no more than a couple of dozen paces to the main doors, but ahead of them, between the bays of bookshelves jutting out from the walls, was an obstacle course of central pillars and free-standing displays, piles of unshelved books and cardboard boxes in the process of being emptied. The closest of these snatched the light from Adam's torch and soaked it up, so that what lay beyond them remained in shadow. The glazed doors and huge display windows at the front of the store were nothing but a sheen of black.

Adam probed with the thin beam of his torch into every alcove, every nook, every cranny, every possible hiding place. The way ahead opened before them and crumpled back into shadow in their wake. They came parallel with the last (or first, if you were entering the store) bay of bookshelves. Now they had the information desk on their right, a long counter studded with tills on their left. The main doors were ten yards ahead, the darkness beyond their panes so impenetrable it was as though someone had given the front of the store a coating of thick black paint.

Adam swept the torch in a wide, slow arc, from right to left. The football-sized pool of light sidled across the information desk, trailing brownish shadows, and was on the point of moving away from it when someone rose up from behind it like a slow jack-in-the-box.

"Adam!" Jacinta cried, at the same instant as Adam spun back on his heels and pinned the figure with torchlight. It was Nigel. He was grinning through the loops of bandage he wore around his face. That, at least, was Adam's first impression, before he realised that the bandages were in fact strips of peeling skin. And the reason Nigel was grinning was because he no longer had any lips. They had sloughed away, leaving his teeth exposed.

"Adam," Nigel said. There was a gruffness to his voice, but it had deteriorated less than Oliver's.

It was Jacinta who answered, her voice flinty, breathless. "Nigel, what's happened to you?"

"I'm coming apart," Nigel said, reaching up and peeling a length of skin from his own head with a sound like tearing paper. "I'm unravelling. I'm not real enough. But I'm one of the last." He sounded almost proud.

"Not real. . . ." repeated Jacinta. She looked at Adam with something like the beginnings of realisation, or a denial of it. "Tell me this isn't happening."

"It isn't," Nigel said. "It's all pretend. So there's nothing to worry about. For me, anyway." He staggered, then righted himself, pushed something across the counter with a scrape and jingle of metal. "Here."

"What is it?" asked Adam.

"Keys. To let yourselves out. I'm going to . . . I need to lie down now . . . Not feeling too. . . ." Without another word he sank back, almost gracefully, behind the information desk.

Adam moved across to pick up the keys, Jacinta clinging to the back of him like a frightened monkey. Neither of them said anything. The time for rationalising and theorising was past; now it was all about going on, surviving from one second to the next. Adam felt as though his thoughts were floating somewhere above his head. They were vague things, just out of reach, but they tugged him along like a puppet. He moved across to the main doors, placed a palm on the cold glass. Even here the darkness outside was impenetrable. He tried to pierce it with the light from his torch, but the white disc that the glass reflected back at him looked like the dying sun of an already dead world. He paused a moment, hoping an alternative to what he was about to do might occur to him, but none did, so he thrust the key into the lock, twisted it and shoved the door open.

Darkness. Silence. Nothing to feel or taste or smell. It was neither hot nor cold. Adam couldn't even seem to push his perception of the ground beneath his feet further than the basic fact that it was a surface to bear his weight. Behind him Jacinta said nothing. Like him, she had probably come to realise how pointless speaking had become.

He took her hand and they started to walk. Their feet made no sound. Adam could not hear his own breathing, couldn't even be sure that time was passing any more. The torchlight began to fail around the same time that Jacinta's hand began to dwindle in his. Adam held on to both for as long as he could, but eventually, inevitably, both his source of light and his companion slipped away and he was left with nothing but his own clenched fists.

At least they were real; at least *he* was. But for how long? Best not to think about that, best not to think about anything. He went on, moving forward, ploughing through the darkness, or something not even as substantial as that. He was left with nothing now but his own desperate hope that if he searched for long enough, eventually he would find something as real as he was.

THE SCARIEST PLACE IN THE WORLD
THE SCARIEST PLACE IN THE WORLD

Holly resented daytime callers. Most of them weren't to know that she worked at home, but even so, her first response when someone rang the bell or banged on the door was to grit her teeth and ball her hands into fists, as if in imitation of the tight knot of resentment she felt clenching in her belly. It had been several weeks after moving in before the old lady who lived next door had got the message. The first time she turned up she'd been clutching a dented biscuit tin containing one of those old-fashioned sponge cakes, the ones with jam and cream in the middle and a light dusting of icing sugar on top.

"Hello, dear," she'd said, her thin shoulders hunched like vestigial wings within her pale green cardigan and her grey hair drifting like a wind-stirred mass of cobwebs. "I'm Mrs. Bartholomew. I'm your new neighbour—or rather, I suppose you're mine, as I've been here for donkey's years. I just thought I'd pop round to see how you're settling in."

Holly had kept the door half-closed, and positioned herself firmly behind it, as if wary the old lady might try to force her way inside. When Mrs. Bartholomew smiled, her face crumpled like a brown paper bag and her beige-yellow teeth sprang forward, reminding Holly of a row of clothes pegs on a washing line.

"We're fine, thanks," Holly had replied, responding to her neighbour's grin with a half-hearted grimace. "We're a bit busy just now. Lots to do."

She'd begun to push the door shut. Quickly the old woman said, "Just the two of you are there?"

Holly had hesitated, then nodded. "Yes, me and my husband, Mike."

"No children?"

"No."

"Ah." The old woman looked thoughtful. "Well, it'll be a lovely house to bring up little ones. When the time comes."

"Yes." Holly inched the door further closed. "Well, thanks for coming round, but we really are busy."

"Oh, I brought you this." Mrs. Bartholomew raised the biscuit tin as though making an offering to an arcane god. "A little house-warming present. Home-made."

Holly had thought of the old woman's bird's-claw, liver-spotted hands buried in cake mix, perhaps even scraping it from under her yellowing fingernails, and her stomach turned over. Mustering a smile she'd said, "That's very kind of you, but Mike and I don't really eat cake."

"Oh." Mrs. Bartholomew looked crest-fallen.

"Sorry," said Holly. "Well, goodbye."

She'd pushed the door shut, and then tensed as, from the other side, she heard the old woman call, "Goodbye for now, dear. Perhaps I'll pop round again when you're less busy."

She *had* popped round again. In fact, she had "popped round" on at least half a dozen occasions over the next few weeks, though Holly had never allowed her over the threshold. In the end Holly had had to tell her that she worked from home, that her time was precious, that she had deadlines to meet, that she couldn't afford to just break off whenever she felt like it. Her voice, when she'd said this, had been a little snappier than she'd intended, and she'd felt bad about it afterwards, thinking that the old woman was probably just lonely and wanted a bit of company. But still . . . her neighbour had to respect the fact that Holly needed to make a living. She had to understand that just because Holly was at home all day it didn't mean that her time was her own to squander on coffee and local gossip. And when Holly *did* get time to herself, in the evenings, she wanted to spend it with Mike—which was natural, wasn't it? They had things to do on the house, after all, plans to discuss.

She soothed her conscience by promising herself that at some point, when things had settled down and they were more on top of the situation, she *would* call on Mrs. Bartholomew and say hello properly. She *would*. But just now she was too busy, too preoccupied. And besides, if the old lady *had* lived on the street for donkey's years, then surely she had other friends to call on? It wasn't as if Holly and Mike ought to feel responsible for her in any way.

Which was why, when the knock came on the front door one Tuesday morning, just as Holly was dropping a camomile teabag into the flip top bin in the kitchen and trying to structure the next sentence of her latest article in her head, she felt that familiar knot in her belly tightening once more. Who was this *now*? Surely not Mrs. Bartholomew *again*? Perhaps it was one of those ex-prisoners selling shoddy and over-priced household wares from a leather holdall—the ones who always made her feel nervous. Or just someone delivering a parcel. Mike was always ordering himself the latest gadgets online. She'd told him to have them delivered to his work address so that she wouldn't be disturbed during the day, but sometimes he forgot.

Pushing open the kitchen door, steaming mug held before her like a weapon, she looked to her right, moving her head slowly, a little fearful of making a sudden move and drawing attention to herself. She didn't *think* whoever was standing outside would be able to see her, but you never knew. After all, she could see the caller through the stippled glass panel of the front door—or at least, she could see a vague dark shape with a pinkish blob on top.

She hovered a moment, willing the caller to go away. If it was someone with a parcel he'd put an attempted delivery slip through the letterbox, whereupon she could rush up to the door and open it before he'd reached the end of the drive, claim she'd been preoccupied with some household chore and hadn't been able to get to the door in time.

But the caller didn't put a note through the door. Instead he knocked again. Three quick taps, timid but insistent. If she'd been upstairs, sitting at her desk, she might have ignored it, but she was damned if she was going to stand in her hallway all day, feeling trapped.

With a grunt of exasperation she marched up to the front door and opened it. Standing outside was a thin young man in a dark jacket, jeans and a white T-shirt with some sort of fuzzy, black-lettered slogan on it that Holly could neither read nor identify. He looked like a student—bony wrists, thick mop of fashionably tousled hair, insipid expression.

"Yes?" she said sharply.

"Hi," he said with a vague smile.

Holly didn't smile back. "Can I help you?"

"Er . . ." The young man looked ill at ease. He wafted a hand vaguely. "This is a bit weird, but . . . I used to live here. A long time ago. I was in the area, so I thought . . . well, it was just a whim really. I just got an urge to see the old place. The house where I grew up." He grimaced. "I haven't been back in . . . I dunno . . . nearly twenty years? My name's Rob, by the way. Rob Norton." He nodded at the side wall of the house next door. "Is Mrs. Bartholomew still there?"

"Yes," Holly said.

Rob Norton smiled. "That's good. It's nice to know that some things never change."

Holly narrowed her eyes. "*When* did you say you lived here?"

"I didn't. The '70s. I was born in '78. We lived here till I was eighteen." Nodding at the expression on Holly's face, he said, "I know what you're thinking. I get it a lot. But I'm older than I look." He gestured vaguely at the house. "Any chance I could have a quick look round?"

"I don't think so," said Holly quickly. "I'm very busy. I've got a deadline to meet. I'm a journalist."

He pressed the palms of his hands together, as if in prayer. "Please. Just five minutes. Two even. It's been such a long time since I've been back, and I don't know when I'll be in the area again."

"How do I know you're who you say you are?" Holly asked.

Rob Norton flourished a hand almost triumphantly at the house next door, like a stage compere introducing a popular act. "You can ask Mrs. B. She'll vouch for me. She knew me from when I was a baby."

Holly pictured it all in an instant, saw immediately how protracted and awkward the situation would become. They would knock on Mrs. Bartholomew's door, and the old lady would answer it. And when she clapped eyes on her old neighbour her face would light up with incredulity and delight. No doubt there'd be a joyous reunion, a babble of questions. Mrs. Bartholomew would invite them in for a cup of tea, and Holly would have to play the killjoy, the party pooper, would—as usual—have to plead the pressure of work and deadlines. So she'd come home, and Rob would probably stay at Mrs. Bartholomew's for a bit. And even though Holly wasn't with them, she'd be unable to settle to her work, because she'd be on edge, waiting for Rob to come back, knowing not only that at some point she'd be disturbed by him again, but also that next door they'd probably be talking about her—Mrs. B. telling Rob how unfriendly she was, how un-neighbourly, how she wished things were back to how they used to be, when he and his family lived next door.

Holly didn't think she could stand all that—the time wasted, the disruption to her schedule, the uncomfortable knowledge that she'd be painted as the villain of the piece. And so she heard herself saying, "Oh, it's okay, there's no need for that. You can have a look round. But it *will* have to be quick. I *do* have a deadline."

"Of course," Rob said, nodding. "Thanks so much. I really appreciate it."

Holly stepped back, tugging the door open reluctantly so that he could enter. He came in, looking around eagerly, peering up the hallway, towards the kitchen, his dark eyes gleaming, the light slithering across them.

Holly took another step back as he closed the door behind him, trapping the shadows and the silence in with them. Outside he'd seemed harmless, skinny, almost frail, but here, inside, right next to her, he seemed taller, rangier, lithe rather than skinny, possessed perhaps of a deceptive strength, a tensile vigour.

What am I doing? she thought. If Mike knew he'd be furious. She wondered if she'd tell him. She knew what he'd say, could almost hear him saying it:

"How could you have been so gullible? Anything might have happened."

You read about these things, don't you? she thought. Strangers wheedling their way into people's homes. And you think: serves them right for being so stupid. But it's different when it's you. After all, *you're* not a newspaper headline; other people are. You're too smart, too careful.

"Where do you want to start?" she asked.

Her voice was a little abrasive. *Too* abrasive? She didn't want to antagonise him. Better to be business-like, though, rather than demure, defensive. The worst thing would be to appear vulnerable, to show any nervousness, any fear.

"This was all wood-panelled when I was a kid," he said, his eyes sparkling. "Well, not wood-panelled . . . you know that cheap stuff? Thin. It came in sheets and you just stuck it on the wall." He gave a sudden laugh, little more than a hitch of breath. "Pretty tacky, I suppose. But people thought it was sophisticated back then."

He sidled past her, away from her, towards the door on the left that led into the front room. "Is it okay if I . . . ?"

She nodded, and he opened the door, pausing before he did so and taking a deep breath as he turned the handle—relishing the moment, or perhaps bracing himself for what he might see.

She guessed that the room must have changed a lot since he had lived here, been redecorated and refurnished several times over. Perhaps even rewired, the light fittings repositioned, the windows replaced. Yet he stood there looking around with a kind of wonder. She saw that he was trembling slightly.

"Are you all right?" she asked to break the silence.

His eyelids fluttered, as if he was about to pass out. He turned his head so slowly towards her she almost expected to hear the bones creak in his neck.

He licked his lips. "I can't tell you how strange this is," he said. "It's like . . . somewhere I've seen in a recurring dream. Or like I've been asleep for a long time and I've just woken up." He shook his head suddenly. "Sorry. You must think I'm a total weirdo. It's just . . . it's hard to explain. Everything is so familiar . . . intensely familiar. And yet at the same time it's different. Like a new reality has been laid over the top . . . Does any of this make sense?"

Holly was a forward-looking person. She was not nostalgic. She had never had any desire to revisit the past, to explore old haunts. Last year she had been invited to a school reunion, but she had declined; the very idea of it made her shudder. Yet she found herself nodding now, to humour him. "It must be very odd coming back," she said.

"It is." He swayed a little on his feet. "Sorry, could I have some water?"

"Sure." He wasn't the only one who found the atmosphere stifling; she was glad of the opportunity to step away from it for a moment. "Sit down. I'll get you some."

She exited the room, hurried to the kitchen, opened the cupboard above the sink and reached instinctively for a glass. Then she thought better of it and took down a plastic beaker instead.

It was becoming heavier in her hand as she filled it with water when a shadow crept across the wall and the cupboard door in front of her. She turned with a gasp, water splashing over her hand.

He was standing right behind her.

"What are you doing?" she cried, immediately appalled at how shrill she sounded.

He backed off, raising a hand. "Sorry, I didn't mean to make you jump." His attention seemed suddenly caught by the room, his eyes flickering from wall to wall, floor to ceiling.

"Strange how small this room seems now," he said. "How narrow."

She felt oddly insulted. "It's plenty big enough for us," she said.

He smiled crookedly. "I just meant . . . when I was a kid this seemed . . . not vast, but . . . bigger, you know? Everything seems bigger when you're a kid, doesn't it? More formidable." He looked out of the narrow window beside the cooker. "I used to think that field out there was massive. But it's not, is it?"

"You sound disappointed." Holly was still holding the beaker. Water was dripping from her hand, forming dark coins on the slate-coloured tiles at her feet.

"Not disappointed," said Rob. "Just. . . ." He looked thoughtful, even sad. "The older you get, the more the world closes in on you. Stifles you."

Holly didn't agree. She thought the opposite was true. But she didn't argue. She held out the beaker. "Do you want your water?"

"Thanks." He took the beaker, but he didn't drink. "Is it okay to look upstairs? My old bedroom."

"Sure," she said, and raised a hand. "After you." She hoped her reason for inviting him to go first—because she didn't want to feel trapped with him; because she knew that if he stayed ahead of her she would always have an escape route—wasn't as evident to him as it seemed to herself.

He turned obediently enough, and as he did so he put the beaker down on the breakfast bar that ran along the left-hand wall of the kitchen. She looked at it, thought about saying something. But why make it an issue? Was it *really* such a big deal that he hadn't drunk the water he'd asked for? Maybe he'd changed his mind. People were entitled to do that. Maybe his feeling of faintness had passed.

She followed him up the stairs, though remained a good few steps behind him. She didn't want to get close enough that he could thrust out an arm and give her a shove. He moved slowly, deliberately, as if wary of disturbing a sleeping incumbent on the floor above. Two steps from the top he halted and turned. When he spoke his voice was sombre, hushed.

"That first door was my bedroom. Is it okay if I . . . ?"

"Be my guest."

He ascended the last two steps, crossed the landing, pushed the door open. It was her study, so the door was already ajar. Pearly light spilled out of it as he stepped forward, softening his outline. When she entered the room behind him he had already crossed to the window beside her desk and was looking at the paved yard below.

"I thought you might have turned it into a garden again," he said. He sounded wistful, disappointed.

"Again?"

He turned to her. His eyes were wide and soft. He looked . . . haunted? Was that too strong a word to describe the expression on his face?

"When we came here it was a garden. Lawn. Flowerbeds. Then my parents . . . my dad really . . . began to breed dogs. Alsatians. And he had the lawn ripped out, paved over. I thought . . . I hoped . . . it might be green again by now."

"It was like that when we moved in," Holly said defensively. "We haven't been here long."

Rob seemed not to hear her. His gaze swept the poky, square room, little more than a cell really. "This was my room."

"Yes, you said."

His eyes fixed on her. They were dark, almost black. And seemed suddenly flat. "You know what a little boy's bedroom is, don't you?"

She shrugged, discomfited. "What?"

"It's the scariest place in the world."

A beat. A silence in which meaning thrummed and throbbed, like the air beneath an electricity pylon.

"Is it?" she said at last, and to her own ears her voice sounded hollow, on the verge of cracking.

He nodded. "He dominated us . . . my dad, I mean. He never touched us, my mum and me, but we were scared of him all the same. He had a way about him . . . a way of grinding us down. . . ."

His eyes drifted away from hers, becoming unfocused. She knew he was looking into his past. "Some people do. There's a force about them . . . a sense that . . . that something terrible could happen at any moment . . . do you know what I mean?"

Holly wasn't sure what to say. Yet she felt compelled to say something. In the end she muttered, "You felt threatened?"

"More than that. I was scared . . . terrified . . . every minute of every day of my life."

His voice had dropped to a whisper. Suddenly he shook himself, like a dog. His head jerked up and his eyes were bright and black again.

"Have you seen him?"

"What?"

"Have you seen *anything*? Since you moved in? Anything . . . unusual?"

"No." She shook her head angrily. "What do you expect me to have seen?"

He half-smiled. "I used to see . . . even after he died. . . ."

"He died?" said Holly. "Your dad, you mean?"

He nodded. "His car was hit by a lorry on the motorway. I was eleven. I cried, and Mum cried, but secretly . . . I was glad. Relieved. I think she was too, but she didn't say so. But then. . . ." His eyes drifted, not to the window, but to the corner of the room *beyond* the window, the one where Holly kept her exercise bike when she wasn't using it. His voice had dropped to a whisper again, and his eyes were full of fear now. "Then he came back. I'd see him at night. I'd wake up and he'd be standing there. A dark shape in the corner. Watching me."

"It was just your imagination," said Holly carefully. "You felt guilty, and afraid."

He looked bewildered. "So you haven't seen him?"

"Of course not."

He nodded slowly. "I couldn't wait to get away. When I did, when I moved out, I thought it'd be over, that I'd never see him again." He gave a sort of sob, and his face twisted for a moment, an expression of fearful anguish. "But it was no good. He followed me. Wherever I went, wherever I lived, I'd wake in the night, and he'd be there, standing in the corner, watching me. . . ."

He swayed, as though about to collapse. Standing beside the window, framed by the light, he looked ethereal, as though the blaze of his own fear was corroding him, devouring him.

Against her better judgement, Holly stepped forward, raising her hands as though to grip his elbows, hold him upright.

"He's not real, Rob, don't you see?" she said. "You only think you saw him because he was such a presence in your life, because he frightened you, and because you felt guilty for being relieved when he died. But you mustn't let him haunt you anymore. He's gone. You're free of him."

Rob shook his head. "I thought if I came back, I might be able to bring him with me, leave him here, lay him to rest."

"Do that," said Holly decisively. "Leave him here. He has no power over me. I don't believe in him."

Rob barely seemed to hear her. His eyes were wild, distracted. "But it's no good," he said. "He'll always be with me. I see that now."

"No he won't," said Holly. "You just have to—"

Her words dried in her throat, her body jerking in horror. Rob had produced a black-handled kitchen knife from his pocket and was now holding it uncertainly in front of him.

Holly's voice, when she rediscovered it, was eerily calm, far calmer than she felt. "Rob," she said, "put that away. You don't need it."

"He won't leave me alone," he said miserably.

"But that won't solve anything, will it? By . . . by using that . . . you'd be letting him win."

Though she said it, she had no idea how he intended to use it. On her? On himself? On his non-existent father? She backed towards the door, not deliberately, almost subconsciously.

He looked at her and his face was wretched. "I'm sorry," he said.

Then he rammed the blade of the knife in his own throat and jerked it sideways.

It was like puncturing a high pressure hose. There was a hiss and a fan of blood spurted from him, rising high in the air and coming down with a spatter like falling raindrops. He reeled and tumbled sideways, his legs simply folding beneath him. Blood continued to gush and jet from his neck as his body bucked, staining everything—the sand-coloured carpet, the walls, the bookcases, the laptop on the desk, even the ceiling—with streaks and spatters.

Holly crammed her fists to her mouth and screamed. She felt a wrench and a wave of dizziness, as though some instinctive, essential part of her was so appalled by what it was witnessing that it was trying to flee, to tear itself from the unresponsive lump of flesh in which it was housed. Barely aware of what she was doing, she turned and stumbled, almost fell, down the stairs. The air felt thick and heavy as soup, and yet at the same time vibrant and piercing, as if filled with a thousand screeching alarms.

"Ohmygod," she whispered, barely aware that she was doing it. "Ohmygodohmygodohmygodohmygod."

She couldn't think straight. Her only thought was to get away, to put as much distance as possible between herself and the terrible thing that had happened upstairs. She felt contaminated, poisoned by it. She rubbed and clawed at her arms, at her clothes, as if she was covered with crawling things that were biting her, trying to burrow under her skin.

At the bottom of the stairs she made instinctively for the light falling in fractured waves through the stippled glass of the front door. Her hand felt large and clumsy as she grasped the door handle, but somehow she managed to twist it, tug it open. She staggered outside, and the light hit her like a slap, causing her to spin around—or perhaps it was the world that was spinning. Next thing she knew her feet somehow became tangled together, and suddenly she was on the ground. She lay there sobbing.

When hands began to tug at her she screamed, but the voice that accompanied them was soft, soothing.

"Now, now, dear, it's all right. You're perfectly safe."

Holly looked up. Mrs. Bartholomew was crouching beside her, the sun turning her feathery grey hair into a halo of white fire.

"You've got to . . . need an ambulance," Holly spluttered.

"An ambulance?" Mrs. Bartholomew looked her over quickly. "Are you hurt? What happened?"

"Not me—him," Holly wailed.

"Who, dear?" asked Mrs. Bartholomew.

Holly's thoughts were racing, hurtling through her head at such a speed she could barely communicate. Forcing herself to think, to concentrate, she said, "You know him. His name's . . . Rob Norton. He used to . . . used to live here."

A strange look came over Mrs. Bartholomew's face. "Rob," she said. "So he's come back, has he?"

"Yes, but he's . . . hurt. Maybe dead. He had a knife and he. . . ." Unable to say the words she mimed stabbing herself in the throat.

Slowly Mrs. Bartholomew rose to her feet, wincing as her knees cracked. She took hold of Holly's hand, and with a tug she encouraged her to stand.

"Come with me, dear."

"Where?"

"I want to show you something."

Holly stood shakily, but resisted when Mrs. Bartholomew started to pull her back towards the open front door that Holly had just tumbled out of.

"No," she said, "I can't. He's in there. I don't want to see."

"It's quite all right," Mrs. Bartholomew said. "Come on, dear."

Such was the gentle authority in her voice that Holly allowed herself to be led. Inside, though, when Mrs. Bartholomew tried to persuade her to go upstairs, she shrank back again.

"No, I can't," she said again.

"All right, dear," Mrs. Bartholomew said gently. "All right, I'll go. You wait here."

She went upstairs. Holly waited, slumped against the wall—the one that Rob had told her used to be covered in sheets of chipboard made to look like real wood—panting as though she had just run a five-miler.

Eventually Mrs. Bartholomew appeared at the top of the stairs. "Come up, dear," she said.

Holly shook her head. "No."

"There's nothing to see," Mrs. Bartholomew said. "Trust me."

Such was the conviction in her tone, combined with a note of reassurance, that Holly sidled across to the foot of the stairs and crept up them like a timid child ready to bolt at the slightest sign of threat. When she reached the top Mrs. Bartholomew took her hand.

"It's all right," she said gently.

The door to the room in which Rob Norton had cut his own throat was ajar. Holly flinched, and almost cried out, as Mrs. Bartholomew stepped towards it, holding her at arm's length, and pushed it open.

The door swung back. The room was empty. Holly stared. There was no blood, no body. Everything was as it should be.

She felt her mind *flex*. That was honestly how it felt.

"I'm going mad," she whispered.

Mrs. Bartholomew shook her head. "No, dear, you're not."

"But he was *there*. I saw him. I spoke to him."

"I'm sure you did. But he died a long time ago. 1997 to be exact. He never got over his father's death, and he came back and killed himself in his childhood bedroom. I expect it was the only place where he felt safe."

"No." Holly shook her head. "He didn't feel safe here. He said it was the scariest place in the world."

Mrs. Bartholomew looked sad. "He's been back several times. Everyone who's lived here since Kath Norton moved out has seen him—spoken to him too. Only once, mind," she added hastily. "He never visits the same person twice."

Holly looked round the room. The pristine laptop, its cursor blinking languidly on the last word she had written. The sand-coloured carpet. The white ceiling, fresh and newly-painted. Her eyes moved past the window to the corner, where her exercise bike stood at an angle.

Who will *I* see at night, she thought. Who will *I* see standing there?

She didn't believe in that sort of thing. She didn't believe in ghosts. But from now on, whenever she came in here in the dark, she would see someone. She felt certain of it. She would see a tall, dark shape, standing there, watching her.

She knew that she would never be alone again.

EATING DISORDER

EATING DISORDER

Clive Decker was eating his breakfast when he felt a sudden, sharp pain in his lower bowel. He gasped so hard he sprayed half his mouthful of chewed-up toast over the kitchen table. His wife, Jo, sitting opposite him, glanced up from her *Daily Mail*, her face crinkling with distaste.

"What on earth are you doing?"

The stabbing pain came again, worse this time. Clive gave an unmanly squeak and doubled over, clutching his gut. Sitting to his left, his son Isaac, distracted from toying listlessly with his bowl of Cheerios, giggled.

Jo's voice hardened, as if she thought her husband's antics were nothing but an attention-seeking exercise. "What's the matter, Clive? Do you need a doctor?"

The pain ebbed slightly, enough for Clive to mutter, "Think I might . . . have a gallstone."

Before Jo could respond, the pain surged again, this time accompanied by a weighty, dragging sensation. Clive gripped the edge of the table and shoved himself backwards, his chair scraping over the expensively tiled floor with a screech that made Jo grit her teeth in dismay.

"Toilet," he grunted.

Sweating, head swimming, he stood up and staggered from the room. As he plunged along the hallway, he was pursued by seven-year-old Isaac's braying laughter and delighted exclamation:

"Daddy's going to poop his pants!"

Clive didn't poop his pants, but it was a close call. After it was over, after he had sweated and groaned and shuddered on the toilet for fifteen minutes, his eyes squeezed shut, his damp forehead resting on arms that were crossed tightly over his trembling lap, he cleaned himself up and rose weakly to his feet. Pulling up his trousers, he turned with some trepidation to examine what he had produced.

Could it have been a gallstone? Or even a kidney stone? He had no idea what such things looked like or how big they were, though he had heard that passing them could be excruciating. Peering into the toilet bowl, wrinkling his nose in distaste, he saw, among the mess of soiled toilet paper and human waste, what appeared to be an eye peering up at him.

He clapped a hand over his mouth to stifle a cry, then looked again. Immediately he realized that what he was looking at was not an eye but a transparent glass marble with a swirly blue core. He let out a whoop of breathy laughter. A marble! Not gallstones! And not (now that the mystery was solved he allowed himself to frame the thought that had lurked in the shadows of his mind) something nasty, like Crohn's disease, or the Big C.

A bloody marble! He bent to examine the object again. He was astonished that something so small, so insignificant, could have given him so much gyp. Now that it was no longer squeezing its way through his system he felt better. Almost back to normal, in fact. Ticketty boo.

And then a thought struck him.

Where had the marble come from?

He straightened up and stared at the patch of lemon-yellow wall above the toilet, thinking hard. Was it possible he had swallowed the thing without realizing it? In a drink maybe? Or a meal with lots of sauce, like the lamb curry he'd eaten a couple of days ago?

He couldn't imagine doing such a thing. Couldn't imagine something the size of . . . well, of a marble, swirling down his gullet without touching the sides. He always chewed his food thoroughly; he wasn't in the habit of opening his throat and gulping it down like a snake. And he sipped his drinks. Even when he'd been out running he took his time with his post-exercise water, swirling it round his mouth before swallowing.

He pondered on the puzzle for several minutes, but in the end decided he would just have to chalk it down as one of life's little mysteries. No doubt there was some simple explanation; perhaps the answer might even come to him in a blinding flash of inspiration. But until it did he'd try to forget it.

After all, it had almost certainly been a one-off, and when all was said and done, it had caused him no *real* harm, had it?

Flushing the toilet and consigning the mystery to oblivion, Clive headed back to the kitchen to finish his breakfast.

When he stepped through the door of the flat that evening, after a tiring day discussing export contracts at work, the first thing he heard was the crash of the piano lid.

The second was Isaac's raised voice:

"I don't want to! It's stupid! I hate it and I hate you too!"

Dropping his briefcase Clive marched down the hallway and burst into the dining room on his left.

"What the hell's going on here?" he bellowed.

Isaac and his piano teacher, Enika, were sitting side by side on the piano stool in front of the Danemann, which Clive's father had bought at auction back in the 1970s. Isaac was red-faced, rigid with aggression, while Enika was straight-backed, unruffled, her hands resting placidly in her lap.

At Clive's voice, Isaac spun round so quickly he reminded Clive of the Tasmanian Devil from the old *Looney Tunes* cartoons. Enika turned more slowly, her movements fluid and graceful, and fixed Clive with her pale green eyes.

Enika was from Iceland, and although she was twenty years younger than Clive, her shimmering blonde hair, flawless complexion and almost preternaturally composed manner never failed to fluster him. In comparison to her ethereal, sprite-like beauty he always felt like a gnarled and uncouth troll.

As ever, she was unfailingly and sweetly polite. "Isaac and I were just having a little disagreement. Weren't we, Isaac?"

Isaac glowered at her. Sullenly he said, "I don't *like* the piano. I don't *want* to learn it. It's stupid."

Clive struggled to control his temper. Recently Isaac's behaviour had been getting worse. The boy was becoming increasingly aggressive, disruptive and uncooperative, both at home and at school. Frankly he was turning into a pain in the arse—though, of course, Jo didn't see it like that. In her opinion Isaac was creative, inquisitive and sensitive, and the reason for his behaviour lay not with the boy himself but with the inadequacy of the educational system for failing to give him the stimulation he craved. Clive thought he and Jo just needed to be tougher with their son; needed to teach him some proper manners, some respect. When, though, after Isaac had thrown one particularly violent tantrum, he suggested the boy might benefit from an occasional clip round the ear, Jo had looked at him with loathing and horror.

"You'd *hit* our son?" she said.

Clive had laughed. "You make it sound like abuse."

"It *is* abuse. All violence is abuse."

He snorted. "Come off it, Jo! I'm talking about a cuff round the head or a slap on the leg, not broken bones and black eyes."

His words, though, had fallen on deaf ears. Indeed, they had only served to widen the gulf that had opened between him and Jo since Isaac's birth. Now, whenever he tried to reprimand the boy, Jo pulled him up on it; several times she'd even accused him of bullying Isaac. Clive couldn't believe she couldn't see what was happening. How was she not aware that their child was becoming an obnoxious, uncontrollable brat?

God only knew what Enika must think of them. Clive felt an urge to apologise for being an inadequate parent, for being one third of a dysfunctional family.

Instead, in as calm a voice as he could muster, he said, "Why do you think it's stupid, Isaac?"

Isaac scowled. "It just is."

Clive knew he ought to be able to handle this situation with the minimum of fuss, knew he ought to be able to dismantle Isaac's childish outbursts with charm, logic and erudition. But the boy's stubbornness was like an impenetrable wall; there was no way round it, no way over it. He felt a sudden wash of despair. What had his life become? But he forced a smile and said, "Grandpa doesn't think it's stupid. And you like the tunes that Grandpa plays at Christmas, don't you?"

Isaac shrugged.

"Of course you do. That's why you wanted to learn the piano in the first place. So that you could play tunes like Grandpa does. So that you could be as *clever* as Grandpa."

Isaac's scowl deepened. "But I can't play like Grandpa."

"No," Clive said, "not yet. But the only reason Grandpa can play so well is because he had someone like Enika to teach him when *he* was a boy, and because he practiced and practiced and practiced. So if you're very good and practice really hard you *will* be as good as Grandpa one day. But it won't happen quickly. It will take time. You'll have to work at it. And that's why Enika's here. So she can teach you."

Isaac stuck out his bottom lip. "I don't want Enika to teach me."

"But if Enika doesn't teach you, how will you learn?"

"I want Grandpa to teach me."

Clive gritted his teeth briefly. "But Grandpa can't teach you. He's busy. And he lives a long way away."

"Well, I don't want Enika. Enika's stupid."

"Isaac!" Clive snapped. "That is very rude. Apologise at once."

"Really, it's all right," Enika said.

"It's *not* all right," Clive retorted, before realising he'd snapped at Enika too. Raising a hand he said, "I'm sorry, Enika, but Isaac needs to learn some manners. Now say sorry to Enika, Isaac, or. . . ." He faltered, wondering what punishment he could implement that Jo would back him up on.

As if the mere thought of his wife had conjured her into being, Jo suddenly said from behind him, "What's going on here?"

Clive instantly felt as if he was standing on shifting sands. It was always how he felt when he criticized Isaac in front of Jo. Instinctively he knew she would take the boy's side against him. Almost aggressively he said, "Isaac was rude to Enika. And he's being very uncooperative."

"Really," Enika said, "it's all right."

Although Clive knew Enika was only trying to keep the peace, her words were all that Jo needed to exonerate her child. With a sinking heart Clive saw a smirk of triumph appear on her face.

"I expect he's just tired," she said. "He's had a long day."

"We've all had a long day," Clive muttered, but Jo ignored him.

Her voice softening, she said to Isaac, "*Are* you tired, little man? Do you want to do your lesson another time?"

Isaac nodded mutely.

"What do you mean, *another time?* He can't just skip lessons willy nilly," Clive said, but Jo gave him a scathing look.

"No need to be such a Nazi about this, Clive. Isaac's tired. It's only one little piano lesson."

"It's the thin end of the wedge," Clive said, and immediately thought: *My God, what have I become?* To deflect any riposte from Jo he added quickly, "Plus, it's Enika's time. If she's prepared to make the effort to come all this way—"

"Enika will be paid in full, of course." Jo turned to Enika. "That's all right with you, isn't it?"

"Yes, of course."

"As for you, little man, why don't you lie on the settee and Mummy will bring you some milk. Would you like that?"

"Yes, thank you, Mummy," said Isaac sweetly.

Clive's blood was boiling. But he knew any protests he made would seem petty and pointless. He glared at Isaac as his son sidled past him. Isaac smirked. In the doorway he paused and turned.

"My daddy pooped his pants this morning," he said to Enika.

Enika's eyes widened slightly. Clive blushed a deep red.

Kill me now, he thought.

Two hours later Clive was vegging out in front of *Masterchef*, cradling a glass of Merlot, when the air was split by a piercing scream.

"Fuck!" he said as his arm jerked and wine slopped into the crotch of his best blue suit. Putting the glass on a nearby shelf he jumped to his feet and turned towards the open door leading out into the flat's long hallway.

"You two all right?" he called.

There was a moment of silence—then Isaac began to scream again. It wasn't a wordless shriek this time, but a stream of words repeated over and over: "I want it I want it I want it I want it I want it *I want it!*"

"Fuck's sake!" Clive muttered and stomped along the hallway to the bathroom, from behind the door of which he could hear not only his son's shrieking voice, but splashing water and various soggy thuds and splats as if wet objects were being thrown at the walls.

The instant Clive stepped through the door, his shoeless foot came down on a sopping towel from which runnels of water were seeping outwards along the gaps between the wooden floorboards. As he lifted his foot with a grimace, water dripping from his sock, he saw a wet flannel slumped on the floor beside the sink, which had clearly impacted with the wall and slithered down it, and a plastic bottle of strawberry-scented shampoo leaking red gel onto the floor beside the toilet.

Isaac, sitting naked in the bath, was slapping his hands down in the water and screeching. Jo, wet and bedraggled, was crouching beside the bath, trying in vain to soothe her son.

"Having fun?" Clive asked, which earned him a glance of contempt from his wife.

"Instead of making smart remarks, it would help if you could look for what he's lost," she snapped.

"What *has* he lost?"

"His boat."

"Which boat?"

"The boat he always has in the bath with him."

Clive had no idea what Jo was talking about, but then bath time had always been her domain.

"What does this boat look like?"

She made an exasperated sound and held her thumb and forefinger three inches apart. "It's yellow. Made of plastic. About so big."

Clive surveyed the devastation his son had wrought, wincing at the water still surging up the sides of the bath and slopping onto the floor as Isaac pistoned his legs in his unceasing, red-faced rage.

"For Christ's sake!" he said. "Why is this boat such a big deal?"

"It's a big deal because he *wants* it."

"Yeah, well, I want a Ferrari, but I'm not going to throw a wobbler because I can't have one."

Jo rounded on him, her fists clenched bloodless, her teeth bared. Water was dripping off her blonde ringlets and trickling down her face. "If you can't contribute anything useful to this situation, why don't you just—" She leaned closer, her voice dropping to a hiss so that Isaac couldn't hear "—*piss off!*"

As if picking up on the antagonism between his parents, Isaac gave an extra loud scream and scooped a double handful of warm, soapy water up and out of the bath, drenching both his parents. Jo spluttered as water hit her full in the face and spattered on the floor. Clive, his trousers soaked, lurched backwards.

"Fucking hell!"

Isaac looked neither repentant nor alarmed by his father's anger. He plunged his hands into the bath again, as though intending to repeat the action. Before he could, Clive lunged forward, slithering a little on the wet floor, and grabbed both his arms.

"Don't you dare!" he shouted. "Don't you bloody dare!"

This time Isaac did look shocked. Not scared exactly, but outraged that Clive had had the temerity to reprimand him. He glared into his father's face. "*Go away! I don't want you!*"

Clive shook him hard. *So* hard that Isaac's head flopped back and forth violently enough to make Isaac bite his tongue.

Instantly the boy wailed again—this time with pain. Clive immediately felt ashamed, but snapped, "For goodness' sake, don't make such a fuss. And stop behaving like a brat!"

Suddenly Jo flew at Clive, digging her nails in to his arm, clawing at his face. *"What the hell are you doing? Get off him! Leave him alone!"*

Unable to defend himself, Clive had no option but to let Isaac go. The boy flopped back into the bath with a splash, his arms red where Clive had gripped them.

"You animal!" Jo screamed. *"You bloody animal!"*

Isaac lolled in the bath, crying, Clive's fingerprints visible on his white arms. After yelling at Clive, Jo turned back to her son, wrapped her arms around him and began to coo softly into his ear. For a moment Clive was confused. Was Jo's response justified? *Had* he gone too far? But then he took a step back and his mind seemed to clear a little.

"For God's sake, Jo," he said, "I hardly touched the boy. Can't you see he's only playing up because you're allowing him to? I mean, throwing a tantrum over a stupid toy, making all this mess . . . it's ridiculous."

Jo gave no indication she'd heard him. She continued to kneel on the wet floor, murmuring softly to her weeping son. Hovering behind her, his socks and trousers wet, Clive wondered whether to keep trying to get his point across or simply sidle away. Tentatively he said, "Look, we need to talk about this. It's important."

In a low voice, still not looking at him, she said, "Just go away, Clive. Haven't you done enough damage?"

"Yes, Daddy," Isaac said, his voice calm now. He looked at Clive over Jo's shoulder. "Go away. We don't want you anymore."

Clive was listening to account manager George Struthers' proposal to maximise profits in the Scandinavian export market when he felt a prickling in his gut. He tensed. Although not exactly painful, it felt as if something had come alive inside him. It felt as if some spiny-bodied creature, which had been curled into a ball, was slowly uncoiling itself.

He cleared his throat nervously and shifted in his seat, hoping the feeling would go away. It didn't. He thought of the marble incident from the day before. Could this feeling be related in some way? But he'd felt fine for the rest of the day afterwards, physically at least, so why should it flare up again now? Perhaps the marble had caused some inflammation, which was only now making itself known? Maybe if he sat up a little straighter in his seat—

Before he could, pain erupted inside him. A clawing, stabbing, searing pain, as if barbed wire was being dragged through his intestines.

Clive cried out and slumped over the boardroom table. For a split-second he was aware of the sudden shock among his colleagues seated around him, the collective intake of breath, the fact that George Struthers had abruptly stopped talking. Then the threat of unconsciousness came surging in like a wave at high tide, attempting to blot out his senses. Through a dimming haze he sensed blurred shapes inclining themselves in his direction as the other eleven people around the table turned towards him.

He was still clinging to the remnants of consciousness when the nearest of those people, Kelly Wilkins, leaned across and touched his arm. She spoke to him, and although her voice was like mushy static beneath the pounding in his head, he knew she was asking him what was wrong, whether he was okay.

Clive wanted to answer, but he couldn't work out how. The only thing that seemed linked to his mind was the pain that occupied his body. Everything else around him seemed to be feeding that pain—the babbling voices, the hands tugging him upright, the juxtaposition of bright light and sooty greyness occupying his vision, like torch beams flashing back and forth through swirling smog.

The pain shifted, moved lower, dragging him down like a ball and chain around the ankle of a murder victim in a lake. All at once, with the clarity of panic, Clive realized what would happen, right here in front of all his colleagues, if he didn't do something about it!

Through sheer force of will he clawed his way through the murk, attempting to regain control of his faculties. He opened his mouth to speak—and immediately felt a hard edge being pressed against his lower lip, cold liquid sluicing across his tongue and down his throat.

Choking he turned his head away, flapping a hand in front of him, feeling it connect with something hard. There was a splash, a clunk, a cry of protest— he must have knocked the glass of water flying.

The babble of voices clarified, words overlapping. ". . . soaking wet/ think he's coming round/anyone called an ambulance?/looks so pale/heart attack, do you think?/give him some air. . . ."

The swirling shapes around him slowly came into focus. Faces. Bobbing like balloons. Blank as masks.

A voice. Imperious. Drilling into his head. "Clive, it's George. Are you back with us? Do you know where you are?"

"Toilet," Clive muttered. "Need . . . got to . . . toilet."

"What did he say?/wants what?/think he needs to be sick. . . ."

"You just hang in there, Clive." George again. "An ambulance is on its way."

The pain had become an unbearable weight, clamouring to get out. Clive felt like he was about to give birth. With an almighty effort he pushed himself upright.

"Need. The. Toilet. Now."

He enunciated each word with care; he spoke as loudly, as clearly as he could. Even so the floating masks twisted into bewildered and bewildering shapes. He put out his hands to push through them, felt his arms, his fingers, being grabbed, squeezed.

"Mark, you take him/make sure he/Ryan, take his other arm/careful, don't/do you think. . . ."

Clive, blinking, trying to focus, trying to remain afloat above the grinding, clawing pain in his lower abdomen, felt himself guided, propelled, through and along what he could only assume were doors, corridors. Although he had no real sense of his body, he nevertheless felt as though he were trying to hold himself together, trying to hold himself *in*.

There came an echoey clatter, the impression of hard light, hard floors.

"Toilet," he muttered, as if identifying the location would make it real.

A mushy, buzzing reply: "Spot on, mate. You can throw up to your heart's content in a minute. Let's just get you into a cubicle."

How Clive did it he wasn't sure. But the next thing he knew he was sitting on a toilet seat, trousers and underpants round his ankles, body bent almost double. It was yesterday all over again. The sweating, the swooning, the pain. When the awful, grinding weight inside him came gushing out, hot and tearing and furious, he thought he would turn inside out. He gripped his head in his hands as if to anchor it, the agony in his lower body so massive, so excoriating, he couldn't even scream.

At last, though, it was over, leaving him in the pulsing aftermath, mouth open and gasping like a fish stranded on a rock. He was drenched in sweat. He probably stank. Certainly what had come out of him did.

Opening his eyes, he raised a hand in front of his face and saw how much it was trembling. But that was all right; he was just relieved to find he was still in one piece. The pounding in his head was getting worse—was his heart about to explode? Then he realised the pounding was outside his body. He looked up, saw the door of the cubicle shuddering.

"Clive? You all right in there? Speak to me, mate."

Clive swallowed and his ears popped, everything suddenly becoming clearer—including his thoughts. Now that it was out of him, whatever *it* was, he felt the pain receding, drawing back, a frothing wave retreating from a slick and shining beach.

"Clive?" The voice came again. "If you can hear me, keep back from the door. I'm going to kick it in."

"No," Clive croaked. He cleared his throat, tried again. "No, I'm fine. I'm . . . feeling better."

"You sure?"

"Yeah, it . . . must have been something I ate. I'm feeling a lot better now."

Relief made whoever was on the other side of the door—Ryan?—try a tentative joke. "Ordinarily I'd say better out than in, mate, but from where I'm standing . . ." He blew air from his mouth, making a "phew" sound.

"Yeah. Sorry about that. Look, you go. I'll clean myself up. I'll see you back in the office."

Ryan sounded uncertain. "Well . . . all right. But if you're not there in five minutes I'll be back to check if you're okay."

Clive heard Ryan's footsteps cross the floor and the door open and close. Once he was alone he let out a long, shuddering breath and slumped forward until his forehead was resting on his knees. Although the pain in his gut was now receding, the experience had exhausted him. He thought if he closed his eyes now he would probably sleep for hours, right where he was sitting.

He might even have done so too if it hadn't been for the fact that Ryan would be back to check on him in five minutes. Instead, therefore, he braced his watery legs by placing his hands flat on the walls on either side of him, and raised his buttocks from the toilet seat with a groan. Fearfully he peered into the bowl between his legs, half-expecting to see blood and maybe worse spattered up the sides of the white porcelain.

He didn't. What he saw was brown, not red, and though it was semi-liquid and stank to high heaven, he let out a sigh of relief.

Then he glimpsed something pale, hard-edged, bobbing in the muck and he tensed again. What was that? A bone?

He peered again—and gasped. No, not a bone. It was, if anything, far stranger, more disturbing than that.

What Clive was looking at was the prow of a small, yellow, plastic boat.

Although the darkness was oppressive, making his eyes ache with tiredness and his head feel stuffed with cotton wool, Clive couldn't sleep. Next to him, a good ten inches of space between their respective backs, Jo was having no such problems. Her breathing, intertwined with the patter of rain against the window, was deep and even. Under other circumstances Clive might have found the sounds an aid to sleep, but right now he was so tense that whenever a vehicle swished by on the wet road outside it sounded to him like the angry hissing of a cat.

Eventually he swung out of bed, wincing as the mattress creaked beneath his weight. This time when a vehicle went by he imagined the night was shushing him. As he stood up he placed a hand on his belly, as if expecting it to be tender, but the only discomfort came from the fact that he'd been tensing his stomach ever since that morning's episode, fearful of another onslaught. After embarrassing himself at work (his colleagues had shown nothing but concern for him for the rest of the day, but Clive felt sure they'd been discussing him—probably even sniggering about him—behind his back) he'd retreated to his office and kept up a pretence of being busy. His mind, though, had been churning, the same questions circling and buzzing like wasps butting against a window:

How had the boat got inside him? How had he swallowed it without realizing?

There were a couple of possible answers he could think of, the most feasible being that he'd chugged it down while sleepwalking, possibly with the aid of a big glass of water or juice. Such a scenario seemed unlikely, but not as unlikely as the only other explanation he could come up with, which was that he'd been drugged, and then, in a highly suggestible state, had been made to swallow, first, the marble, then the boat.

Even if this second option *were* possible, why would anyone do that to him? What would be the point? Could it have been done as a prank, to embarrass him? Or had someone (Jo?) genuinely been trying to poison him or choke him? No, he couldn't believe that. It was beyond crazy. Even if someone did want him dead there were a thousand and one easier and more reliable ways to go about it.

All the same, lying in bed, the darkness pressing in on him, his thoughts shooting off in wild directions, he couldn't help but recall the stonily knowing look on Isaac's face when he had regarded Clive over Jo's shoulder in the bathroom the previous evening; couldn't help but hear an echo of the words his son had spoken in his eerily calm voice: *Go away. We don't want you anymore.*

Padding along the hallway to the kitchen, pouring a glass of milk and glugging it down by the light of the open fridge, Clive wondered what on earth he was thinking. Musing on whether his wife might be doing this to him was bad enough, but was he honestly now contemplating the possibility that his seven-year-old son had something to do with his . . . affliction? I mean, what did he think Isaac was, for God's sake? Some sort of devil child, like Damien from *The Omen*?

Feeling guilty of the route his thoughts had taken, Clive finished his milk, tiptoed out of the kitchen into the flat's main corridor, then turned not back towards his own bed but in the opposite direction, towards Isaac's room. He felt a sudden compulsion to check up on his son, to silently reconnect with him, watch him sleep for a few moments and remind himself how innocent, how vulnerable, how easily malleable his little boy still was.

Pausing outside Isaac's door he listened. Out here in the hallway the rain beating down outside sounded like nothing but a faint, steady crackle of background static. Aside from that, all was silent. Clive opened the door of his son's room and stepped inside. The first thing he saw was Isaac's slowly revolving night light, casting a dim, swirling pattern of stars and spaceships across the walls and ceiling. The second thing was Isaac himself. The boy was sitting up in bed, staring at Clive, his eyes glowing yellow.

Clive's body lurched in shock, the movement seeming to dislodge an avalanche of coldness, which rippled through him, making him shudder. His instinctive response was to step back out of the room and pull the door quickly closed to provide a barrier between himself and his son. But resisting the temptation, he said hesitantly, "Isaac? Are you okay?" When the boy failed to respond he added softly, "It's just me. It's Daddy."

Isaac remained motionless and silent. Peeling his hand from around the door handle, Clive stepped further into the room. Isaac's yellow eyes seemed to slide to follow his movements. But eerie though the effect was, Clive had now recovered enough of his wits to realize it wasn't his son's eyes that were glowing, but the light of the night light reflected in them.

"Isaac?" he said again. "Can you hear me?" Still receiving no answer he padded closer to the bed. He was relieved that Isaac's head didn't turn slowly to track him. Instead the boy continued to stare at the door through which Clive had entered the room—or appeared to.

He's asleep, Clive thought. *Asleep with his eyes open.* And indeed, when he got close enough to the bed he saw how slack Isaac's face was, how lacking in intent or expression.

Clive put a hand on Isaac's shoulder. He was surprised at how thin, how fragile, the boy seemed, which made him further realize how little physical contact he had with his son, how seldom he held him, hugged him.

Was that his fault or Jo's? Did she deliberately keep Isaac to herself out of selfishness or jealousy? Clive wasn't sure, though the relationship between himself and his own father had never been a particularly tactile one. Was he, therefore, subconsciously continuing that tradition? Should he make more of an effort to bond with Isaac? He'd never felt inclined to pamper the boy, because Jo seemed to do more than enough for the both of them. Plus Isaac's recent behaviour had discouraged Clive from showing affection towards him—but perhaps that was the problem? Perhaps Isaac played up in a bid for some fatherly attention? Clive decided he would talk it over with Jo—though not now. Tomorrow. When his head was clearer and he wasn't so befuddled by tiredness.

"Come on," he said softly, applying gentle pressure to Isaac's shoulder, pushing him down towards the bed. "Lie down, Isaac. Go to sleep." Although he didn't know why, he expected Isaac to offer resistance, but the boy seemed relaxed, compliant. With a soft exhalation of breath, he lay down and closed his eyes.

"Good lad," Clive said, and felt his own eyes unexpectedly tear up. "Good boy."

Standing in the queue for his pre-work coffee next morning, Clive thought about how and why his best-laid plans had gone awry, and what he could do to redeem the situation.

An hour ago he'd been full of good intentions, determined to turn over a new leaf. "Morning, gang!" he'd said cheerily as he entered the kitchen. He was barely deterred when Jo and Isaac, at the breakfast table before him as usual, ignored him. Even Isaac's reaction when Clive ruffled his hair as he strode past to take his place at the table—the boy flinching, as if he expected his father to deliver the cuff round the ear that Clive had suggested to Jo might bring their son into line, then scowling and pointedly smoothing his hair down with the palms of his hands—drew no more than an affectionate chuckle from Clive, as if he and Isaac were sharing a well-rehearsed joke.

Before sitting down Clive leaned across to kiss Jo on the cheek. His wife, reading her paper, reacted much as Isaac had—by flinching, and then rearing back from Clive's puckered lips, an expression of surprise, even outrage, on her face.

"What the hell are you doing?" she said.

Clive's grin never left his face. "I'm just saying good morning."

She narrowed her eyes. "Why? What's wrong with you? What have you done?"

"Nothing." Clive's smile faltered only slightly. "I'm just . . . in a good mood, that's all. I've been doing some thinking."

Jo looked suspicious. "About what?"

Clive sat down, flashing Isaac another smile. Isaac stared back at him.

"I just thought Isaac and I ought to spend more time together, that I should take him out somewhere—just the two of us."

"Why?"

"Well, because . . . we don't do it often enough. It would be good for us to have some father-son bonding time. Plus it would give you a break."

"I don't *need* a break," said Jo icily. "As it happens I *like* spending time with my son."

"Well, so do I—or at least I would if I got the chance. And I didn't mean a break, I just meant . . . well, we all like a bit of time to ourselves now and then, don't we? Just to do our own thing?"

Jo glared at him. "No. We don't. Some of us aren't as selfish as others."

Although Clive's smile stayed in place, it felt fixed to his face now, stiff as a mask. Trying to keep the irritation from his voice, he said, "It's not a question of being selfish. It's a question of balance, of managing your time. You and Isaac spend almost all your time together, and I just thought—"

"Is that how you see it?" she said harshly. "All our time? He's at school all day, and I'm at work. The *small* amount of time we do spend together is very precious to me."

"As it should be," said Clive reasonably. "Look, I don't know why you're getting so irate. All I want is to spend more time with my son. Is that so bad? I thought you'd be pleased."

Before Jo could respond, Isaac said, "I don't want you."

Clive turned towards Isaac. Over his untouched breakfast his son was staring at him fiercely.

"You see?" said Jo, quietly triumphant.

Clive's head whipped back in her direction again, and suddenly the anger spiked inside him.

"See what?" he said. "See how you've turned him against me? My own son? What's wrong with you, Jo? Why have you become so petty, so jealous, so . . . twisted up inside? All I want is for us to be a family. The *three* of us. A happy, healthy, *together* family. Whereas what you seem to want is to take sides. To make Isaac dependent on you." His lips curled in a sneer. "You're poisoning him. That's why he's turning out like he is."

"Turning out like he is?" Her bark of laughter was a knowing rasp rather than an expression of humour. "*Now* you're showing your true colours. You only want to be alone with Isaac so you can manipulate him."

"Like I've just accused you of doing, you mean?"

She rolled her eyes as though his comment was beneath contempt. "Let's ask Isaac wants he wants, shall we?"

"Well, of *course* he'll agree with you."

"Yes, because *I* treat him like a human being instead of a troublesome possession. I talk to him, *listen* to him."

"That's not fair and you know it."

Jo deliberately turned her head away and smiled sweetly at Isaac.

"You know what Mummy and Daddy have just been talking about, don't you, Isaac?"

He nodded.

"Daddy wants to take you out, to somewhere where it'll just be you and him. Would you like that?"

Isaac shook his head.

"Look, I know it's not something you're used to, Isaac," Clive said, trying to sound gentle, encouraging, "but we'd have fun, I promise. We could go to the park or the cinema. We could get chips in—"

"I don't want you," Isaac said, his voice low, his eyes a glare of hatred. Then, so abruptly that it made Clive jump, he started to screech. *"I don't want you! I don't want you! I don't want you!"*

He swept his bowl of cereal off the table. It shattered on the floor, milk and Cheerios going everywhere.

Clive stared at his son, aghast. Jo smirked.

"I think that's fairly conclusive, don't you?" she said.

The memory was still vivid in Clive's mind as he reached the front of the queue. According to her name badge the barista who smiled at him was called Alice. Although pretty, she was thin to the point of frailty, her corn-coloured hair tied into plaits.

"Large decaff latte?" she said.

Clive knew it was pathetic, but he couldn't help feeling a swell of pride that "Alice" remembered not only him, but also what he drank.

"That's the one," he said, smiling at her, and reached for his wallet as she passed his order on to the coffee-making team and rang his purchase up on the till.

But his wallet wasn't there. The inside pocket of his jacket was empty. Puzzled Clive tried his other pockets, to no avail.

"Shit," he said.

Alice looked at him expectantly, a vague smile on her lips.

"I've lost my wallet," he told her. "It should be in my pocket, but it isn't."

Her eyes flickered briefly to the queue behind him, which Clive imagined was already becoming restless. "Oh dear," she said blandly. "You could pay by cash? It's only £2.65."

Grimacing, he delved into his pockets, almost certain that they didn't contain even that amount of money.

Sure enough, his pockets yielded a measly 72p in loose change.

"Sorry about this," he said. "My money's in my wallet, which is God knows where. I could pay you tomorrow?"

Alice looked vaguely apologetic. "The tills would be wrong. I'll just have to cancel your order."

"Couldn't you put a note in the till? I mean, I come in here every morning. You must know I'm good for it?"

She shook her head. "Sorry, it's not up to me. I could ring head office?"

She cast a more meaningful glance at the queue behind Clive to express how inconvenient that would be.

Flushed with anger and embarrassment, Clive muttered, "All right, don't bother. It doesn't matter." He stomped out of the shop, certain that everyone was not only staring at him, but smirking at his humiliation. By the time he reached his car his forehead was damp with sweat and his body felt prickly-hot inside his suit. Adjusting the aircon to blast out cool air, he pulled aggressively away from the kerb, wondering where his wallet had gone.

It can't have been stolen. He must have left it somewhere—but where? He couldn't remember taking it out of his jacket last night. Maybe he'd left it on the counter of the bagel shop where he'd bought lunch yesterday? He'd have to ring them when he got to work. And if it wasn't there, then he'd have to contact his bank.

He was crawling through traffic on the narrow road beside the sprawl of buildings that constituted the hospital when he felt the first cramp in his stomach. He gasped and would have stamped on the brake if the car hadn't already been almost stationary. Twenty seconds later, just as he was starting to hope the cramp had been nothing but a bit of wind brought on by stress, the pain came again, and this time it made him cry out. It was so agonising, so all encompassing, that it felt as though his body had suddenly become filled with burning coals from his throat to the base of his bowel.

He jerked forward, his head thumping the steering wheel. His vision swam and he thought he was going to be sick; despite the cool air his skin began to ooze sweat, which instantly turned clammy. Barely aware of what he was doing he pulled into the side of the road, his wheels scraping the kerb, and came to a lurching halt on double yellows. The car behind him blared its horn, but to Clive it sounded like nothing but the roar of his own pain. Fumbling his door open, he blundered across the street, heading for the hospital's main entrance. He was only half-way there when a flock of black birds seemed to erupt out of the fire inside him and engulfed his mind.

White.

White that hurt his eyes.

Sounds around him. Clattering. Voices. The shuffle-squeak of footsteps.

Slowly he became aware that he was flat on his back, a pillow beneath his head.

"He's coming round," someone said.

A face looming to his right. Plump. Smiling. Female.

"Back with us, are you, Mr. Decker?" the face said.

"Where am I?"

His voice was a whisper, but it still seemed to reverberate inside him, to hurt deep down. He winced.

"You're in hospital. You've had an operation. Try not to move."

Suddenly it all came back to him. The coffee shop. The pain in his stomach. Everything going black before he could reach the hospital.

"Was it the wallet?" he asked, each syllable causing a fresh vibration of pain in his core. "Was it inside me?"

The nurse hesitated, torn between providing comfort and sheer curiosity. Her voice hushed, as if she didn't want anyone to overhear, she asked, "How did it get there?"

He closed his eyes. His thoughts were turning over in his head. It felt as though they had been doing so, subconsciously, all the time he was under the knife.

"Lost things," he whispered, opening his eyes again.

The nurse leaned closer, close enough for him to smell the fruity scent of the shampoo she used. Like kiwi fruit. Or melons.

"Things get lost," he said. "Disappear. Then they turn up inside me."

"Things?"

"A marble. A toy boat. My wallet."

"You mean this has happened before?"

His innards were throbbing, pulsing, as if with anger that he was giving away their secrets.

"Yes."

"I see."

From her voice, it was clear she thought he was doing this to himself. That he was disturbed in some way.

"It's not me," he said. "I don't swallow the things or . . . put them inside me. They just appear."

"Like magic, you mean?" Her voice was a studied monotone, as if she was being careful not to let on what she was really thinking.

"No," he whispered, and frowned in an effort to express himself. "I don't know how they get there. They just do. But it's not me."

"All right," she said, and however much she tried not to, she couldn't help but sound patronizing. "Don't worry about it now. Just relax. Try and get some sleep. We'll take you up to the ward in a little while. I'll arrange for someone to talk to you."

"I'm not mad," Clive said. "I don't need a psychiatrist, if that's what you're thinking."

"I know you're not mad," she said as if the matter had never been in doubt. "Now try not to worry."

"You think I'm bonkers, don't you?"

The next morning Clive was half-sitting up in bed, his shoulders and head supported by pillows. At his bedside, one leg crossed over the other, was an attractive woman in her forties with glossy chestnut hair and healthily-tanned skin that looked as though it came not from a sunbed or out of a bottle, but from a relaxing week or two in the Mediterranean. She wore a crisp white blouse, a charcoal-grey skirt and dark sheer mesh stockings or tights that made a faint *zizzy* sound whenever she adjusted position. She managed to convey an air both of approachability and extreme efficiency.

Introducing herself as Dr. Meyer, she had asked Clive if he felt up to a brief chat, and when he had said yes she had pulled the curtains around the bed in three brief strokes before sitting down.

She laughed now, tossing back her head as if he had made a particularly funny joke. "I wouldn't describe anyone as 'bonkers', Mr. Decker."

"So what's the phrase you use nowadays? What's the politically correct terminology? Mentally challenged?"

She pursed her lips and scrutinized him, albeit not coldly. "Mental illness is a huge umbrella that covers a variety of conditions. Some are relatively mild, others extremely severe."

"So what condition have I got—in your opinion?"

"Well, that's jumping the gun rather. I'm simply here for an initial chat."

"You're here to assess me, you mean?"

"If you like. But please don't feel as though I have any pre-conceptions. I've read your medical report and I'm interested in your version of events leading up to your admittance yesterday."

"You mean you want me to tell you how those things got inside me?"

She paused. "I know you underwent surgery to remove a wallet—your own wallet—from your digestive system, where it was causing a blockage that could have proved hazardous to your health. But I understand you also told one of the nurses in Recovery that this wasn't the first item you'd ingested?"

"I didn't ingest them." When she half-raised her eyebrows, he added, "And I didn't . . . stick them up myself either. They just . . . appeared inside me."

She shifted in her seat, her tights making that *zizzy* noise again as her legs rubbed together. Gently she said, "Forgive me, Mr. Decker, but you do know that's impossible, don't you?"

Clive felt a surge of anger, but forced himself to smile. "Of course I do. I'm not delusional. I know how crazy this sounds. And believe me, I've wondered myself how those things got inside me. I've wondered whether I swallowed them in my sleep, or even whether I was drugged and *made* to swallow them."

"By who?"

"I've no idea. To be honest, I'm just speculating. Don't you think, though, that if I *had* swallowed those things, particularly the wallet, there'd be evidence of some sort? That I'd have a sore throat, at least?"

"Well, I don't know. I'm no expert."

"The surgeon who removed the wallet showed it to me. It was pretty much intact. It hadn't been crushed or damaged in any way. He told me he was baffled, that it was as though I'd been cut open and the wallet placed where they found it. But I hadn't been. It just appeared." Before Dr. Meyer could comment he raised his hands. "And yes, I *do* know that's impossible, but those are the facts."

Dr. Meyer regarded him for a moment. Then she said, "I understand the other items you . . . the other items that appeared inside you belonged to your son?"

Clive nodded.

"And were they things that your son particularly treasured?"

Clive snorted. "You mean was I devouring my son's belongings to show my . . . what? Dominance over him? Control over him? Or perhaps you think I was doing it to punish him?"

"Does he *need* punishing?" she asked.

Clive shook his head. "I know what you're getting at. But this isn't about power. The items themselves aren't significant. The first was a marble. No one even knew it was missing until I . . . until it came out of me. The second was a toy boat that Isaac plays with in the bath. But the third was my own wallet. So what's your psychological take on that? Was that my protest against capitalism? My way of consuming my own identity?"

Dr. Meyer sat with pursed lips and a vaguely smug expression. Instead of responding to Clive's tirade, she asked, "Have your wife and son been to visit you since you were admitted to hospital yesterday, Mr. Decker?"

"What business is that of yours?"

Her friendliness, her sheer *reasonableness*, was beginning to get on his nerves. Smiling she said, "Your response to my question seems unnecessarily aggressive. Why is that?"

"You know exactly why it is," Clive said. "It's because you're trying to twist the situation to fit your own daft theories. You know my wife and son haven't been to visit me, so you automatically assume there's something wrong between us. But for your information I was unconscious most of yesterday, and by the time I was in any fit state to receive visitors it was past Isaac's bedtime. So they're coming today. Very soon, in fact. Satisfied?"

Dr. Meyer's smile couldn't have been warmer. "Perfectly."

"Can I ask you something, Jo?"

Jo paused on the threshold of their bedroom, her back to him. "What?"

Clive's throat was dry. Did he really want to know the answer to the question he was about to ask? Probably not, but he asked it anyway.

"Do you still love me?"

He saw his wife's shoulders stiffen, and felt his spirits slump. Her reply was without emotion. "Course I do."

Staring at her back, he said, "I'd prefer you to be honest. Don't feel you have to be nice just because of. . . ." He hesitated, unsure what to call it. ". . . my condition."

"I'm not just being nice."

"Why don't you turn round and tell me you love me then? Tell me to my face."

There was a moment's silence, then she sighed. "I'll be late for work."

"It'll only take ten seconds. It'll take less than the time we've already spent discussing it."

Slowly, reluctantly, she turned to look at him. "This is stupid," she said.

Gently he said, "I just don't want any bad feeling between us. Whatever you think, I'd rather we were honest with each other."

"I am being honest. Now can I go?"

Clive had been home for two days now, laid up, recovering. In between taking painkillers for his bruised and swollen stomach he'd read a lot, slept a lot, kept in touch with work via email, and watched the occasional DVD on his iPad. Jo had left him sandwiches and snacks by his bedside when she went to work, and had brought him his evening meal on a tray. If he needed the loo when she wasn't there he manoeuvred himself across the floor to the en suite with the aid of a walking frame, though it took a while and hurt like buggery.

Isaac had been in to see Clive three times a day since Clive had been home from hospital. Dutifully he appeared in the morning before heading off to school, again around 4pm when he got home, and for the third and final time in his pyjamas, fresh from his bath, to say goodnight before going to bed. These encounters, which almost certainly wouldn't have occurred if Clive hadn't requested them, had been stilted and awkward, Isaac on each occasion monosyllabic, clearly anxious to get away. But Clive consoled himself with the fact that at least the boy hadn't thrown one of his tantrums and flat-out *refused* to see him. Perhaps if he continued to show friendliness towards Isaac, to treat him—for now, at least—with kid gloves, the boy would eventually come round.

Clive looked now at Jo, at the exasperated expression on her face. It was as if she was holding up a shield against him, blocking his attempts to steer the conversation towards what had been on his mind since he'd woken up in hospital. Knowing this was neither the right time nor place, but unable to contain himself any longer, he suddenly blurted, "Is it possible to will something on to someone, do you think?"

He watched her closely for her reaction, and didn't know whether to feel relieved or disappointed when she simply shook her head, her expression unchanged. "What are you talking about now?"

"I'm talking about the power of the mind. I'm asking whether you think it's possible to wish, say, bad luck on to someone by willpower alone?"

Her exasperation deepened to bafflement, irritation. "For God's sake, Clive, get a grip. I don't know what you're on about, and I don't think you do either."

"*I* know what I'm on about. I'm asking whether someone deliberately meant to cause me harm."

"Someone?"

"Anyone."

She stared at him. "By doing what?"

He took a deep breath. "I didn't swallow those things, Jo. They just appeared inside me. They just—" He flapped a hand. "One minute they weren't there, the next they were."

Although she continued to stare at him, there was now no expression on her face. "Do you realize what you're actually saying?"

"I do. And I know it sounds crazy. But I'm *not* crazy. You *know* I'm not crazy."

"Do I? You're saying crazy things."

"Am I, though?"

"Yes, you fucking are! How can you possibly doubt it?"

"I just. . . ." He paused. He just what? Eventually he said, "I just want to say that I'm not out to hurt anyone, or make anyone unhappy. I just want us to be a family. I just want the best for us. And if you think I'm doing things wrong—you *or* Isaac—then please tell me. Tell me and we'll discuss it. There's no need for anyone to get hurt. No need for all this . . . bad feeling."

There was silence. Jo stared at him. Her face was still, but her eyes were alive. He could almost see her thoughts turning.

"Say something," he said.

She sighed. It was a deep sigh. Deep and regretful. Her voice was as flat as her expression.

"I'm going to work."

Something woke him. Pain? Was it another pain in his gut? No, he felt okay—aside from the ache of his surgical wound, of course. He didn't even need to piss—which was a relief, as struggling to the bathroom in the middle of the night was not high on his list of favourite pursuits.

So what *had* woken him? A sense that he was in danger?

No, not quite that—but close. It had been more a sense that . . .

That he was not alone.

Maybe it had simply been a dream, or the vestiges of one. Even so, he felt an urge to check, if only to settle his mind enough to drift back to sleep. With a grunt of effort he raised his head from the pillow.

Isaac was standing by the side of the bed, not two feet away, staring at him.

Clive jumped, the involuntary movement causing his wound to flare with pain, making him cry out. Beside him Jo slept on undisturbed, her back to him as usual.

Isaac was motionless, little more than a silhouette in the darkness. Although Clive *felt* as though his son was staring at him, in truth the boy's face was nothing but a featureless oval, his eyes black pools.

Clive's heart was thumping hard, but he was determined not to be intimidated. This was only his seven-year-old son, for God's sake!

"Hey, Isaac," he whispered. "Are you okay?"

There was no response.

With an effort that made him grit his teeth, Clive shuffled his body into a semi-sitting position. He reached for the switch of the bedside lamp, hesitated a moment, glancing across at Jo, then clicked it anyway.

Rose-coloured light bloomed, pushing back the shadows. Jo didn't stir. Clive half-expected Isaac to blink and rub his eyes, but the boy remained statue-still. And now Clive saw that his first instincts had been correct: Isaac *was* staring at him.

Was he actually *seeing* anything, though? Because although his eyes were wide open, his pupils fixed on Clive, Isaac was otherwise expressionless, his face blank as a mannequin. He gave every indication that he was sleepwalking, or in a trance.

Wasn't it said that you should never wake a sleepwalker, that you should simply lead them back to bed, make sure they were safe? But Clive couldn't really do that, not in his condition. It would take too long, and besides he would need both hands to support himself on the walking frame.

Jo then? Perhaps he should wake her up, let her steer Isaac back to bed? But Clive felt oddly reluctant. He got so little time on his own with his son that even here, even now, when he was the only one awake, he felt as though he should hold on to this moment, make the most of it.

He reached out, touched Isaac gently on his pyjama-clad arm. Isaac didn't flinch. His son's pyjamas depicted Spider-Man leaping forward, a skein of web flowing from his outstretched hand.

Looking into Isaac's wide, staring eyes, Clive whispered, "Isaac? Can you hear me?"

When Isaac didn't respond Clive said, "Isaac, this is Daddy. You need to go back to bed. Do you understand? You need—"

And then he fell silent. Because something had just occurred to him. He was remembering the last time Isaac had stared at him like this—a couple of nights ago, when Clive had gone into Isaac's room to find the boy sitting upright in bed. On that occasion, as now, Isaac had seemed to be staring not *at* him, but *into* him. And the next day. . . .

The next day Clive's wallet had ended up inside him. It had caused a blockage in his digestive system, which had nearly killed him. Which, indeed, might well have killed him if he hadn't been lucky enough to have been driving past the hospital at the time.

"No," he murmured, "no." He looked again at Isaac, at his son's staring eyes, and a shiver went through him.

"It isn't you, is it, Isaac?" he said. "You're not doing this to me without knowing it, are you?"

The thought both terrified and saddened him. He had an urge to take evasive action—cover Isaac's eyes with his hand or pull the blankets over his face to break the connection between them. Instead he reached out and shook Jo's shoulder.

"Jo," he said, "wake up."

As soon as Jo began to groan and grumble, Isaac turned away and walked sedately towards the door on the far side of the room. By the time Jo had cracked open one sleepy, bloodshot eye and scowled at Clive the boy had gone.

"Wassit?" she mumbled.

"Isaac was here," Clive said. "Just now. I woke up and he was staring at me. I think he was sleepwalking."

At the mention of their son's name, Jo jerked fully awake. Sitting up she looked around. "Where is he?"

"He's gone now. Back to his room maybe."

"Why didn't you wake me?"

"What do you think I've just done?"

But she wasn't listening to him. She shot him another scowl, then threw back the duvet and stalked barefoot across the room and out of the door, calling their son's name.

Clive shuffled slowly back down into the bed until he was again lying flat. He looked up at the ceiling and thought of Isaac's blank eyes staring at him, marking him.

No, he thought. *You're being ridiculous.*

But that didn't stop him from placing a protective hand on his belly, like a mother soothing her unborn child.

By 4 PM the next day Clive was beginning to relax, at least a little. After Jo had returned to bed the previous night, having reported that Isaac was tucked up and sleeping peacefully, Clive had spent the next few hours drifting in and out of a light sleep punctuated by panicky, barely-remembered dreams. He had finally risen, wrung-out and gritty-eyed, at 7 AM, when Jo's alarm had gone off, whereupon he had decided that instead of lying in bed he would make the effort to get up, shower and dress—just so that he would be ready in case he needed, at some point, to make a dash to the hospital. It was while he was laboriously pulling on his socks, gritting his teeth against the pain it caused him to bend forward at the waist, that Isaac ghosted into the room.

Clive only noticed him when he straightened up with a groan. Although he didn't jump like he had the night before, it still disturbed him to see that Isaac was not only standing motionless, but also that he was gazing at Clive with an intense expression.

"Hey, Isaac," he said, trying not to sound nervous. "How are you this morning? All ready for school?"

At first he thought the boy was simply going to keep on staring. Then Isaac gave a single slow nod.

"That's good," Clive said with an enthusiasm he didn't feel. "So . . . how did you sleep last night?"

Isaac moved his mouth so little he might have been practicing ventriloquism. "Fine."

"Do you remember waking up?"

"No."

Clive's grin widened so much his dry lips felt as if they were about to split. "Hey, did Mummy tell you what you did?" When Isaac didn't reply, or perhaps before he could, Clive blurted, "You sleepwalked."

Isaac seemed unsurprised by the revelation. "Did I have my eyes closed?" he asked blandly.

"No, they were open. Which is weird, isn't it? Sleeping with your eyes open?"

Isaac gave a sulky shrug. "Did I see you when I sleepwalked?"

Clive felt his heart beat a little faster. "Do you *remember* seeing me?"

"I saw you in my dream. Then you weren't there anymore. Goodbye, Daddy."

Goodbye, Daddy. It was what Isaac said every morning—dutifully, monotonously—but it preyed on Clive's mind for the rest of the day. Had Isaac said it a little differently that morning? Had he said it in a way that suggested he didn't expect his father to be there when he arrived home from school?

At 4:05 Clive glanced at the clock. Jo and Isaac would be back within the next few minutes, and Enika would arrive at 4:30 to give Isaac the second of his twice-weekly piano lessons. If Isaac played up today how would Clive react? He didn't have the energy to be angry, added to which he was determined to foster a better relationship with his son. On the other hand Isaac couldn't be allowed to get away with murder. (Clive winced at the choice of phrase, which rose to his mind before he could stifle it.)

When, several minutes later, he heard Jo's key in the lock and the thumping clatter of Isaac's boisterous entry into the flat, he exhaled as if he'd survived some ordeal.

"Hi!" he called from the front room, where he was sitting in an armchair and gripping the TV remote as if it was a panic alarm. "I'm in here!"

If Isaac was surprised to see his father he didn't show it. He thumped into the room, tugged the remote from Clive's hand—who, after biting back a reprimand, gave it up without protest—and changed the channel. As Isaac threw himself on the settee, his eyes already fixed on the antics of *Ben 10*, Clive asked, "So how was school?"

Isaac grunted a half-word, which might have been "Alright."

"You haven't forgotten Enika will be here soon, have you?"

Another grunt.

Jo's groan preceded her into the room. "What a day! I'm shattered." She narrowed her eyes at Clive, as if resentful of his lack of mobility. "How are you feeling?"

"Not too bad," he said. "A bit better. Look, why don't you go and have a nice bath? I'll keep an eye on Isaac."

Immediately she looked suspicious. "He needs his milk and biscuits. He's always hungry when he gets in from school. I'm not sure those dinners they give them are up to scratch."

"I can do that," Clive said. "I'd like to. And it'll be good for me to be up and about a bit more. I don't want to sit here atrophying, do I?"

In truth he wanted the chance to quiz Isaac further about last night—more specifically about the "dream" he claimed to have had which had featured Clive—and if he were lucky he'd get ten minutes to do that before Enika arrived.

When Jo continued to look uncertain, Clive said, "Go on, love, treat yourself. You deserve it. We'll be all right here, won't we, Isaac?"

Although Isaac, his attention still fixed on the TV, didn't reply, at least he didn't protest about the prospect of being left alone with his father. It may have been his indifference that encouraged Jo to say, "Well, all right. But don't forget his milk and biscuits. He likes those chocolate chip cookies in the cupboard. He has three of them."

Clive waited until Jo had locked the bathroom door and he could hear the bath water running before he said, "Can I ask you something, Isaac? About your dream last night?"

Isaac continued to stare at the screen.

"Isaac, can you hear me? I want to talk to you for a second."

Isaac's head swivelled slowly to regard him, in a manner that struck Clive as peculiarly snake-like. Light from the TV washed over Isaac's features, making them appear chalky, lifeless. In a low voice he said, "I want my milk and biscuits."

"I'll get them in a minute," Clive said. "Could we have a chat first?"

"I want my milk and biscuits *now*."

I want doesn't get. That was what Clive's mother used to say. Yet although the words perched in his throat, Clive couldn't bring himself to release them. Isaac was glaring at him so fiercely that, in spite of himself, Clive felt unnerved.

He's a seven-year-old boy, he thought, not for the first time, and then, with more than a hint of desperation, *He's my son.*

He switched on the smile that he was beginning to regard as a disarming mechanism. "All right, I'll get you your milk and biscuits. But then we have a little chat. Deal?"

Isaac shrugged.

Using the walking frame, Clive struggled up from the chair and shuffled into the kitchen. He moved from cupboard to fridge to cupboard, getting together cookies and milk, plate and glass. It was a laborious process, but by 4:23 he was done, which still gave him seven minutes before Enika—

The doorbell rang.

Shit, Clive thought.

He shuffled out of the kitchen and along the hallway, pushing the walking frame before him. He was still a few metres from the door when the bell rang again.

"Clive?" Jo called from the bathroom.

"I've got it," he called back, trying not to sound irritated.

He opened the door. Enika stood there, several minutes early, as immaculate and efficient as ever. She was already wearing a smile of greeting, but when she saw Clive her brow wrinkled.

"Mr. Decker? Whatever has happened? Are you injured?"

"A minor operation," he said tersely. "I'm fine." Before she could comment further he added, "Look, would you go through to the dining room and wait a few minutes? I just want a quick chat with Isaac before his lesson."

She raised her shoulders in an easy-going shrug. "Sure. No problem."

Jo always referred to the dining room as the "music room" because that was where they kept the piano, but Clive had always thought that a bit pretentious—nice though the Danemann was, it was the only musical instrument they owned. He shuffled back along the hallway, Enika walking slowly behind him, until he reached the dining room on his left, which faced Isaac's bedroom across the corridor, and adjusted his weight on the frame so that he could reach out and open the door for her.

"It's all right, Mr. Decker," she said quickly, slipping past him, "I can manage. You have your talk with Isaac. Take as much time as you need."

Clive nodded gratefully and recommenced his slow progress towards the main room at the end of the corridor as Enika opened the dining room door and slipped inside. He had gone no more than a few steps, however, when she reappeared.

"Mr. Decker?"

He turned with an effort. "What is it?"

"Sorry, but I don't understand. How can I give Isaac his lesson today?"

Clive stared at her. "What do you mean?" But before she could reply a horror of realisation swept through him.

"No," he said in a strangled voice. "Christ, no, it can't be."

Swinging the walking frame in a circle, he shuffled back towards her. From the main room behind him he heard Isaac laugh. All but shoving Enika out of the way, he pushed the dining room door fully open and leaned inside.

It was as he had feared.

The patch of floor on the far side of the dining table was empty.

The piano was gone.

ESSENCE

As soon as she walks through the door they know that she's the one.

It's like a sixth sense, like they've been genetically augmented to home in on the vulnerable, the uncertain. They play it cool, however, saying nothing, their flat shark's eyes never even meeting in a flicker of mutual recognition. Pa continues to sip his pint of bitter, his solid, weighty body relaxed into a round-shouldered slouch. Beside him, Ma still toys with her rum and Coke, turning the greasy tumbler round and round on the stained wooden table-top. They appear unaware of their surroundings, uninterested in the choppy clamour around them.

But in truth they are focused wholly on the girl, who is still clearly acclimatising, having stepped from the frosty November night and into the over-warm, sour-smelling fug of The White Hart.

The girl is slight, her complexion too peachy-smooth, her features too delicate, to be from this neighbourhood. The faces that bob and leer around her, gulping at drinks, engaged in braying, aggressive conversation, are coarse, or mottled, or cunning, or sometimes all three. She is like a fallow deer that has inadvertently stumbled into the midst of a wolf pack.

Both Pa and Ma see her eyes widen imperceptibly, her shoulders stiffen with tension, as she looks around, her head making little darting motions, her golden hair shimmering as it flickers and bounces around her face.

Then, as if nervous of making a move which might incite hostility, she tilts her right wrist towards her face and carefully peels back the cuff of her soft grey hoodie. She glances down, then up again. Checking her watch. Then checking to see whether anyone has noticed how expensive it is. In that instant, despite their lack of mutual consultation, both Pa and Ma know her story.

She is new in town, a student maybe, judging by the dinky little backpack she is wearing. A friend has arranged to meet her here, and she is wondering whether she is too early, or too late, for the appointment. Is wondering, in fact, whether she is in the right place.

She probably is. The White Hart is a no-man's-land kind of pub, frequented by locals and occasionally by students, but not particularly cherished by either. Dirty-walled and dirty-windowed, it gives the impression of trying hard *not* to be noticed. Its sign is faded and colourless with age. It perches in a dark, forgotten street of largely shuttered and abandoned businesses, somewhere between the edge of a decaying council estate and a neighbourhood of once-grand houses which have now run to seed, their chilly, high-ceilinged rooms sliced and diced into bedsits for itinerants: students, casual labourers, the dispossessed.

The only reason people come here at all these days is because it is *convenient*. Within walking distance of the main road, and therefore of the bus route into town; grim, but not *too* dangerous; quiet, but not entirely dead. It is a meeting-place, a stopping-off point, a stepping-stone. It serves a similar purpose to a city centre bus station, and has a corresponding lack of allure.

All of which makes it perfect for the purposes of Pa and Ma. They know they won't be remembered here; they know they can blend in; they know they can move on quickly if things go wrong, to any one of numerous such hunting-grounds dotted throughout the city.

They watch the girl decide whether she's going to stay or not. If she doesn't it's of no importance. They know there will be plenty more opportunities. They know that the city is full of young flesh, impressionable minds. This is a game not of desperation, but of patience, persistence. They are hungry, but they are not reckless. It is better to take small bites, when they can, than to gorge themselves. They know that if they were to feast without compunction, they would risk exposure, and subsequently face a future of nothing but famine.

When the girl eventually takes a deep breath and marches almost defiantly to the bar, they show no response. They watch as she slides her lean frame between bulkier shoulders. As soon as the barman gravitates towards her, Ma finishes what is left in her glass and stands up. Without looking at Pa she walks unhurriedly to the bar, her eyes fixed on her target, her expression blank. She arouses no interest. She is drab, invisible—a plain, dumpy, middle-aged woman in colours that deflect attention. She positions herself directly behind the girl, knowing that she remains unnoticed.

248

The girl leans forward to take a jingling handful of change from the barman, her tight-fitting jeans stretching over a bottom that is almost breathtaking in its perfection. Ma is close enough to the girl to smell her. She smells of youth and freshness, of springtime, new growth. Ma breathes it in, relishes it, is aroused by it, even as she feels a giddy, enraged desire to destroy it utterly.

The girl pockets her change, and as she picks up her glass of Coke, Ma steps forward, a practised move, so subtle it is almost balletic in its execution. The girl turns. Instantly surprise and alarm cloud her face as she bumps into Ma, her elbow jolting. Coke splashes out of her glass and down the front of Ma's grey cardigan.

"Oh my God! I'm so sorry. I didn't see you there," the girl says.

She looks distraught, though Ma guesses she is more fearful of the reaction she might provoke than of the fact that she has stained this dull-looking woman's shapeless item of clothing.

"Oh!" Ma says, as though startled by the collision, and drops the purse she is holding. She bends to pick it up, and then staggers slightly. "Oh," she says again, her voice fainter this time.

She feels the girl's hand clutching her arm, hears her anxious voice: "Are you all right?"

What do you care? Ma thinks. *You only ask because you don't want to draw attention to yourself.*

Weakly, raising her head like a tortoise emerging from its shell, Ma says, "Yes, I . . . I'm sure I'll be fine. I just felt a bit dizzy there for a minute."

The girl is biting her lip, an expression of concern on her face. Ma's eyes flicker down to the purse at her feet, and immediately the girl says, "Oh, let me pick that up for you."

"Would you, dear?" Ma says. "That's very kind."

She steps back to allow the girl room to lean forward. Staring down at the girl's blonde head she allows herself a moment of indulgence. She imagines herself naked before the girl, imagines twisting her hands into the girl's shimmering hair and forcing her face into the sour, damp crevice between her meaty, dimpled thighs.

Then the girl rises with the purse and holds it out. Instead of taking it, however, Ma sways slightly. "Oh," she says for the third time. "I think I'd better sit down."

"Here," the girl says, stepping forward quickly. "Let me help you."

She has no hand to spare, though, and Ma sees she is in a quandary. She hesitates a moment, then stuffs Ma's purse into the side pocket of her hoodie.

With her left hand now free, she curls it slightly awkwardly under Ma's right arm.

"That's where I'm sitting," Ma says, nodding towards Pa. "That's my husband, Gerald."

Gerald is not Pa's real name, but he'll know that's what she's calling him tonight. They had decided on names earlier, as they always do before a hunt. Tonight he's Gerald and she's Phyllis.

She allows the girl to lead her to the table, knowing that this is the most dangerous time. Knowing that if she and Pa are going to be noticed and remembered, then this is when it will happen. She doesn't think that they *will* be noticed, though. If any of the pub's customers are looking their way right now, their attention will be on the girl. She's the one who catches the eye. She's the beacon whose glare will reduce those she's with to dim silhouettes.

Ma knows that people are spectacularly unobservant. They *think* they remember everything until pressured to recount precise details, whereupon they discover that their recollections are hazy, that the finer points have become smudged and blurred.

Pa is hunched over the *Times*, which he has folded into quarters. He is doing the crossword, holding the newspaper in his left hand, a stub of pencil in his right. Pa has a look of intense concentration on his face, his eyes narrowed behind his spectacles. He doesn't look up as they approach the table. He appears to be lost in thought.

Ma knows that the girl will find the sight of Pa reassuring. The fact that he is engrossed in the *Times* crossword, and that he is wearing spectacles, will give her the impression that he is educated, reliable, unthreatening. The further fact that he appears not to have noticed their approach will cement this impression. The girl will be used to men staring at her, admiring her, assessing her physically. But Pa will seem to be above all that. She will think of him as a fatherly figure, someone to be trusted.

Only when their presence is too close to ignore does he look up. And then he barely glances at the girl before his attention focuses fully on his wife. His face creases in concern and he puts down his newspaper and pencil in one swift motion. Struggling to his feet, and wincing as he does so, he reaches out, as though to catch her should she fall.

"My dear," he says, his voice a gentle rumble, "whatever's the matter? You look terribly pale."

Ma tries to laugh it off, to wave it away, but she knows that the sound she makes is hollow, her movements feeble. "I'm fine," she says. "I just felt a bit dizzy, that's all. It's nothing."

Despite her words, Pa's face looks no less concerned. "Sit down, sit down," he urges, waving towards her chair.

Ma *does* sit down, plumping into the chair a little more weightily than she needs to. Pa's eyes rove anxiously over her face, and only then does he glance at the girl.

As if prompted, the girl begins to speak, the words spilling out of her. "I'm afraid it's my fault. I accidentally bumped into your wife and spilled my drink on her and made her drop her purse. She reached down to pick it up and went a bit dizzy. I have it here. Her purse I mean. . . ."

She snatches it from her pocket, as if afraid that she might otherwise be accused of trying to steal it. She places it on the table, her face flushed.

Pa eyes the purse, and then looks up at the girl again. He takes his time before replying. When he does, his words are accompanied by a warm smile. "Thank you, miss. . .?"

"Veronica," the girl says. "My friends call me Roni."

"Thank you, Veronica," Pa says. "You've been very kind."

Veronica demurs modestly and haltingly, but Ma cuts across her words with a groan. "I'm terribly sorry, Gerald," she says, "but would you mind getting me a drink? I'm feeling rather faint."

Pa immediately looks away from the girl as if he has entirely forgotten about her. As if all that concerns him now is the welfare of his beloved wife.

"Certainly, my dear," he says. "What would you like?"

"Oh, anything soft," she replies. "It doesn't matter."

"Right you are," he says, and turning awkwardly, he reaches for a walking stick propped against the wall. He hobbles from behind the table, leaning heavily on the stick. Wincing again, he lets out a low but quickly stifled grunt, which gives the impression that he is attempting to cover up the fact that his leg is causing him considerable pain.

Spotting this, the girl puts her glass down on the table and raises her hands, as though to physically impede his progress.

"Please," she says, "let me get you both a drink. It's the least I can do."

Pa smiles and shakes his head. "No, no, my dear, you've done more than enough. You go back to your friends."

The girl pauses. Pa knows he has given her a get-out clause, but he is not concerned; it is all part of the game. Though the pause seems prolonged, it is really no more than a second or two before the girl is shaking her head.

"Honestly," she says, "I'd *like* to buy you both a drink. Besides, my friend's not here yet. I was supposed to meet her ten minutes ago, but she hasn't turned up."

Pa looks at Ma, doubt on his face. Ma sighs, and wearily says, "Don't look at *me*, Gerald. *You* decide. But do it quickly please. I really do need that drink."

"It's already decided," the girl says firmly. "I'm buying." She swivels to face the bar and throws a question back over her shoulder. "Gerald, what can I get you?"

"Oh . . . er . . . half a pint of bitter, please," he says, grunting as he lowers himself gingerly into his seat. It's a convincing performance, and one he maintains despite the fact that the girl is already marching back towards the bar and doesn't see it.

Ma and Pa sit in silence until the girl returns. They do not look at each other. The game is going well, though their faces betray no trace of triumph. They are both aware that there is a long way to go yet before the girl is theirs. If her friend arrives, which is more likely than not, then the girl will slip from their grasp. But the prospect does not concern them. Many such girls have slipped from their grasp over the years. The majority that do serve only to make the victory of procuring the few that don't all the sweeter. Indeed, it amuses Ma and Pa to think that there are hundreds of girls alive today who have no idea how thin was the ice upon which they once skated.

No doubt most of those girls don't even remember the nice couple with whom they once had the briefest of encounters. If the friend of this girl, Veronica, appears as arranged, full of apologies for her lateness, Ma and Pa know that they will all too soon be forgotten. It doesn't bother them. It's the way things are. People are inherently selfish, inherently callous. They resent dwelling on the needs and misfortunes of others. Out of sight, out of mind.

The girl returns with the drinks, and after thanking her, Pa casually invites her to join them. The girl glances at the door, as if weighing up her chances of reaching it before they can bring her down (although both Ma and Pa know that she is actually wondering about her friend's whereabouts), and then gratefully accepts their invitation. She clearly feels less vulnerable in their company than she would do if she were waiting alone.

They chat, though because Ma is still feigning recovery, it is Pa and the girl who do most of the talking. Occasionally one or other of them will break off to ask Ma how she is feeling. "A bit better," she replies weakly, or "Not too bad." The girl texts her friend, but after receiving no reply calls her, only to reach a voicemail message. "Where are you?" she asks, her voice thin with frustration and restrained anger. She frowns at the phone as she puts it away. Ma and Pa look sympathetic.

Almost half an hour passes. Eventually Pa lifts his glass, tilts back his head and drains the last of his beer. Placing his glass back on the table with a decisive thump, he gives a gasp of satisfaction.

"That's my lot," he says, and smiles at Ma. "Shall we make tracks, Phyllis?"

Ma nods, then casts an anxious look at the girl. "But what about you, dear? What will you do?"

The girl looks momentarily indecisive, then straightens, shakes back her hair and sighs. "I might as well go too," she says. "It looks as though I've been stood up."

"Oh dear, I wonder where your friend is," Ma says. "I hope nothing's happened to her."

The girl looks resigned rather than worried. Dismissively she says, "I'm sure she's fine. She's a bit like this, I'm afraid. Unreliable."

"Oh dear," Ma says again.

The girl smiles, evidently touched by her concern. "It's okay. It's no big deal."

"I hope you haven't far to go?" Pa asks.

"No, not really. Fulwood Park. It's only a bus ride away."

Ma looks almost shyly at Pa. "We could give Veronica a lift, couldn't we, Gerald? We go right through Fulwood Park."

Pa looks a little doubtful. "Well, I *suppose* we could. But she might not want to, Phyllis. I mean, she doesn't really know us from Adam. We could be anyone."

Ma gives a silvery laugh. "Don't be silly, Gerald. You'll accept a lift, won't you, Veronica?"

The girl looks wary. "Well, I don't know. . . ."

Frowning at Ma, Pa says, "Of course you don't. Don't pressure the poor girl, Phyllis. You're making her uncomfortable." Turning to the girl with a look of apology, he adds, "Don't feel as though you have to say yes, Veronica. We'd quite understand if you weren't keen. Wouldn't we, Phyllis?"

Ma looks a bit put out, like a child who feels she's been unfairly reprimanded. Glancing at her, the girl says quickly, "Well, obviously I'd love a lift, but only if you're absolutely sure. . . ."

Ma beams. "Of *course* we're sure."

Pa looks at the girl and secretly raises his eyebrows in a *what-is-she-like?* gesture, making the girl smile. "That looks as though it's settled then," he says.

They leave with the girl, Pa moving slowly, aided by his walking stick, Ma with her hand resting lightly on his back. They don't look around to see whether anyone notices their departure. They know that even if they *have* been seen, witnesses will remember only false details: Pa's spectacles, his walking stick. Aside from that they'll recall only that Ma and Pa were a normal, middle-aged couple. Plain-looking and drably clothed. Nothing to distinguish them.

The night is cold. Ma thinks of the air like a thin, flexible sheet of ice closing over her face. The white vapour of her breath curls and dissipates, each exhalation a fragment of her life breaking free and instantly, irretrievably lost.

At least, she thinks, the girl's young, sweet breaths, which are currently coiling in the air, are more limited than her own. This pleases Ma. It gives her a sense of longevity, of immortality almost.

"Here we are," Pa says, gesturing down the dark street. He and Ma have parked their car around fifty metres from the pub, deliberately positioning it in the bowl of shadow between one glimmering street light and the next. Cloaked in darkness it is impossible to tell what colour the car is. Like its owners, it is drab and nondescript. Pa takes his key fob from his pocket and presses a button, and the car responds with a brief, complicit flash of its lights.

"You sit in the front, dear," Ma says. "Then you can give Gerald directions."

"Are you sure?" the girl asks.

"Oh, quite sure. Besides, I'll be able to spread out a bit in the back. Put my feet up."

They get into the car, Pa making a big show of easing his stiff leg into the foot well. Finally he's settled, whereupon he hands his walking stick to Ma in the back, pulls his seatbelt across his round stomach and clicks it into place. Beside his bulk the girl, waiting patiently, seems child-like. She has taken off her backpack, which now rests between her feet like a sleeping pet.

"Are we all set?" Pa says, glancing at the girl and then at Ma in the back. They both nod and he starts the engine.

Ma knows the girl will be relaxed, unsuspecting. Like the *Times* crossword, and Pa's spectacles, and his walking stick, she will find the interior of the car reassuring. It is clean and tidy, but not so pristine that it hints at obsession, at a need to control and dominate. There is a National Trust membership sticker in the top corner of the windscreen—symbolic of respectable, middle-class gentility—and a three-quarter full packet of chewy mints in the shallow well between the seats.

There is nothing visible that is sharp, nothing that can be construed as a weapon. Ma and Pa are very careful about this. They make certain they are never in possession of any of the tools that they use on the girls. Even at home they keep the tools hidden, and restrict their activities to the basement. They pride themselves on their restraint, their attention to detail. It is thanks to their meticulous natures that they have never been caught.

They have been active for almost twenty-two years, and the light of suspicion has never once wavered in their direction. In the eyes of the world they are decent, law-abiding citizens. Good neighbours. Pillars of the community.

They make only one exception to their rule, and although it constitutes a tiny risk it is a necessary one. In a hidden compartment in the lining of her handbag Ma keeps a small hypodermic syringe filled with a strong, swift-acting anaesthetic. As Pa chats to the girl in the front seat, Ma takes the hypodermic from her handbag and removes the plastic cap that protects the needle. Then she leans forward ever so slightly, pushes the needle into the exposed flesh of the girl's neck and depresses the plunger.

So swift and skilled is she at this that the syringe is empty before the girl reacts. By the time she jerks forward in her seat, clapping her hand to her neck as if stung by an insect, Ma has withdrawn the needle and is settling back in her seat. She catches a glimpse of the girl's face as she twists, and relishes the brief expression of shock, accusation, and, yes, terrified realisation in the girl's eyes. Then those eyes lose focus and the delicate peach-coloured petals of the eyelids slide closed over them. The girl's head nods forward and she slumps to one side in her seat, limp and compliant, her poise and vitality suddenly gone.

The anaesthetic affects the girls in different ways. The majority merely fall into a deep and abrupt sleep, though some lose muscular control to such an extent that they evacuate bladder and bowels. There was a girl four years ago who had an epileptic seizure, which almost resulted in Pa losing control of the car. And there were two girls who suffered such an adverse reaction to the drug that they died on the journey back to the house—a bitter disappointment for Ma and Pa, as it denied them their pleasure just when it seemed they were home and dry.

Steering the car with one hand, Pa reaches across and pushes the girl's head down so that it is beneath the level of the window. Now anyone who happens to glance casually at them when they drive past will not see an unconscious girl slumped in the front seat.

"I want to take my time with this one," Ma says. "I want to make her suffer."

Pa laughs. "You really hate the pretty ones, don't you?"

"I hate the ones who think they've got it all," Ma retorts. "Who think they're untouchable."

Ma and Pa are both eager to start their night's work, but Pa drives steadily, carefully. It wouldn't do to be pulled over for speeding, or to otherwise draw attention to themselves. In truth they live nowhere near Fulwood Park, and now that the girl is unconscious, Pa takes a right, and then another right, until they are heading in the opposite direction.

They lapse into silence, but are occupied by thoughts of how they will use the girl. Of the implements they will employ to penetrate her. Of how loudly they will make her scream. Of how much they will make her plead.

Their house is neat, modest, unassuming. They live in a quiet neighbourhood, suburban, respectable. The crime rate is low and the local children are generally well-behaved. Each house is equipped with a small garden front and back, and its own garage. The streets are sparsely populated at this time of night, and indeed, as they pull into their cul-de-sac, Ma and Pa see only a single figure ahead of them—a man hunched in a bulky overcoat, a dog trotting at his side.

Pa slows the car as they approach the open gate into their own drive and reaches across the girl's body to snap open the glove compartment. He withdraws a slim black device the size of a mobile phone, points it out of the window and presses a button. Almost silently the door of the garage which abuts their house begins to ascend. Pa places the remote control in the well between the front seats and drives smoothly through the gate, up the drive and into the garage.

Even now Ma and Pa do not hurry. Though they are eager, their actions are rehearsed, methodical. Pa gets out of the car and closes the garage door with the remote control, before placing it back in the glove compartment. Ma waits until the door has descended far enough to conceal them from view before clicking on the light. Then, while she unlocks the inner door that leads directly into the kitchen, Pa unclips the girl's seatbelt and lifts her out of her seat. He drapes her over his shoulder in a fireman's lift, her body so limp that she resembles a rag doll. Her golden hair hangs between her dangling arms like a shimmering, silken waterfall.

Ma imagines burning off that hair with a blowtorch, continuing until the girl's scalp is raw and bleeding. She imagines the girl's flesh crisping like roasted pork, hot meat juices running down the girl's face and into her screeching mouth.

She chuckles at the prospect, the sound low and throaty with lust. As Pa carries the girl into the house, Ma snatches up the girl's backpack, locks the car and switches off the garage light. By the time she switches on the kitchen light, Pa is already halfway across the room. He knows the house so well that he has already side-stepped the kitchen table in the dark.

"I'll take her down," he says. "You put the kettle on."

Ma nods. It is part of the ritual. Pa will take the girl to the basement and make her secure, then he will come back upstairs and the two of them will plan their evening's entertainment over a nice cup of tea.

Ma fills the kettle and switches it on. She hums contentedly as she takes two mugs down from the cupboard and drops a tea bag into each. To Pa's mug she adds two spoonfuls of sugar. It is a vice he has been unwilling to relinquish. It is because of him that she still buys biscuits—his favourites are chocolate HobNobs and bourbon creams. She worries about his heart, but at the age of fifty-six he is as strong as an ox. She thinks it is their joint hobby which keeps him young and fit. He does enjoy it so.

The kettle boils and she fills each mug three-quarters full. She pokes at the tea bags with a spoon, stirring them around. Hers she removes first. Pa likes his tea brick-red, just as his own father did, but Ma prefers hers the colour of sun-warmed flesh. She adds milk, then stirs the tea and drops the metal spoon into the sink. Carrying the mugs to the table, she wonders where Pa has got to.

A wriggle of alarm snakes through her. Surely he hasn't started without her? She shakes her head. No, he would never do that, they have always done everything together. Even when Pa is having his way with the girls at the beginning, he knows how much Ma likes to watch. Knows how she likes to savour the terror and revulsion on their faces, to hear them begging him to stop.

Even so, this particular girl is prettier than most, and Pa has his appetites. Perhaps he has been unable to resist a quick dabble with his fingers, or with his tongue. Ma *supposes* that would be understandable, but even so, she feels a little disappointed, a little hurt, at the prospect.

She puts the mugs on the table and turns towards the kitchen door, meaning to go to the top of the basement steps and call down to him. But as she turns she freezes, her heart lurching with shock, her eyes widening with astonishment.

The girl—Veronica—is standing in the kitchen doorway.

She looks neither groggy nor dishevelled nor confused. On the contrary, she appears fresh and alert, her eyes gleaming. There is even a half-smile on her face, as if she enjoys the impact her unexpected appearance has made.

A myriad questions rush instantly through Ma's head. What is the girl doing here? How did she escape? Where is Pa? How has the girl overcome the effects of the anaesthetic so quickly?

Ma wonders whether she should speak to the girl, lie to her, try to bluff it out. But there is something in the girl's expression that tells Ma she knows precisely what has been happening, and why. And so instead of speaking, Ma wheels towards the knife block beside the electric cooker, her hand already reaching for the jutting black handle of the carving knife.

Ma doesn't know how, but suddenly she is lying on the kitchen floor. It happens so abruptly that it is only in retrospect that she recalls being hit by a solid weight that moved so swiftly it might have been a car. Except that that is impossible. So what has happened? Has she been shot? Struck down by a sudden seizure or heart attack? Her ribs and back are hurting, her eyes are unfocused and she cannot move her arms. Then she blinks and sees that the girl is sitting astride her. Peering down at her with eyes that are glittering strangely, the girl's golden hair softly caresses Ma's face.

"You thought you were the hunters," the girl says, "but you're not. *I* am."

There is a blur of movement and suddenly everything goes black.

How long Ma is unconscious for she has no idea. When she comes to she is no longer lying on the kitchen floor. It takes several moments for her vision to focus, and when it does the first thing she sees are stone walls and a stone floor. Her thoughts are so jumbled that she doesn't immediately realise she is in her own basement. It is only when she spots Pa, in the centre of the room, strapped into the iron chair which they call The Throne, that she becomes fully aware of her surroundings.

Pa is slumped forward, groaning slightly, though Ma can see no obvious injuries to his body. There is no blood on his clothes, no bruises on his face. Yet somehow he has been overcome, restrained. How can this be?

It is not until Ma tries to move that the pain kicks in. As if it too has been sleeping, it awakens in her shoulders and back and ribs, threading glassily through her muscles, embedding itself in her bones, her joints. It swiftly rises to such a pitch that she cries out, and instinctively attempts to curl up, to draw her body inwards. But she cannot move. Her arms are locked in an upright position, her immovable feet planted firmly on the ground, a metre or more apart.

As the cramps set in, excruciating enough to reduce her cries to nothing but tortured gasps, she looks down and sees the shackles encircling her ankles. And suddenly she realises she has been clamped to the wall, just as she in turn has clamped numerous girls to this same wall over the past twenty-two years.

She glances up, and although it is only a small movement it causes such agony to tear through her body that everything whites out for a second.

When her vision clears, seconds or perhaps minutes later, she sees the face of the girl swimming before her. At first she thinks it is an illusion, but then the girl speaks.

"You've been hanging there for a while," the girl says. "I'm sorry it's so uncomfortable. I think the dead weight of your body, pulling downward, has dislocated at least one of your shoulders."

Ma tries to respond, to vent her fury, or perhaps simply to plead for release, but the pain has robbed her of her ability to speak. The girl's face still swims in her vision. Ma sees regret there, compassion. The girl speaks again.

"I expect you're confused. Wondering what's happened. And I *know* you're in pain, for which I truly apologise. I mean, all things being equal, you probably deserve it. But I've never gone in for that eye for an eye Old Testament stuff. Just because *you* like inflicting pain doesn't mean that whoever metes out your punishment should get the same satisfaction for inflicting it on you. It'd be a pretty sick world if we *all* got gratification from the suffering of others, wouldn't it?" The girl smiles, as if she's made a joke. "A *sicker* world, I should say."

Ma watches the girl as she crosses the basement and comes to a halt in front of Pa. The girl peers into Pa's face, as if to check whether he is conscious, and then turns back to Ma.

"I ought to explain who I am," she says. "Or rather *what* I am. Because I can guarantee that you'll never have come across anything like me before. And I don't want you to get the wrong idea. I don't want you to think that

I'm doing this because I *like* doing it, or even that I'm some kind of avenging angel, acting on behalf of all the girls you've killed. Although, having said that, I can't deny that there's a certain poetic justice to this situation, or that I don't feel *some* satisfaction in knowing that you'll never torture and kill another innocent girl. But as I say, that's not my main motivation for what I'm about to do. You see, for me, this is all about *survival*."

Ma is not sure whether she's momentarily blacked out, because all at once the girl is standing directly in front of her once more. Earnestly the girl says, "What you have to understand, Phyllis, is that there are two kinds of serial killer in this world. There are those that *choose* to kill, like you and Gerald, and there are those that *have* to. And when I say 'have to' I'm not talking about people who are driven to kill by some form of psychological deviance. No, I'm talking about killing in the same way that you would talk about eating or breathing. I'm talking about killing in the sense that if you didn't kill you would die. And I mean, *literally*, die. Because for some people killing is like oxygen or food. For some people, there is no way to survive without it."

She pauses, peering into Ma's eyes. "I hope you're getting all this," she says. "I hope you understand what I'm saying. Because you see, Phyllis, I'm one of those people. Which doesn't mean that I'm cruel—on the contrary, I'd say I was quite compassionate. It just means . . . well, it's simply the way I am, the way I was born. I'm not a monster. I'm a human being, just like you. But I'm also . . . *different*. A freak of nature, I suppose you'd call me.

"I'm faster and stronger than you could ever be. I live longer—much longer—and I'm pretty much impervious to the illnesses that afflict most human beings, and also to the drugs that you use. I eat and drink only for the pleasure of it, not because I have to. My *real* sustenance, you see, as I've already said, comes from killing—or rather, not from the act of killing itself, but from absorbing the memories and emotions of fellow human beings at the point of death. Absorbing their *essence*."

She shrugs, as if to say: *I know it's crazy, but there you are.* "When I was growing up," she continues, "this was a big problem for me. I didn't *like* killing people, but I had to. For a while I survived on old people, who were nearing the end of their time, or people with terminal illnesses, who just wanted relief from their pain. Then I hit on the idea of feeding on those who feed on others. That way I get not only the memories and emotions of my chosen subjects, but the residual emotions of those on whom they've inflicted pain.

"Because that's the way it works, you see. The more extreme the memories and emotions, the longer they sustain me." She waves a hand between her captives. "I mean, you two will keep me going for simply *ages*. I won't have to kill again for a long time after this. Now, isn't it nice to know that out of all your evil some good will ultimately come? True, it's not much of a consolation to all the girls you've tortured and murdered over the years, but at least there's a *kind* of cosmic balance."

She smiles gently and says, "Right then, who's first? I can't pretend it won't hurt, but at least it'll be quicker than the ordeal you were planning for me." She raises her head and twitches her nose as if sniffing the air. "I'll start with you, Gerald, if I may? I don't wish to be cruel, but your wife is more frightened than you are, and when she sees what's in store for her she'll go out of her mind with terror. And that, frankly, will be all the sweeter for me. Now, are you ready? Brace yourself."

Ma opens her mouth, but she still can't scream, not even when the girl walks up to Pa, places her hands almost tenderly on the sides of his head and pushes her thumbs into his eyes.

Ma can't scream, but Pa certainly can.

Over the next few hours he screams more than enough for the both of them.

PUPPIES FOR SALE

It was Beth who saw the sign.

"Can we have one, Daddy? Can we? *Please!* You said we could."

I glanced at Carol. She had her superior face on—lips pursed, eyebrows raised slightly. "Don't expect any support from me," she said. "You dug the hole, you climb out of it."

I could only grin. It was true. I hadn't actually promised the kids a puppy, but I'd said we'd think about it when Hamish died, which was tantamount to the same thing. And now that little Hamish had ascended to the great hamster wheel in the sky (we were on our way back from a movie and pizza trip to cheer up the kids after the trauma of the past few days, as a matter of fact), Beth in particular had been reminding me of my hastily uttered words on a regular basis.

"Not from here, Beth," I said, glancing at my nine-year-old daughter's bobbing blonde head in the rear view mirror.

"Aw, why not?"

"Because we have to think about these things, not rush into them. We don't even know what breed of dog they are."

"Can't we go and see? We don't have to buy one. Can't we just *look*?"

Now, don't get me wrong. I was no pushover when it came to my kids. In fact I reckon Carol and I were pretty strict compared to other parents we knew. We limited the kids' hours of TV viewing and computer game playing; we gave them chores to do—cleaning their shoes for school, emptying the dishwasher, tidying their rooms; we insisted they respect their own and other peoples' property.

I'm not sure what it was, therefore, that made me indicate and pull into the layby a few hundred yards beyond the farm we'd passed. Spur of the moment. Fate. Outside influence. Call it what you will.

"You're terrible," Carol said, but she was smiling. "You're as bad as they are."

"It can't do any harm, though, can it?" I said. "We'll just go and see."

"Yeah. Sure we will."

Beth's little face was alight with excitement. Eleven-year-old Daniel was trying to look cool as always, as if this was no big deal to him, but I could tell he was all but bursting with anticipation too.

"All right," I said, adopting stern dad mode, "we'll go and have a quick look. But I want both of you to understand that that doesn't mean we're going to buy a dog. We don't know what kind they are, we don't know how old they are, we don't know how much they cost. So if me and Mum say no, we don't want you throwing a wobbler, Beth, and showing us up in front of people."

"I won't," Beth said and solemnly drew a cross on the breast of her *Charmed* t-shirt with a forefinger. "Promise."

I turned the car round and we drove back to the farm. It was an unassuming place, just off the main road that connected the urban sprawl of Leeds to our quiet little town in the sticks. The sign that had attracted our attention was on the verge just before the turn-off, a square wooden placard painted with bold black letters—PUPPIES FOR SALE—atop a stout post that had been hammered into the ground. Oddly the sign looked permanent, suggesting that puppies were always on offer there, plentiful as eggs or pots of jam.

We parked in a muddy yard, the kids excitedly unfastening their seatbelts even before I'd switched the engine off.

"We don't all have to go," I said. "I'll suss things out first."

Beth opened her mouth to protest, then thought better of it. "Okay, Daddy," she said demurely.

A stone porch sheltered the front door of the farmhouse. On a ledge at waist level was a sheep's skull and a broken, one-eyed doll, plastic skin jaundiced and grubby with age, its clothes colourless rags.

"Welcome to the Yorkshire Chainsaw Massacre," I murmured. "The lucky ones died first."

I knocked on the door.

The woman who answered was not my immediate idea of Leatherface's local equivalent. She was stout and dowdy, a grey cap of hair framing a pouchy, wrinkled face.

"Sorry to disturb you," I said, "but we noticed your sign on the road."

The woman's yellow, veined eyeballs swivelled to peer around me. "Oh yes. Got little ones, have you?"

I followed her gaze, glancing back at the car. "Yes, two."

"Well, bring them in, why don't you? The little ones love seeing the puppies."

If she'd been a man I might have made my excuses there and then. Instead I found myself saying, "Can I ask what sort of dogs they are?"

"Black labs, lovey," she said, and I swear she looked at me as if she *knew*.

Black labs. My parents had bred Labradors for fifteen years when I was a kid. We'd had eight at one point, before our old girl, Jilly, had been the first to pop her clogs at the grand old age of thirteen.

My folks were down to five, and I was at university, when my dad popped *his* clogs after suffering a massive stroke half-way up a mountain in Wales. Mum and Dad had gone there to celebrate their thirtieth wedding anniversary. When my dad died the dog-breeding days died with him. Mum was getting too old and arthritic to cope on her own. Her five remaining dogs aged and died gradually over the next decade. She'd been dog-less now for the past dozen years, during which I'd considered taking up the mantle on several occasions. I looked at the woman, trying to keep my expression neutral.

"Okay," I said. "Well, if you're sure it's no trouble. . . ."

"No trouble at all, lovey."

I motioned to Carol and she and the kids got out of the car. The four of us followed the woman into the house, straight into a high-ceilinged kitchen with a stone-flagged floor and an open fire and massive dark items of wooden furniture, antique but ugly. A bearded man in a dirty blue pullover was sitting at an oak table with a mug of tea and a cigarette. Smoke and steam battled for dominance above his grizzled head. I caught Beth staring and tensed a little. She could be primly puritanical about smoking, which was both amusing and admirable in the right circumstances. Before she could enlighten the man as to the appalling damage he was inflicting on his heart and lungs, I said, "Good afternoon."

"Ow do," he replied.

"These people have come to see the puppies, Jud," said the woman.

He grunted.

"They're through here," she said, and led us into a laundry area containing a huge old sink with a wooden draining board and a vast iron radiator that was pumping out heat. Sheets and tea towels dried on a clothes dolly suspended on a pulley beneath the ceiling.

"Oh, they're gorgeous!" Beth cried, and scampered, puppy-like herself, across to a large basket alcoved between a washing machine and a dryer. The basket contained a half dozen or so squirming black bundles suckling at the swollen teats of a rather haughty-looking Labrador bitch.

"Careful, Beth," Carol said. "New mums can be a bit funny with strangers. She might think you're after her babies and bite you."

"Oh no," said the woman, "not our Ebony. She's daft as a brush, aren't you, old girl?" As if to demonstrate she stumped across and fondled Ebony's ears. The dog wagged her tail briefly, but she still looked wary of the strangers in her midst.

Beth looked at the woman squatting in front of the basket beside her and asked in her politest voice, "Do you think Ebony will let me stroke her puppies?"

"I'm sure she will, lovey," the woman replied. "Why don't you give Ebony a little stroke first, though, just to show her how friendly you are."

I tensed again as Beth stretched out a hand towards the Labrador's head, but Ebony was fine. Not friendly exactly, but not hostile either. I glanced at Carol and she gave a resigned smile. It was her way of acknowledging that the deal was already as good as sealed.

We called the puppy Jet, for obvious reasons. It was Dan who came up with the name. For the first few weeks everything was as fine as it can be when you've got a new pup in the house. Naturally the little bugger pissed and shat all over the place and got his gnashers into anything and everything. That didn't stop the kids, not to mention Carol and me, from loving him, though. Indeed, Beth continued to adore him even when he destroyed the Little Mermaid doll she'd had since she was a baby. And Dan, who seemed to be transforming into a sullen, image-conscious teenager a couple of years early, became all soppy with Jet when he thought no one was watching him.

In fact, when Dan started acting strangely, Carol and I initially put it down to the onset of adolescence, to the hormonal changes we knew would soon be rampaging through his body. If I recall correctly, it began as he was recovering from the bug that had laid him low over most of our final Christmas. He had been feverish for several nights, sweating so much that Carol and I had had to change his bedding daily, and sometimes more frequently than that. Throughout that time he had been up and down, unable to sleep, weepy and delirious with virus and fatigue.

Carol and I had taken turns to comfort him, dose him with Calpol, cool him down with cold flannels against his forehead. Several nights of broken sleep meant that we were both shattered too, though, at a low ebb, querulous and irritable with the kids, with Jet, with each other.

Jet was about four months old by this time, already twice the size he'd been when we bought him. He wasn't quite house-trained, but he was getting there. Despite my lack of energy, Beth and I would take him for long walks in the afternoons during the Christmas holidays, while Carol stayed behind to look after Dan. I know I was tired, and that the weather was cold and drizzly, the sky grey, the ground heavy underfoot, but I look back on those times now with the yearning of a man who has been given a taste of paradise only to have it snatched cruelly away. As the days pass, my previous life seems more and more like a dream to me. Sometimes I even wonder if it existed at all. If there *is* a Heaven, if there *is* something good beyond all this, then those long leaden plods in the rain with my beautiful daughter's little hand clasped tightly in mine, is the closest approximation to it that I can think of.

New Year's Day was when the bad stuff really began. Not that I believe the date holds—or held—any particular significance. The incident which I now regard as the absolute starting point, as the first in a long line of dominos to fall, occurred that evening, some time between ten and midnight.

Carol and I, exhausted, had gone to bed early. I was out like a light, and my sleep was as deep and dreamless as anaesthesia. I was all the more disorientated, therefore, when a crash that sounded like a bomb hitting the house ripped me out of unconsciousness. Before I even knew what I was doing, I was out of bed and running towards the sound. However, quick as I was to respond, Carol was ahead of me. She was in Beth's room a few paces before I was, and I heard her scream, "Dan!" before I saw him.

My son was lying on his back on the floor beside his sister's bunk bed. The expression on his face was shocking. He looked as terrified as I had ever seen anyone look in my life. His skin was white as bone, but his eyes were stark and dark-rimmed. At that moment he looked lost to us, utterly, irrevocably.

"Dan!" I snapped as if he had done this deliberately, just to give us a fright. When he didn't respond I turned my attention to Beth, who was sitting up in bed, her head inches from the ceiling, tousled, sleepy, confused.

"What happened?" I demanded, and felt Carol give my arm a brief squeeze, which I translated instantly: *Steve, calm down.*

"He was climbing up my ladder, shouting that people were after him. He woke me up. When I asked him what people, he threw himself backwards on to the floor."

"Oh God," Carol said. "He might have damaged his back or his neck. Or his head."

"Don't try to move him," I said, kneeling beside her as she reached out. "Dan," I said, "it's Dad. Can you hear me?"

His eyes flickered towards me, but for a moment remained wild and unfocused. He resembled nothing more than something primitive reacting to a sound.

Brain damage, I thought, my guts clenching in panic. But then a change came over him. His eyes focused; the tautness went from his face.

"Dad?" he whispered.

I took his hand, enfolded it in mine. "I'm here, Dan," I said, "don't worry."

"Dan, it's Mum," said Carol. "Are you all right?"

He looked as if he didn't understand the question and she glanced at me fearfully.

"Do you hurt anywhere?" I asked. "Does your back hurt or your head?"

He blinked as if mentally assessing himself. "No."

"Are you sure?" said Carol. "Try to move. Try to sit up."

"But slowly," I added, stretching out my hands as if to prevent him leaping to his feet and exacerbating any damage he might have done to himself.

Slowly, aided by Carol and myself, Dan raised himself into a sitting position. He was breathing heavily, puffing out his cheeks as if to blow away the thick dust of confusion that clogged his mind.

"Can you tell us what happened?" Carol coaxed.

He frowned. "They were after me. I was trying to get away."

"Who were after you?" I asked.

"Don't know. People. They wanted to hurt me. I had to fight them."

"Why did you throw yourself off Beth's ladder, Dan?" asked Carol.

"They were shouting at me. I was scared."

He was beginning to look distressed again. Carol stroked his sweaty head.

"It's okay, buddy," I said. "No one's after you. It was just a dream. You're safe now."

I made him a hot chocolate, then we got him back into bed. Carol lay beside him as he drifted off to sleep. I went back to bed myself, but thought I'd be too shaken to sleep again that night. However Carol's side of the bed was still empty when I nodded off.

"I can't stop thinking how much worse it might have been," Carol said the next morning.

We were in the bathroom. She was soaking in a hot bath; I was shaving, my bloodshot eyes staring back from the mirror.

"It was lucky he didn't land on anything," she went on. "You know what Beth's like for leaving things lying around. I mean, what if her CD player had been sitting on the floor, or a plastic box of toys, or that metal case she keeps all her hair things in?" She shuddered. "God, he could have broken his back or split his skull open."

I spun round so suddenly that flecks of shaving foam flew across the room and landed like snowflakes on the wooden floor. "Yeah, but he didn't, so don't think about it. No use worrying about what *might* have happened."

Carol scowled. "All right, you don't have to have a go at me. I was only saying."

I flapped a hand in apology. "I know. It's just . . . well, he's okay, thank God. Let's just be thankful for that."

Carol stirred the bath water languidly with her hand, creating ripples which made her body appear to shimmer. At the age of forty she was still slim and well-toned. Didn't stop her moaning about cellulite and stretch-marks, though.

"It's just worrying," she said. "I mean, you know what Dan's like. He's always been so . . . centred, so calm, insular even. It was scary seeing him out of control. What if he does something like this again? What if he really hurts himself next time?"

"He won't," I said firmly. "It was a one-off. Stop fretting about it."

"It's just . . ." She looked momentarily uncomfortable, as if unsure whether to say what was on her mind. "Oh, I know this is going to sound stupid, but I can't help wondering . . . what if he's got problems? Psychological ones, I mean. What if this is the start of something?"

I felt amused and annoyed at the same time. However I could see how much this was bothering her, so I tried to be as understanding, as comforting as I could.

"He hasn't. It's this fever, that's all. What happened last night was just the tail-end of it."

I could see she was desperate for reassurance. "Do you *really* think that's all it is?"

"I'm certain of it. A hundred percent."

I think of those words now and feel nothing but a gut-deep, bone-deep shame. Of course I was not to blame for what happened, yet I can't help feeling that ultimately I let them all down. I tell myself I should have seen the connections sooner, I should have stepped in, nipped the situation in the bud, saved them. What happened was preventable. That's the worst thing. But I was blind to that, and now it's too late. Now all I have left is revenge, which is not enough. Which will never be enough.

For the next few days Dan seemed fine. Tired and withdrawn, admittedly, but not excessively so, and certainly no more than might have been expected of someone recovering from the effects of an energy-sapping virus.

"Do you think he'll be all right to go to school tomorrow?" Carol asked as we laid out the kids' uniforms for their first day back after the Christmas holidays.

"He'll be fine," I said. "He just needs a good night's sleep."

It wasn't a crash that woke me this time, but it was just as distressing, in its own way. It was the sound of sobbing that pulled me, gasping like a drowning man, from sleep. I opened my eyes to see a figure looming by the bed, blacker than the darkness which framed it, swaying slightly as it wept.

"Dan?" I murmured. "Is that you?" Knowing that it was.

He hitched in a breath as if to respond, then simply began sobbing all the louder.

I sat up, alarmed at the intensity of my son's apparent despair. I reached out and grasped his shoulder, tugged him towards me. His skin felt rubbery, boneless. "Hey," I said, "what's all this?"

"What's the matter, Danny?" Carol said softly and sleepily from behind my shoulder. I hadn't realised she was awake until she spoke.

We dragged Dan into bed with us, plumped a pillow behind him, pulled the duvet up to his chest. We smothered him in comfort and tenderness even as we probed him with questions, but at first he wouldn't or couldn't answer, was too tightly in the grip of his own misery even to acknowledge us.

Eventually, though, we eked a few answers out of him, though they weren't exactly what you might call enlightening. Dan didn't know *why* he was crying. He simply felt tired and unhappy, too tired for school, too unhappy to see his friends.

"I thought you liked school?" I said.

"I do."

"So why don't you want to go?"

"I don't know."

"Is there something you're worried about you're not telling us?"

"No."

"Has someone been bullying you?"

"No."

"Are you worried about the lessons, about not being able to cope?"

"No."

"If there *was* something wrong, you would tell us, wouldn't you, Dan?"

"Yes."

"Because you know we'd help you, don't you? You can always rely on us."

"I know."

"But we can't help you if you don't tell us."

"I know."

We let Dan stay off-school that day. Once we'd calmed him down he crawled back into bed and slept until lunchtime.

"This virus has really wiped him out," I said to Carol. "Just give him time to catch up on his sleep today and he'll be fine tomorrow."

I took Jet with me when I went to pick Beth up from school that afternoon. I knew she'd appreciate the opportunity to show him off to her friends, plus I thought we could get into the habit of heading home the long way, which involved trudging across a couple of farmers' fields, following the thread of the River Wharf for half a mile or so, and then cutting up through the ancient churchyard with its leaning, moss-splotched graves.

Beth, however, wasn't as enthusiastic as I thought she'd be when she spied me standing at the school gates. Not even the sight of Jet straining at his lead, wriggling with excitement at the touch of every passing child, appeared to invigorate her.

"Hi, Daddy," she said wearily, and then, bending down and stroking the dog's head, "Hi, Jet."

"Are you all right, honey?" I asked as we turned along the viaduct walk that would lead us into the first farmer's field.

"Fine."

"How was school?"

"Okay."

"Was it nice to see your friends?"

"Yeah."

She spoke with little conviction, which surprised me. Beth normally loved school. Her reports glowed with praise for her energy and enthusiasm and creativity. Now, though, she sounded like Dan, who—bless him—was a plodder, who was more often than not described as a "quiet but pleasant" member of class, who was "studious," who made "steady progress" in all his subjects.

"You don't sound very sure," I said, trying not to make too big an issue of it.

"I'm just tired."

"Not you too," I said. "Must have been all the excitement of Christmas."

"I've got a tummy ache."

"Have you? When did that come on?"

She shrugged.

"Do you feel up to a walk?"

"Yeah. Whatever."

Neither of us said much as we followed our meandering route home in the gathering dusk of that winter's afternoon. The gloomy sky seemed like a reflection of our mood. When we arrived home, Beth took off her shoes without a word and dumped herself in front of the TV. Dan was already there, but he didn't look up when Beth walked in, and neither did she acknowledge him. I looked at the two of them for a moment, staring like zombies at the screen.

"Aren't you two going to even say hi to one another?"

"Hi," they responded dutifully and simultaneously without averting their gaze from the TV.

"The Stepford kids," I said, raising my eyebrows. Leaving Jet with the kids in the hope he might enliven them (how horribly ironic those words sound now; I might as well have left them a live hand-grenade to play with) I went to seek out Carol.

I found her in the kitchen, making spaghetti bolognese.

"You don't have to get upset," I joked feebly, "they're only onions."

She dumped the chopped onions and garlic, which had been making her eyes water, into a pan of hot olive oil, which received them with an angry eruption of sizzling. As she washed her hands and dabbed at her streaming eyes with kitchen roll, I said, "I hope Beth's not coming down with what Dan had."

When I told her about our walk, she suggested, "Back to school tiredness?"

"Let's hope that's all it is," I said.

It was Beth who woke us up that night. When the sound of her whimpering cries tugged me out of much-needed sleep, it seemed at first like the continuation of a cruel joke.

"I don't believe this," I groaned, rolling onto my back.

"Nnn," said Carol, still ninety per cent asleep.

Feeling as though the muscles of my body had been pulverised by thousands of tiny hammers, I hauled myself out of bed.

"Hey, baby," I said softly, entering Beth's room, "what's the matter?"

She was half-asleep, not really with it. "Tummy hurts," she groaned.

"Come here," I said, stretching out my arms. "Let's get you some medicine."

I lifted her from her bunk bed and carried her into our room. Carol was already sitting up, pushing her long dark hair out of her face.

"Another casualty," I said, and offered Beth to her mother's welcoming embrace. In the semi-light Beth's face looked like a miniature version of Carol's—the same delicate bone structure, the same dark eyebrows, the same pointed chin.

I padded downstairs and into the kitchen for the Calpol. An excitable black-furred body bounded up to me as I opened the door, a cold wet nose snuffling at my bare ankle.

That was when it happened. I suppose you'd call it a vision. As if from nowhere an image leaped into my head that suddenly and momentarily made me feel as though I was no longer in my own kitchen at home, but somewhere else entirely.

I saw the old couple. The ones who had sold Jet to us. They were leaning over me, staring down, and they had a look on their faces that I can only describe as *hungry*.

I jerked so violently that Jet scampered back with a startled yelp, and in that instant the connection was broken. I tottered forward and gripped the edge of the sink, trying to catch my breath.

I was trembling from head to foot. I looked at the window and saw my own ghostly image reflected back at me. What the hell had happened? Was I so tired that I was hallucinating? Or, impossible as it seemed, could it be that I had actually nodded off on my feet for a second and started to dream?

Jet, having got over his startlement, was now wagging his way towards me again. However, anxious to avoid a repeat of what had happened, I said firmly, "Basket."

He obeyed, albeit reluctantly. I fed myself a glass of water, then grabbed the Calpol and went back upstairs.

"How's she doing?" I asked, though the answer was obvious. Beth was curled up in Carol's arms, her face creased in pain.

"Not so good," Carol said, kissing the top of Beth's tousled head.

"Here, sweetheart, have some of this." I poured medicine into a plastic spoon. "It'll make you feel better."

I slept in the spare bedroom and woke, exhausted, to the sound of Carol calling my name. For a moment I considered feigning deafness, turning to face the wall and pulling the duvet over my head, but then I sighed and dragged myself to my feet. Plodding from the bed to the door was like wading through quicksand. The room was steeped in a pearly light, which suggested it was around 7 AM.

I didn't have to ask what was wrong. Stepping into our bedroom, I saw that Carol was flanked in bed by our children, Beth whimpering and frowning in a light sleep, as if having a bad dream, Dan curled up on Carol's other side, tears gleaming on his cheeks.

For a split-second I was gripped with an angry sense of injustice. A jagged thought flashed through my mind: *Oh, for fuck's sake, what's the matter now?*

One look at Carol, though, was enough to make me swallow my resentment. She looked utterly drained, which reminded me that at least I had managed to grab a few hours undisturbed sleep. I moved across and touched her cheek.

"Do you want me to take over?"

"I just want my children to be well," she said, her tired irritability reflecting my own.

I moved around the bed to where Dan was curled like a foetus, sobbing every bit as lustily as the day before. "Hey, big feller, what's up?"

It was the same story. He didn't know. He felt exhausted and unhappy. That day we had two kids off school. The daylight, as it often does, allowed us to re-evaluate, put things into perspective.

Carol and I sat in the kitchen, drinking coffee. We both looked and felt shell-shocked, as if this was a little oasis of quiet in the midst of a fierce and bloody war.

Beth's stomach ache didn't concern us unduly, not then. We put it down to a bug that was going around, told ourselves she'd be right as rain in a day or two.

No, Dan was our main concern.

"What's *wrong* with him?" Carol all but wailed.

I rubbed a hand over my face. The backs of my eyeballs ached; my emotions were brittle, thoughts sluggish.

"He's just exhausted," I said. "This fever obviously took it out of him more than we realised."

I sounded like a broken record. Even I wasn't sure if I believed what I was saying any more.

"I think it's more than that," Carol said. "I think he's worried about something he's not telling us."

"You mean you think he *is* being bullied at school?"

"I don't know. It seems the most likely explanation, but. . . ."

"But what?"

"He says it's not that. He says he doesn't know what it is. I know Dan's . . . quiet, secretive even, but usually, eventually, he tells me what's wrong."

"Do you want me to call Mrs. Pettigrew, see if she can enlighten us?"

"I'll do it. You never ask the right questions, only ever end up getting half the story."

"Oh, thanks."

"Sorry, Steve, but you do."

I shrugged, grumpy but too tired to argue. "All right. Whatever."

Mrs. Pettigrew was Dan's form teacher and year head. Carol called her that afternoon. She was concerned, but could offer no explanation for Dan's behaviour. She said that, as far as she was aware, Dan had settled into secondary school relatively quickly, was a conscientious pupil and seemed to be coping well with the extra work load.

"It did cross our minds that perhaps someone was picking on him," Carol admitted.

"I think you need have no worries on that score, Mrs. Butler," Mrs. Pettigrew said briskly. "We take a very strict line on bullying here, and pride ourselves on identifying it quickly and stamping it out. And we're particularly vigilant with our year sevens. No, if our new young people were being bullied, believe me, we'd know."

It was agreed that Carol, Dan and I would have a meeting with Mrs. Pettigrew and the school psychologist the following day in an effort to get to the bottom of Dan's anxiety.

"Psychologist?" I said when Carol put the phone down. "He doesn't need a psychologist. He's not mad."

"Keep your voice down," she hissed, glancing towards the lounge door, where the kids were huddled in blankets, watching TV. "Of course he's not mad. We're just going for a chat."

"But it's just the bug he's had," I protested for the hundredth time, and saw Carol roll her eyes in exasperation. "He just needs to catch up on his sleep."

As did we all. However it was not to be. That night Beth woke up screaming.

"*Fuck!*" I shouted, hurtling upright from my bed, swathed in a tangle of duvet. "What's going on?"

Carol was already flapping her way out of the door in her white nightshirt. I pulled on my boxers, almost falling in my haste, and went after her.

By the time we reached Beth she had stopped screaming, but only because she was sitting up in bed, sobbing into her hands. Bathed in the soft, peachy glow of the night-light, Carol climbed up the ladder to Beth's bunk, reaching out in comfort.

I wondered dazedly whether there was some blight on our house, whether we—or at least our children—had been cursed for some reason.

"It's okay, baby," Carol crooned, "Mum and Dad are here. Nothing to be scared of."

"There were some bad people," Beth whimpered. "They wanted to get me."

"No one's going to get you," Carol assured her, climbing into the bunk, which creaked alarmingly, and wrapping her arms around our daughter. "You're perfectly safe. You've had a silly dream, that's all."

Instantly I thought of the dream Dan had had a few nights before, which had prompted him to hurl himself from the top of Beth's ladder, and of my own experience in the kitchen the previous night.

"Who *were* the people?" I asked. "The ones in your dream."

Carol frowned at me. "Steve."

"I was just asking."

"Well, don't. She doesn't want to be reminded of it."

"My tummy hurts," groaned Beth.

"What, still?" I said.

"Do you want Daddy to make you a hot chocolate?"

Beth gave a feeble nod.

"Shall we ask Daddy to make us *both* a hot chocolate?"

I held up my hands. "All right, I surrender. Far be it from me to come between women and their chocolate."

I was about to leave the room when, out of the corner of my eye, I saw something black and furry moving in the shadows between Beth's bed-frame and the chest of drawers at its foot. My first ridiculous but jolting thought was that it was some monstrous creature—a giant, man-eating spider perhaps. In my sleep-raddled state I might well have shrieked like a sissy if, in almost that same instant, I hadn't recognised the black bundle for what it really was. It was Jet. Of *course* it was Jet. The dog emerged from the hiding place which I assumed he'd scooted to in terror when Beth had started to scream, wagging his tail uncertainly.

"Hey, little feller," I said, reaching down and picking him up, "what are you doing here?"

I didn't see it even then, didn't make the connection. If I had . . . well, who knows how things might have turned out?

"Beth," Carol said, though not as sternly as she would have done in normal circumstances, "did you fetch Jet out of the kitchen?"

"No," Beth said, but she avoided eye-contact with her mother.

"Are you *sure*?"

"Yes." Now Beth sounded indignant. "He came up by himself."

"But you didn't take him down again, did you?"

Beth pursed her lips, then shook her head.

"*I'll* take him," I said. "Come on, you little monster."

I carried Jet downstairs and plonked him in his basket. When I left the room with three mugs of hot chocolate five minutes later, I made sure the door was firmly shut behind me.

Beth slept fitfully between us for the rest of that night and didn't go to school the next morning. Dan did, albeit unwillingly, but because Beth was off only Carol attended the lunchtime meeting with Mrs. Pettigrew and the psychologist.

"Well, that was a fat lot of good," she said when she arrived home that afternoon. She had washed and styled her hair and made herself up for the occasion, but she still looked tired. There were lines around her mouth that I was certain had not been there a few days before, and the skin round her eyes looked swollen, pouchy.

"What did they say?" I asked.

"I think the conclusion was that Dan is just being a bit moody."

"Right," I said heavily, knowing she had more to tell me. I watched as she took off her coat and flung it on the stairs as if it had offended her.

"I suppose it was Dan's fault as much as theirs," Carol muttered a few minutes later, sipping coffee as if she needed the caffeine both to keep her awake and fuel her dissatisfaction. "He sat there like a zombie, hardly saying anything, answering their questions in monosyllables. I tried to be Miss

Chatty to compensate. I was embarrassed, Steve, embarrassed by our own son. And I was angry too. This so-called psychologist didn't ask him any questions that we couldn't ask him ourselves—that we *haven't* been asking him for the past week. After Dan had gone and there were just the three of us, I was hoping she'd come up with something a bit more insightful, but no. She just came out with the usual guff about Dan being at a difficult age, about secondary school being a big upheaval and how he needed time to adapt, about how behaviour is often affected by hormonal changes coupled with a greater awareness of self and yada, yada, yada. . . ." She flapped her hands in a dismissive, exasperated gesture.

"Well, maybe that's all it is," I said. "Maybe this psychologist didn't come up with anything because there's nothing *to* come up with. I mean, that's the best-case scenario, isn't it? We can live with that whole 'difficult age' thing."

Carol sighed. "I guess." She sat up abruptly, as if rallying herself, and pushed her hair back from her face. "How's Beth?"

"Asleep."

"Wish I was," said Carol and looked at her watch. "In fact, I think I might get my head down for an hour. Fancy a nap?"

"I've got work to do. Got to finish this golf course design by the end of the week and I'm already way behind."

Carol walked across and kissed me on the nose. "Go on then, Mr. Architect, back to your computer. Go and earn your poor sick family some money."

After that, things settled down for a while, in relative terms at least. Beth was still listless, off her food, sleeping poorly, but she went back to school and, being the little trooper she was, made such an effort to be her old cheerful self that no one would have guessed what she was going through— or so her teacher, Mrs. Newsome, later told me. As for Dan, I tried to speak to him on several occasions. I sat on his bed just before lights out a few times, in the hope that a cosy chat *mano a mano* would draw him out of himself; I took him into town to spend his Christmas money one Saturday when Beth was at a school friend's sleepover and bought him a hot chocolate with all the trimmings in Starbucks; I played chess with him, and computer games, and Cluedo, thinking that all he required was a little male bonding to reveal his inner self.

No good. None of it. No good at all. I don't know, maybe what happened *wasn't* preventable, despite what I said earlier. Maybe the instant we all clocked that sign at the side of the road our fate was sealed. Maybe *nothing* would have made a difference. Or maybe—and this is the thought that really haunts me, that I keep coming back to time and again—I just didn't try hard enough, didn't see what was really happening until it was too late. Maybe they were laughing at me all along, joking about what a dumb, useless sap I was, what a *bad* husband and father. It tears me apart, that thought, but it also fuels me, sustains me. It will enable me, I believe, to do what needs to be done, to see what will perhaps be the final meaningful task I will ever perform in my life through to the bitter end.

I can still picture my son's face, telling me that nothing was wrong, that he was fine, that he just felt bad sometimes like everybody else, and that all he wanted was to be left alone.

All *I* wanted, on the other hand, was simply to believe him. Sometimes I almost did.

Dan wasn't a bad lad. He was my poor, lost little boy. He was my son and I loved him. I always will.

I can't remember what came first—the blood in the toilet or the call from Dan's school. Maybe it all happened on the same day. Certainly from this point on our joint lives seemed to converge, as if we were all passengers on a runaway train, hurtling towards some inevitable but terrible conclusion.

The blood in the toilet. Let's start with that. It wasn't my blood, it was Beth's.

I kissed my daughter goodbye at the school gates that morning as usual, masking my gnawing anxiety from her. As soon as I got home I picked up the phone and called my friend, Doug, who was a doctor.

"What can I do for you, Steve?" Doug asked. He was a great guy, but he had a formality to his manner that some people found off-putting. Additionally I knew he would have just started morning surgery, and would be anxious not to start falling behind with his appointments.

"It's Beth," I said. "I'm worried about her."

"Why, what's up?"

"Well, this morning she went to the loo and forgot to flush it, like kids do sometimes, and I noticed there was blood in her poo, quite a bit of it."

Doug retained a professional calm, which was all I would have expected, but which reassured me nonetheless. "Does she have any discomfort when she passes her stools?"

"She has done this last week or so. She's either been constipated or had diarrhoea. And she's been complaining about this stomach ache for weeks. She's been washed out, off her food. . . ."

"Hmm," Doug said. "Bring her in after school and I'll run a few tests. Try and bring a stool sample if you can."

"What do you think's wrong with her?"

"It could be any number of things. Or it could be nothing much at all. I wouldn't like to speculate until we've run the tests and got the results back."

It was around lunchtime when the school called. I was in my study working and heard Carol pick up the phone and say hello. My stomach lurched just as it had when I had seen the blood in the toilet bowl, as Carol said, "Oh my God."

I walked into the hall. Carol was gripping the telephone receiver tightly, as if fearful of dropping it. The colour had drained from her face. Her eyes were wide and dark.

"Yes, of course," she said. "We'll come straight away."

"What's wrong?" I asked the instant she moved the receiver away from her ear. "Is it Beth?"

"No," she said, "it's Dan. He . . ." She uttered a disbelieving laugh ". . . he's attacked someone."

"Attacked?" I repeated the word almost angrily. "What do you mean, attacked?"

"A serious physical assault on a fellow pupil, Mrs. Pettigrew called it. The police are there."

"For fuck's sake," I said. "Couldn't they have called us first?"

"It was the girlfriend of the boy Dan attacked who called the police." Carol shook her head and for a moment I thought she was going to cry. "It never rains. . . ."

"Come on, let's get over there." I grabbed my jacket and the car keys, feeling hollow and sick. On the drive over I noticed that Carol's hands, though lying limply in her lap, were shaking, as if she was struggling to hold herself together.

I don't know what I expected when we pulled in through the school gates. Police cars, with maybe Dan sitting in the back of one of them in handcuffs; a crowd milling about; perhaps even a seedy journalist or two. But all was quiet, the playground empty. Carol and I walked across to Reception, she gripping my hand as if it was the only thing holding her up, me stealing surreptitious glances at the windows of the classrooms surrounding us, half-expecting to see accusatory eyes watching our progress.

"Mrs. Pettigrew called us," I told the dumpy receptionist, whose orange tan made her dark eyes resemble lumps of charcoal. I spoke defiantly to mask the sense of embarrassment, almost shame, that I felt. "Mr. and Mrs. Lister. Daniel's parents."

The blandness of her expression convinced me she knew exactly what we were there for. She made a couple of calls and said, "Mrs. Pettigrew will be along in a moment, if you'd like to take a seat."

We barely had when Mrs. Pettigrew appeared, a tall, business-like woman with short grey hair. "Mr. and Mrs. Lister," she said, grasping each of our hands and giving them a brief, firm shake, "thank you for coming so promptly. If you wouldn't mind following me. . . ."

She led us across the square entrance hall and down a long corridor, her shoes squeaking on the shiny vinyl floor. She stopped at a door bearing a small steel door-plate engraved with the word HEADMASTER. She rapped once, then pushed the door open, indicating that we should enter.

It occurred to me as we stepped inside that the room's occupants had arranged themselves as if for a scene in a movie. The school headmaster, Mr. Trevis, was sitting upright in his chair, hands resting on the desk in front of him, fingers laced together. Dan, by contrast, on the other side of the desk, was slumped in his seat, gazing unfocusedly down at his knees, or perhaps at the patch of floor visible between them. Sitting on the far side of Dan was a uniformed policeman with sergeant's stripes, bespectacled and moustached, overweight but in a solid rather than flabby way.

The sergeant looked up and nodded briefly. As I nodded back, Mr. Trevis lifted his chin and pushed his shoulders even further back as if to make himself as imposing as possible. Only Dan failed to acknowledge our presence.

"Mr. and Mrs. Lister, please sit down," Mr. Trevis said. As we lowered ourselves into our seats, Carol said a little shrilly, "So what happened exactly?"

"That's a question I'm sure we would all appreciate an answer to," Mr. Trevis said. "Unfortunately, thus far, Daniel has been less than forthcoming."

Carol leaned across and touched Dan's forearm. He stiffened a little, but otherwise ignored her. "Dan, what's been going on?"

I could already feel it building in me again, could feel myself getting angry. After the stress of the last few weeks it didn't take much to break the surface. Now Dan's silence and Mr. Trevis's pomposity were enough of a combination to make me snap, "Will you please answer your mother's question!"

Dan flinched, slid a sullen look my way. I glowered back at him. "Nothing," he muttered.

"*Nothing?* How the hell can you say *nothing?* We're not here because nothing happened, Dan. Mrs. Pettigrew told us you attacked someone. Is that true?"

He shrugged, but I could see his lips tightening as he tried to contain the unhappiness we'd seen far too much of recently. "It wasn't like that."

"So what *was* it like? You'd better bloody tell us because, believe me, you're in serious trouble here."

Carol, sitting between Dan and I, gripped my arm. "Don't, Steve."

"Don't what? Have a go at him? What are we supposed to do? Slap his wrist and tell him not to do it again?"

Now anger and resentment flashed in Carol's eyes. "You're not helping."

Miserable on the inside but still angry on the outside, I sat back, folding my arms. "All right, then, *you* get him to tell us what's going through that head of his. Believe me, I've tried. It's like squeezing blood from a stone."

In the simmering silence that followed, I felt ashamed of my outburst, wished that I could withdraw from this excruciating situation.

"Dan," Carol said softly, "you have to tell us what happened. Your dad's right. You could be in serious trouble."

"It wasn't my fault," Dan said.

"So whose fault was it?"

"It was him. Parker. He was having a go at me."

"Parker?" said Carol.

"Matthew Parker," clarified Trevis. "The boy who was attacked."

"Where's *he* now?" I asked, trying not to make it sound like an accusation.

"York District Hospital. One of our supply teachers, Mr. Cook, drove him there to have his injuries attended to."

Carol blanched.

"What injuries?" I asked.

"Cuts and bruises mainly," the sergeant said.

"And a broken wrist," added Trevis a little tetchily.

"A suspected broken wrist, yes," the sergeant said.

"It was clearly broken," Trevis said. "Matthew claims that Daniel stamped on it."

Carol looked too upset to talk. A ghost of a smile played over Dan's face and he shook his head.

"Dan," I said, "is that true?"

"No," muttered Dan indignantly.

"So what happened?"

"He hit me. That's how he broke his wrist. If he *did* break it. It's not my fault if my head's tougher than his arm, is it?"

"So what are you saying? That *he* started the fight?"

"He was calling me names. Showing off in front of his stupid girlfriend. He wound me up. He's always winding people up. He thinks he's cool, but he's just an arsehole."

"That's not what I asked, Dan? Who threw the first punch?"

He shrugged, turning sullen again. I looked from Trevis to the sergeant. "What's going to happen?"

There was talk of suspension, of possible exclusion, of criminal prosecution even, but in the end the incident blew over. Or perhaps I should say that this particular incident was superseded by what happened afterwards. In the meantime Dan came home with us to "cool down". Carol tried to talk to him, but it was like banging her head against a brick wall. I wanted to rage at Dan, but knew it would be equally counter-productive. In the end I grounded him for a month and took away his computer games, but he simply shrugged, which made me feel nothing more than petty and ineffectual.

I'm ashamed to say that as it turned out, Dan's behaviour—or rather, our response to it—became quickly shunted down our list of priorities. It wasn't that we didn't care. Far from it. It was simply that within a short space of time, Carol and I had to contend with emotional overload. I'm jumping ahead of myself, but certain things happened which made us feel as if we were being bombarded from all sides, as if we didn't know which way to turn. Correction: it felt as if that runaway train I mentioned earlier was being bombarded from all sides, with us inside it. We were reeling from the constant motion, the constant barrage, unable to do little but cling on and hope that the impact at the end of the line wouldn't be too devastating.

It becomes a jumble from now on, days and events overlapping, running into one another. It was some time around now, I think (around *then* I should say), that I started to realise what was happening. What was *really* happening. Not that I could stop it. I remember this:

I guess you'd call it a dream, although I now believe (I *know*) that it was more than a dream. I remember a weight on my chest. I remember feeling stifled, panicky, wanting to wake up but being unable to do so. I remember that clearly—*wanting to wake up*—which implies conscious thought. I remember seeing *them*. Their hungry eyes. Watching me. Feeding off me.

Drinking in my confusion, my fear, my misery. Getting stronger on it. Like vampires.

Just like vampires.

It was that thought that enabled me to surface, to crash out of the murky depths and into the light, gasping and spluttering, almost sobbing. For several seconds the dream clung to me like . . . like weed, like pond slime, and it was in that long, confused moment that I gained an impression, conversely both vague and vivid, of a warm, suffocating weight releasing itself from my chest, and then of something sleek and black slipping away from me, down from the bed and out of the room.

I remember thinking, in my befuddled state, that somehow my nightmare had escaped from my sleeping mind, had come out of me like some evil black tumour and was now free somewhere in the house. I thought of my children, and my fear for them had me leaping out of bed on shaky legs. I was naked and dream-fever sweaty, and the chill January (or February; it might have been February by this time) air clung to me, making my skin contract, making me shudder inside. It was dark. I had no idea what time it was—somewhere in the dead hours, four or five.

"Wossmatter?" Carol murmured from her side of the bed.

"Nothing," I muttered. "Go to sleep."

I checked on my children. For once they were sleeping peacefully. They had both suffered from nightmares recently, nightmares of being pursued by "bad people," but this night their faces looked free of trouble, achingly vulnerable, heart-rendingly innocent.

Carol had not thought it unusual that their recent dreams had seemed to run parallel. "We're all suffering at the moment," she had said, "all experiencing the same things." She seemed to cling to the hope that it would blow over, that the lighter days and the warmer nights would bring a healthier outlook for us all.

And what did *I* think? I don't know. Tunnel vision mentality. I think I was just pushing it all to the back of my mind, taking it step by step, trying to cling on as the runaway train hurtled through the night.

Beth's face looked marble-pale that night, her skin thin as gossamer; she looked as though a gentle breeze would blow her away. Dan's face looked slack and smooth as a toddler's; it hurt my heart to think of how it had been etched with anguish so often these past weeks.

I looked down at them for a long time, listening for movement, for the presence of some other living thing in each of their rooms, and then I went downstairs. The kitchen door was ajar, and at that moment something clicked; a connection was made. I went in and turned on the light.

Jet was in his basket, head up, looking at me, as if he had been waiting. His tail thumped the blanket beneath him, but for the first time it didn't strike me as a friendly sound, reminded me rather of someone slapping a lead pipe into an open palm to test its weight, its efficacy as a weapon.

I stared at the dog for a moment, and then very softly I said, "Was it you?"

Jet gazed at me blandly, his tail continuing to thump . . . thump . . . thump. . . .

"It *was* you, wasn't it?" I said. I approached the basket, knelt in front of him. After a moment's hesitation I took his head in my hands. Gently. I looked into his eyes, saw nothing but my own trapped and miniaturised reflection.

"Are you there?" I said. "Can you hear me?"

I suddenly realised what I was doing. I released Jet's head, patted the side of his muzzle. "It's not your fault is it, boy?" I said. "It's them. What are we going to do about it, eh?"

I stood up, thinking hard. Eventually I left the kitchen, shutting the door behind me. I went back to bed, crawling in next to Carol, and lay between now cool sheets, not sleeping but thinking about what I should do.

After I had dropped Beth off at school I got in the car and drove back to the farm. I told Carol I was going to town to get some computer software I needed for my next design project. The lie came easily, which made me feel a little ashamed; we were not in the habit of keeping secrets from one another.

It was one of those days where it never seems to get properly light, the air murky and grey, dark colours nothing but blocks of black. I drove up the rutted track until the stunted trees unmeshed their branches and revealed the farmhouse.

It was even more squat and shabby than I remembered. A slight tremor went through me as I got out of the car, but the desire to protect my children was greater than my fear for myself. I approached the house, wondering whether they knew I was here, my eyes darting from one small black window to another in an effort to detect a flicker of movement. The sheep's skull grinned at me as I knocked, the impact jarring up through my cold knuckles. I bit my bottom lip to stop it from trembling. The door opened.

If the woman recognised me she didn't show it. She looked at me with an amiable, even quizzical expression.

All the anxiety and stress of the past weeks, the sheer, impotent fury that had spluttered out of me now and then, but which for the most part had remained dormant, curdling my stomach, suddenly rushed to the surface. I felt my skin grow hot, felt sweat spring out on my forehead. "Is your husband in?" I asked curtly.

"Jud? Yes, he's having his breakfast. Who shall I say-"

"I want to speak to him. To both of you."

The old woman looked taken aback. Perhaps she and her husband weren't used to being found out, tracked down. Perhaps they had been doing this for years with no comeback.

"I suppose you'd better come in then," she said doubtfully. She stood aside and I marched past her, into the kitchen.

Just as before, Jud was sitting at the table. His ruddy face shone beneath his unkempt beard. He was shovelling bacon and scrambled eggs into his slot of a mouth and barely looked up as I entered.

I glanced again at his wife, who had closed the door behind me and now stood with her arms folded. Now I thought about it, she looked healthier too, rosier. I thought of my children, of the life that was being sucked out of them, and my anger twisted up a notch. Clearing my throat to stop my voice from strangling, I said, "I know you know why I'm here."

Jud glanced at me, but didn't respond. "Do we?" said the woman.

"Don't play games!" I didn't quite shout, but my voice echoed in the stone-flagged room.

That got Jud's attention. He put down his knife and fork with a clatter and swiped the back of a hairy hand across his mouth.

"What's your problem, sonny?" he growled.

I took a lurching step towards him. "My *problem* is what you and your wife are doing to my children. Don't think I don't know, and don't try to deny it."

Jud stood up. Despite his age he was a bear of a man. At least six feet four, he had a broad chest and shoulders, powerful arms. If it came to a physical battle, he ought to win hands down, regardless of his advancing years—but I was fighting for my children's lives and was prepared to take on all-comers.

Glancing at his wife he said, "Do you know what this feller's on about, our Flo?"

"Not a word," she said. "I don't even know who he is. Hang on a minute, though," she added immediately, "didn't you buy one of our Ebony's pups a while back? Aye, that's it. You had two little 'uns with you. A boy and a girl."

I watched this charade, dumbstruck. Her sheer gall, her measured insouciance, astounded me. What did she hope to achieve by denying what we all knew to be true?

"You know who I am," I said. I jabbed an accusatory finger in her direction. "You know who I am and you know what you did."

"*That's enough!*" roared Jud. He had planted his fists on the table and was leaning forward, as if he intended to vault it like an ape. "I don't know what you reckon we've done, sonny, but I'm not having you coming into *my* house, upsetting my wife—"

"*Upsetting your wife!*" I all but squawked. "After what you've done to my family, I have every right—"

"*What we've done!*" Now it was Jud's turn to interrupt me. "Well, that's just it, isn't it? We don't know *what* we've done, or what *you* reckon we've done. If you ask me, you've got a screw loose, sonny. I think you need to see somebody."

"I'm not stupid," I said, "and I'm not mad. I know how you use that dog. I've seen you watching us through him."

Jud was crimson, his eyes bulging. His wife, by contrast, looked ashen, evidently alarmed by the fact that her hideous little secret had been exposed.

"Look, let's calm down, shall we?" she said. "If you could just explain what you think we've done, young man, then perhaps we could put it right, or help you to."

I swung to face her. "Just leave my family alone," I hissed. "I'm on to you. I know what you're doing and how you do it, and if you try anything else I'll know."

She cast a despairing look at Jud, who growled, "We haven't been near you *or* your family, and neither do we intend to be. Now bugger off out of my house before I chuck you out!"

"I'm warning you," I said. "Leave us alone or I'll call the police."

"And tell 'em *what*? There's a few things *I'd* like to tell 'em, believe me."

He was right, of course. The police would never believe my story. I crossed the floor to the door of the cottage. The old woman stood aside to let me pass. I opened the door and felt the cold morning air washing over me, drying the sweat on my face. "You're parasites, the both of you," I said. "You live off other people. You make me sick. If I hear of this happening to anyone else, I'll . . . I'll stop you. I swear I will."

It wasn't much of a parting shot, and I didn't feel as though I had handled the situation well, but my mind was all over the place and it was the best I could do. At least they knew now. At least they knew that *I* knew. It might be enough to make them stop. And if it wasn't . . . well, I'd cross that bridge when I came to it.

I drove back up to the main road and parked on the grassy verge. I got out of my car and, with cars speeding past me on their way to and from Leeds, tried to remove the sign that had drawn us to the farm in the first place. It was harder than it looked. The sign was set too deeply into the earth to be uprooted and the post was too sturdy to be broken with a kick. In the end I had to content myself with picking up a rock and defacing the words on the sign itself, making them unreadable. At least in the short term it would stop other families being drawn into the web.

Carol was waiting for me when I got home. "Doug wants to see us," she said.

She looked pale and aged by worry, almost withered by it. Or maybe it wasn't worry that had done this. Maybe the . . . the vampires were taking not just my children's life energy, but my wife's too, sapping it right out of her.

I took her hand. Sure enough it was cold, as if bloodless. "When?" I asked gently.

"Today. Noon."

I smiled, kissed her forehead. "It'll be all right," I said. "Don't worry. From now on, everything will be fine."

As soon as we stepped into Doug's office and sat down he said, "I won't beat about the bush." He walked to the window, glanced out as if to check the weather, then stood with his back to it, facing us. "I'm afraid Beth has got cancer."

Carol gasped, and for an instant I was so certain she was about to collapse that I shot out my hands and grabbed her. I felt my own stomach looping as if I was on a rollercoaster. I could barely croak, "What . . . I mean . . . what sort?"

For an instant Doug's professional mask slipped. He looked anguished by the bad news he'd evidently been dreading to impart. He licked his lips, made an effort to compose himself. "Initial evidence would suggest that it's centred in the stomach with secondaries in the oesophagus and bowel. We'll know more after surgery."

"Surgery?" whispered Carol.

"I've arranged an appointment for tomorrow. If you're agreeable, they'll be operating at three PM. The surgeon will be Oscar Fleetwood. He's a good man. One of the best."

"So soon?" I said. "Is it really that serious?"

Doug tried to smile, and almost managed it. "Better to catch these things sooner rather than later. We've got to give Beth every chance there is."

"You make it sound as if there isn't much."

Doug winced. "I'm sorry, I didn't mean to."

I was still holding Carol. She stirred in my arms, raised her head. She looked ravaged, her eyes red with tears. In a blurred, broken voice, she said, "How serious is it, Doug? What's going to happen to my baby?"

Again that grimace, as if he was in pain. "Honestly, guys, if I could give you an exact prognosis I would. But I'm not going to bullshit you. All I can say at the moment is . . . it looks pretty virulent."

Carol crumpled, began to cry. She sounded so wretched, so devoid of hope, that it frightened me. I could only hold her, unable to summon a single word of comfort. Later, when the kids were asleep, I said, breaking the silence that had formed around us like a shell, "I know what caused this."

She looked at me as if she had been asleep or was drunk. "What?"

"I know what made Beth sick. I know why Dan is behaving like he is."

She frowned, irritated by my obtuseness. "What are you talking about?"

She was lying on the settee, a blanket around her as if she was sick. I moved across the room from the armchair, took her hands (still cold) in mine and looked into her eyes with as much earnestness, as much sanity as I could muster.

"It's Jet," I said.

"Jet?" She looked utterly bewildered. "What do you mean?"

I tried to keep my voice light, as if by doing so it would dilute the sheer craziness of what I was about to say. "Well, not Jet himself, but the ones who sold him to us. The old couple. You remember?"

Still that bewildered look, undercut with an irritability that suggested I was distracting her from what was really important. "Steve, you're not making sense."

"Just hear me out." Clutching her hands as if to prevent her pulling away, I told her about the kids' dreams and my own, about my experience in the kitchen, about the connections I'd made, the conclusions I'd reached.

I had hoped that the words alone would be enough to convince her, but even as I was speaking I became aware of how relating the events seemed to reduce them, made them sound arbitrary, fantastical.

"Don't you see?" I said, frantic to make her believe, "Jet's a conduit. They're using him to get to us. They're channelling our energy through him, absorbing it into themselves. They're like vampires, Carol. It's not Jet's fault, but if we get rid of him it'll effectively cut off their supply line and then . . . well, who knows? Things might get better. *Beth* might get better."

It was no use. Carol didn't just look bewildered by the time I'd finished, she looked angry and scared. She squirmed, trying to pull away.

"Let go of me, Steve," she whimpered. "You're hurting my arms."

I let go, and was astonished to see dark red finger marks on her skin where I'd been gripping her. "I know I'm right—" I began.

"*Right?* Have you actually *heard* yourself? It's crazy talk, Steve."

"It's not crazy—"

"*It is!* Look, I know we're under a lot of stress, but going off into . . . into cloud cuckoo land won't help anybody."

I sat back on my haunches with a groan. "All right," I said. "Suppose what I'm saying *is* crazy—"

"It is."

I held up my hands. "Either way, doesn't it make sense to get rid of Jet? I mean, we're going to have to devote all our time to Beth from now on. We haven't got time to look after a dog as well. And dogs are not exactly hygienic, are they? He could be a source of infection."

"Beth loves that dog. He makes her happy. It's going to be hard enough for her as it is over the next . . . however long, without taking away the things that make her happy as well."

"But he's killing her," I protested.

She sat bolt upright on the settee and suddenly she was shrieking at me. "*No, he's not! It's the cancer that's killing her! It's the fucking cancer, you fucking stupid man!*"

The next few weeks were hell. Beth's surgery revealed that the cancer was even more widespread and aggressive than had at first been feared. She was subjected to an intensive course of chemotherapy, which made her constantly sick and which caused all her lovely blonde hair to fall out. By the beginning of April she was so weak she could barely stand. She looked like a famine victim, her eyes sunk deep in the hollows of her skull, thin yellowish flesh clinging so tightly to her skeleton that through it you could see the outline of her teeth, her ribs, her shoulder blades, each individual phalanx and metacarpal bone in her hand.

We were back and forth to the hospital on an almost daily basis. Our life was defined by the different stages of Beth's illness. Throughout that time I kept Jet away from her as much as I could, without making it too obvious.

If Carol noticed she didn't comment. She never again mentioned the conversation we'd had on the day we'd found out about Beth; I assumed she'd decided to ignore it, or regard it as a minor mental aberration on my part, brought on by shock. As surreptitiously as I could I continued to watch Jet closely, looking for signs that Jud and his wife had ignored my warning.

In the background Dan simmered away, still quiet and withdrawn, but seemingly okay. Things had settled down at school and he didn't seem to be experiencing the nightmares and emotional trauma that had plagued him at the beginning of the year. I took this as tentative evidence that Jud and his wife had cut the link, decided to leave us alone. I felt vaguely guilty that some other poor family might be suffering as we had, but with Beth to occupy me the twinges were few and far between and certainly not strong enough to goad me into action.

In the event the question of whether Jud and his wife were still linked to us through Jet quickly became irrelevant. Despite the best efforts of a dedicated team of doctors and nurses, Beth's condition deteriorated. She was transferred to our local hospice on Monday 10th April and lapsed into a coma in the early hours of Wednesday 12th. Carol and I were sitting at her bedside around noon that day when one of the hospice nurses tapped on the door and entered.

"Sorry to barge in, but there's a police officer here to see you," she said.

Carol and I looked at each other. We were so exhausted, at such a low ebb, that the news barely raised a flicker of alarm between us.

I gave her hand a quick squeeze. "I'll go." I followed the nurse along several corridors to where a uniformed constable was standing uncomfortably between a matching pair of plump sofas, upholstered in royal blue and gold, which faced each other across the plushly-carpeted expanse of the Reception area.

"Mr. Lister?" The PC was lean and ginger-haired.

I was so tired, so pre-occupied, that I had no conception of why he might be there, ludicrous though that sounds. "Yes," I said.

"Mr. Lister, I'm PC Wainwright. I know this is a bad time for you, but we thought you ought to know. It's your son, Daniel, he . . ." he hesitated "Well, there's no easy way of putting this. He's in some trouble, I'm afraid. Peril perhaps I ought to say. . . ."

I was so close to the end of my tether that the young PC's stumbling delivery made me snap, "What's he done, constable?"

Wainwright puffed out a breath, composing himself. "He's up on the school roof, Mr. Lister. He's armed with a knife and he's taken a fellow pupil hostage. He's threatening to kill both the girl and himself."

I hadn't thought I could sink any lower, but what little energy I had left suddenly seemed to be rushing out of me, escaping through the pores in my skin. My head spun and I stumbled. I made a grab for the arm of the nearest sofa to steady myself, missed it and would have fallen if Wainwright hadn't stepped forward and grabbed my arm.

"Just sit down a minute, Mr. Lister, get your breath back," Wainwright said. "I'll get you some water."

Despite my spinning head, my listlessness, I was gripped by a sense of urgency. "Need to see Dan," I said, each word an effort.

"Drink this first."

I had no sense of time passing, but suddenly he was thrusting a plastic cup full of water into my hand.

I sipped and immediately felt sick. After fighting down the nausea I sipped again. Three sips later I felt able to stand. "Let's go," I said.

I called Carol from the police car. All I told her was that Dan was in trouble again. When she asked what kind, I lied and said I wasn't sure, but that I'd handle it. "Stay with Beth. I'll be back as soon as I can," I said.

On the way to the school I asked Wainwright whether Dan had given any reason for what he had done.

"We're trying to get him to talk, but he's not saying much, apart from the fact that he wants to be left alone and that he'll kill the girl and himself. We were hoping you might be able to give us some insight into his behaviour."

I thought of telling this earnest young constable what I had told Carol— about Jet, about Jud and his wife, about nightmares and visions. I pictured myself using words like "conduit" and "vampires" and "life essence" and then I pictured Wainwright telling his colleagues there was no wonder the son was a nutter; he was simply taking after his old man.

I shrugged. "He's been unhappy since the turn of the year. He's always been a quiet boy, but recently he's become sullen, withdrawn. His mother and I have tried to talk to him, but. . . ." My voice choked off as emotion overcame me. Wainwright glanced at me, but didn't say anything.

Eventually, feebly, I said, "We just thought it was part and parcel of becoming a teenager . . . you know. . . ."

I felt I ought to be asking a million questions, but my mind was reeling and I could think of only one. "Who's the girl?"

"Her name's Fiona Summerfield," said Wainwright. "She's the girlfriend of a boy I believe your son was feuding with earlier this term."

Feuding. It seemed a strange, almost medieval word. "Matthew Parker," I said. I had never met the boy, but I remembered his name.

On this occasion the entrance road to the school *was* full of vehicles. There was a police van, four police cars, three vans bearing TV company logos and plenty of regular cars, quite a number of which had men sitting in them as if waiting for something. Beside one of the TV vans were two men and a woman. One of the men was holding a camera and the other a fluffy mike on a long pole that resembled a giant cotton bud. The woman was wearing a bottle-green suit and holding a smaller microphone. The man with the camera pointed it at us as we passed, making me hunch my shoulders instinctively. Wainwright groaned.

"Bloody press already. Who told *them*?"

"Someone who works at the school," I suggested. "A caretaker or dinner lady."

"They ought to have more sense."

The school playground had been cordoned off. More journalists were waiting patiently behind a makeshift barrier of police tape. As we approached, several raised cameras in our direction. I tried to resist the urge to put my hand in front of my face, thinking it would only encourage them.

Wainwright lifted the barrier and I ducked through. Uniformed police officers and a couple of men in suits were standing around, apparently aimlessly. People were either silent or talking in low murmurs. By the main building a fire engine was parked, its helmeted occupants standing around a jump net. They reminded me of overgrown kids in fancy dress waiting for a go on a trampoline.

It was an odd, surreal atmosphere. I wondered whether it was all over, whether Dan had come down and was now sitting somewhere—in the staff room maybe—having a cup of tea, being gently questioned by a police officer. Wainwright led me over to the shorter and stouter of the two suited men. He had grey hair, too much of which sprouted from his ears, and shaving cuts on his throat.

"Sir, this is Mr. Lister, Daniel's father," Wainwright said. "Mr. Lister, this is DCI Chadwick."

We shook hands. Chadwick had a powerful grip.

"Do you want me to talk to Dan?" I asked.

"Not at the moment, sir, if you don't mind. A trained officer is currently trying to establish a dialogue with your son. For now your presence is enough. We'll let him know you're here. And may we say that you're concerned for his safety and for the safety of the young lady?"

I nodded, swallowed as emotion rushed through me again. Trying to keep my voice from cracking I said, "Tell your officer to tell him that his mother and I love him very much, and that we . . . we just want him back safely with us."

Time passed—though there persisted the odd sense that it was at a standstill, that nothing at all was happening. I was tense, sick with worry, wound up like a spring, frustrated at not being able, or rather allowed, to do anything to help.

I've gone through it over and over in my mind, have wondered whether I should have insisted on speaking to Dan myself, whether I could have made a difference. I could see him and the girl, his hostage, as nothing more than a pair of occasionally bobbing heads, black against the sky, above the parapet of the school's tallest building. Were they bobbing because they were becoming animated, perhaps arguing or fighting, or were they simply leaning forward to peer down at what was happening below? Could Dan see me in the playground? Did he ask for me? Did he give a thought to Carol and me at all? If so, I never found out.

He jumped just after five. He threw the girl off first. We knew something was happening because we heard screaming and pleading from up above us. The girl's terror cut through the air like a biting wind on a spring day. I looked up, saw their black shapes struggling, converging and breaking apart. Then, abruptly, shockingly, she was falling, a black sprawl of limbs against the glint of the windows. She made no sound. The firemen rushed forward with their safety net, positioned it, caught her. By this time Dan was falling too. He had jumped a second or two after pushing the girl. There was no one to break *his* fall. People ran towards the building. I ran with them, my head filled with the insane notion that somehow I could catch my son, save him. He hit the ground and broke apart, smashed like a soft fruit full of bright red pulp. They say that the mind blots out the greatest traumas, the most terrible sights, but it's not true. Whenever I close my eyes I see Dan's body bursting open on the concrete. I think I'll probably see it for the rest of my life.

The irony is that the one they managed to catch, the girl, was already dead. Dan had killed her before throwing her off the roof, slashed her throat with a knife taken from our kitchen, the same knife that I'd been using the day before to slice onions, chop capsicums.

Most people were kind to us afterwards, on the surface at least. However, beneath that kindness I detected a sense of . . . wariness, suspicion, a tacit insinuation in almost every case that somehow Carol and I were to blame for what our son had done. Murderers are not born, after all, but made. They are products of their upbringing, warped by their experiences. I didn't need to be a mind reader to know that this was what people were thinking. There were articles about it in the paper. For a little while Dan became a *cause celebre*, a topic of discussion in pubs, on factory floors, on TV debate programmes.

A minority were more vocal. Twice Carol was pilloried in the street by mothers who made it clear they considered her unfit to number amongst them; a brick was thrown through our living room window; we received crank calls, death threats through the post, other letters that were little more than crazed rants.

A week after Dan's suicide, the day after his funeral, in fact, Beth died. Our gentle, beautiful girl slipped away one Wednesday afternoon at 3:30, the time when her classmates' parents would be picking them up from school. Carol and I were with her, sitting either side of her bed, each holding one of her tiny, fragile hands. The day she died a chasm opened beneath us. While she'd been alive, even after Dan's death, we had had a purpose, a reason for getting up in the morning, somewhere to go. But now there was nothing. We had both been stripped away—psychologically, emotionally, spiritually— to such an extent that we no longer even had each other. We were ghosts, empty, trapped by our grief. We ate and we slept, but it was all automatic, there was no structure to it, no sense of progress, no notion of the future.

"What's the point?" Carol said to me one day in a rare moment of communication.

"Of what?" I said.

"Of this. Of any of it. Of existing. Why do we bother carrying on?"

"I don't know," I said. "Because . . ." I struggled to think of an answer ". . . I don't know."

It was the last conversation we ever had. Later that day I was sitting in my study, staring at the last piece of work I'd done on my computer screen, trying and failing to work out why the fuck it mattered, how I could ever have considered it *important*, when I heard her car drive away. It was an hour later, when I went to find Jet to take him for a walk—another aimless pursuit, another example of simply going through the motions—that I realised she had taken the dog with her.

The police arrived later. I don't know what time, but it was dark. I was sitting in the house without lights on, obscurely comforted by the sense that I was smothered, cocooned in shadows, by the sense that as the darkness thickened around me, the world and its harsh, dreadful realities were receding, becoming more abstract.

Resenting the intrusion, I turned the hall light on and pulled the front door open. I knew from the looks on their faces what they were here for. I'd become used to that same expression of dread on every face I'd seen lately. They introduced themselves, told me they had some bad news, that they thought I ought to sit down.

"I'm afraid your wife met with an accident earlier this evening," the taller of the policemen said. "Her car went off the road. Paramedics did all they could, but they couldn't save her. She died at the scene."

"The dog too," the shorter and younger of the policemen added, then winced as if he had said something crass, inappropriate.

"So that's it," I said to them. "I'm on my own now."

I felt oddly calm. I don't know what they thought of me. Probably that I was in shock, stunned to near-catatonia by the devastating sequence of events that had shattered my life in less than a month.

Maybe their assumption was correct. Maybe I *was* in shock. But it was a lucid, clear-headed sort of shock. In a strange way the news of Carol's death didn't surprise me. I had been expecting it. It felt almost as though it was inevitable.

That didn't stop me wondering about the *nature* of her death, though. Had she, after all, been thinking about what I had told her? Had she been weighing up the evidence, or perhaps discovering new evidence of her own, and thus slowly coming round to my point of view? Had she set out to confront Jud and his wife? Had they put some sort of influence on her, forced her off the road? Had they used Jet as a murder weapon, got him to attack her while she was driving?

Or was I making the wrong assumptions? Perhaps her death was suicide? Or even the accident it appeared to be?

Strange how the mind sifts and turns and questions, as though by discovering the truth it can somehow turn back time, alter the consequences.

The one thing that Carol's death did was to clear the confusion, cut away the loose ends. Nothing mattered now. There was no one to worry about, no one whose feelings I had to consider. There was a single path stretching straight out ahead of me. I knew what I had to do.

How do you kill vampires? With stakes? With holy water? With crucifixes? With garlic? Well, let's see, shall we. I'm going to have a hammer in one hand and an axe in the other, and I'm going to go at them for all I'm worth, and if they're still moving after that lot, then I'll get the tent pegs I've brought with me out of the car and I'll drive them into their rotten black hearts.

And then what? Well, then my mission will be done. My life will be over. I'm going now. A short walk up the lane, a knock on the door . . .

Wish me luck.

WAITING FOR THE BULLET

The first thing we saw was the smoke. It curled into the air from fuck knew how many barbecues and burger vans, giving a dirty grey underbelly to the fluffy white clouds. Before then the sky had been nothing but pure, pigeon-egg blue, the sun high and hot and blinding, like a permanent camera flash reflected off a steel plate. The roads were baking blacktop layered with white dust from the surrounding desert, which kicked up in clouds behind us. Whenever we found ourselves behind a slow-moving truck—it hadn't happened often, maybe twenty or thirty times on the entire four hundred mile drive—we had had to close the windows to avoid choking to death, though that had trapped the stink of Jed's skunk in with us. It was the lesser of two evils. Just.

Couple of minutes after the smoke the Frisco site became visible on the horizon. All we saw at first, appearing and disappearing as the ground rose and fell, was a random selection of roofs—spikes and jags and domes. But then we crested a rise and suddenly we saw the whole panorama laid out before us.

"Fuck me," Abi muttered from the back seat.

I touched the brake of the camper van, slowing the vehicle to a crawl, so we could take it all in. Within the vast circle of the high perimeter fence a bizarre shanty town had formed, composed of pre-fabs and marquees and the multi-coloured triangles of thousands of tents. We could hear music playing, see people milling like insects over a corpse.

"Bullet time!" Jed announced gleefully, his pink-eyed, bearded face appearing between the front seats.

Fran, sitting beside me, asked anxiously, "Where are you going to park, Chris?"

I thought that was pretty obvious. On the right-hand side of the road, before the Frisco site itself, a quarter-mile square of desert had been transformed into one huge parking lot. Some of the vehicles were so caked with dust they looked as though they had been there for years. People were sitting on lawn chairs beside their mobile homes, reading or eating or praying. I could see kids playing ball or Frisbee. There was even one guy with a beard down to his navel, who had painted himself blue, doing some kind of tai-chi.

I cranked the van into gear and cruised down the hill. Just before we came parallel with the first of the parked vehicles, a guy in a sweat-stained grey T-shirt and khaki shorts stepped up on to the verge and started gesturing to us. His left arm was stuck out at a right angle and his right arm was windmilling, in the familiar gesture of a traffic cop ordering a vehicle to pull over. I slowed to an idling halt and instructed Fran to wind down her window.

"Hi," I called, leaning across.

The guy stepped up, put his hand on the window frame and peered in at us. He was maybe twenty-five, tall and tanned, his tousled hair bleached by the sun. He grinned, though the grin was intended mostly for Fran. I felt a brief stab of ownership as he ran his gaze over her tight, salmon-pink top and white shorts.

"Hi," he said. "How long you folks here for?"

"We got a four-day pass with an option to extend," I told him.

"Care to show me?"

I shrugged. "No offence, but we have no idea who you are."

The guy held up a finger as if I'd made a good point and produced a grubby laminated card from the pocket of his shorts. Beneath the words OFFICIAL FRISCO STEWARD was a picture of him with darker hair and his name, Brad Chesuik. His steward number, some eight or nine-digit affair, was on there too, but I couldn't be bothered to read it.

I handed the card back and dug our pass out of the glove compartment. I had a moment where I wondered whether the ID he'd showed me was fake, and whether I'd be able to catch him if he took off, but he barely glanced at the pass before giving it back to me.

"That's cool," he said. "Follow the channel through there. Someone'll show you where to park."

"Can't we park inside?" asked Fran.

"Not without a thirty-day pass."

"But all our stuff's in the van. Are we supposed to walk all the way back to it when we want something?"

"Sorry," Brad said, but he didn't look as though he *was* sorry and I couldn't really blame him.

"It's okay," I said, putting a hand on Fran's knee, "we'll manage."

"Yeah," said Abi from the back. "What're we gonna need anyway? Money and water. It's no big deal."

Fran and Abi had started this trip as best friends, but their relationship had begun to fray almost from the off. Me and Fran had been together almost two years, and I had always known that Fran was more uptight than she usually let on, especially when she was outside her comfort zone. It was one of the things I found endearing about her; it brought out the protective male in me. What surprised me, though, was that Abi, who had known Fran since they were both five, seemed to be finding all this out for the first time. Had their relationship really been so shallow before? Or maybe Abi had changed? She certainly didn't seem the easy-going, fun-loving girl I'd always taken her to be. She was more moody and self-obsessed than I'd expected—she got angry and irritable at the slightest thing. One night we'd got pissed in a bar in Texas and Abi had disappeared. I thought she'd staggered out to be sick and went to see if she was okay. I found her in the front seat of the camper van, sobbing. But when I asked her what was wrong, she just said she was "homesick."

Anyway. We'd been in the States nearly four weeks now and this was our last major stop-off before flying home next Thursday. Once we'd spent a few days at the Frisco site we'd drive the camper van back to San Fran and that'd be it.

What "it" actually was I wasn't entirely sure, but it felt like . . . I dunno . . . the end of innocence. The end of the adventure. I know that sounds a bit wanky, but the thing was, all four of us had finished Uni in the late spring and had worked our butts off in menial jobs through June and July so that we could afford this trip. We hadn't actually said as much, but I think we all saw this as our last big blow-out before settling down. On August 2nd we'd flown out in a state of near-delirious excitement, and back then the days stretching ahead of us had seemed endless, a glorious buffer between ourselves and real life.

But those days were now nearly all gone. It was hard to believe. Before heading off, Fran and I had talked about this being a life-changing experience, but had it been? I honestly don't know. I think we thought we'd arrive home with a fresher, more focused, more mature perspective on our individual futures—but at that moment all I was really sure about was that I was knackered from all the driving, and the nightly drinking, and the lack of sleep. And as for the others, well, it didn't seem to me as if any of them had undergone any great epiphany. Fran had spent most of the last four weeks worrying; Abi had spent it lurching from one foul mood to another; and Jed had spent it stoned out of his skull.

It felt good to finally get out of the camper van and stretch my legs and back. Abi was right—we didn't need much. Some water, some sun-block, my wallet and my green Oakland Athletics baseball cap to prevent me getting sunstroke.

It was weird to finally be here, to be walking up to the Frisco site, past all the parked-up vehicles and the reinforced food vans and the opportunists selling shitty souvenirs. We'd seen these places on TV. In the early days especially they'd been all over the news. Atmosphere-wise, I hadn't known what to expect, but now that I was actually here, I felt the same kind of eager anticipation I felt at somewhere like Glastonbury. I didn't feel scared, or even apprehensive, probably because out here hardly anyone was wearing protective gear. There were a few family groups—mum, dad, kids—sweltering in bullet-proof vests, but that was about it. Maybe there'd be more inside, I thought. Or maybe, after seven years, people had just become blasé.

Jed, typically, was a sucker for all the souvenir shit. He bought a bullet on a key-chain (it wasn't even a genuine replica) and a Stetson whose hatband was imprinted with the slogan: I SURVIVED THE FRISCO SHOOTOUT.

"Don't count your chickens," Abi said. "We're here for four days, remember."

"Yeah, well, if I *do* take a bullet I won't really care, will I?" he grinned.

We arrived at the main gates, above which a big sun-bleached sign proclaimed: Welcome to Frisco. The main site was ringed with police vehicles, behind which a chain-link fence topped with razor wire stretched away on both sides. Armed cops in helmets and flak jackets were patrolling bad-temperedly, their faces red and sweating, eyeballing the steady dribble of people going inside. I suppose, when you thought about it, it was pretty amazing that even seven years after the first fatality these sites were still so popular. In fact, they had grown and expanded over the years; the whole thing was a social phenomenon, crazy and inexplicable, but undeniable all the same. The reason why people continued to flock to these places had been written about and analysed in newspapers, magazines, and academic theses throughout the world. Psychologists had a phrase for what motivated the permanent residents, those who had become addicted to the *idea* of being constantly in the firing line: "Shootout Syndrome", they called it.

At first we had planned to go to the OK Corral site in Tombstone, Arizona, but when I went online to book tickets I found that there was a three-year waiting list. Some of the other sites had waiting lists too—the Wild Bill Hickok site in Springfield, Missouri, for example—so in the end we had opted for the Frisco site, mainly because it would be a relatively short drive to the airport afterwards.

As we stood in the queue, Fran sidled up to me. "Why are we doing this, Chris?"

It was a question she'd asked several times before, except then it had always been: "Why would we *want* to do that?"

"It'll be a laugh," I'd always told her, but now that we were actually here, I felt something more considered was called for.

"Because . . . it's an experience," I said. "Nothing like this has ever happened before, and people still don't really understand how it works. And it's historically fascinating. And it's just . . . well, it's a thrill, isn't it?"

"Is it?" she said.

"Course it is. Isn't it a buzz to tempt fate? Doesn't it make you feel alive?"

She shook her head. "Not really. I don't see the point of putting ourselves at risk."

Fran had never understood my predilection for tombstoning and bungee jumping and body boarding. She'd never been an adrenaline junkie. But I needed it. It was my drug, my high—though, unlike Jed, I didn't feel the need to be out of my fucking tree twenty four hours a day.

"We're not really *at risk*, though, are we?" I said. "There've only been— what?—twenty fatalities in the past seven years? Statistically we're more likely to die in a plane crash."

She winced. "Don't remind me." She was not a good flyer either, and was hardly relishing the flight home.

I smiled. Fran was like the yin to my yang. Or the yang to my yin. Whatever. I put my arm round her.

"Don't worry, I'll look after you," I said.

Getting into the Frisco site was like passing through the security check at an airport. You put all your money and belts and shit in a plastic tray, then walked through a metal detector. Then, once you were through, you were frisked to make doubly sure you weren't carrying any concealed weapons.

The reason for the security was because when the sites had first started up, some nutters had seen them as a kind of weird invitation to bring along their own guns and let fly. Random murders had been committed on the twisted premise, submitted by several killers in their defence, that anyone who visited a site was presumed to have a death-wish and was therefore fair game.

Of course, not all the murders were random. Some were more calculated. In one famous case some guy bought an original 1873 Peacemaker, had some bullets made for it, and then used it to kill his wife at the Blazer's Mills site in Lincoln County. He was only caught because a ballistics expert realised that the killing bullet was made from an alloy that wasn't around in the nineteenth century.

Once we were inside, we just stood for a few minutes, taking it all in. It was like a cross between some massive bazaar and a kind of warped, ramshackle Disneyland. The shootout sites attracted all sorts of people—thrill-seekers; tourists in helmets and protective vests; research scientists; religious weirdos; opportunists out to make a fast buck; the reckless; the suicidal. There were street entertainers—acrobats and jugglers, fire-eaters and magicians. And there were Wild West enthusiasts, strutting around in their Stetsons and their waistcoats and their cowboy boots, looking a bit pathetic because their holsters were empty of the replica pistols they'd had confiscated at the gate.

"So what do you wanna do?" I asked.

Abi shrugged. "Get hammered."

"Score some dope," said Jed.

Fran, who was clutching my hand tightly, sighed. "Let's just look around," she suggested and pointed at a wooden street sign. "The main street's that way. Let's start there."

We started walking, stopping now and again to see the sights. A bored-looking Chinese girl in a pink and white cowgirl outfit that was all sequins and tassels thrust a leaflet at me. The leaflet was advertising the Frisco Museum and gave a brief history of the Frisco Shootout. I whistled.

"Hey, listen to this. Around four thousand rounds of open fire were expended during the Frisco Shootout, which lasted for approximately thirty-three hours."

"How can a shootout last thirty-three hours?" asked Abi scathingly.

"It was actually more of a siege," I said. "A bloke called Elfego Baca was wanted for questioning about the murder of a ranch foreman, but holed himself up in a house, which was then attacked by around eighty cowboys. It says here that the cowboys fired over four thousand shots into the house, but Baca wasn't hit once. During the siege, Baca killed four of his attackers and injured eight others. In the end a friend of Baca's convinced him to surrender and he walked out of the house unarmed."

Abi shrugged as if this was the most boring thing she had ever heard, but Jed raised his eyebrows, impressed.

"Four thousand shots," he said. "Fuck, man. If those bullets show up, we are gonna be Swiss cheese."

I felt Fran tense beside me.

"They won't," I said.

"They might," said Jed, grinning as if he relished the idea.

"Not while we're here," I said. "The chances are infinitesimal."

"Isn't that what everyone thinks?" said Fran tersely.

"What?" I said.

"That they'll be all right? That the chances of them being here when the bullets show up are so small it isn't even worth thinking about? But it's going to happen *one* day, isn't it? *Somebody's* going to get hurt?"

"Not necessarily," I said. "This thing's pretty random. The Frisco bullets might *never* show up."

Jed nodded. "Yeah, those scientist guys might find a way to, like, close the wormhole or whatever."

"Or they just might never show up anyway," I said. "It hasn't happened everywhere."

"It's happened in enough places," Fran said.

"Eleven," I said. "Eleven sites in seven years."

"God, you are such a geek," muttered Abi.

I frowned. "I knew we were coming here, so I googled the information. Isn't that understandable?"

"For you maybe."

I felt my temper rising. I'd done all the fucking driving, I'd booked the tickets, and all Abi could do was behave like a twat.

"What's your fucking problem?" I snapped. "Why do you always give everyone such a hard time?"

Abi glared at me. Unlike Fran, who was small and blonde and pretty, Abi was stocky and a bit . . . well, butch, I suppose. And just before the trip she had dyed her hair a deep, almost-black maroon. It didn't suit her.

"Maybe it's the company," she said. "Maybe it's having to hang around with Mr. Pointless Trivia and Mrs. Oh-I've-Got-Nothing-To-Worry-About-So-I'd-Better-Invent-Something."

She said that last bit in a simpering falsetto.

"Oh, fuck off," I snarled.

"Ooh, how articulate," she sneered back at me.

I felt myself starting to shake with anger. My ears felt as though they were burning and melting on the sides of my head.

Aware that I was spitting and starting to lose control, I said, "No, tell me, really, what *is* your fucking problem? Are you just angry because you're too fat and ugly to get laid? Are you blaming everyone else for the fact that you look like a fucking bull dyke?"

As soon as the words were out of my mouth, I regretted them. I felt awful, not least because Abi looked at me with an expression of utter desolation and burst into tears.

"Hey, look, I'm sorry . . ." I mumbled, reaching towards her.

"Fuck off!" she screamed, flinching back so violently that she stumbled, almost losing her balance. *"Don't fucking touch me!"*

Then she turned and ran. I made to go after her, but Fran pulled me back.

"I'll go."

She hurried after Abi.

"But I won't know where you are," I called.

"I'll text you."

The girls disappeared into the crowd, leaving me and Jed standing there. Jed patted me on the shoulder. He looked genuinely amused.

"Nice one, mate."

"Fuck off," I replied.

We walked on. I felt miserable now, ashamed of what I had said.

"Why does Abi have to be such hard work?" I asked Jed.

He shrugged. "Like you said, maybe she just needs to get laid."

"No, but seriously, Jed, has she said anything to you?"

"Why should she say anything to me?"

I sighed. I didn't need this shit. Why didn't people just *talk* to each other, get stuff out in the open, air their grievances if they had any? Why did everyone have to be so fucking uptight?

"So what do you wanna do?" I said.

Jed gestured off to the left. The muffled throb of music was coming from a red and white striped marquee, the top of which towered over the huts and vans thronging the streets. "Head towards the sound of salvation, man," he said. "Sex and drugs and rock n'roll. The only real truth."

"You talk some utter shit sometimes," I said.

Jed grinned, as if I'd paid him the highest possible compliment, and led the way.

More sights: kids in bullet-proof vests queuing up for a Wild West Ghost Train, the outside emblazoned with skeletal gunslingers; a bunch of drunken guys wearing comically huge foam Stetsons; a Yogi-type guy wearing nothing but a turban and a loincloth, sitting cross-legged on the dusty ground, a yellow snake coiling around him. It was a colourful mish-mash of styles and cultures, a vast melting pot of humanity. The shootout sites were unique in that people were drawn to them for a variety of reasons—celebration, introspection, historical curiosity, scientific research. But that wasn't the strangest thing. The strangest thing was that all of this—this whole amazing, ludicrous, terrifying phenomenon—had blossomed from the death of just one woman.

Minnie LaChance. A forty-nine-year-old housewife from Trinidad, Colorado. Seven years ago, Minnie's husband, Earl, had arrived home from his engineering job at a local gas drilling company to find Minnie lying dead in their back yard. It seemed that she had been hanging out washing when someone had shot her in the thigh, shattering her femur and severing her femoral artery. She might still have survived if she had received prompt medical treatment, but she had lain undiscovered for over seven hours, during which time she had bled to death.

At first it was thought that there might have been a racial motive for the killing—Minnie and Earl were black in a town where only 0.5% of the population were African American—but further investigation revealed a curious fact. The bullet that had killed Minnie had been fired from an 1866 Derringer. This was not especially unusual in itself—there were still plenty of old guns around in full working order—but what *was* unusual was that it had not merely been the murder weapon which was vintage but the actual bullet. The bloodied slug extracted from Minnie LaChance's thigh was found to be an original .41 Rimfire Cartridge, a 130 grain lead bullet propelled by thirteen grains of black powder. The Trinidad PD worked hard on the case for several months, determined to bring the killer to justice, and yet, despite the oddity of the bullet, forensic evidence proved to be frustratingly non-existent and Minnie LaChance's killer was never found.

Eight months later in Coffeyville, Kansas, during the annual October celebration in remembrance of the 1892 Dalton Raid, four of the town's citizens, including one eleven-year-old girl, suffered fatal gunshot wounds. A further nine victims received hospital treatment for injuries sustained by what at first was thought to be a lone gunman on a killing spree. However, events took a turn for the strange when it transpired that not a single witness to the shootings could actually recall seeing a man with a gun. Indeed, those citizens who *had* been in the vicinity of the killings all claimed more or less the same thing—that the bullets had not only seemed to come from nowhere, but from several directions at once.

As in the LaChance case, the murderer (or murderers) of the Coffeyville Four, as they became known, was never found. Also as in the LaChance case, it was subsequently discovered that the victims had been struck by a variety of vintage bullets from vintage guns. Perhaps not surprisingly, rumours began to circulate that a group of unknown and unseen psychos had decided to celebrate the anniversary of the Coffeyville Shootout in their own unique way—by re-enacting the incident as accurately as they could.

It took two similar incidents, however—in Hunnewell, Kansas, nine months after the Coffeyville killings, and in San Antonio, Texas, just three weeks later—in which a total of five more people were either killed or wounded by vintage bullets, for someone to finally stumble upon the truth.

That "someone" was a freelance journalist called William Marby, who, seven months after the San Antonio killings, sold an article to *The Fortean Times* entitled "Bullets From The Past?" In his article, Marby postulated the outrageous theory that the murder victims of the four seemingly random incidents had in fact all been killed by stray bullets fired by various gunmen back in the late nineteenth century—bullets which had, in effect, *moved forward through time*. There was a lot of nonsense in the article about "time ricochets" and "temporal pockets," but for the first time Marby pointed out what no one had previously noticed—that all four incidents had occurred on the sites of significant Old West shootouts. At the end of the article, Marby included a map of the U.S., supplemented by a list, pinpointing where future incidents might possibly occur. Of course, neither he nor his article was taken seriously—until his predictions began to come true.

Now, of course, Marby was world famous. He had five bestselling books to his name and travelled the world, talking about his various researches into the unknown. Sometimes he even gave lectures at the shootout sites themselves—those, like Frisco, where the bullets had yet to fly. The American public loved him for this, his willingness to put his life of fame and riches on the line by tempting fate via the very phenomenon he had identified, and through which he had made his fortune. There was a neatness about it, a braggadocio which appealed to them. And if, in the course of one of his lectures, he should ever actually be *killed* by one of his famous "bullets from the past," well then, that would be the neatest trick of all, one for which he would most likely be made a national hero.

The inside of the marquee was like an oven. I hadn't taken more than three steps through its arched entrance when sweat started to pour from my skin. The place stank of hot rubber and unwashed flesh and cannabis smoke. I took off my baseball cap and swiped an arm across my forehead, and wondered whether maybe Fran hadn't been right, after all: why the fuck *were* we here?

Jed put a hand on my shoulder and leaned in. "Off to see a man about a dog," he yelled above the music, before disappearing into the crowd.

Alone, I began half-heartedly pushing my way through the dripping, stinking audience towards the stage. The band was a punky country-and-western outfit, all manic fiddles and scything guitars. The lead singer had a shaved head tattooed with Celtic symbols and a thick handlebar moustache which curled up to the lobes of his multi-pierced ears. As the swirling wail of the song came to an end, he frenziedly ripped off his sweat-sodden shirt and hurled it into the crowd. Beating his gleaming, muscular, tattooed chest with his fists like a depilated King Kong, he screamed, "Come on, fucking bullets, I fucking dare you!"

The crowd whooped like fanatical supporters at a political rally.

I stood just behind the mosh pit and watched the band rip the fuck out of another song as the crowd surged and heaved in front of me. Despite the energy and the noise, I felt miserable and isolated and bored. I checked my phone to see whether Fran had texted me, but there was nothing.

My clothes were so wet it felt like I'd jumped into a swimming pool full of warm, barely-set jelly. I looked around, trying to spot Jed, but in the red-tinted gloom it was impossible. I decided to head towards the exit, and shivered as I stepped outside the marquee, even though it was thirty degrees out there. I squinted into the sun and, although my hair was matted and drenched with sweat, put my cap back on. A line of shaven-headed Buddhists wearing white robes went by, chanting softly and clashing little finger-cymbals.

I texted Jed: **Where r u?** Then I texted Fran: **Whats going on? U ok?** Then I began to walk, heading in the vague direction of the main street, thinking about the future.

Did I want to settle down, get a job? The prospect frightened and depressed me. I had talked to Fran about running my own business, starting up a company selling adventure holidays to thrill-seekers like myself. She'd been encouraging, enthusiastic even, but the truth was, I hadn't really thought it through. I liked the idea of doing the research, checking places out, experiencing the holidays myself, but I didn't know the first thing about business. Paperwork, tax, advertising, getting premises, building up a client base—all that stuff seemed beyond me, a crushing, daunting weight of toil and responsibility.

Whenever I'd expressed doubts, Fran had said, "You can go on a business course," or "You can do book-keeping at night school," or "You can get a bank loan to start you off." I'd nodded, but inside I'd been horrified; she might as well have suggested I wrap heavy chains around myself and jump in the river.

Thing is, I *knew* I was being immature, I *knew* I had to face up to real life sooner or later, but . . . I dunno. I just didn't feel ready for it yet.

Another thing: Fran was assuming we'd get a flat together when we got back, start life as an "official" couple. To be honest, though, I wasn't sure I wanted that either. I mean, Fran was brilliant and we got on really well, but did I actually *love* her? Was she *the one*? I'm not sure I knew what true love was, what it was supposed to feel like. Isn't it all tingly excitement and choirs of angels and never wanting to be parted from the other person?

I found a bar en route to the main street and went inside. I ordered a beer and sat down at a spare table and texted Jed again: **Am in Red Eye Bar. Just head towards Main St. C u soon?**

The bar, all dark wood and green and white checked tablecloths on round tables, was about a quarter full. A family—Mum, Dad, two small boys—were sitting by the front window beneath a flashing neon sign advertising Budweiser. They were eating burgers and drinking sarsaparilla in tall glasses; the boys had curly plastic drinking straws in theirs. A balding middle-aged man was sitting alone, staring sadly into space, nursing a beer. In the shadows at the back of the room, beside a small stage, was a quartet of what I can only describe as good ole boys in lumberjack shirts with the sleeves cut off to reveal their brawny arms.

I stared out of the window and drank my beer. My phone remained silent. It was almost four in the afternoon. The smell of burgers reminded me that I hadn't had lunch. Draining the last of my beer, I walked up to the bar and perused one of the laminated menus.

"Get you, buddy?" said the barman.

"I'll have a cheeseburger and fries with a side order of coleslaw. And another Coors," I said.

"You got it."

When I lowered the menu, one of the good ole boys was standing at the bar, about three feet away, looking at me. He had a crew cut and a thick sandy moustache. His hairy upper arms were thicker than my thighs. Sweat glistened like tiny diamonds on the velvety side of his head where the sun hit it.

"Hi," I said with a half-smile. He didn't smile back.

"English, huh?" he said.

"Yeah."

"So what part of England you from?"

"Sheffield," I said.

"That in London?"

"No, it's about a hundred and fifty miles north."

He continued to regard me, his eyes half-closed, as if I was some exotic creature. I felt uncomfortable. I paid the barman, took my beer and half-turned away.

"Nice speaking to you," I said.

"Well, now, ain't that rude," replied the man loudly.

I turned back. "Pardon?"

The man had been leaning on the bar, but now he straightened up, rotating his head so that his neck muscles crackled. He was a good seven inches taller than me.

"Here we are in the middle of a nice little chat, and you just up and leave. I call that rude."

I sensed violence thrumming off him. It hit me like a wave, drying out my mouth, making my guts ripple.

"Sorry," I said, trying to keep my voice steady. "I didn't mean to cause offence."

"Oh, you didn't mean to cause offence, huh?" said the man quietly.

"No," I said. "I'm here for a quiet drink and something to eat, that's all."

"You just a little English fag, is that it?" said the man.

I couldn't see the correlation between my comment and his. I felt a bead of sweat ooze from under the brim of my baseball cap and trickle down my face. "Sorry?" I said.

"What you sorry for?" he demanded, as if I'd bad-mouthed him.

"I mean . . . pardon?" I said, and licked my lips. I was still holding my beer. My mouth was so dry I was desperate to take a sip, but was afraid that if I made any move he would see that as provocation enough to hit me. Trying again, I said, "Look, I'm sorry if I've offended you. I don't want any trouble."

"You don't, huh?" said the man.

"No."

I could sense that the good ole boy was about to go for me. I had already decided to throw the beer in his face and run like hell when the barman appeared from nowhere.

"You okay, gents?" he asked.

The good ole boy looked at him, as if sizing *him* up too. "Oh yeah, we're just fine. My little English buddy and me, we're just shooting the breeze."

The barman's gaze flickered from the good ole boy to me. I could see he had taken in the situation at a glance.

"Your burger'll be ready in just a moment, sir," he said. "If you'd like to take a seat I'll bring it right over."

"Thanks," I said.

"And what can I get for *you*, sir? Four more Buds, is it?"

I slipped away while the good ole boy was distracted. I considered heading right out of the door, but I'd just spent fifteen bucks on a burger and a beer, so fuck that—why should *I* be intimidated? I caught the eye of the mum sitting by the window and she gave me a sympathetic smile. I smiled back, though my lips felt as dry as old rubber bands.

I gulped my beer and kept my head down. I didn't want to look up and find that the good ole boy was still staring at me. I didn't want to give him an excuse to come over.

I jumped when I heard footsteps approaching my table, but it was only the barman with my food. He had put it in a takeaway box. He leaned forward conspiratorially.

"Entirely up to you, friend, but I thought I'd give you the choice of eating here or elsewhere," he murmured.

I nodded gratefully. "Thanks."

"My pleasure. You take care now."

I risked a glance over at the good ole boys. They were refreshing their glasses from a jug on the table. I picked up my box of food and headed for the door. I didn't look back.

Outside I began to walk away from the Red Eye Bar at a brisk pace. Every instinct urged me to break into a run, but I resisted, knowing that that would only draw attention. I was just beginning to relax when I heard a shout behind me:

"Hey!"

My heart lurched and my muscles tensed. I was getting ready to leg it when the voice came again:

"Chris! Wait!"

It was Jed. Relief shuddered through me. I waited for him to catch me up.

"You okay, man," he said. "You look like shit."

I barked a laugh. "Yeah, I'm fine. Just met a guy in a bar who took a dislike to my face."

"Well, that's understandable. What's that? Food? It smells like food."

"Burger and fries. You want some?"

"*Do* I? I got the munchies like you wouldn't believe."

We found a bench and sat down, me still keeping a wary eye out for the good ole boys. My run-in with them had ruined my appetite, so Jed ate most of the food, wolfing down the burger like it was the first thing he'd eaten in days. He was polishing off the fries when my phone chimed. It was from Fran:

In Frisco Tavern on Main St. Everything ok. Join us? xx

I texted back: **C u there in 5 xx**

The Frisco Tavern was like a big Wild West saloon, with swing doors, sawdust on the floors, a guy playing honky-tonk piano. A wide wooden staircase led to an upper balcony, where ample-breasted women in low-cut velvet gowns winked and catcalled to the clientele below. I think they were just window dressing. If they weren't, they would surely have been pissed off at the big Mohawk standing at the bottom of the stairs with his massive arms crossed, forbidding access to all and sundry. As Jed and I walked in, I spotted Fran near the back of the room waving frantically.

She and Abi were sitting at a table in an alcove beyond the end of the bar. I mimed lifting a glass to my mouth. She nodded and raised an almost-empty wine glass. With her other hand she made a V sign. I gave her the thumbs-up, then headed to the bar.

The place was busy, the atmosphere relaxed, convivial. The staff was in period costume. The barman had oil-slick hair in a centre parting and a small waxed moustache. Behind the bar was a huge mirror, the name of the place engraved across it in gold leaf. Optics held bottles of brightly-coloured liquid, each of which was stamped with a black skull-and-crossbones. Above the bottles was a sign: DARE YOU TRY THE FRISCO FIRE-WATER COCKTAIL? $9.50

I leaned closer to the barman so he could hear me above the clamour. "What's in the Frisco Cocktail?"

He grinned. "State secret. Tell you this, though—it's good."

I turned to Jed. "Wanna try?"

"Go for it," he said.

We took the drinks across to the girls. Fran gave me a wide-eyed look which could have meant anything.

"Hey," I said.

"Hey," she replied.

Abi avoided eye-contact.

"You okay, Abi?" I asked.

She glanced at me, her face unreadable. "Yeah," she said, and took the wine I held out to her. "Thanks."

Fran was still giving me the look, though how she expected me to interpret it I have no idea. She waggled her eyebrows and swivelled her eyes meaningfully.

Clearing my throat, I said, "Hey, Abi, sorry about earlier. I was totally out of order. I behaved like an utter cunt."

Abi shrugged, took a sip of her drink. "S'okay," she muttered.

"No," I said, "it's not. I said some bad things. Things I didn't mean. I'm really sorry."

Abi sighed, and this time when she looked at me she held my gaze. "You're forgiven," she said. "And I'm sorry too. I've been a right mardy cow these past few weeks."

"No, you haven't," I said automatically.

"Yeah, I have. And I *know* I have." She raised her glass, and her voice. "Now let's forget about it—and get totally pissed!"

"Yeah!" Jed yelled, downing his cocktail in one.

The next few hours were the best we'd spent together since arriving in the States. That might just have been my interpretation based on the immensely efficacious effects of several Frisco Fire-Water Cocktails, but somehow it felt as if the air had been suddenly and magically cleared, as if for the first time in weeks there was no hidden agenda, and that the only reason we were there was to have fun.

And we *did* have fun. We were on a high, all four of us. It was one of those nights where you start laughing at stupid stuff and then find that you can't stop; where the stars seem in perfect alignment and you're absolutely certain of your place in the universe and the people you're with; where it seems completely feasible that you might live forever, and that if you did, forever would continue to be as amazing and brilliant as it was right then.

I have no idea what time it was when the shadow fell over our table. That's how I remember it—something large and dark, blotting out the light.

"Well, lookee here," said a voice. "If it ain't the little English fag and his fag friends."

It was the good ole boy from the Red Eye Bar. All I could see through my booze-goggles was the glint of his eyes and the porcupine-like quills of his moustache. I was aware, in an intense slow-motion kind of way, of Abi peering up and saying in a slurring, sniggering voice, "Who the fuck are you?"

Then Jed began to laugh and point. "I am the walrus," he said, "coo-coo cachoo."

As he and Abi exploded into giggles, the good ole boy seem to swell, to get bigger.

"What did you say, boy?" he muttered.

Realising he was being addressed, Jed blinked at the good ole boy. He seemed to have no inkling of the guy's mood. Or if he did, he just didn't care.

"Are you in the Village People?" he said. "Are you the—"

The good ole boy's fist exploded into the centre of Jed's face. In my drunken state it seemed so massive that it appeared to obliterate Jed's features. Then Jed fell back, his eyes already glassy with unconsciousness, his nose a mangled, bloody mess.

That was when it all turned bad. Suddenly I no longer felt indestructible, merely incapable. I tried to stand, but my legs wouldn't respond, and I ended up sprawling across the table, scattering glasses. All at once there was uproar. Fran crying. Abi screaming obscenities. Glass smashing and furniture breaking. Things being overturned.

I felt hands on me. I pinwheeled, flailed, fought them off. Other people were yelling. I had a confused impression of wrestling bodies, flying fists.

I slipped, or maybe I was pushed; I don't remember. All I know is that suddenly I was under the table, sitting in something wet. Then Fran was with me, her tear-stained face close to mine.

"You okay?" I asked.

She nodded, but she was upset, shaking so much her teeth were chattering. "Who are those people?"

"Bunch of pissed-up muscle heads," I said. "They had a go at me earlier. Don't think they like the English."

Someone crashed against the table we were sheltering beneath. It sounded like there was a full-on bar brawl happening above us.

"I don't like it here," Fran said.

I put my arms round her. "It *is* a bit lively," I agreed.

"I want to go home."

"We will," I said. "In a few days."

"I want to go home *now*."

I frowned, irritated. "We can't," I said. "Our flights are in four days. We've got tickets."

"I want to go *now*. Abi needs to go *now*."

"What's Abi got to do with it?"

Fran paused, then said, "She's got cancer."

"*Cancer?*"

"Ovarian cancer. She needs an operation. She found out just before we came away."

"But . . . why did she come then?"

Fran gave a wan smile. "Last fling. Last big adventure before going home to face it all."

"Last?" I said. "You don't mean . . . I mean, she *is* going to be all right, isn't she?"

Before Fran could answer, the table we were sheltering beneath was lifted up and away from us. I thought the good ole boys had found us, but it was the huge Mohawk who had been guarding the stairs.

"You," he said. "Out."

I scrambled to my feet. "What? I didn't do anything."

"*Everybody* out," he said.

I looked around. The place was wrecked. Furniture broken, smashed glass all over the floor. The big mirror behind the bar had black zig-zag lines radiating out from a central crater of shattered glass. People were flowing towards the exit, herded by armed cops. Some were limping, others bloodied and bruised.

"Where're Jed and Abi?" I said.

The Mohawk just looked at me.

"We were attacked," I said. "My friend Jed was the first to get punched."

Fran put a hand on my arm. "They're probably outside, Chris," she said. "Come on."

We went outside. It was dark now, getting cold. Instead of reviving me, the air hit me like a fist in the guts and I reeled away to throw up. Suddenly I felt wretched. I just wanted to lie down, slip into unconsciousness. Fran tugged on my arm.

"Come on."

"Where?"

"Let's find Abi and Jed and go."

I allowed myself to be led. I had no idea where we were going. My head was swimming. I didn't ask questions. I concentrated purely on putting one foot in front of the other.

For a while we were in a crowd, bodies ebbing and flowing around us. I was vaguely aware of people sitting around camp fires, singing and laughing. We passed various establishments lit up like beacons, belching with music. The smell of food from street-vendors made my stomach roil. We passed someone who was fire-eating, attracting oohs and ahhs as he breathed flames into the night sky. We passed patrolling cops, armed and armoured. Then the noise and people slipped away and we were somewhere else. Somewhere dark.

"Where are we?" I said.

Fran put a finger to her lips. "Shh. People are sleeping."

"Where are we?" I asked again, whispering this time.

"Campsite," Fran murmured. "Thirty day pass area."

"Why are we here?"

"This is where Abi said she'd meet us. Look."

She held her phone up. There was a text, presumably from Abi, but it just looked like little black insects jittering on a tiny light box. It made me feel sick again. I looked away.

"Where?" I said.

Instead of answering, she took my hand and dragged me along. I felt limp and rubbery, my head bobbing. I just wanted to sleep.

"Abi," Fran was whispering, "Abi."

Then something slammed into my back.

I felt for a moment as though my spine and ribs had exploded. I fell forward and something landed on top of me. I had a confused impression that I'd been attacked by a bear, a big grizzly. This *was* America, after all.

My head was crushed into the ground, my face turned to the side. I saw

Fran's feet kicking. I saw her phone drop to the floor. Then I heard muffled voices, grunts. Fran was forced forward, onto her knees. Suddenly I realised what was happening. An ambush. The good ole boys had ambushed us. In a flash of sobriety I realised they must have taken Abi's phone. The text hadn't been from her at all. It had been bait.

They made me watch while they raped Fran over and over. They used her like she was nothing, an object, a series of holes for them to abuse. They slapped and punched her until her face was unrecognisable. They made her say she loved it, made her ask for more. They used a beer bottle on her, a splintered branch. They giggled and joked as they tore her open. I tried to scream for help, to beg them to stop, but they shoved rocks and dirt into my mouth. I wept and struggled, but I could do nothing. I could do nothing.

It reached a point where I knew it would never be over. Even when it was, I knew it never would be. They went eventually, those good ole boys. They left us lying in the dirt. They left Fran, my beautiful, gentle Fran who had never hurt anybody, broken and torn and lying in the dirt.

I crawled to her. I was crying. Empty. I told her I was sorry over and over. I don't know if she heard me.

Before coming here I had thought: Even if the bullets *do* come they probably won't hit us. The chances of any of us getting hurt are infinitesimal.

But what I hadn't considered was that bullets are personal, individual, that they come in all shapes and sizes. Each of us has a bullet out there somewhere with our name on it. And when it hits, no amount of statistics or rational argument or magical thinking or any of the other bullshit we wrap around ourselves and convince us will keep us safe is going to make a blind bit of difference.

The bullet hits, we're gone.

End of story.

AUTHOR BIO

Mark Morris has written over twenty-five novels, among which are *Toady*, *Stitch*, *The Immaculate*, *The Secret of Anatomy*, *Fiddleback*, *The Deluge* and four books in the popular *Doctor Who* range. He is the author of two previous short story collections, *Close to the Bone* and *Long Shadows, Nightmare Light*, and several novellas. His short fiction, articles, and reviews have appeared in a wide variety of anthologies and magazines, and he is editor of *Cinema Macabre*, a book of horror movie essays by genre luminaries for which he won the 2007 British Fantasy Award, its follow-up *Cinema Futura*, and two volumes of *The Spectral Book of Horror Stories*. His script work includes audio dramas for Big Finish Productions' *Doctor Who* and *Jago & Litefoot* ranges, and also for Bafflegab's *Hammer Chillers* series. His recently published work includes the official movie tie-in novelization of Darren Aronofsky's *Noah*, two novellas—*It Sustains* (Earthling Publications), which was nominated for a 2013 Shirley Jackson Award, and *Albion Fay* (Spectral Press)—and the first two books of his Obsidian Heart trilogy, *The Wolves of London* and *The Society of Blood* (Titan Books). Book three in the trilogy, *The Wraiths of War*, will be out in October 2016.

PUBLICATION HISTORY

"Fallen Boys" was first published in *The End of the Line* edited by Jonathan Oliver (Solaris, 2010)

"Biters" was first published in *21ˢᵗ Century Dead* edited by Christopher Golden (St. Martin's Griffin, 2012)

"The Name Game" was first published in *The British Fantasy Society Yearbook 2009* edited by Guy Adams (BFS, 2009)

"The Red Door" was first published in *Terror Tales of London* edited by Paul Finch (Gray Friar Press, 2013)

"White Wings" is original to this collection

"The Complicit" is original to this collection

"Vicious" was first published in *Classics Mutilated* edited by Jeff Conner (IDW, 2010)

"Bad Call" was first published in *The Second Humdrumming Book of Horror Stories* edited by Ian Alexander Martin (Humdrumming, 2008)

"Feeding Frenzy" was first published in *Night Visions 12* edited by Kealan Patrick Burke (Subterranean Press, 2006)

"The Scariest Place in the World" was first published in *Hauntings* edited by Ian Whates (Newcon Press, 2012)

"Eating Disorder" is original to this collection

"Essence" was first published in *Psycho-Mania!* edited by Stephen Jones (Robinson, 2013)

"Puppies For Sale" was first published in *British Invasion* edited by Christopher Golden, Tim Lebbon & James A. Moore (Cemetery Dance Publications, 2008)

"Waiting for the Bullet" was first published in *Gutshot* edited by Conrad Williams (PS Publishing, 2011)